HACK/S

VOLUME ONE: FIRST CUT

A TIM SEELEY/STEFANO CASELLI
PRODUCTION

DEDICATION TO MY DAD, FOR INTRODUCING ME TO HIS B-MOVIE COLLECTION
TO MY MOM, FOR PUTTING UP WITH MY DAD'S B-MOVIE COLLECTION

THANKS TO: ALL MY HACK/SLASH COLLABORATORS, CRAIG THOMPSON,
DANIEL ALTER, ADRIAN ASKARIEH, CHAD WISE, TODD LINCOLN,
MARTIN SCHENK, CHRIS CRANK, DAVE RICHARDS, RYAN ROTTEN,
KEVIN SOUTHWELL, SANDRA KAMMERER, ROBERT KIRKMAN,
JIM HARPER, LLOYD KAUFMAN, AND, MOST IMPORTANTLY, TO
HACK/SLASH FANS WHO, LIKE A GOOD SLASHER, KEEP COMING BACK.

REPRINT SERIES DESIGN & PRODUCTION MONICA GARCIA

REPRINT SERIES EDITOR JAMES LOWDER

IMAGE COMICS, INC.

ROBERT KIRKMAN CHIEF OPERATING OFFICER
ERIK LARSEN CHIEF FINANCIAL OFFICER
TODD MCFARLANE PRESIDENT
MARC SILVESTRI CHIEF EXECUTIVE OFFICER
JIM VALENTINO VICE-PRESIDENT

ERIC STEPHENSON PUBLISHER
TODD MARTINEZ SALES & LICENSING COORDINATOR
JENNIFER DE GUZMAN PR & MARKETING DIRECTOR
BRANWYN BIGGLESTONE ACCOUNTS MANAGER
EMILY MILLER ADMINISTRATIVE ASSISTANT
JAMIE PARRENO MARKETING ASSISTANT
SARAH DELAINE EVENTS COORDINATOR

KEVIN YUEN DIGITAL RIGHTS COORDINATOR
DREW GILL ART DIRECTOR
JONATHAN CHAN PRODUCTION MANAGER
MONICA GARCIA PRODUCTION ARTIST
VINCENT KUKUA PRODUCTION ARTIST
JANA COOK PRODUCTION ARTIST
WWW.IMAGECOMICS.COM

HACK/SLASH Vol. 1: FIRST CUT
ISBN: 978-1-60706-605-7
First Printing

INTRODUCTION

When I first met Tim Seeley, he seemed so much more
well-adjusted than me: smiling, sociable, free-spirited... a
party dude, even. This was at community college in central
Wisconsin, where I was struggling with what to do with my
life — depressed, confused, still living with my parents,
distraught about religion. I'd just rediscovered the comics
medium and was hacking out a comic strip for the school
newspaper when Tim and I were introduced. Immediately he
was welcoming and gregarious, bouncing around with positive
energy while hot girls flocked to his side. And he was a far
more prolific and inspired cartoonist than I, proving that you
didn't need to be a social misfit to make comics.

Now, after having read *Hack/Slash*, I see that Tim's not really
that well-adjusted after all.

This book's brimming with sex and violence — dismembered
limbs, buckets of blood, and gratuitous panty shots. But under
that (the surface elements, not the panties) is a sentiment
I can identify with: growing up in small-town Wisconsin —
the isolation, repression, and puritanical oppression of the
Midwest and the plight of being continually picked on by
rednecks. Tim's choice of themes is no wonder, knowing that
the "Cheese State" is recognized as an occult vortex with a
disproportionate number of serial killings. Home to Ed Gein and
Jeffrey Dahmer, to name a few, and Burlington, Wisconsin — a
town built over ancient burial mounds, just like in frickin'

Poltergeist. Wisconsin's a state with its very own Paranormal
Research Group (in Janesville).

So our childhoods were haunted by racists, gun-crazy hunters,
endless stretches of unlit gravel backroads, and — above
all — the fear that one will be eternally trapped in this rural
wasteland. But the best of the slasher genre is all about
confronting our fears with humor, absurdity, and over-the-top
sensibilities, and Tim certainly taps into that playfulness in
Hack/Slash. The tone of it all often gets giddy and hilarious.
Oh, and Stefano Caselli can really draw.

Obvious at a glance, I now recognize that Tim, like myself,
grew up as a skinny loser social misfit, but was able to
transcend the darkness and transform himself into a mostly
healthy adult. Mostly.

If you're ever in Wisconsin, you gotta try the cheese curds.

—Craig Thompson
Portland, Oregon. March 2005

Craig Thompson was born in Traverse City, Michigan in 1975
and raised outside a small town in central Wisconsin. His
award-winning graphic novels include *Good-bye, Chunky Rice*;
Carnet de Voyage; *Habibi*; and *Blankets*.

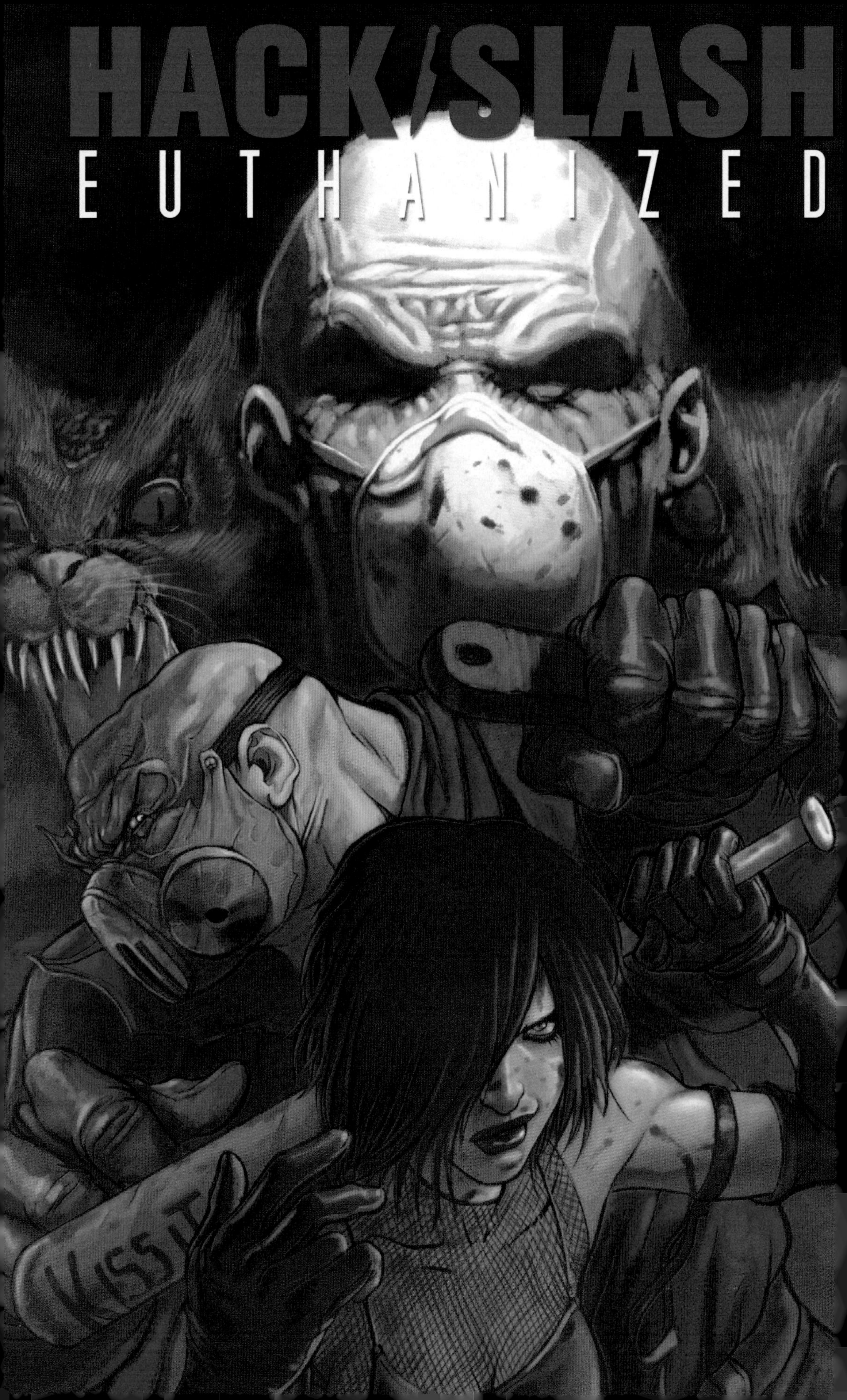
HACK/SLASH
EUTHANIZED

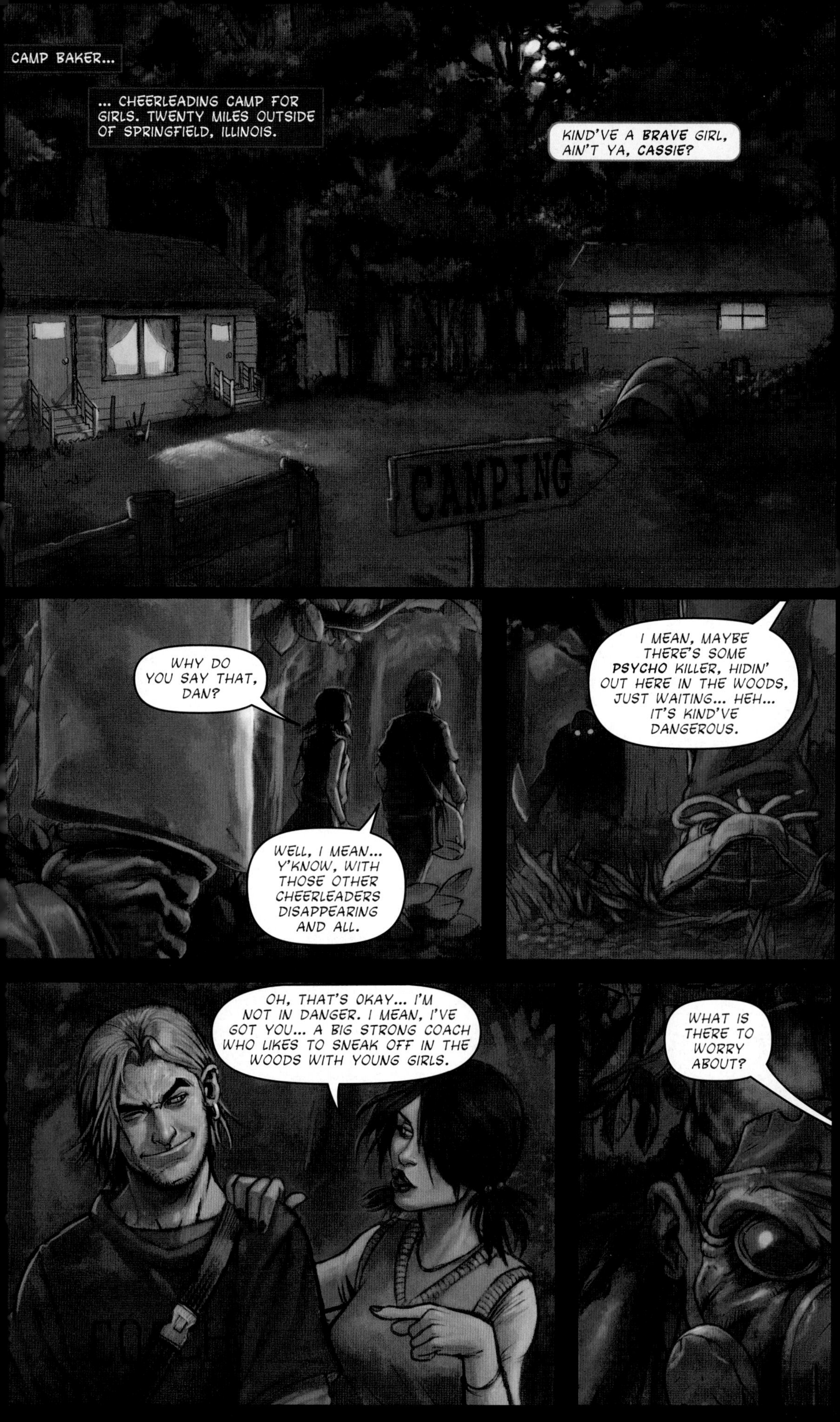
CAMP BAKER...
... CHEERLEADING CAMP FOR GIRLS. TWENTY MILES OUTSIDE OF SPRINGFIELD, ILLINOIS.
KIND'VE A BRAVE GIRL, AIN'T YA, CASSIE?
CAMPING
WHY DO YOU SAY THAT, DAN?
WELL, I MEAN... Y'KNOW, WITH THOSE OTHER CHEERLEADERS DISAPPEARING AND ALL.
I MEAN, MAYBE THERE'S SOME PSYCHO KILLER, HIDIN' OUT HERE IN THE WOODS, JUST WAITING... HEH... IT'S KIND'VE DANGEROUS.
OH, THAT'S OKAY... I'M NOT IN DANGER. I MEAN, I'VE GOT YOU... A BIG STRONG COACH WHO LIKES TO SNEAK OFF IN THE WOODS WITH YOUNG GIRLS.
WHAT IS THERE TO WORRY ABOUT?

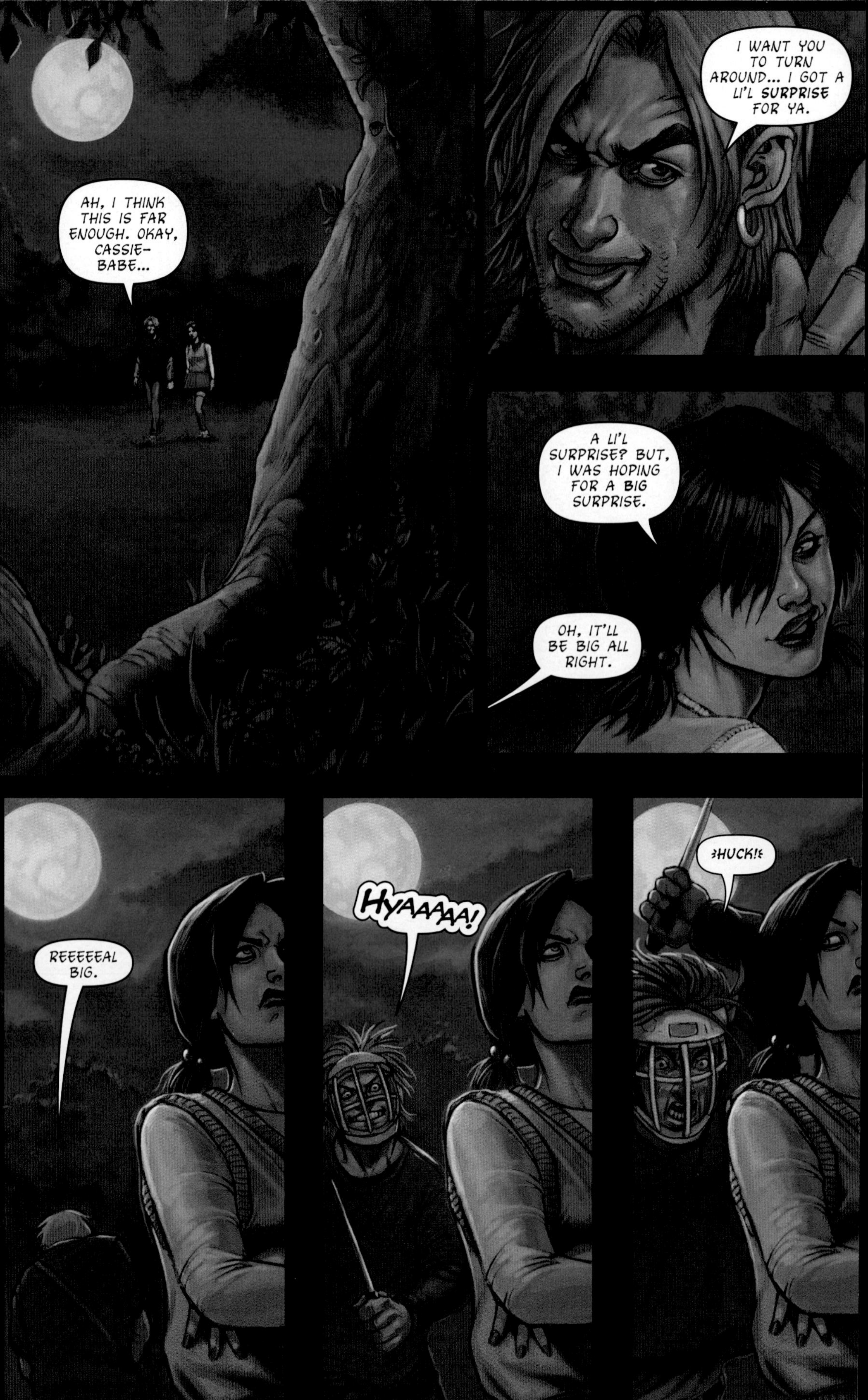
AH, I THINK THIS IS FAR ENOUGH. OKAY, CASSIE-BABE...
I WANT YOU TO TURN AROUND... I GOT A LI'L SURPRISE FOR YA.
A LI'L SURPRISE? BUT, I WAS HOPING FOR A BIG SURPRISE.
OH, IT'LL BE BIG ALL RIGHT.
REEEEEAL BIG.
HYAAAAA!
HUCK!

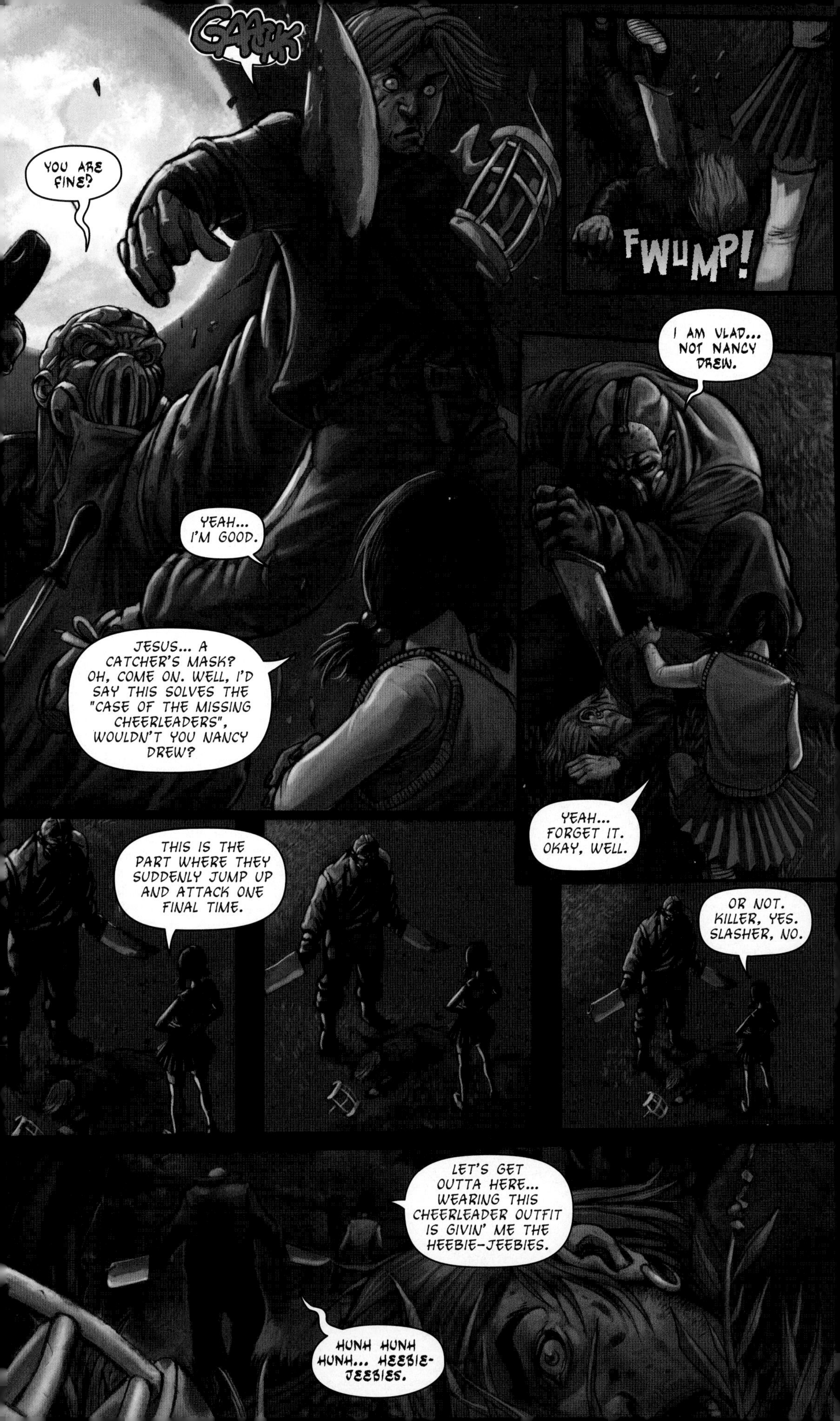
GAAAK
YOU ARE FINE?
FWUMP!
YEAH... I'M GOOD.
JESUS... A CATCHER'S MASK? OH, COME ON. WELL, I'D SAY THIS SOLVES THE "CASE OF THE MISSING CHEERLEADERS", WOULDN'T YOU NANCY DREW?
I AM VLAD... NOT NANCY DREW.
YEAH... FORGET IT. OKAY, WELL.
THIS IS THE PART WHERE THEY SUDDENLY JUMP UP AND ATTACK ONE FINAL TIME.
OR NOT. KILLER, YES. SLASHER, NO.
LET'S GET OUTTA HERE... WEARING THIS CHEERLEADER OUTFIT IS GIVIN' ME THE HEEBIE-JEEBIES.
HUNH HUNH HUNH... HEEBIE-JEEBIES.

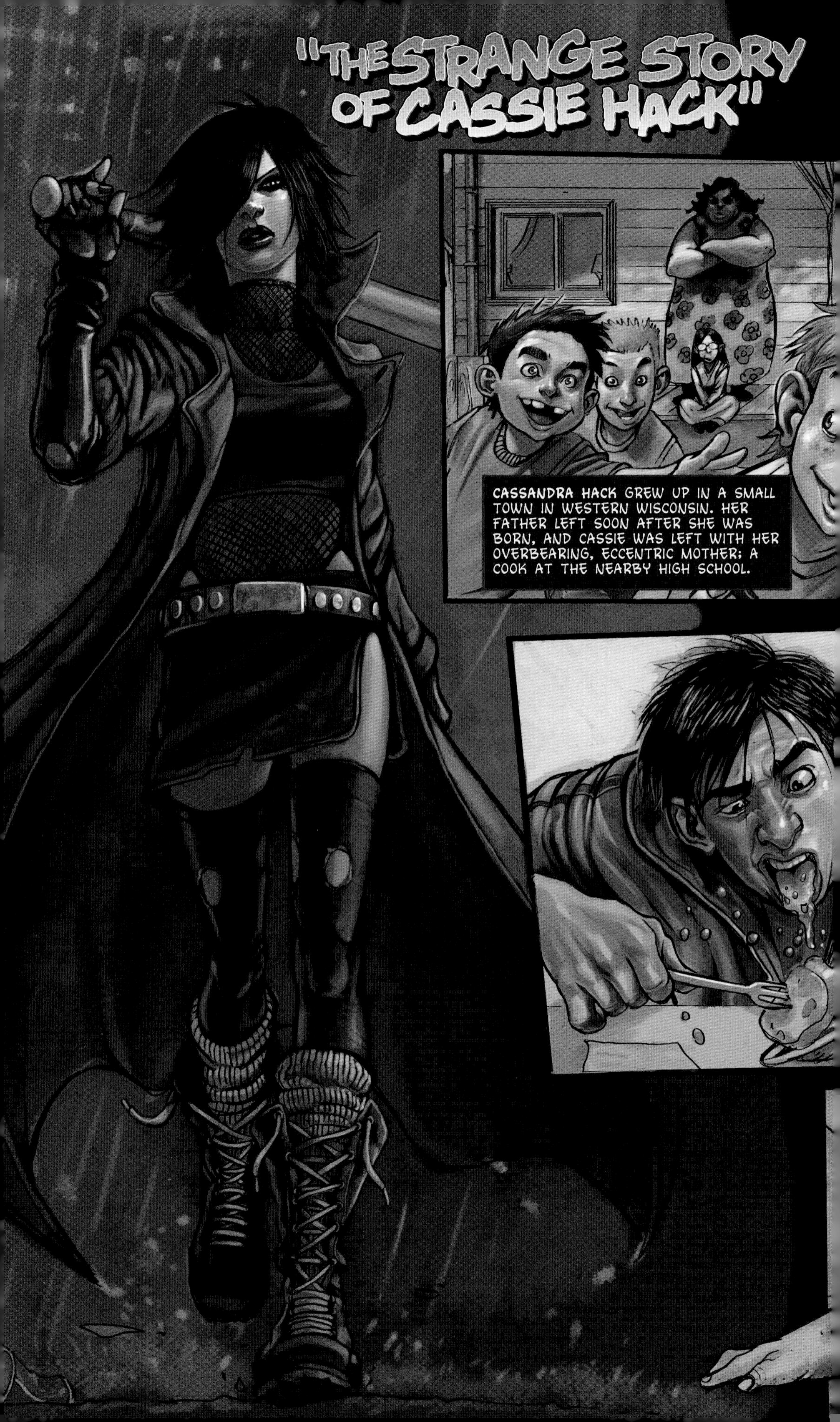
"THE STRANGE STORY OF CASSIE HACK"
CASSANDRA HACK GREW UP IN A SMALL TOWN IN WESTERN WISCONSIN. HER FATHER LEFT SOON AFTER SHE WAS BORN, AND CASSIE WAS LEFT WITH HER OVERBEARING, ECCENTRIC MOTHER; A COOK AT THE NEARBY HIGH SCHOOL.

CASSIE GREW INTO A BITTER TEENAGER, CONSIDERED A FREAK BY HER CLASSMATES. HER MOTHER WATCHED UNHAPPILY AS HER DAUGHTER WAS CHASTISED AND TORMENTED.

THAT'S WHEN STUDENTS BEGAN TO DISAPPEAR.

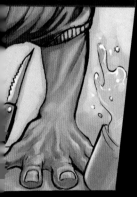

DISAPPEARENCES RESPONDED TO A SUDDEN RANGE "MYSTERY MEAT" G SERVED IN THE HIGH OOL CAFETERIA, AND IT 'T TAKE LONG BEFORE CLUES POINTED TO...

MRS. HACK... THE SCHOOL LUNCH LADY. HACK HAD BEEN MURDERING STUDENTS SHE FELT HAD TREATED HER DAUGHTER UNFAIRLY, AND SERVING THEM WITH A SIDE OF FRIES AND CHOCOLATE MILK.

WHEN CONFRONTED, HACK PLUNGED HER HEAD INTO A POT OF BOILING GRAVY, LEAVING HER TEENAGE DAUGHTER AN ORPHAN.

CASSANDRA WAS PLACED IN A FOSTER HOME, AND ATTENDED A NEW SCHOOL... BUT NEWS OF HER CONNECTION TO THE NOTORIOUS 'LUNCH LADY' MADE HER EVEN MORE UNPOPULAR THAN BEFORE.

SOON, GIRLS BEGAN TO DISAPPEAR, SIGNALING THE HORRIFIC RETURN...

FEELING RESPONSIBLE FOR THE DEATHS, CASSIE HUNTED DOWN AND DESTROYED THE LUNCH LADY... HER MOTHER.

...OF THE LUNCH LADY, REBORN AS A VENGEFUL 'SLASHER' FROM BEYOND THE GRAVE.

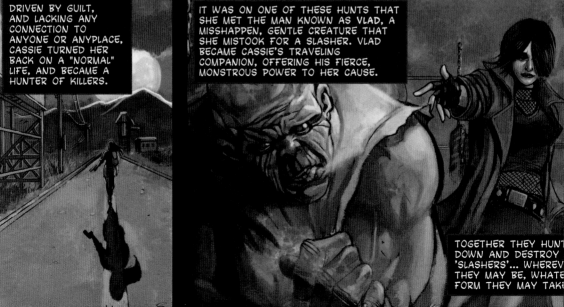

DRIVEN BY GUILT, AND LACKING ANY CONNECTION TO ANYONE OR ANYPLACE, CASSIE TURNED HER BACK ON A "NORMAL" LIFE, AND BECAME A HUNTER OF KILLERS.

IT WAS ON ONE OF THESE HUNTS THAT SHE MET THE MAN KNOWN AS VLAD, A MISSHAPPEN, GENTLE CREATURE THAT SHE MISTOOK FOR A SLASHER. VLAD BECAME CASSIE'S TRAVELING COMPANION, OFFERING HIS FIERCE, MONSTROUS POWER TO HER CAUSE.

TOGETHER THEY HUNT DOWN AND DESTROY 'SLASHERS'... WHEREV THEY MAY BE, WHATE FORM THEY MAY TAK

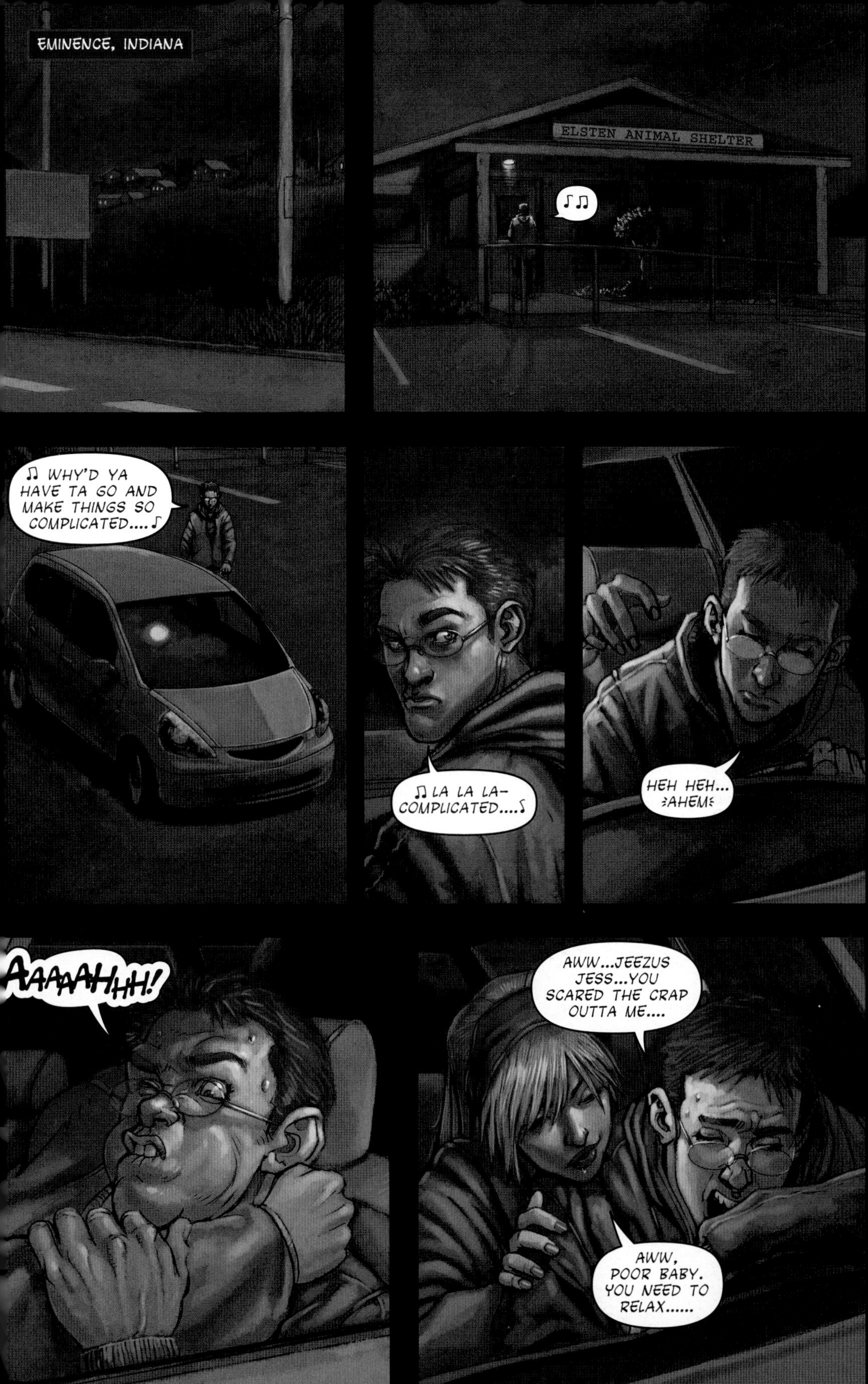
EMINENCE, INDIANA
ELSTEN ANIMAL SHELTER
♪♫
♫ WHY'D YA HAVE TA GO AND MAKE THINGS SO COMPLICATED.... ♪
♫ LA LA LA-COMPLICATED.... ♪
HEH HEH... AHEM
AAAAAHHH!
AWW...JEEZUS JESS...YOU SCARED THE CRAP OUTTA ME....
AWW, POOR BABY. YOU NEED TO RELAX......

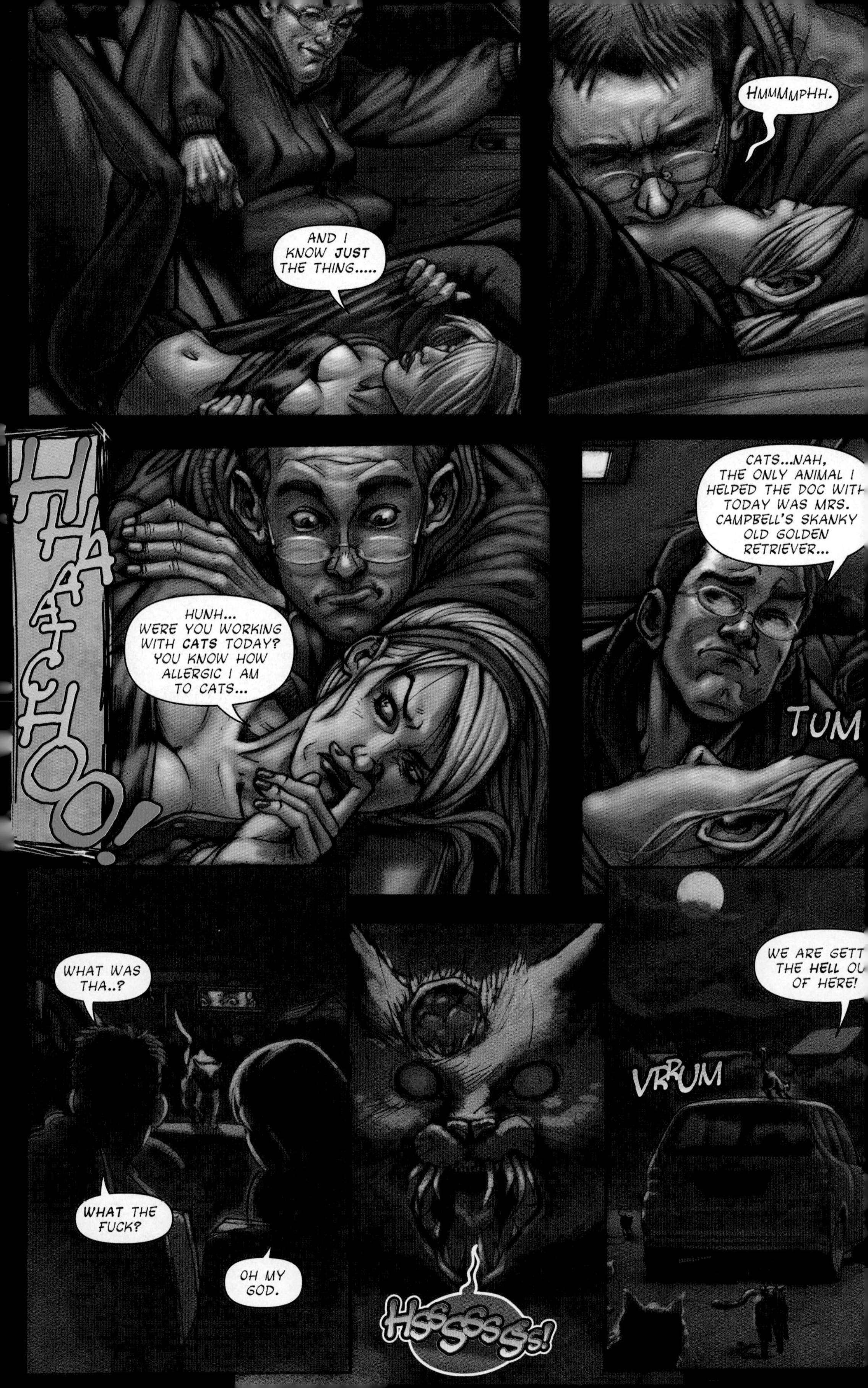
AND I KNOW JUST THE THING.....
HMMMMPHH.
HAAATCHOO!
HUNH... WERE YOU WORKING WITH CATS TODAY? YOU KNOW HOW ALLERGIC I AM TO CATS...
CATS...NAH, THE ONLY ANIMAL I HELPED THE DOC WITH TODAY WAS MRS. CAMPBELL'S SKANKY OLD GOLDEN RETRIEVER...
TUM
WHAT WAS THA..?
WHAT THE FUCK?
OH MY GOD.
HSSSSSSS!
WE ARE GETT THE HELL OU OF HERE!
VRRUM

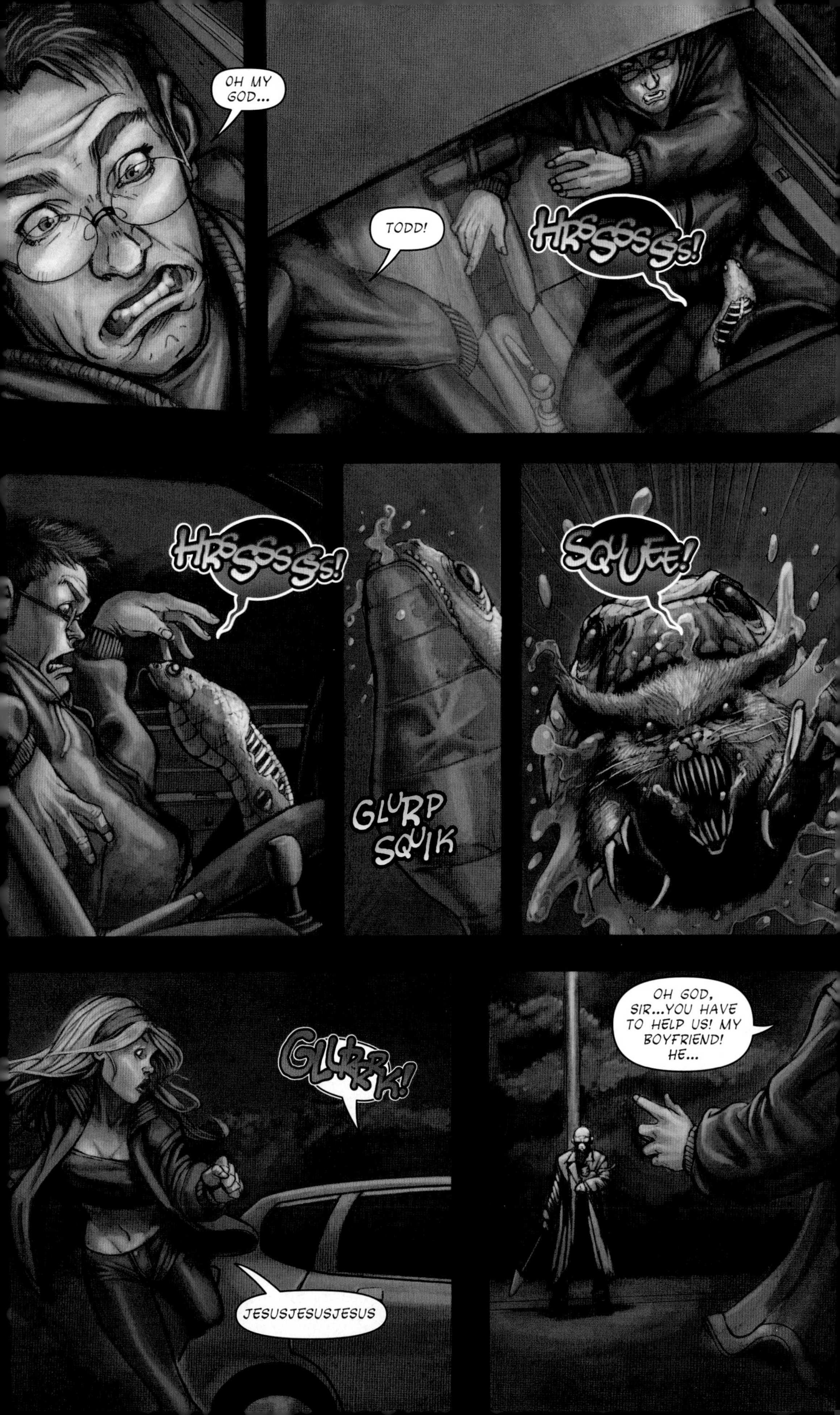
OH MY GOD...
TODD!
HRSSSSSS!
HRSSSSSS!
GLURP SQUIK
SQUEE!
GLURRK!
JESUSJESUSJESUS
OH GOD, SIR...YOU HAVE TO HELP US! MY BOYFRIEND! HE...

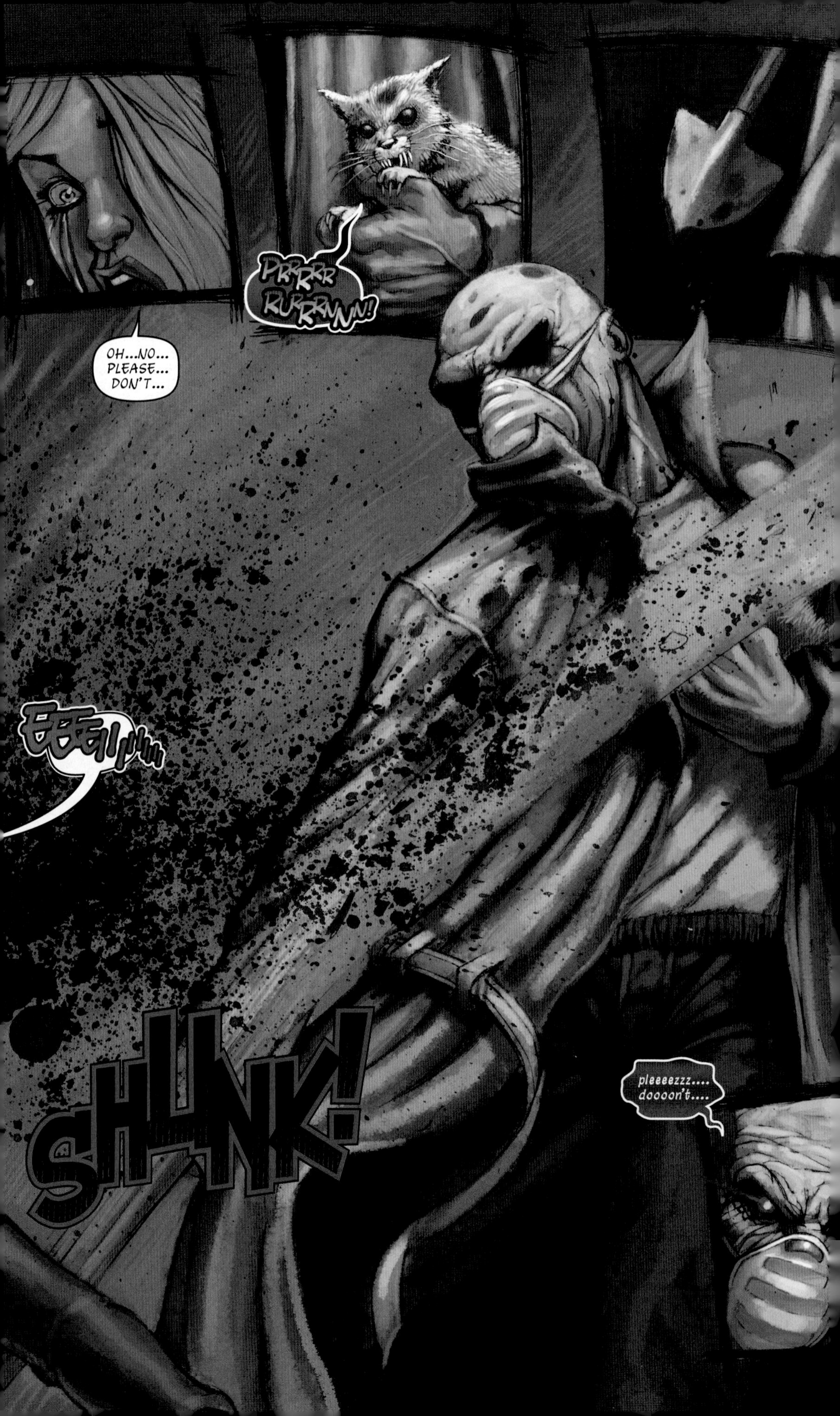
PRRRRR KURRRNNN!
OH...NO... PLEASE... DON'T...
SHUNK!
pleeeezzz.... doooon't....

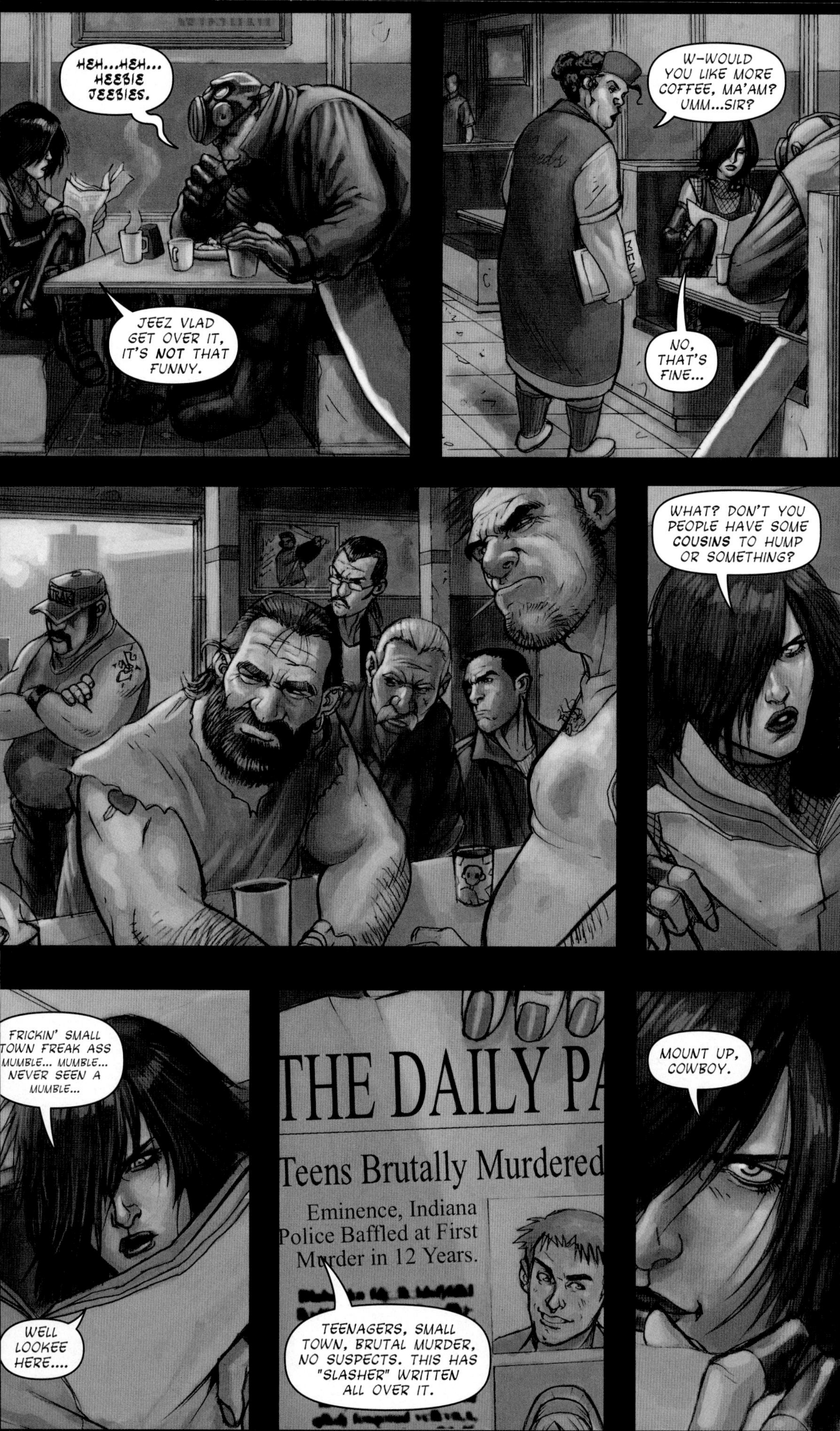
HEH...HEH... HEEBIE JEEBIES.
JEEZ VLAD GET OVER IT, IT'S **NOT** THAT FUNNY.
W-WOULD YOU LIKE MORE COFFEE, MA'AM? UMM...SIR?
MENU
NO, THAT'S FINE...
TRAK
WHAT? DON'T YOU PEOPLE HAVE SOME **COUSINS** TO HUMP OR SOMETHING?
FRICKIN' SMALL TOWN FREAK ASS MUMBLE... MUMBLE... NEVER SEEN A MUMBLE...
WELL LOOKEE HERE....
THE DAILY PA
Teens Brutally Murdered
Eminence, Indiana
Police Baffled at First
Murder in 12 Years.
TEENAGERS, SMALL TOWN, BRUTAL MURDER, NO SUSPECTS. THIS HAS "SLASHER" WRITTEN ALL OVER IT.
MOUNT UP, COWBOY.

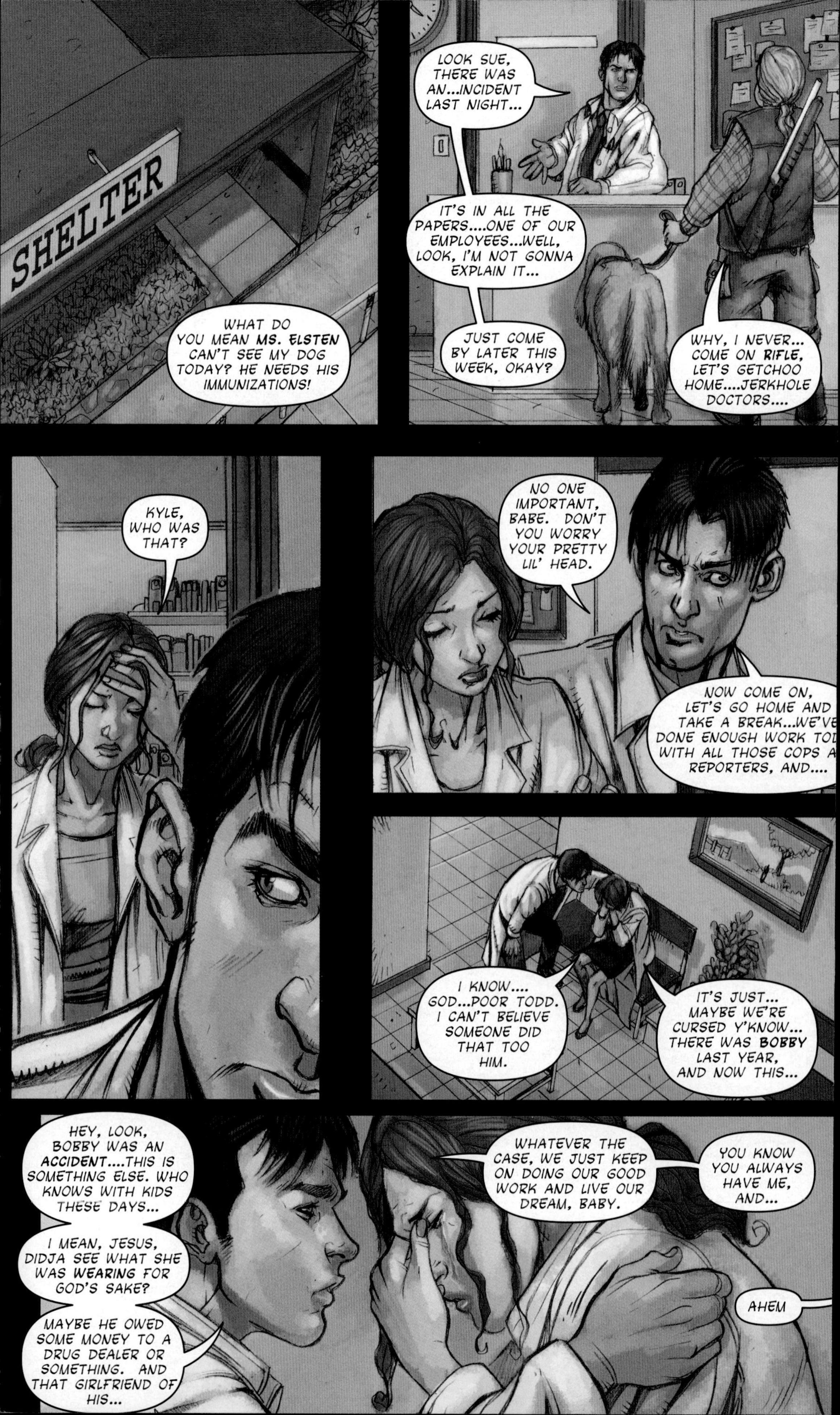
SHELTER
WHAT DO YOU MEAN MS. ELSTEN CAN'T SEE MY DOG TODAY? HE NEEDS HIS IMMUNIZATIONS!
LOOK SUE, THERE WAS AN...INCIDENT LAST NIGHT...
IT'S IN ALL THE PAPERS....ONE OF OUR EMPLOYEES...WELL, LOOK, I'M NOT GONNA EXPLAIN IT...
JUST COME BY LATER THIS WEEK, OKAY?
WHY, I NEVER... COME ON RIFLE, LET'S GETCHOO HOME....JERKHOLE DOCTORS....
KYLE, WHO WAS THAT?
NO ONE IMPORTANT, BABE. DON'T YOU WORRY YOUR PRETTY LIL' HEAD.
NOW COME ON, LET'S GO HOME AND TAKE A BREAK...WE'VE DONE ENOUGH WORK TOD WITH ALL THOSE COPS A REPORTERS, AND....
I KNOW.... GOD...POOR TODD. I CAN'T BELIEVE SOMEONE DID THAT TOO HIM.
IT'S JUST... MAYBE WE'RE CURSED Y'KNOW... THERE WAS BOBBY LAST YEAR, AND NOW THIS...
HEY, LOOK, BOBBY WAS AN ACCIDENT....THIS IS SOMETHING ELSE. WHO KNOWS WITH KIDS THESE DAYS...
I MEAN, JESUS, DIDJA SEE WHAT SHE WAS WEARING FOR GOD'S SAKE?
MAYBE HE OWED SOME MONEY TO A DRUG DEALER OR SOMETHING. AND THAT GIRLFRIEND OF HIS...
WHATEVER THE CASE, WE JUST KEEP ON DOING OUR GOOD WORK AND LIVE OUR DREAM, BABY.
YOU KNOW YOU ALWAYS HAVE ME, AND...
AHEM

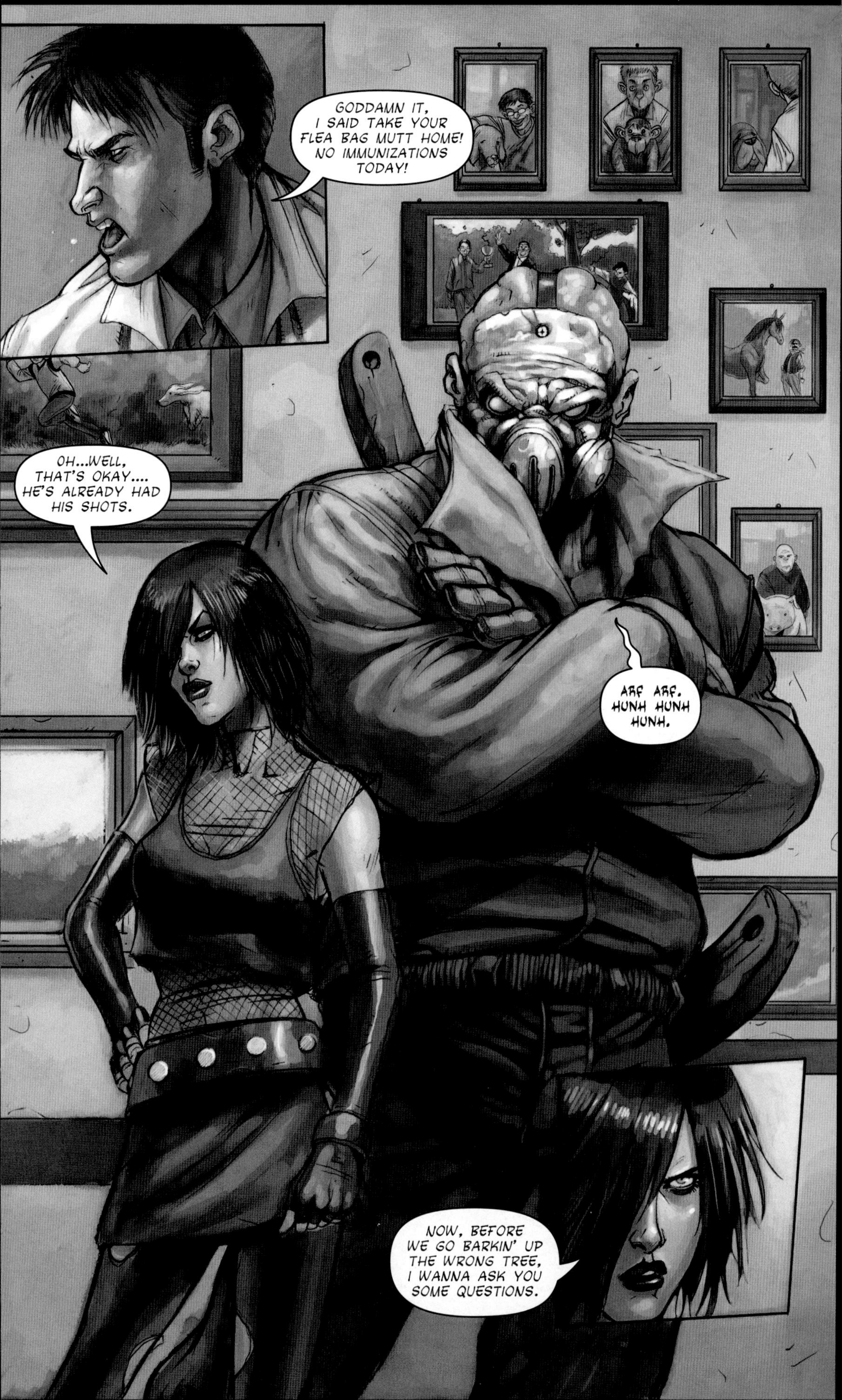
GODDAMN IT, I SAID TAKE YOUR FLEA BAG MUTT HOME! NO IMMUNIZATIONS TODAY!
OH...WELL, THAT'S OKAY.... HE'S ALREADY HAD HIS SHOTS.
ARF ARF. HUNH HUNH HUNH.
NOW, BEFORE WE GO BARKIN' UP THE WRONG TREE, I WANNA ASK YOU SOME QUESTIONS.

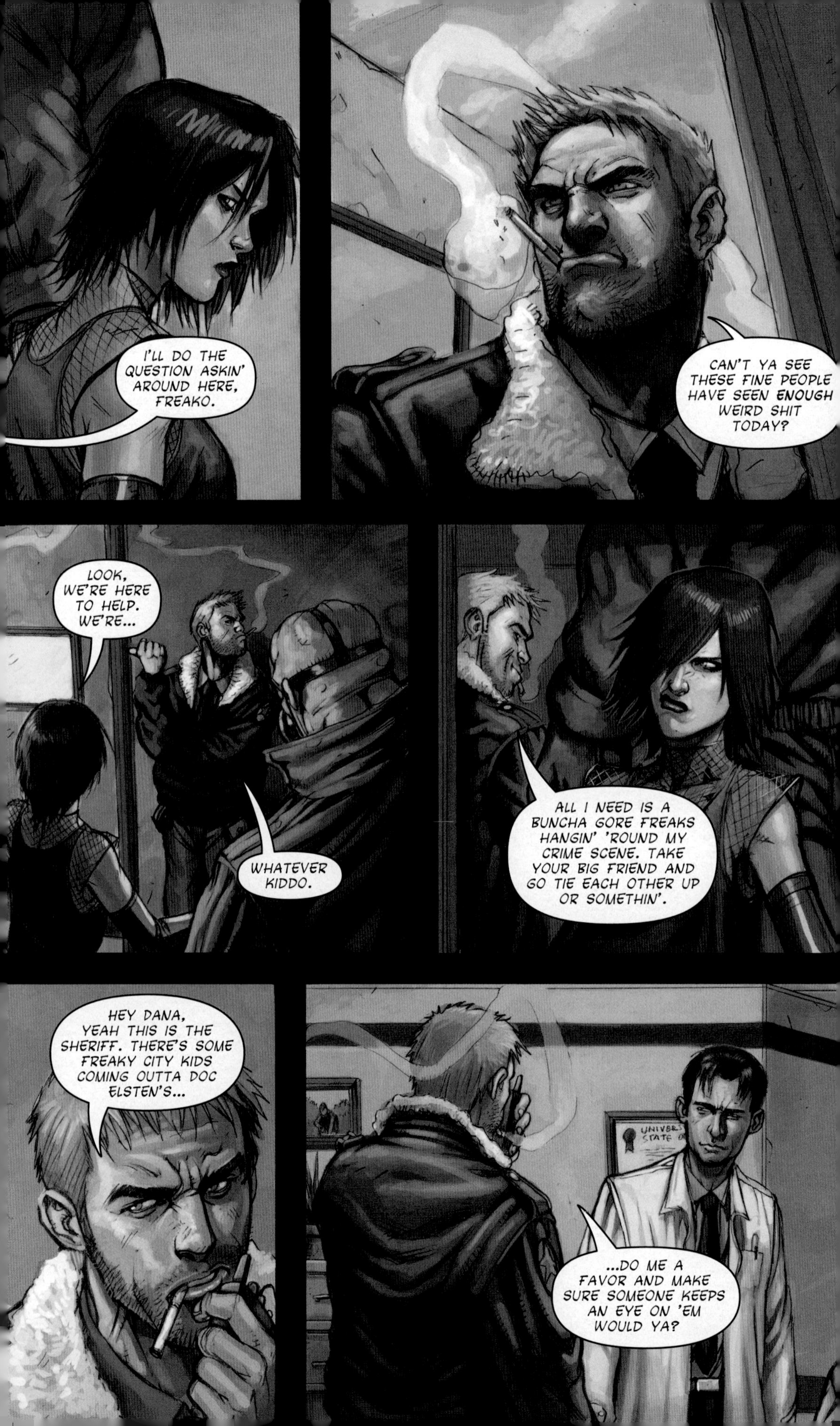
I'LL DO THE QUESTION ASKIN' AROUND HERE, FREAKO.
CAN'T YA SEE THESE FINE PEOPLE HAVE SEEN ENOUGH WEIRD SHIT TODAY?
LOOK, WE'RE HERE TO HELP. WE'RE...
WHATEVER KIDDO.
ALL I NEED IS A BUNCHA GORE FREAKS HANGIN' 'ROUND MY CRIME SCENE. TAKE YOUR BIG FRIEND AND GO TIE EACH OTHER UP OR SOMETHIN'.
HEY DANA, YEAH THIS IS THE SHERIFF. THERE'S SOME FREAKY CITY KIDS COMING OUTTA DOC ELSTEN'S...
...DO ME A FAVOR AND MAKE SURE SOMEONE KEEPS AN EYE ON 'EM WOULD YA?

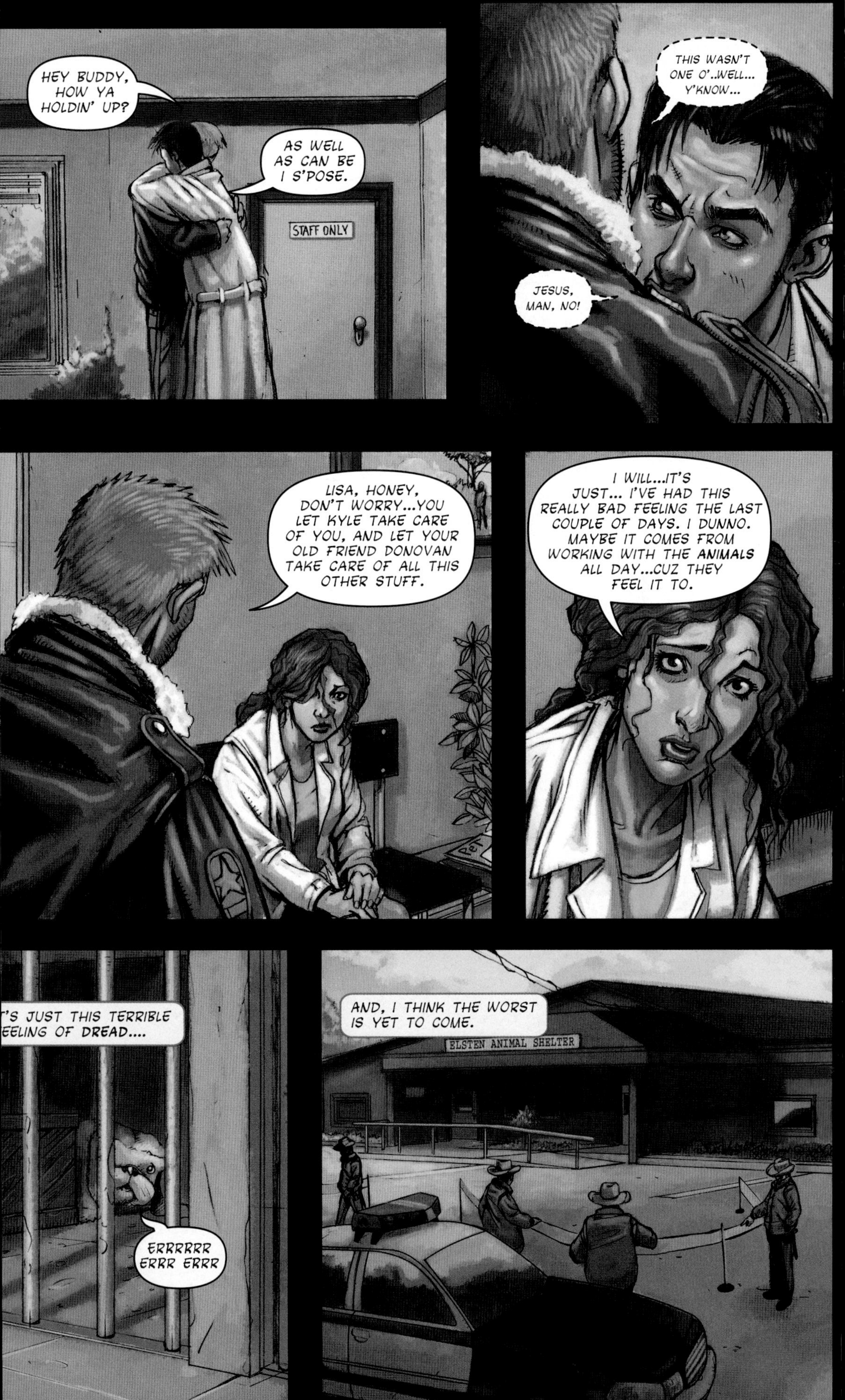
HEY BUDDY, HOW YA HOLDIN' UP?
AS WELL AS CAN BE I S'POSE.
STAFF ONLY
THIS WASN'T ONE O'..WELL... Y'KNOW...
JESUS, MAN, NO!
LISA, HONEY, DON'T WORRY...YOU LET KYLE TAKE CARE OF YOU, AND LET YOUR OLD FRIEND DONOVAN TAKE CARE OF ALL THIS OTHER STUFF.
I WILL...IT'S JUST... I'VE HAD THIS REALLY BAD FEELING THE LAST COUPLE OF DAYS. I DUNNO. MAYBE IT COMES FROM WORKING WITH THE ANIMALS ALL DAY...CUZ THEY FEEL IT TO.
'S JUST THIS TERRIBLE EELING OF DREAD....
ERRRRRR ERRR ERRR
AND, I THINK THE WORST IS YET TO COME.
ELSTEN ANIMAL SHELTER

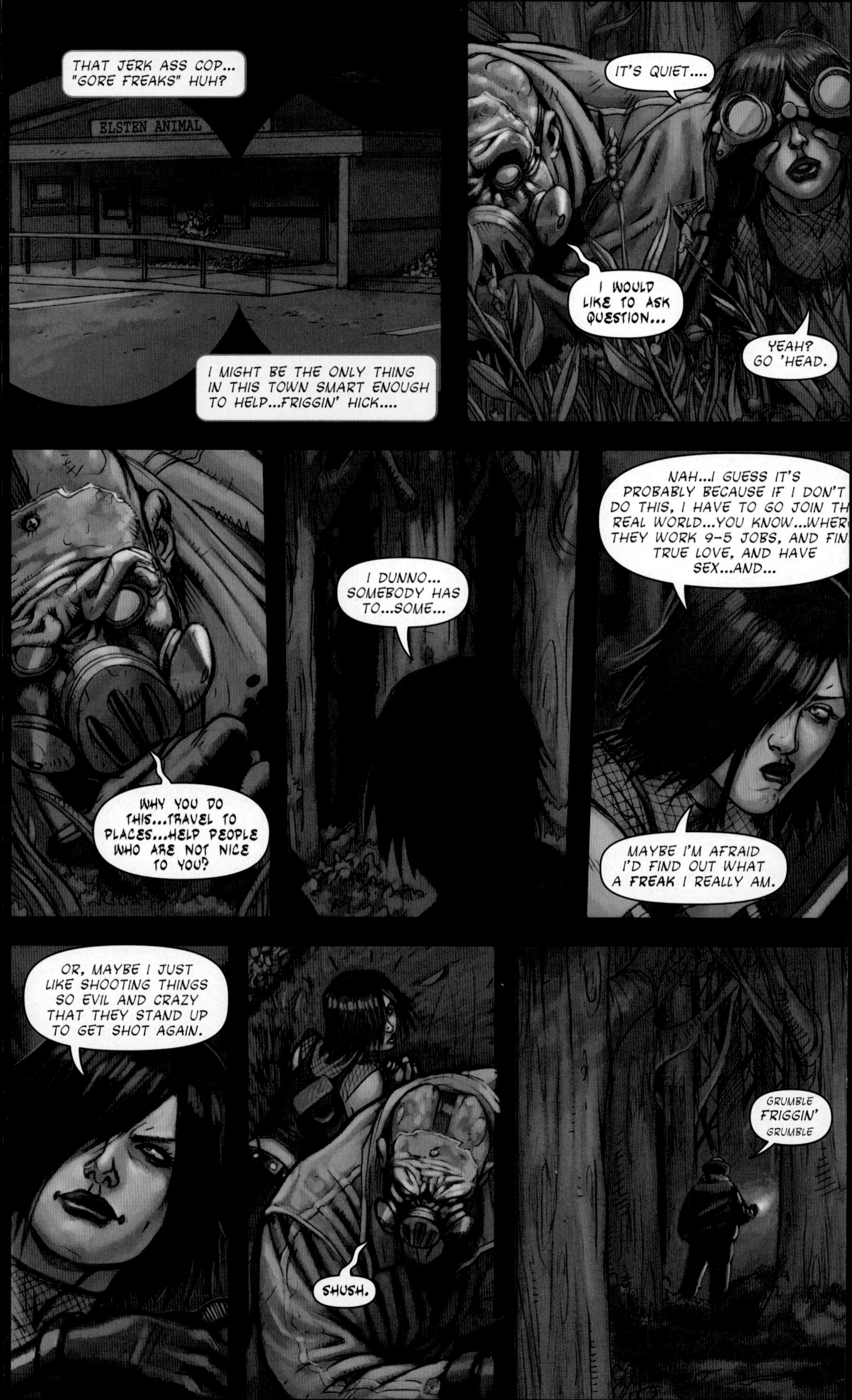

THAT JERK ASS COP... "GORE FREAKS" HUH?
ELSTEN ANIMAL
I MIGHT BE THE ONLY THING IN THIS TOWN SMART ENOUGH TO HELP...FRIGGIN' HICK....
IT'S QUIET....
I WOULD LIKE TO ASK QUESTION...
YEAH? GO 'HEAD.
WHY YOU DO THIS...TRAVEL TO PLACES...HELP PEOPLE WHO ARE NOT NICE TO YOU?
I DUNNO... SOMEBODY HAS TO...SOME...
NAH...I GUESS IT'S PROBABLY BECAUSE IF I DON'T DO THIS, I HAVE TO GO JOIN TH REAL WORLD...YOU KNOW...WHER THEY WORK 9-5 JOBS, AND FIN TRUE LOVE, AND HAVE SEX...AND...
MAYBE I'M AFRAID I'D FIND OUT WHAT A **FREAK** I REALLY AM.
OR, MAYBE I JUST LIKE SHOOTING THINGS SO EVIL AND CRAZY THAT THEY STAND UP TO GET SHOT AGAIN.
SHUSH.
GRUMBLE FRIGGIN' GRUMBLE

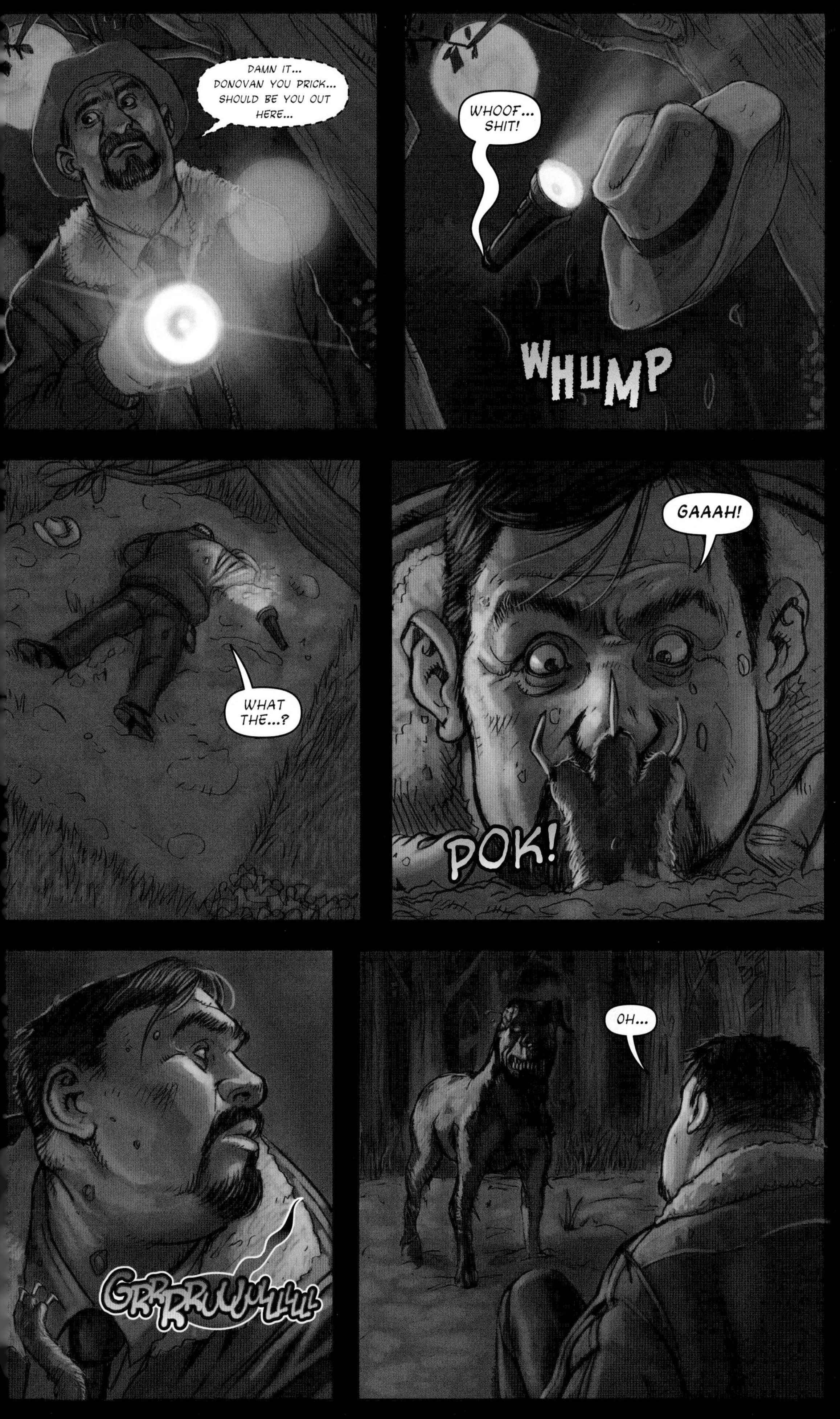
DAMN IT... DONOVAN YOU PRICK... SHOULD BE YOU OUT HERE...
WHOOF... SHIT!
WHUMP
WHAT THE...?
GAAAH!
POK!
GRRRRUUULLLL
OH...

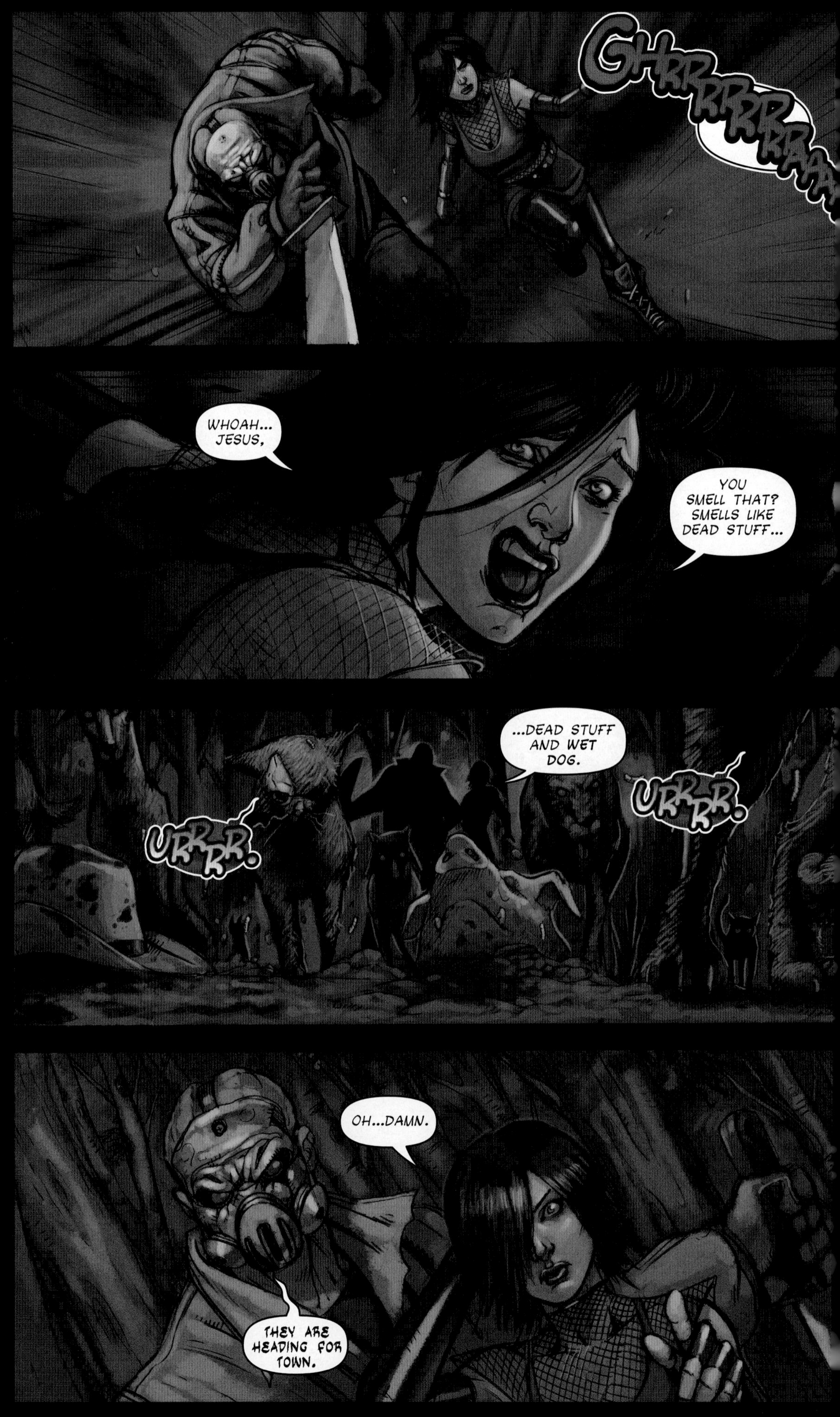
GHRRRRRRRAAAA
WHOAH... JESUS,
YOU SMELL THAT? SMELLS LIKE DEAD STUFF...
URRRR.
...DEAD STUFF AND WET DOG.
URRRR.
OH...DAMN.
THEY ARE HEADING FOR TOWN.

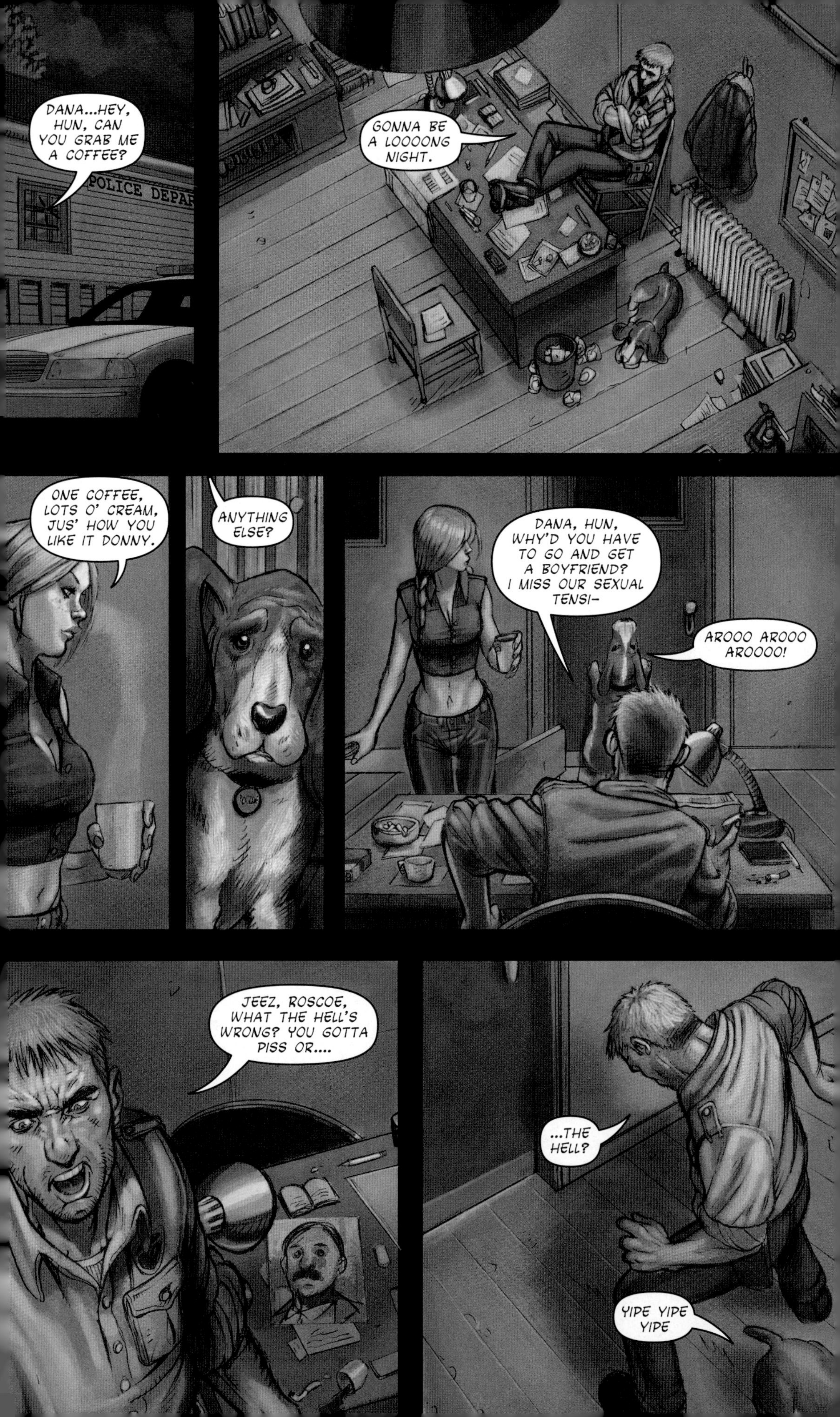
DANA...HEY, HUN, CAN YOU GRAB ME A COFFEE?
POLICE DEPAR
GONNA BE A LOOOONG NIGHT.
ONE COFFEE, LOTS O' CREAM, JUS' HOW YOU LIKE IT DONNY.
ANYTHING ELSE?
DANA, HUN, WHY'D YOU HAVE TO GO AND GET A BOYFRIEND? I MISS OUR SEXUAL TENSI-
AROOO AROOO AROOOO!
JEEZ, ROSCOE, WHAT THE HELL'S WRONG? YOU GOTTA PISS OR....
...THE HELL?
YIPE YIPE YIPE

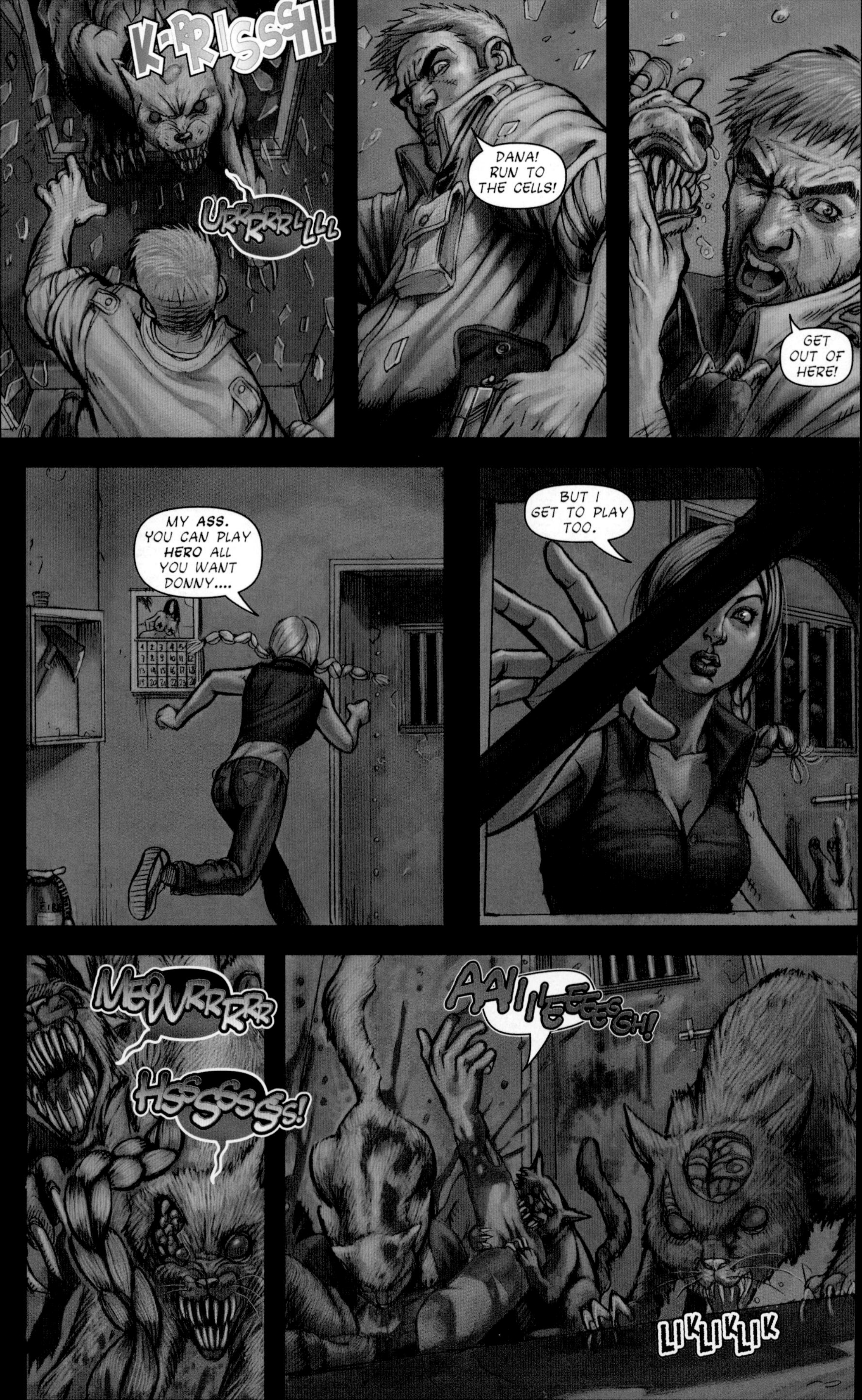
K-RRISSSH!
URRRRRLLLL
DANA! RUN TO THE CELLS!
GET OUT OF HERE!
MY ASS. YOU CAN PLAY HERO ALL YOU WANT DONNY....
BUT I GET TO PLAY TOO.
MEOWRRRRRR
HSSSSSSS!
AAIIIEEEEEGH!
LIKLIKLIK

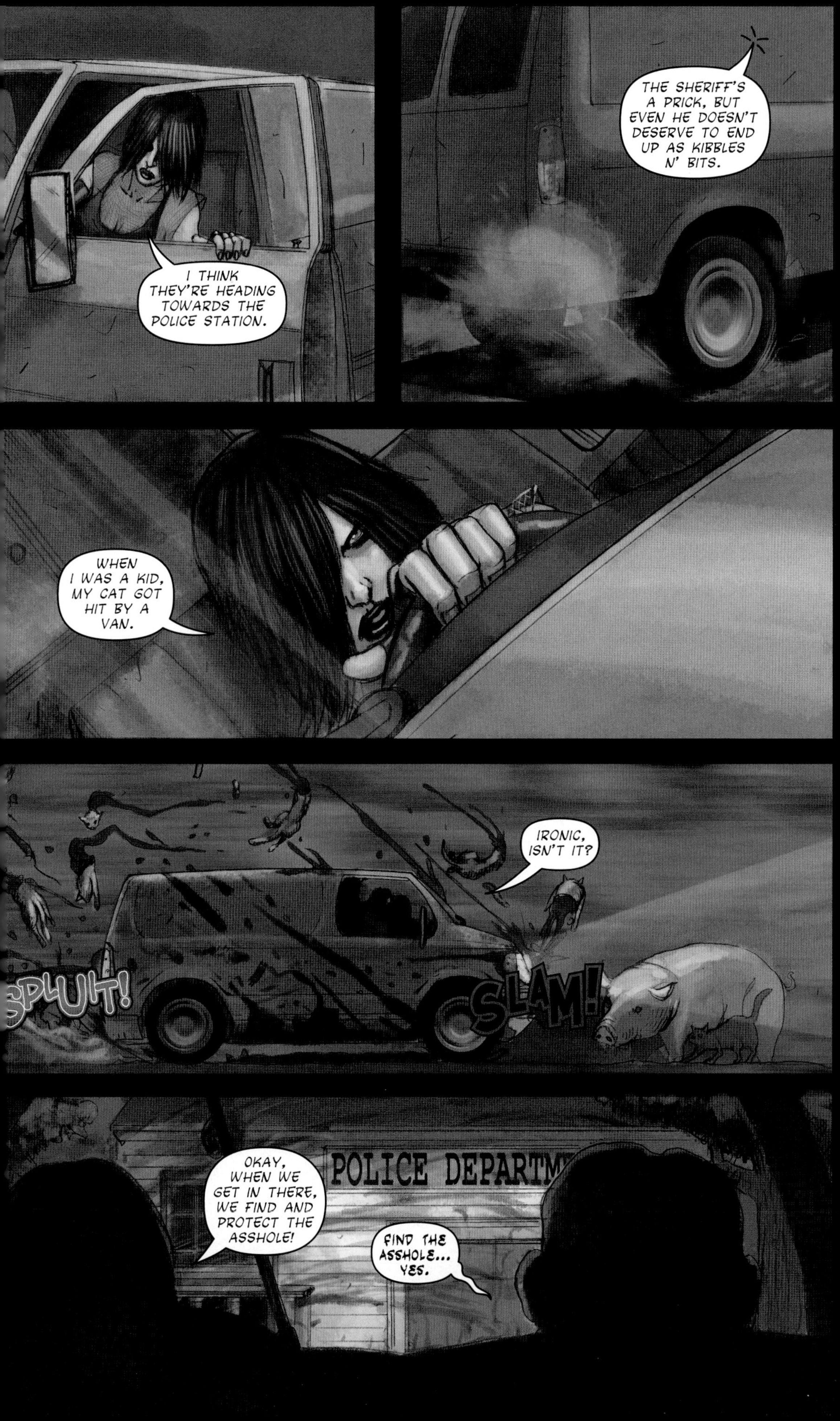
I THINK THEY'RE HEADING TOWARDS THE POLICE STATION.
THE SHERIFF'S A PRICK, BUT EVEN HE DOESN'T DESERVE TO END UP AS KIBBLES N' BITS.
WHEN I WAS A KID, MY CAT GOT HIT BY A VAN.
IRONIC, ISN'T IT?
SPLUIT!
SLAM!
POLICE DEPARTM
OKAY, WHEN WE GET IN THERE, WE FIND AND PROTECT THE ASSHOLE!
FIND THE ASSHOLE... YES.

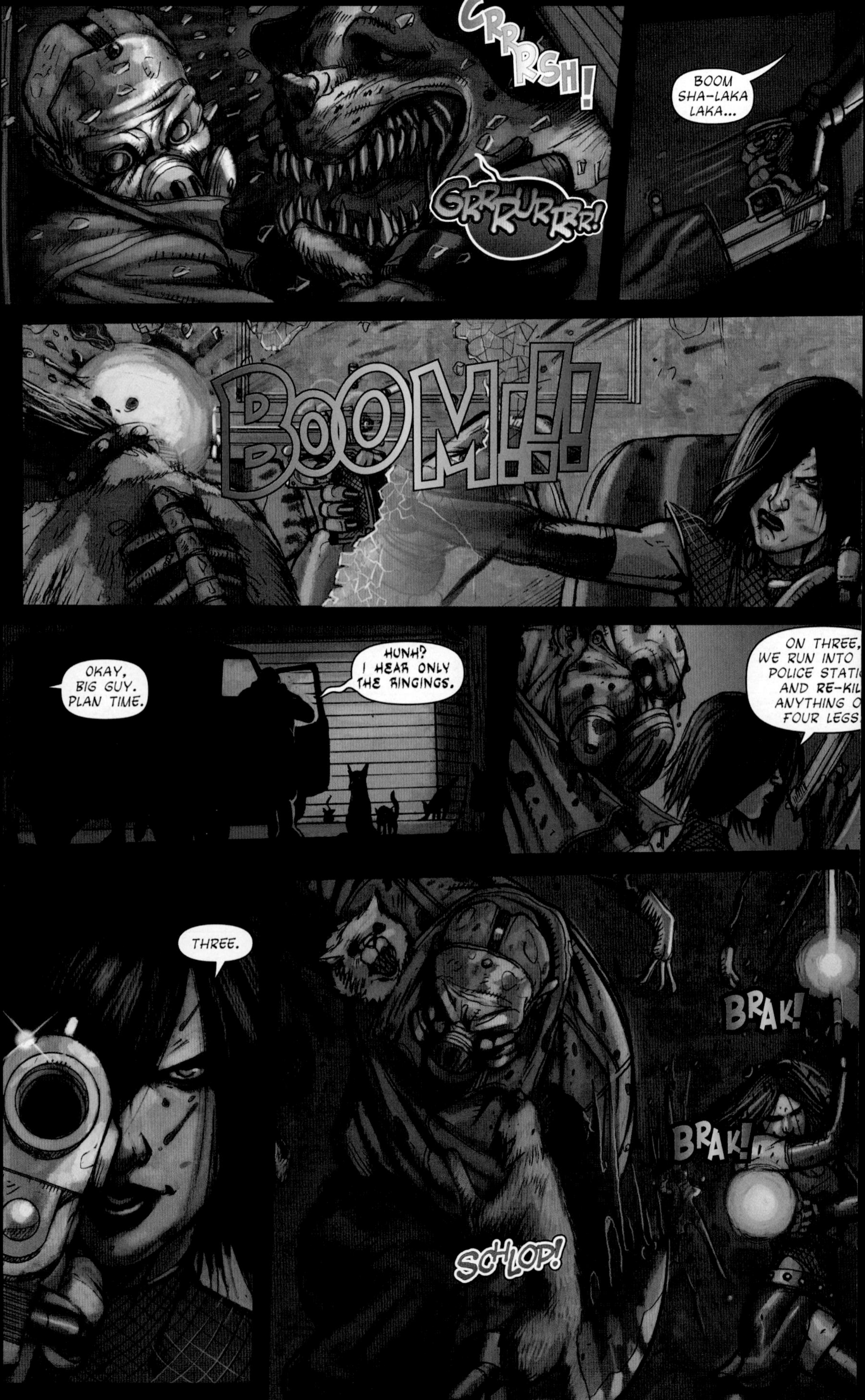
CRRRSH!
GRRRURRRR!
BOOM
SHA-LAKA
LAKA...
BOOM!!
OKAY,
BIG GUY.
PLAN TIME.
HUNH?
I HEAR ONLY
THE RINGINGS.
THREE.
BRAK!
BRAK!
SCHLOP!

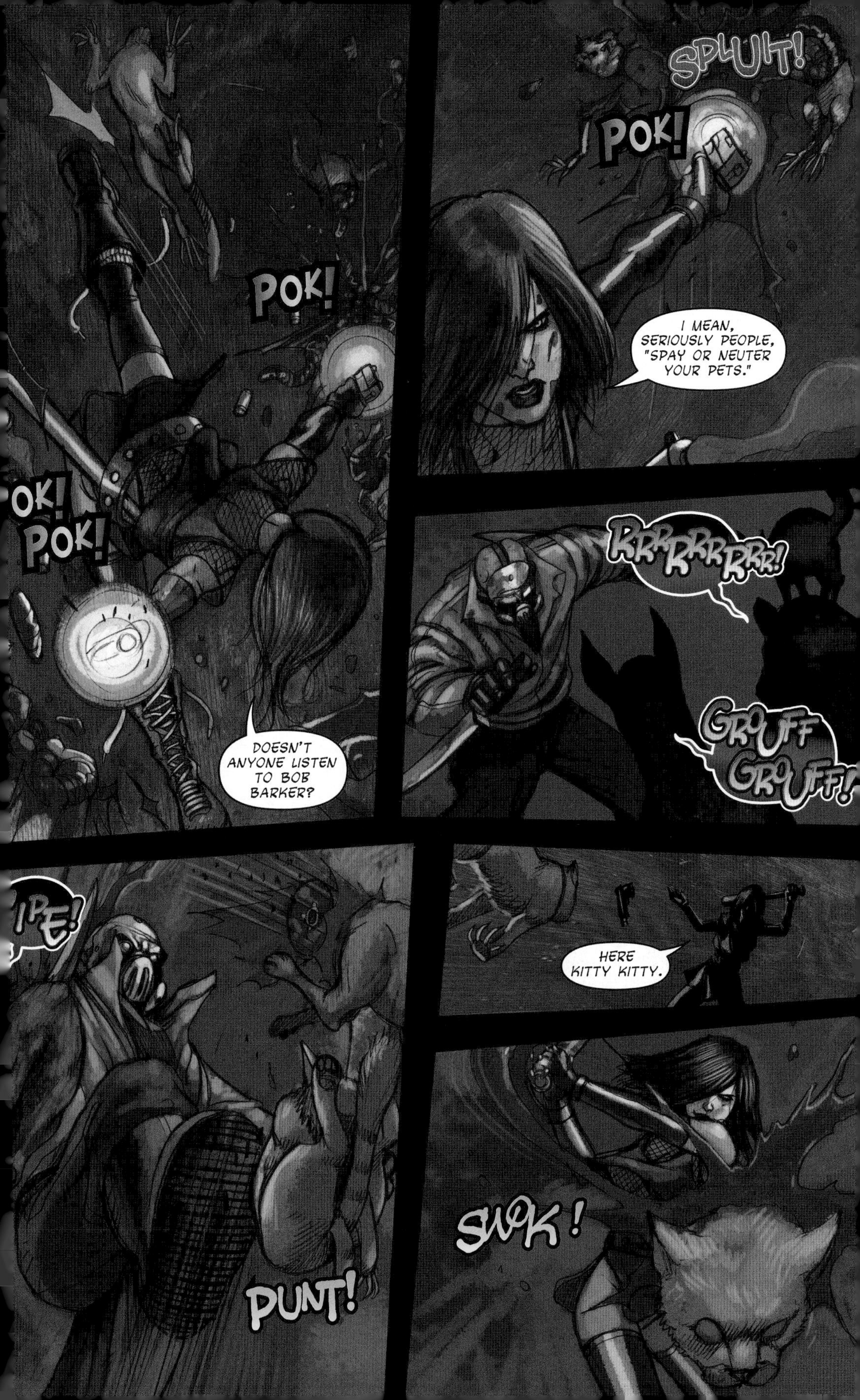
POK!
OK! POK!
DOESN'T ANYONE LISTEN TO BOB BARKER?
SPLUIT!
POK!
I MEAN, SERIOUSLY PEOPLE, "SPAY OR NEUTER YOUR PETS."
RRRRRRRRR!
GROUFF GROUFF!
IPE!
PUNT!
HERE KITTY KITTY.
SWOK!

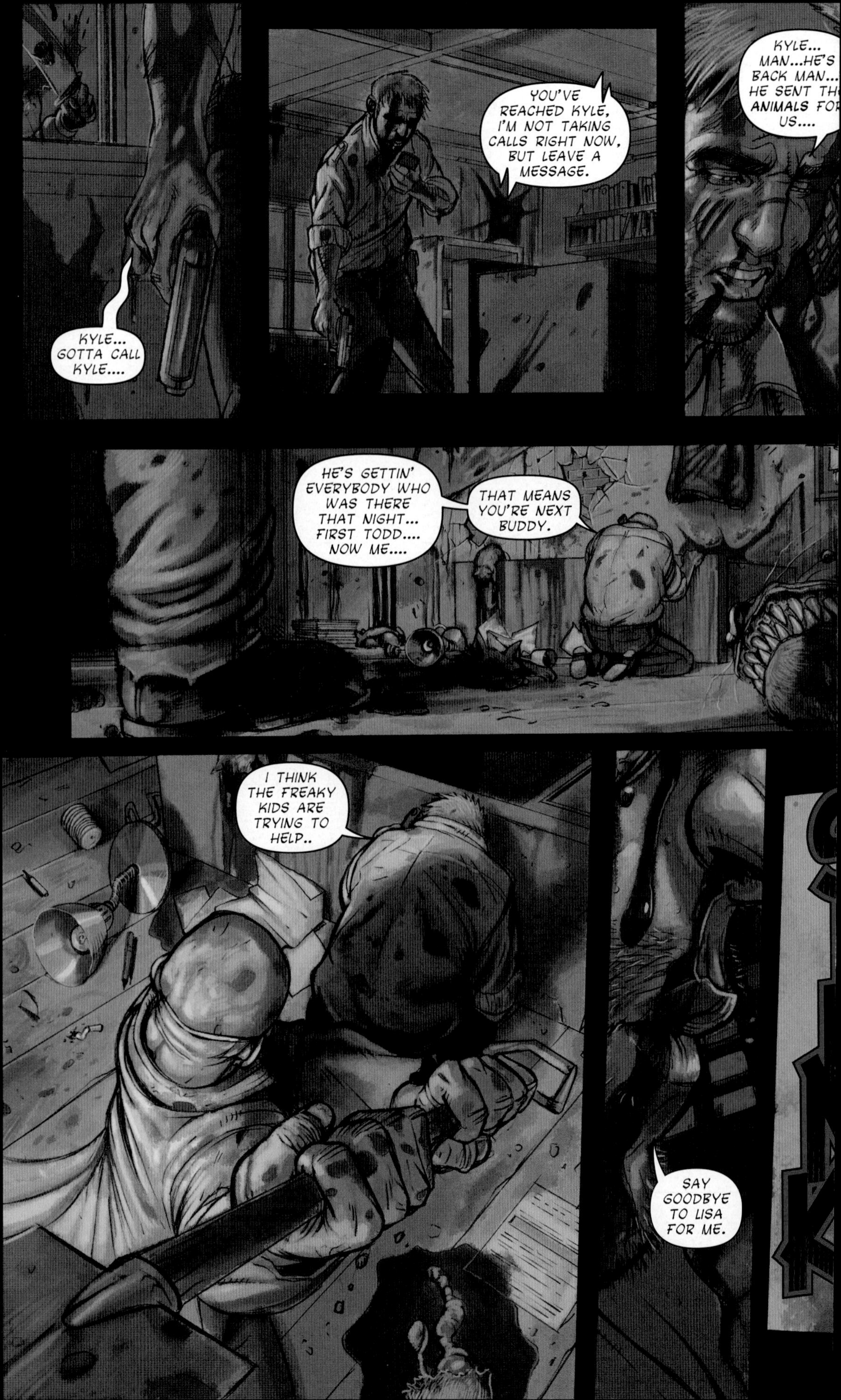
KYLE... GOTTA CALL KYLE....
YOU'VE REACHED KYLE, I'M NOT TAKING CALLS RIGHT NOW, BUT LEAVE A MESSAGE.
KYLE... MAN...HE'S BACK MAN... HE SENT TH ANIMALS FO US....
HE'S GETTIN' EVERYBODY WHO WAS THERE THAT NIGHT... FIRST TODD.... NOW ME....
THAT MEANS YOU'RE NEXT BUDDY.
I THINK THE FREAKY KIDS ARE TRYING TO HELP..
SAY GOODBYE TO LISA FOR ME.

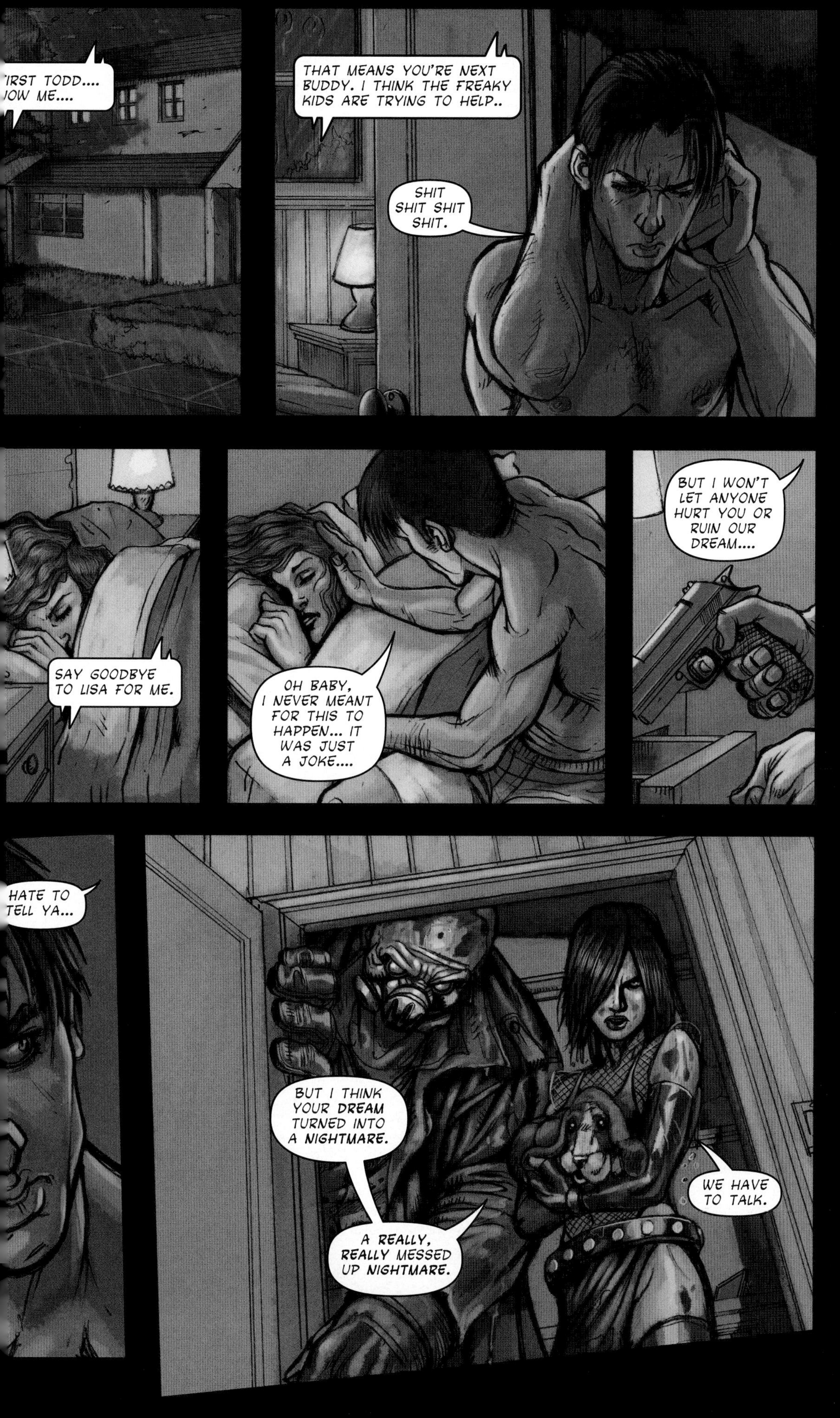
IRST TODD....
IOW ME....
THAT MEANS YOU'RE NEXT BUDDY. I THINK THE FREAKY KIDS ARE TRYING TO HELP..
SHIT SHIT SHIT SHIT.
SAY GOODBYE TO LISA FOR ME.
OH BABY, I NEVER MEANT FOR THIS TO HAPPEN... IT WAS JUST A JOKE....
BUT I WON'T LET ANYONE HURT YOU OR RUIN OUR DREAM....
HATE TO TELL YA...
BUT I THINK YOUR DREAM TURNED INTO A NIGHTMARE.
A REALLY, REALLY MESSED UP NIGHTMARE.
WE HAVE TO TALK.

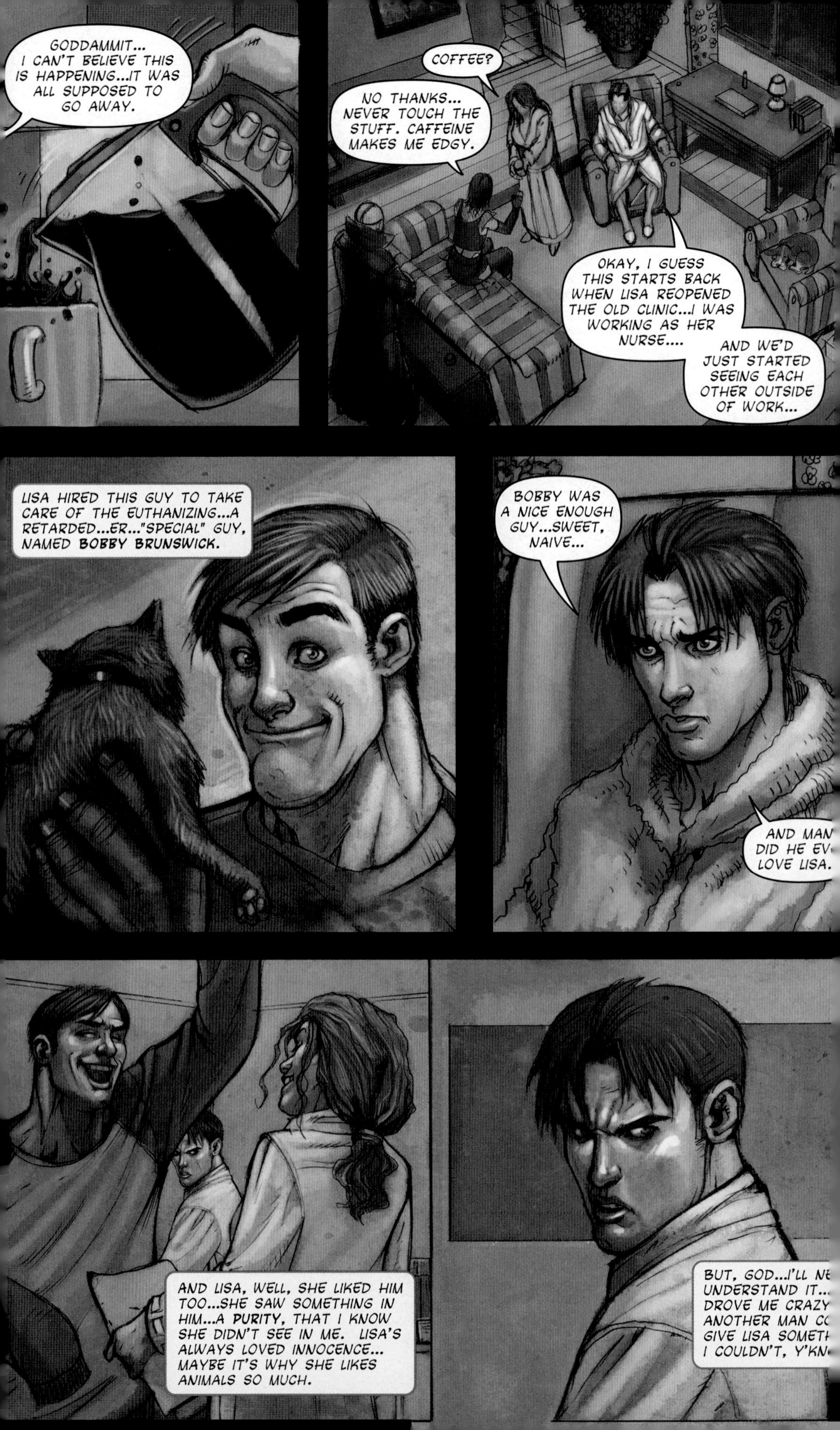
GODDAMMIT... I CAN'T BELIEVE THIS IS HAPPENING...IT WAS ALL SUPPOSED TO GO AWAY.
COFFEE?
NO THANKS... NEVER TOUCH THE STUFF. CAFFEINE MAKES ME EDGY.
OKAY, I GUESS THIS STARTS BACK WHEN LISA REOPENED THE OLD CLINIC...I WAS WORKING AS HER NURSE....
AND WE'D JUST STARTED SEEING EACH OTHER OUTSIDE OF WORK...
LISA HIRED THIS GUY TO TAKE CARE OF THE EUTHANIZING...A RETARDED...ER..."SPECIAL" GUY, NAMED **BOBBY BRUNSWICK**.
BOBBY WAS A NICE ENOUGH GUY...SWEET, NAIVE...
AND MAN DID HE EV LOVE LISA.
AND LISA, WELL, SHE LIKED HIM TOO...SHE SAW SOMETHING IN HIM...A **PURITY**, THAT I KNOW SHE DIDN'T SEE IN ME. LISA'S ALWAYS LOVED INNOCENCE... MAYBE IT'S WHY SHE LIKES ANIMALS SO MUCH.
BUT, GOD...I'LL NE UNDERSTAND IT... DROVE ME CRAZY ANOTHER MAN CO GIVE LISA SOMETH I COULDN'T, Y'KN

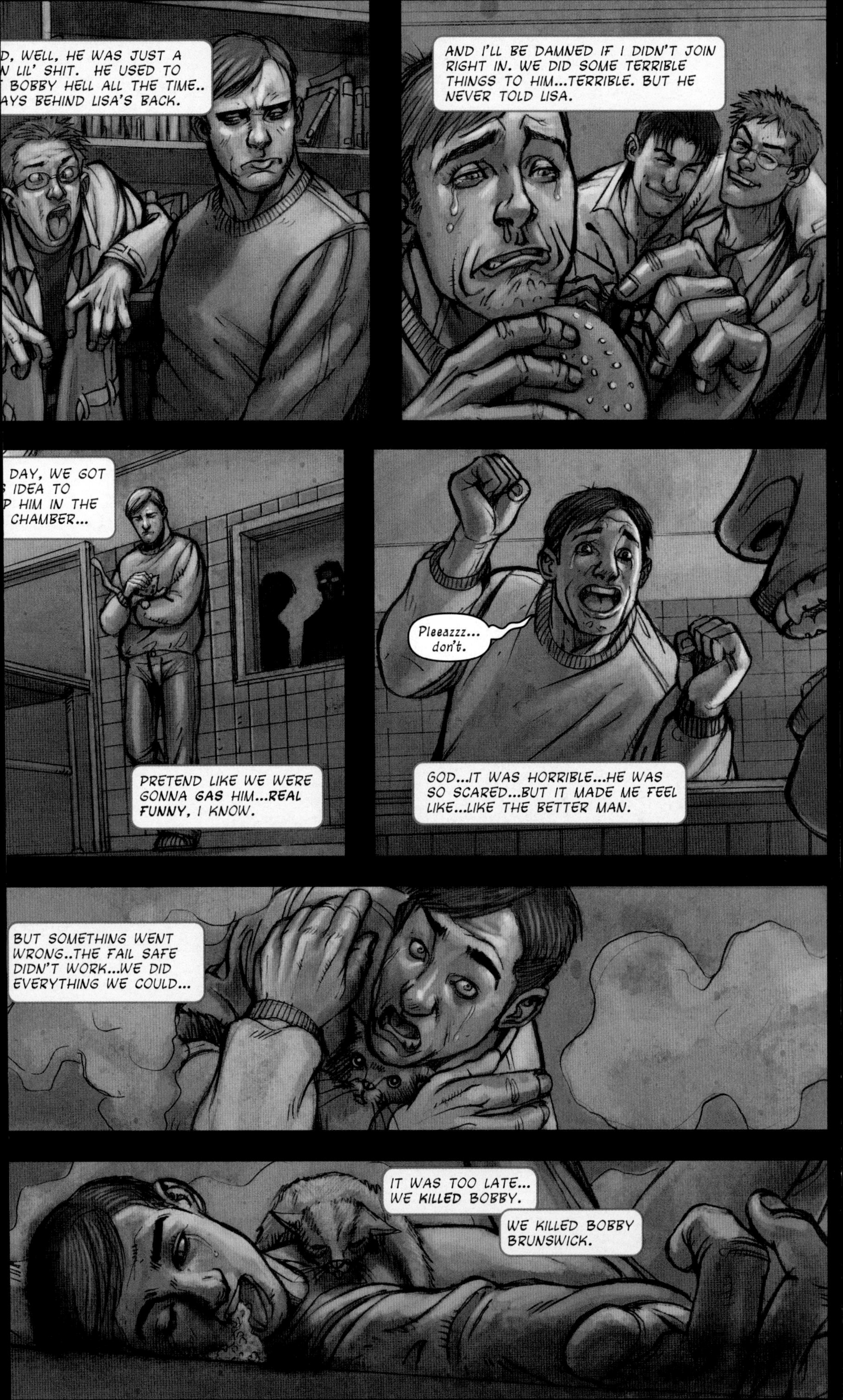
D, WELL, HE WAS JUST A
N LIL' SHIT. HE USED TO
BOBBY HELL ALL THE TIME..
AYS BEHIND LISA'S BACK.
AND I'LL BE DAMNED IF I DIDN'T JOIN RIGHT IN. WE DID SOME TERRIBLE THINGS TO HIM...TERRIBLE. BUT HE NEVER TOLD LISA.
DAY, WE GOT
IDEA TO
P HIM IN THE
CHAMBER...
PRETEND LIKE WE WERE GONNA GAS HIM...REAL FUNNY, I KNOW.
Pleeazzz... don't.
GOD...IT WAS HORRIBLE...HE WAS SO SCARED...BUT IT MADE ME FEEL LIKE...LIKE THE BETTER MAN.
BUT SOMETHING WENT WRONG..THE FAIL SAFE DIDN'T WORK...WE DID EVERYTHING WE COULD...
IT WAS TOO LATE... WE KILLED BOBBY.
WE KILLED BOBBY BRUNSWICK.

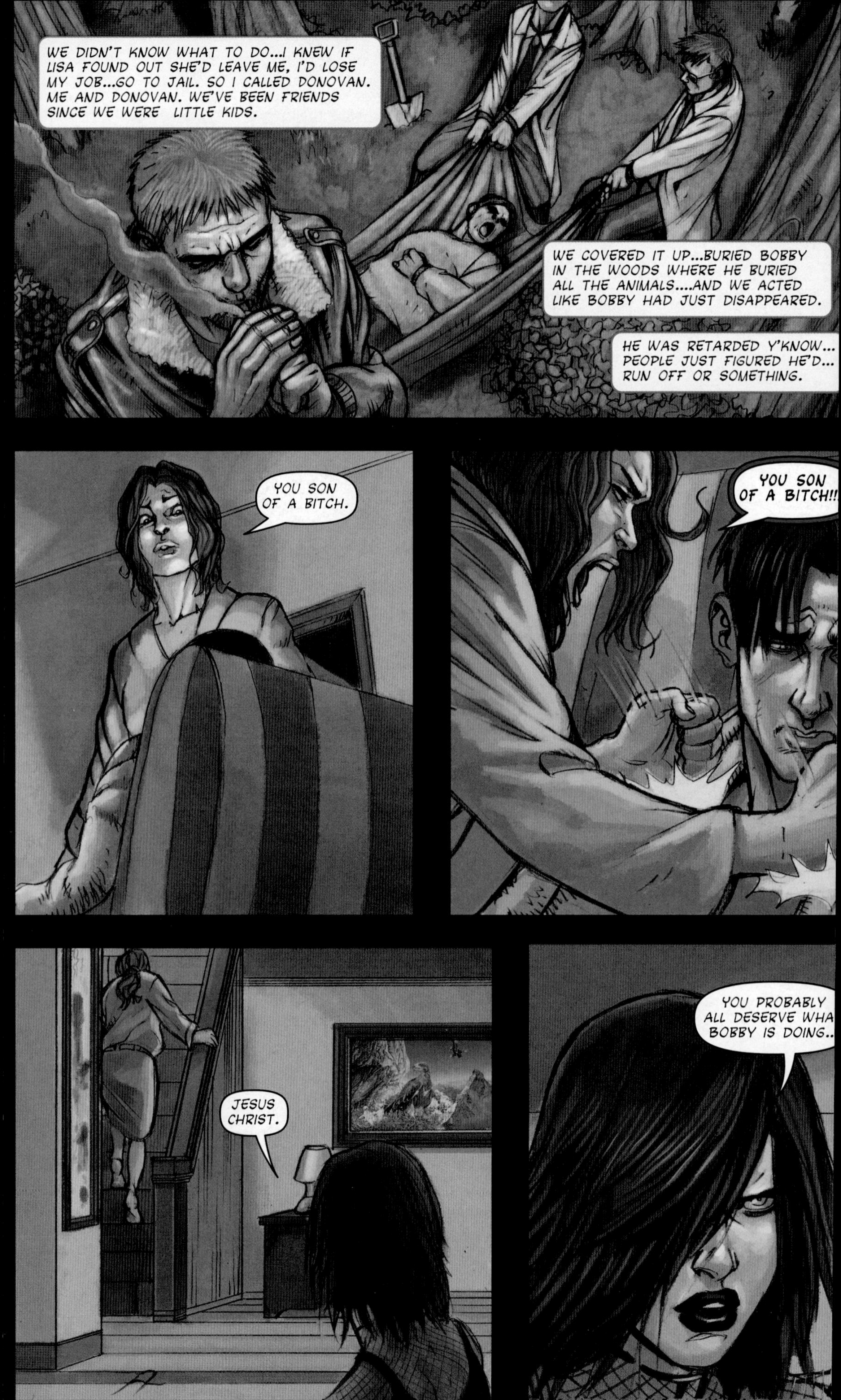
WE DIDN'T KNOW WHAT TO DO...I KNEW IF LISA FOUND OUT SHE'D LEAVE ME, I'D LOSE MY JOB...GO TO JAIL. SO I CALLED DONOVAN. ME AND DONOVAN. WE'VE BEEN FRIENDS SINCE WE WERE LITTLE KIDS.
WE COVERED IT UP...BURIED BOBBY IN THE WOODS WHERE HE BURIED ALL THE ANIMALS....AND WE ACTED LIKE BOBBY HAD JUST DISAPPEARED.
HE WAS RETARDED Y'KNOW... PEOPLE JUST FIGURED HE'D... RUN OFF OR SOMETHING.
YOU SON OF A BITCH.
YOU SON OF A BITCH!!
JESUS CHRIST.
YOU PROBABLY ALL DESERVE WHA BOBBY IS DOING..

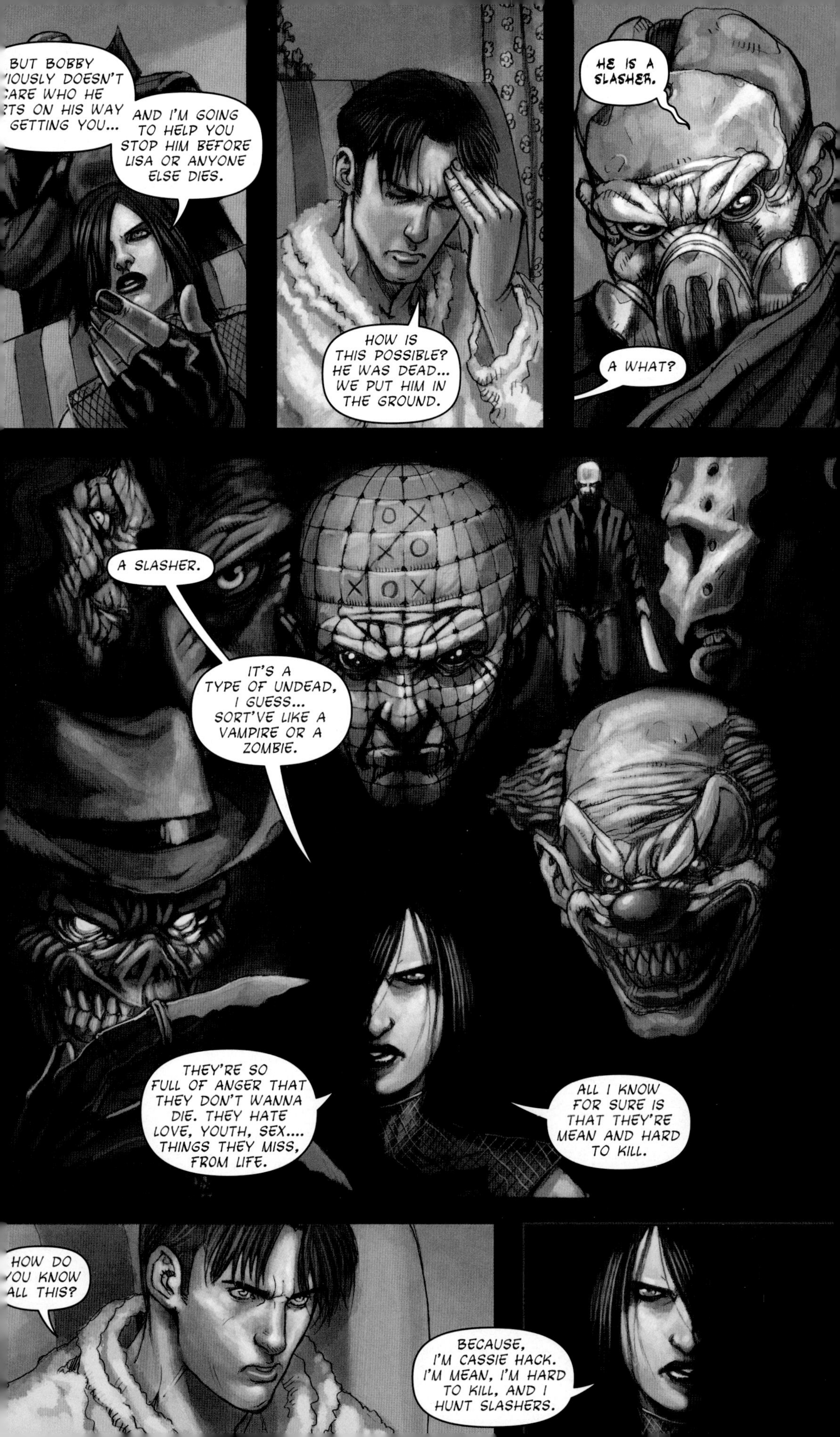
BUT BOBBY IOUSLY DOESN'T CARE WHO HE RTS ON HIS WAY GETTING YOU...
AND I'M GOING TO HELP YOU STOP HIM BEFORE LISA OR ANYONE ELSE DIES.
HOW IS THIS POSSIBLE? HE WAS DEAD... WE PUT HIM IN THE GROUND.
HE IS A SLASHER.
A WHAT?
A SLASHER.
IT'S A TYPE OF UNDEAD, I GUESS... SORT'VE LIKE A VAMPIRE OR A ZOMBIE.
THEY'RE SO FULL OF ANGER THAT THEY DON'T WANNA DIE. THEY HATE LOVE, YOUTH, SEX.... THINGS THEY MISS, FROM LIFE.
ALL I KNOW FOR SURE IS THAT THEY'RE MEAN AND HARD TO KILL.
HOW DO YOU KNOW ALL THIS?
BECAUSE, I'M CASSIE HACK. I'M MEAN, I'M HARD TO KILL, AND I HUNT SLASHERS.

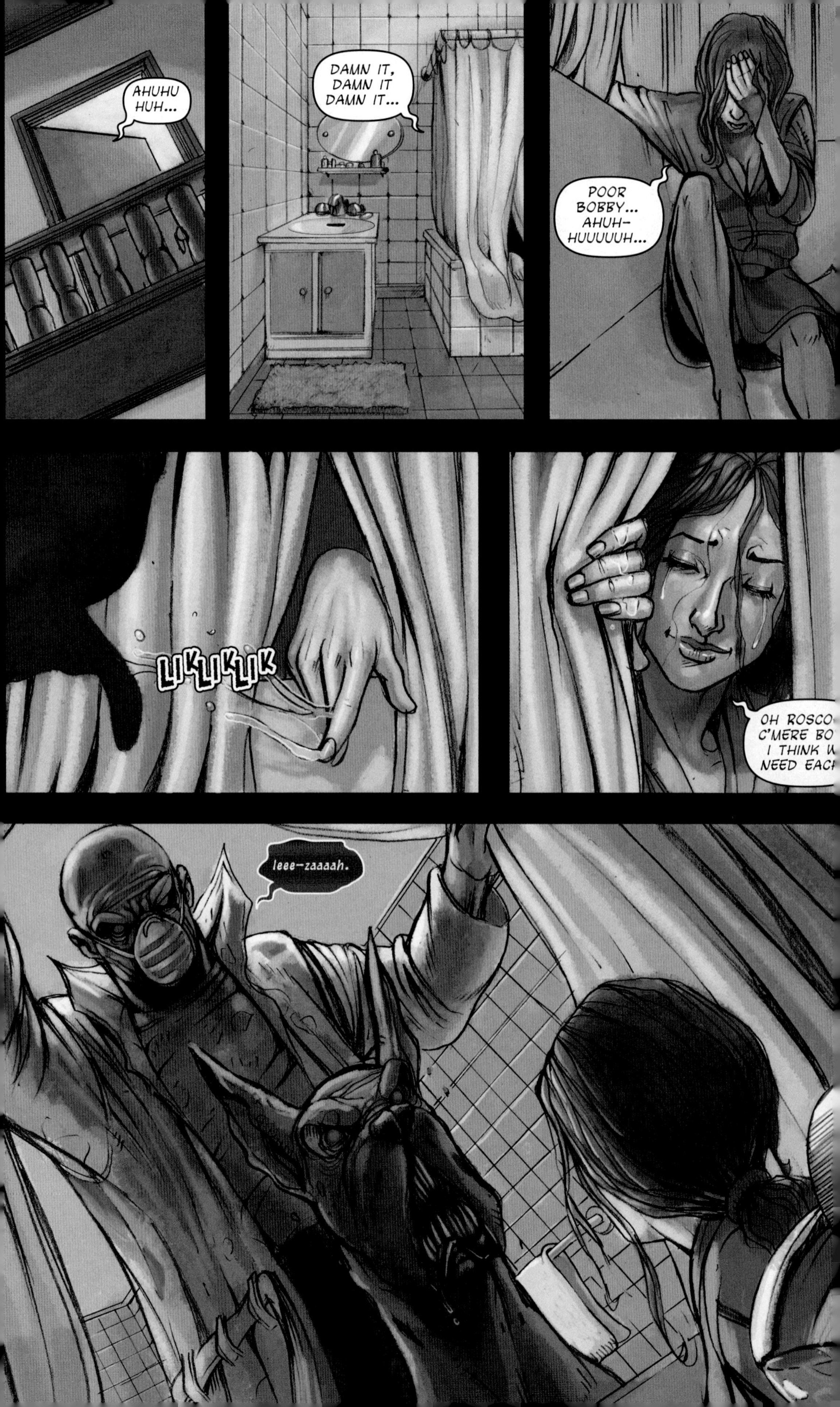
AHUHU HUH...
DAMN IT, DAMN IT DAMN IT...
POOR BOBBY... AHUH-HUUUUUH...
LIKLIKLIK
OH ROSCO C'MERE BO I THINK W NEED EACH
leee-zaaaah.

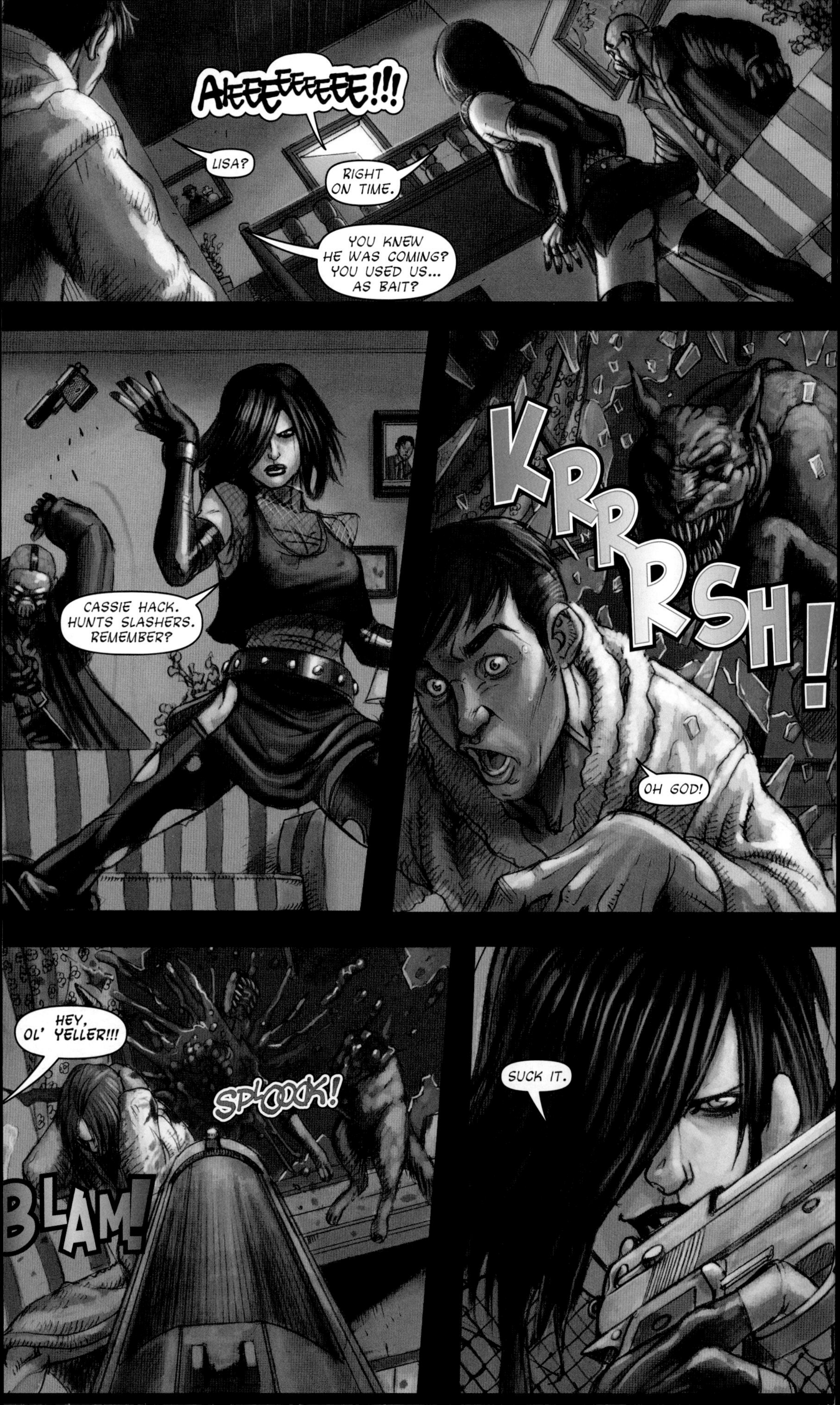
AIEEEEEEEEEE!!!
LISA?
RIGHT ON TIME.
YOU KNEW HE WAS COMING? YOU USED US... AS BAIT?
CASSIE HACK. HUNTS SLASHERS. REMEMBER?
KRRRSH!
OH GOD!
HEY, OL' YELLER!!!
SPLOOCK!
BLAM!
SUCK IT.

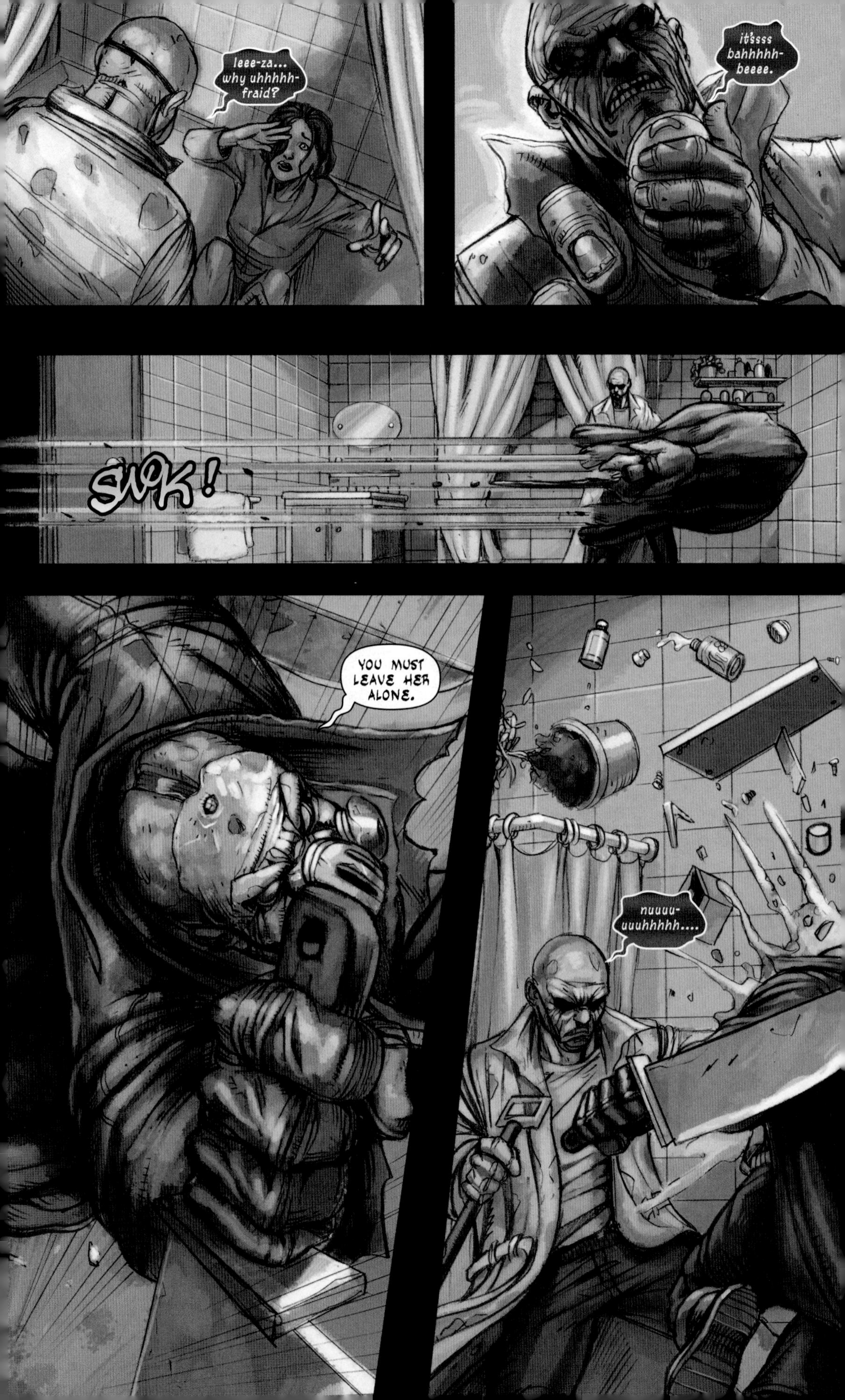
leee-za... why uhhhhh-fraid?
it'ssss bahhhhhh-beeee.
SWK!
YOU MUST LEAVE HER ALONE.
nuuuu-uuuhhhhh....

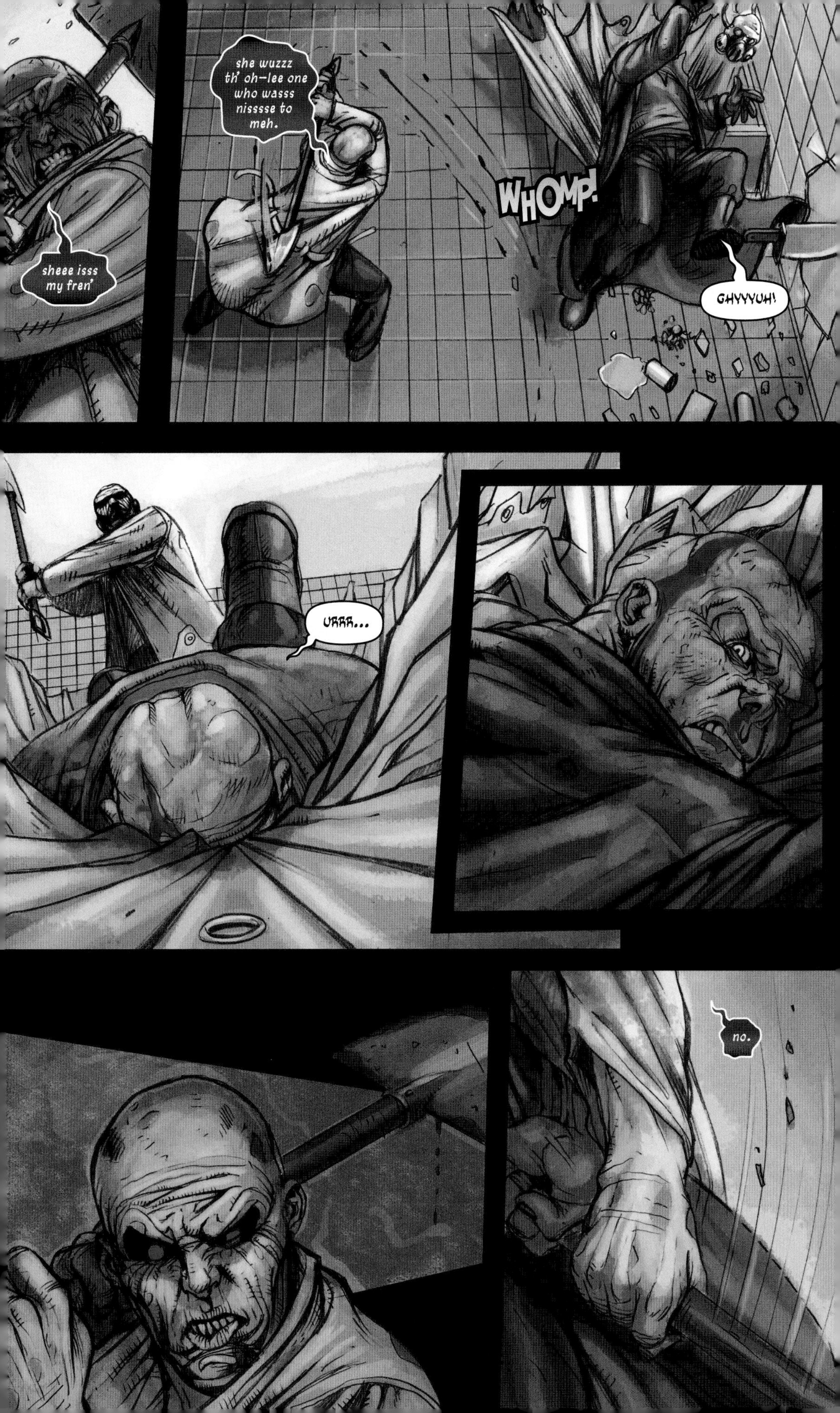
sheee isss my fren'
she wuzzz th' oh-lee one who wasss nisssse to meh.
WHOMP!
GHYYYUH!
URRR...
no.

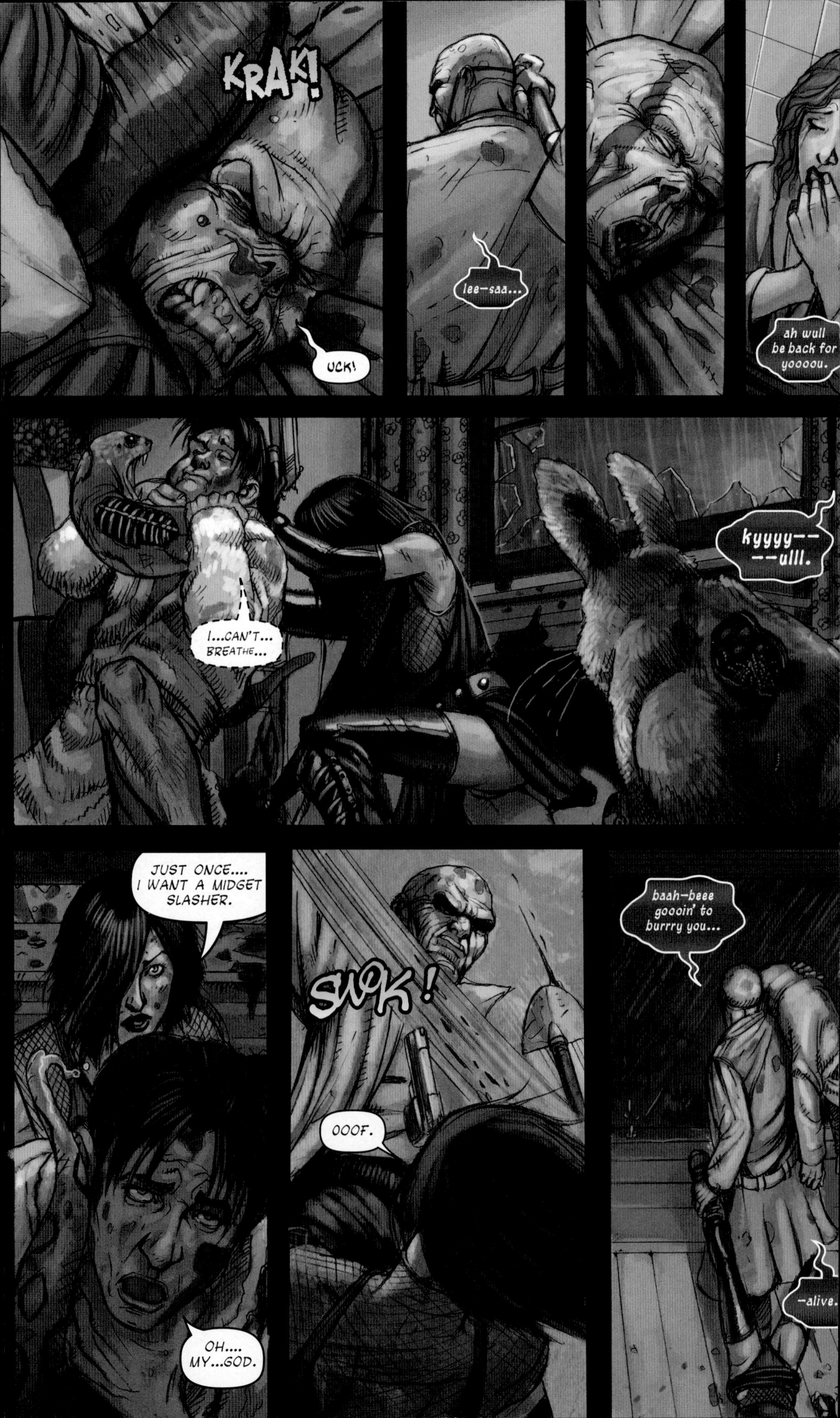
KRAK!
UCK!
lee-saa...
ah wull be back for yoooou.
I...CAN'T... BREATHE...
kyyyy-- --ulll.
JUST ONCE.... I WANT A MIDGET SLASHER.
OH.... MY...GOD.
SWK!
OOOF.
baah-beee gooin' to burrry you...
-alive.

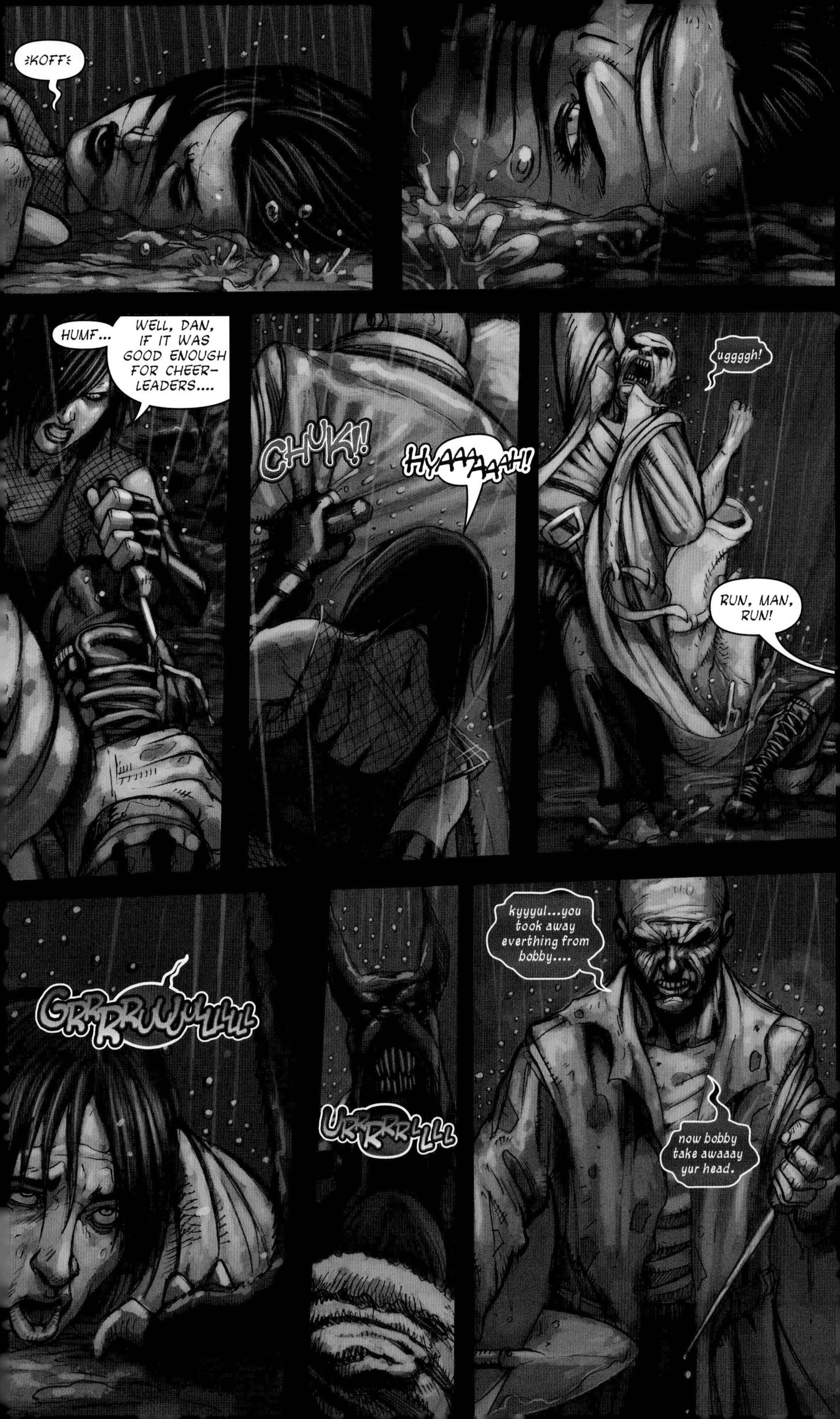

KOFF
HUMF...
WELL, DAN, IF IT WAS GOOD ENOUGH FOR CHEER-LEADERS....
CHUK!!
HYAAAAAAH!
uggggh!
RUN, MAN, RUN!
GRRRRUUULLLL
URRRRLLL
kyyyul...you took away everthing from bobby....
now bobby take awaaay yur head.

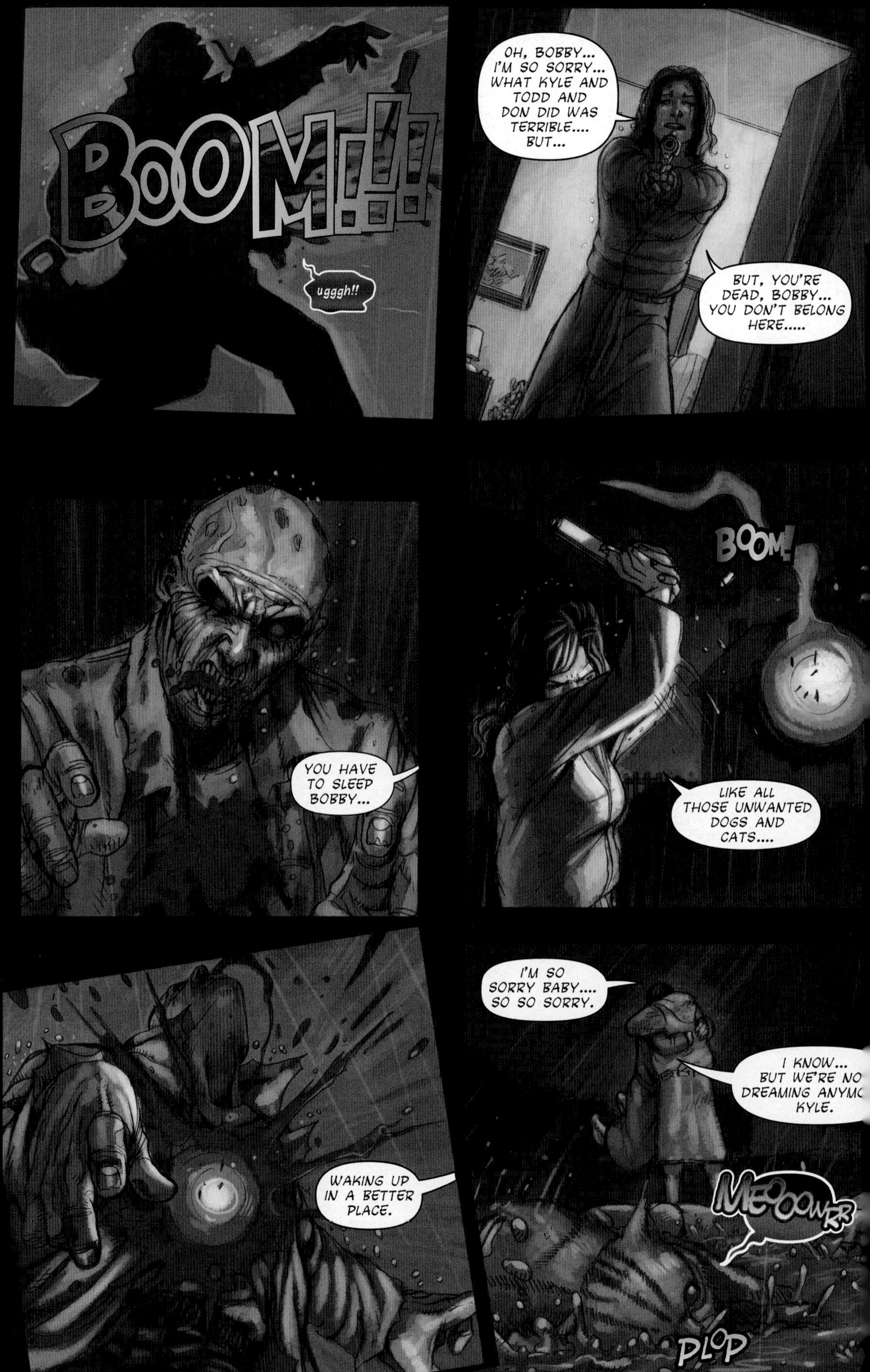
BOOM!!!
uggggh!!
OH, BOBBY... I'M SO SORRY... WHAT KYLE AND TODD AND DON DID WAS TERRIBLE.... BUT...
BUT, YOU'RE DEAD, BOBBY... YOU DON'T BELONG HERE.....
YOU HAVE TO SLEEP BOBBY...
BOOM!
LIKE ALL THOSE UNWANTED DOGS AND CATS....
WAKING UP IN A BETTER PLACE.
I'M SO SORRY BABY.... SO SO SORRY.
I KNOW... BUT WE'RE NO
DREAMING ANYMO
KYLE.
MEOOOWRR
PLOP

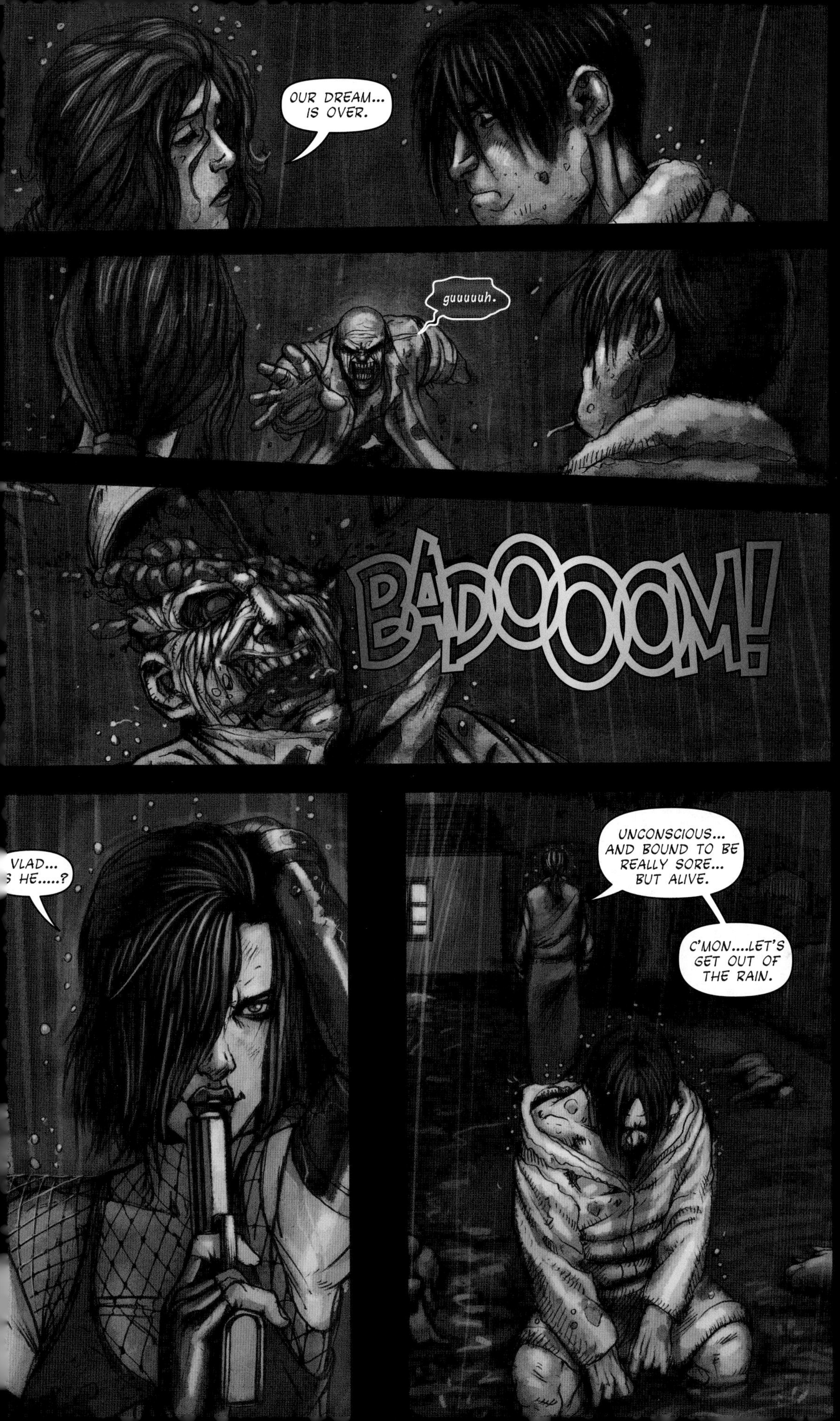
OUR DREAM... IS OVER.
guuuuuh.
BADOOOOM!
VLAD... S HE.....?
UNCONSCIOUS... AND BOUND TO BE REALLY SORE... BUT ALIVE.
C'MON....LET'S GET OUT OF THE RAIN.

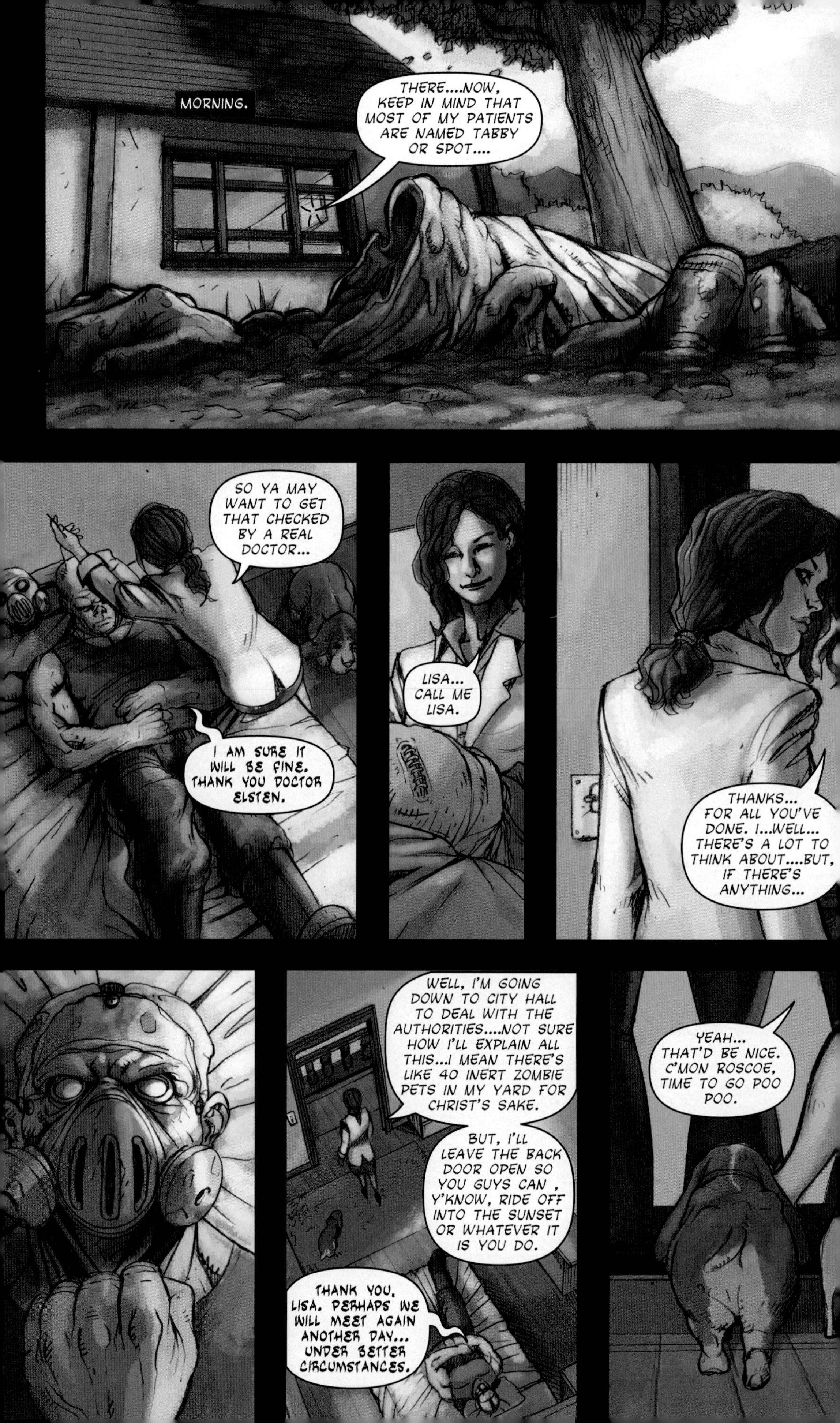
MORNING.
THERE....NOW, KEEP IN MIND THAT MOST OF MY PATIENTS ARE NAMED TABBY OR SPOT....
SO YA MAY WANT TO GET THAT CHECKED BY A REAL DOCTOR...
I AM SURE IT WILL BE FINE. THANK YOU DOCTOR ELSTEN.
LISA... CALL ME LISA.
THANKS... FOR ALL YOU'VE DONE. I...WELL... THERE'S A LOT TO THINK ABOUT....BUT, IF THERE'S ANYTHING...
WELL, I'M GOING DOWN TO CITY HALL TO DEAL WITH THE AUTHORITIES....NOT SURE HOW I'LL EXPLAIN ALL THIS...I MEAN THERE'S LIKE 40 INERT ZOMBIE PETS IN MY YARD FOR CHRIST'S SAKE.
BUT, I'LL LEAVE THE BACK DOOR OPEN SO YOU GUYS CAN , Y'KNOW, RIDE OFF INTO THE SUNSET OR WHATEVER IT IS YOU DO.
THANK YOU, LISA. PERHAPS WE WILL MEET AGAIN ANOTHER DAY... UNDER BETTER CIRCUMSTANCES.
YEAH... THAT'D BE NICE. C'MON ROSCOE, TIME TO GO POO POO.

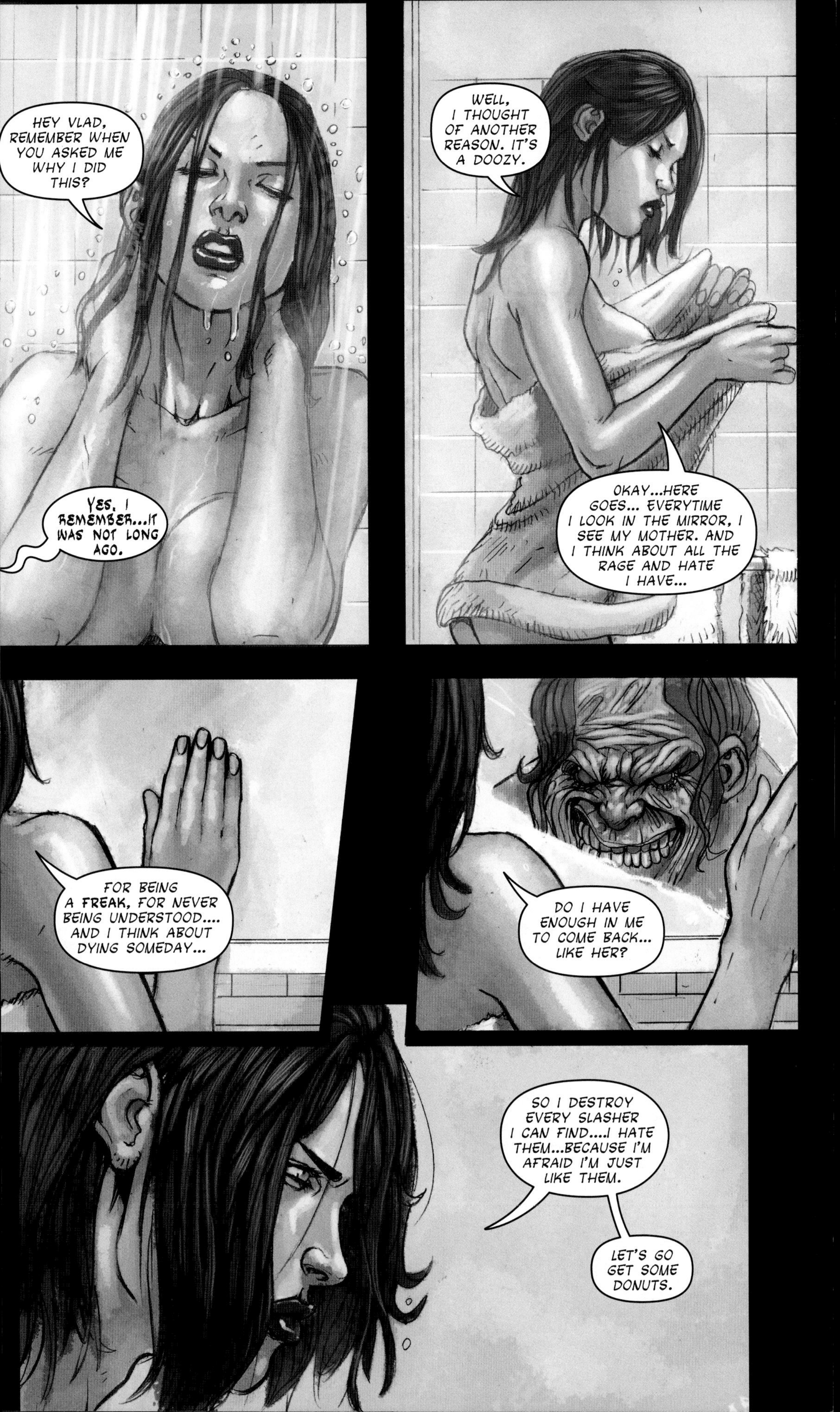
HEY VLAD, REMEMBER WHEN YOU ASKED ME WHY I DID THIS?
YES, I REMEMBER...IT WAS NOT LONG AGO.
WELL, I THOUGHT OF ANOTHER REASON. IT'S A DOOZY.
OKAY...HERE GOES... EVERYTIME I LOOK IN THE MIRROR, I SEE MY MOTHER. AND I THINK ABOUT ALL THE RAGE AND HATE I HAVE...
FOR BEING A FREAK, FOR NEVER BEING UNDERSTOOD.... AND I THINK ABOUT DYING SOMEDAY...
DO I HAVE ENOUGH IN ME TO COME BACK... LIKE HER?
SO I DESTROY EVERY SLASHER I CAN FIND....I HATE THEM...BECAUSE I'M AFRAID I'M JUST LIKE THEM.
LET'S GO GET SOME DONUTS.

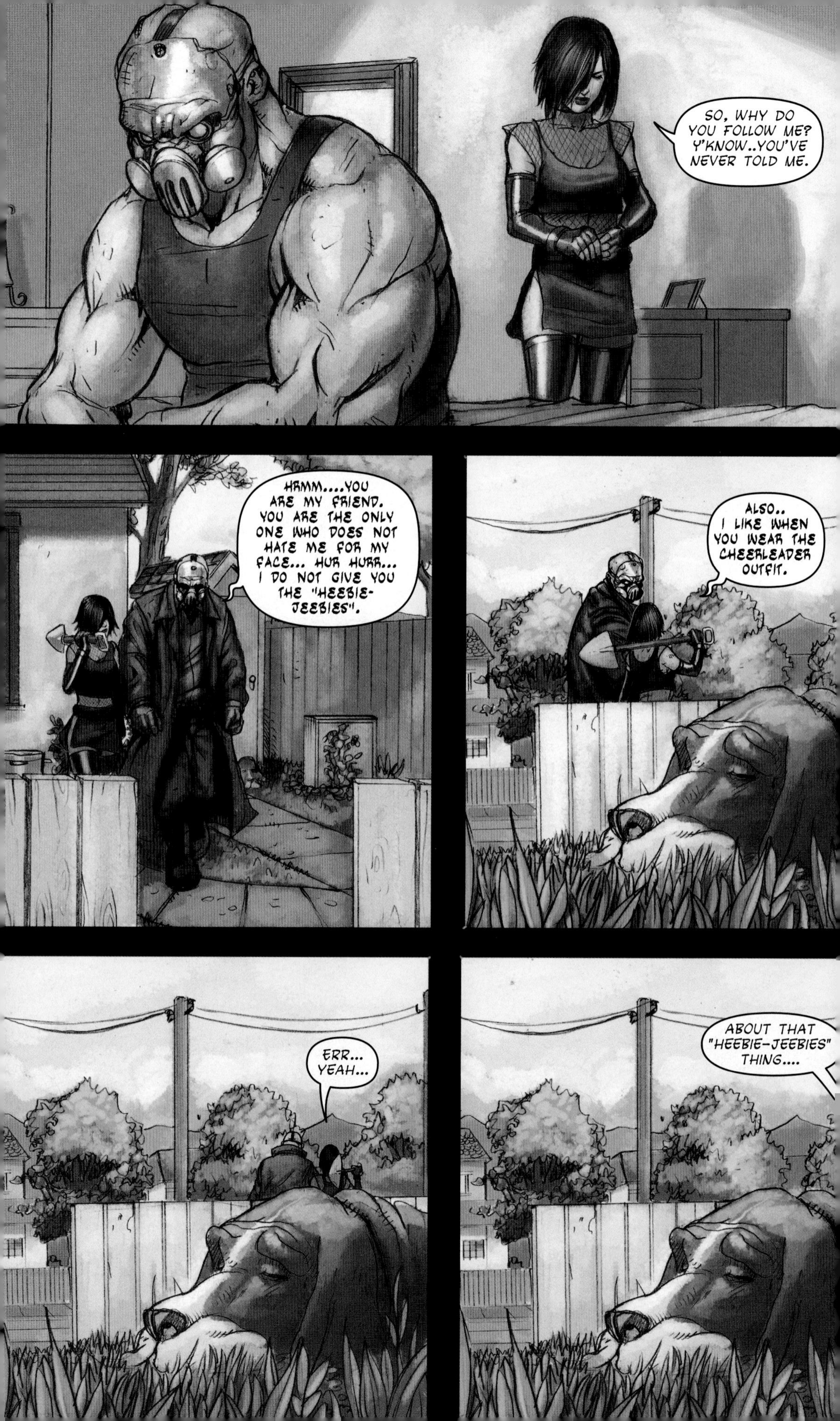
SO, WHY DO YOU FOLLOW ME? Y'KNOW..YOU'VE NEVER TOLD ME.
HRMM....YOU ARE MY FRIEND. YOU ARE THE ONLY ONE WHO DOES NOT HATE ME FOR MY FACE... HUR HURR... I DO NOT GIVE YOU THE "HEEBIE-JEEBIES".
ALSO.. I LIKE WHEN YOU WEAR THE CHEERLEADER OUTFIT.
ERR... YEAH...
ABOUT THAT "HEEBIE-JEEBIES" THING....

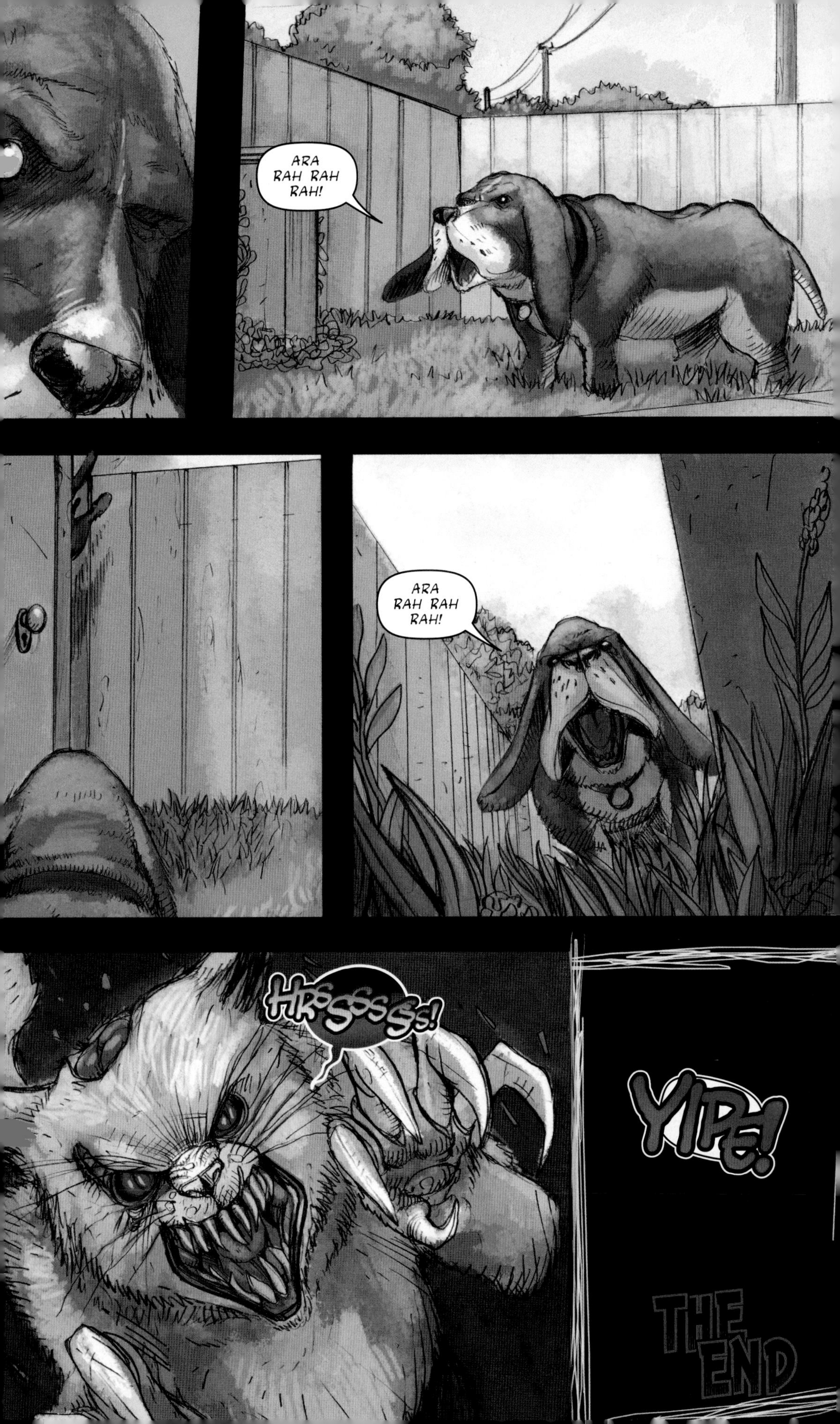
ARA RAH RAH RAH!
ARA RAH RAH RAH!
HRSSSSSS!
YIPE!
THE END

HACK/SLASH
GIRLS GONE DEAD

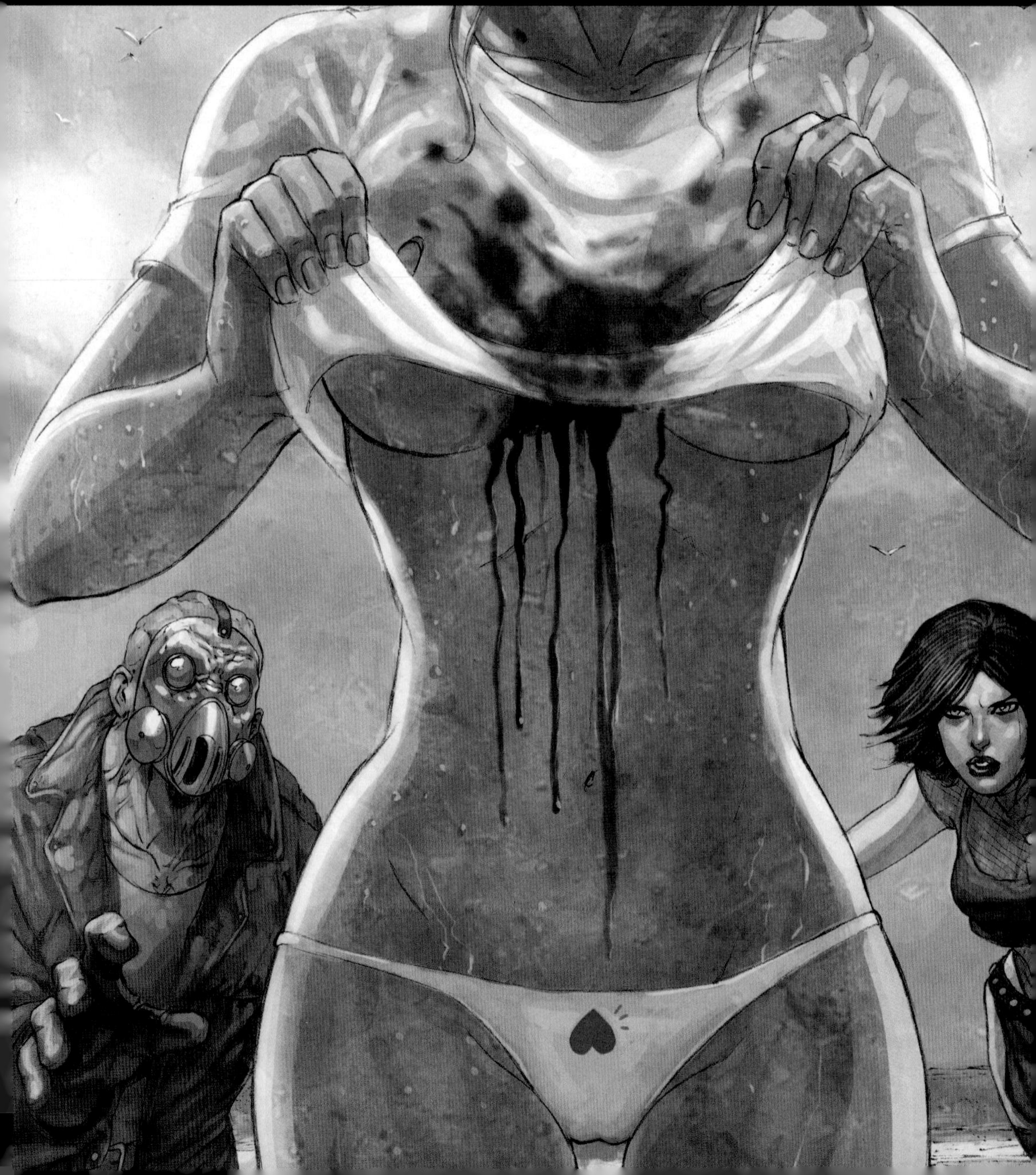

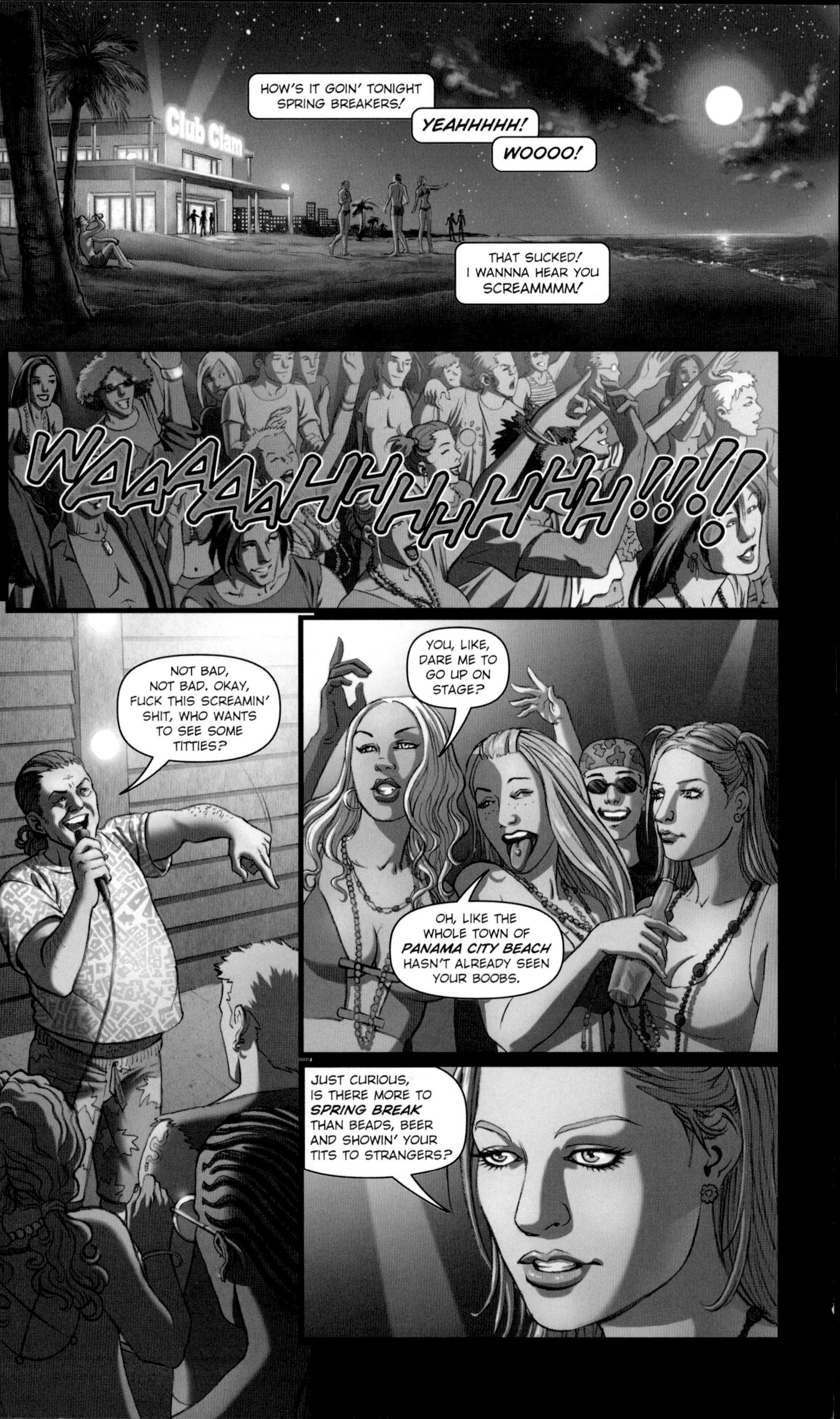
Club Clam
HOW'S IT GOIN' TONIGHT SPRING BREAKERS!
YEAHHHHH!
WOOOO!
THAT SUCKED! I WANNNA HEAR YOU SCREAMMMM!
WAAAAAHHHHHHH!!!!!
NOT BAD, NOT BAD. OKAY, FUCK THIS SCREAMIN' SHIT, WHO WANTS TO SEE SOME TITTIES?
YOU, LIKE, DARE ME TO GO UP ON STAGE?
OH, LIKE THE WHOLE TOWN OF ***PANAMA CITY BEACH*** HASN'T ALREADY SEEN YOUR BOOBS.
JUST CURIOUS, IS THERE MORE TO ***SPRING BREAK*** THAN BEADS, BEER AND SHOWIN' YOUR TITS TO STRANGERS?

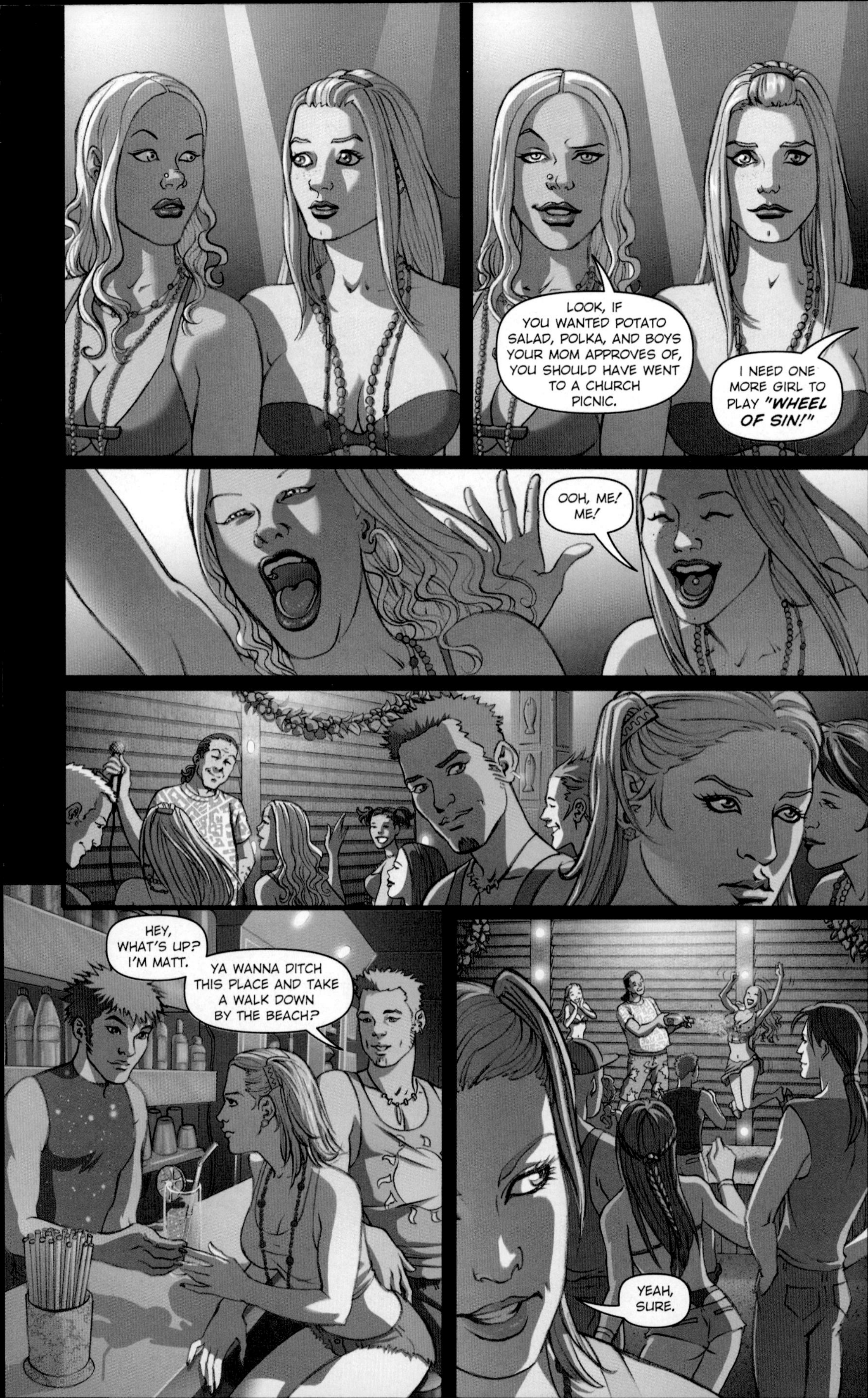
LOOK, IF YOU WANTED POTATO SALAD, POLKA, AND BOYS YOUR MOM APPROVES OF, YOU SHOULD HAVE WENT TO A CHURCH PICNIC.
I NEED ONE MORE GIRL TO PLAY "WHEEL OF SIN!"
OOH, ME! ME!
HEY, WHAT'S UP? I'M MATT.
YA WANNA DITCH THIS PLACE AND TAKE A WALK DOWN BY THE BEACH?
YEAH, SURE.

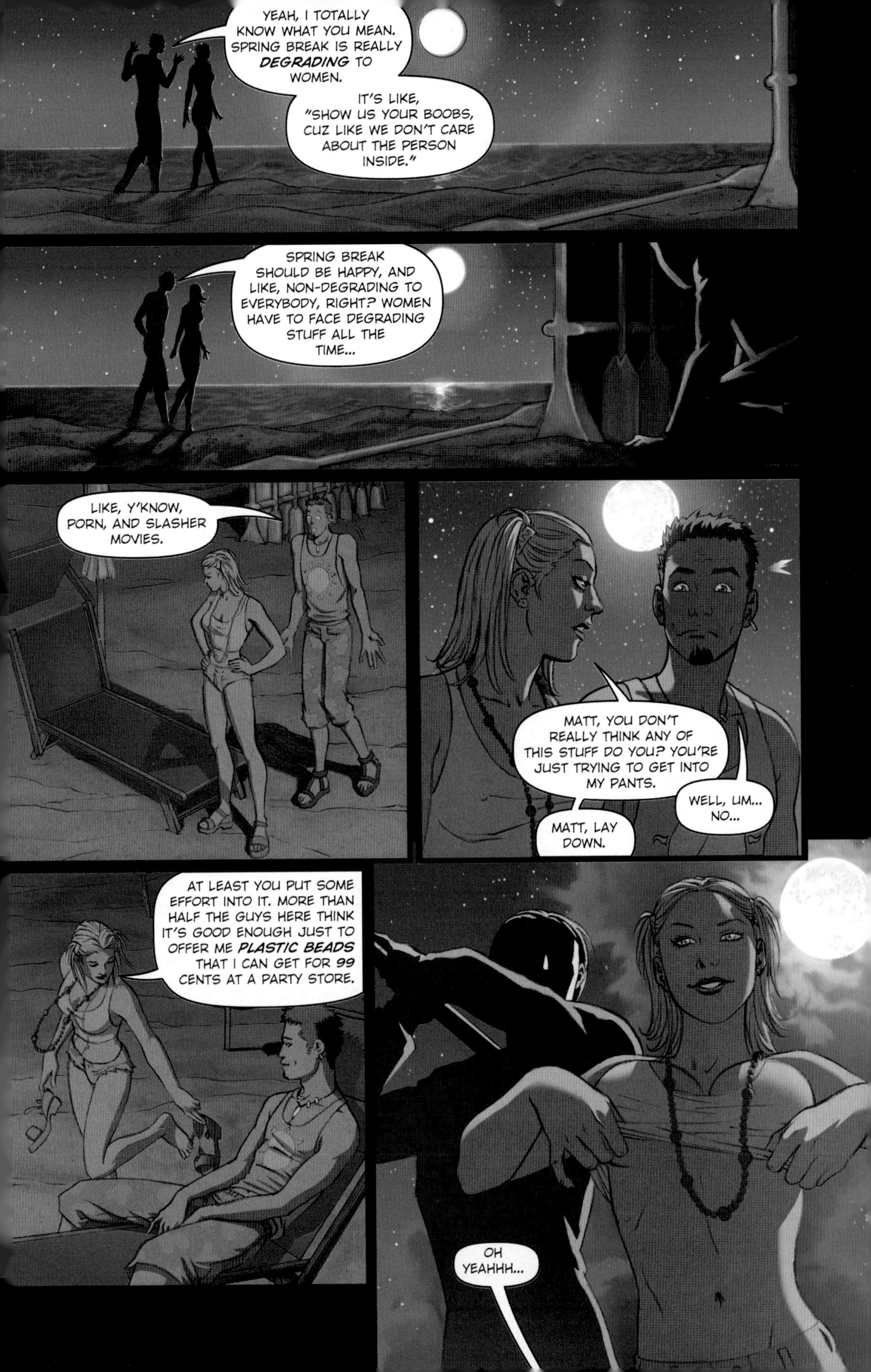
YEAH, I TOTALLY KNOW WHAT YOU MEAN. SPRING BREAK IS REALLY *DEGRADING* TO WOMEN.
IT'S LIKE, "SHOW US YOUR BOOBS, CUZ LIKE WE DON'T CARE ABOUT THE PERSON INSIDE."
SPRING BREAK SHOULD BE HAPPY, AND LIKE, NON-DEGRADING TO EVERYBODY, RIGHT? WOMEN HAVE TO FACE DEGRADING STUFF ALL THE TIME...
LIKE, Y'KNOW, PORN, AND SLASHER MOVIES.
MATT, YOU DON'T REALLY THINK ANY OF THIS STUFF DO YOU? YOU'RE JUST TRYING TO GET INTO MY PANTS.
WELL, UM... NO...
MATT, LAY DOWN.
AT LEAST YOU PUT SOME EFFORT INTO IT. MORE THAN HALF THE GUYS HERE THINK IT'S GOOD ENOUGH JUST TO OFFER ME *PLASTIC BEADS* THAT I CAN GET FOR 99 CENTS AT A PARTY STORE.
OH YEAHHH...

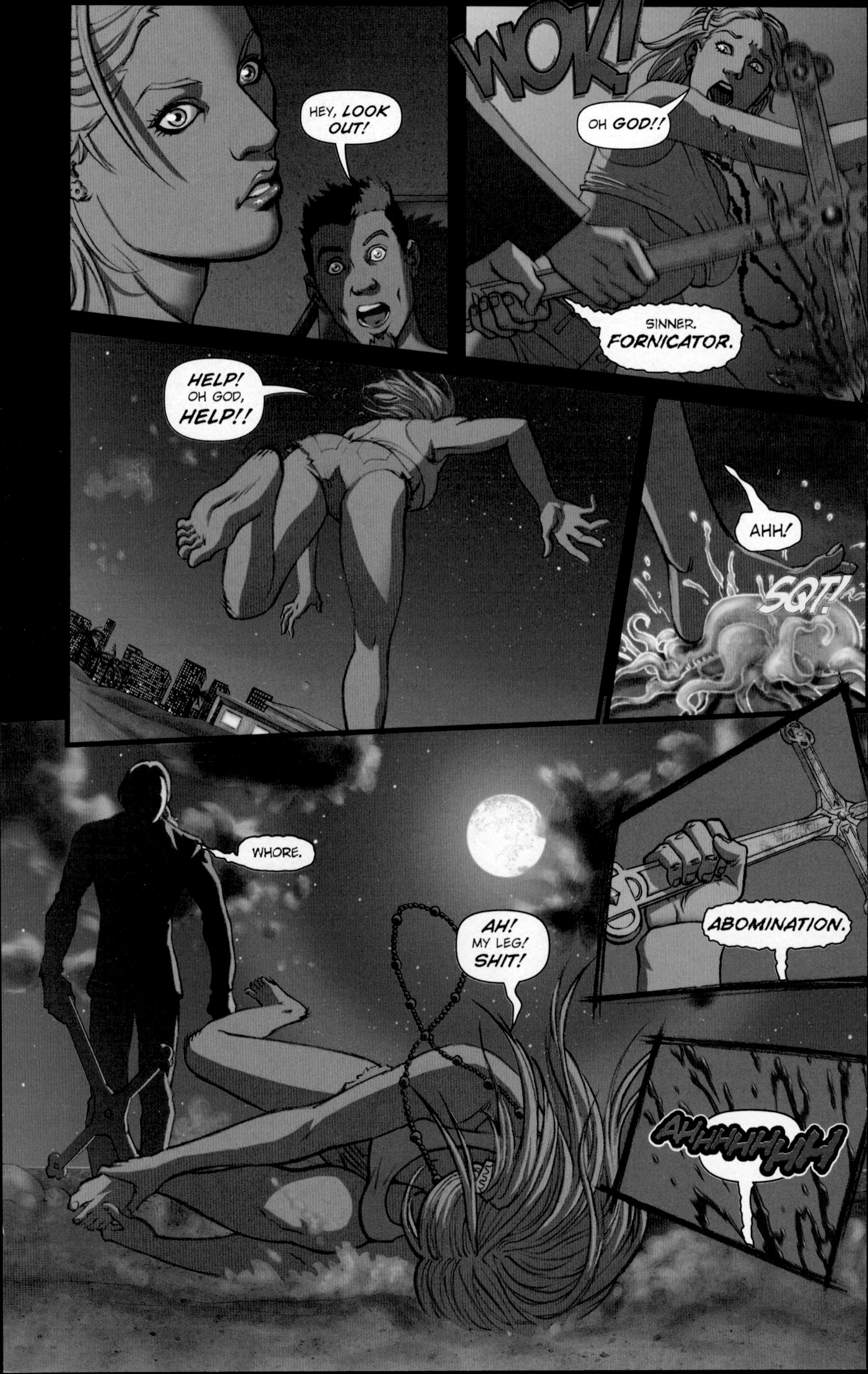
HEY, LOOK OUT!
WOK!
OH GOD!!
SINNER. FORNICATOR.
HELP! OH GOD, HELP!!
AHH!
SQT!
WHORE.
AH! MY LEG! SHIT!
ABOMINATION.
AHHHHHHH

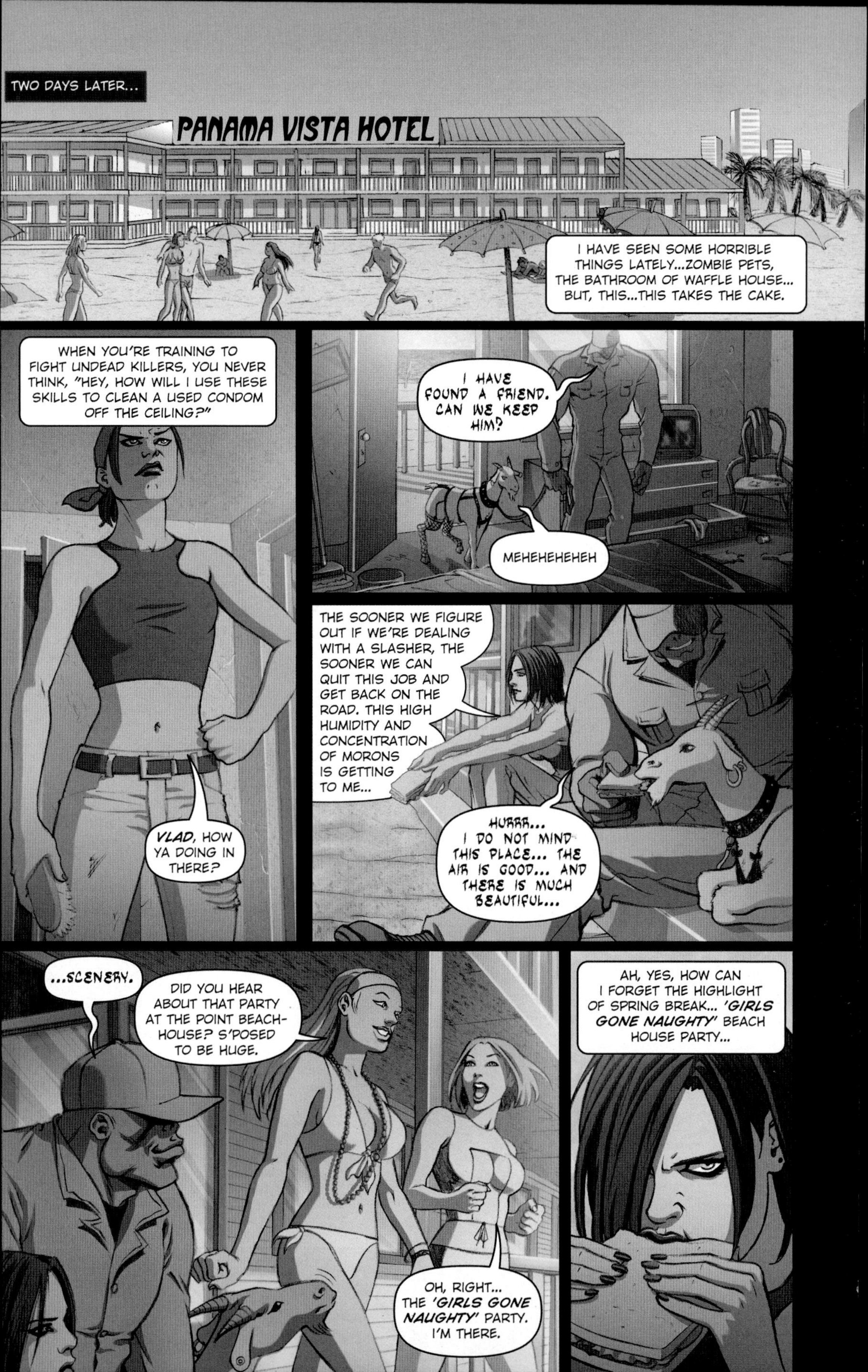
TWO DAYS LATER...
PANAMA VISTA HOTEL
I HAVE SEEN SOME HORRIBLE THINGS LATELY...ZOMBIE PETS, THE BATHROOM OF WAFFLE HOUSE... BUT, THIS...THIS TAKES THE CAKE.
WHEN YOU'RE TRAINING TO FIGHT UNDEAD KILLERS, YOU NEVER THINK, "HEY, HOW WILL I USE THESE SKILLS TO CLEAN A USED CONDOM OFF THE CEILING?"
VLAD, HOW YA DOING IN THERE?
I HAVE FOUND A FRIEND. CAN WE KEEP HIM?
MEHEHEHEHEH
THE SOONER WE FIGURE OUT IF WE'RE DEALING WITH A SLASHER, THE SOONER WE CAN QUIT THIS JOB AND GET BACK ON THE ROAD. THIS HIGH HUMIDITY AND CONCENTRATION OF MORONS IS GETTING TO ME...
HURRR... I DO NOT MIND THIS PLACE... THE AIR IS GOOD... AND THERE IS MUCH BEAUTIFUL...
...SCENERY.
DID YOU HEAR ABOUT THAT PARTY AT THE POINT BEACH-HOUSE? S'POSED TO BE HUGE.
OH, RIGHT... THE 'GIRLS GONE NAUGHTY' PARTY. I'M THERE.
AH, YES, HOW CAN I FORGET THE HIGHLIGHT OF SPRING BREAK... 'GIRLS GONE NAUGHTY' BEACH HOUSE PARTY...

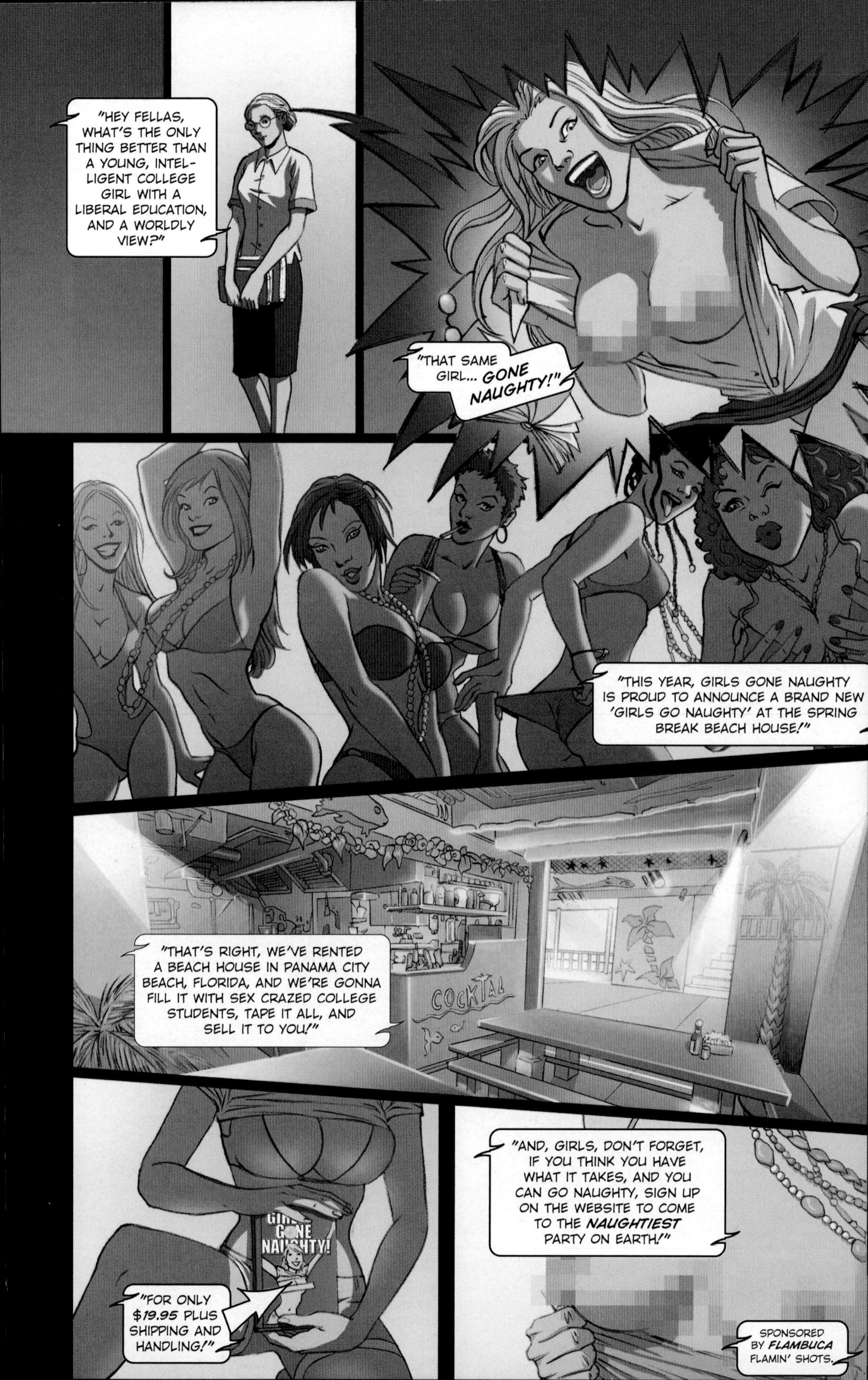
"HEY FELLAS, WHAT'S THE ONLY THING BETTER THAN A YOUNG, INTEL-LIGENT COLLEGE GIRL WITH A LIBERAL EDUCATION, AND A WORLDLY VIEW?"
"THAT SAME GIRL... GONE NAUGHTY!"
"THIS YEAR, GIRLS GONE NAUGHTY IS PROUD TO ANNOUNCE A BRAND NEW 'GIRLS GO NAUGHTY' AT THE SPRING BREAK BEACH HOUSE!"
"THAT'S RIGHT, WE'VE RENTED A BEACH HOUSE IN PANAMA CITY BEACH, FLORIDA, AND WE'RE GONNA FILL IT WITH SEX CRAZED COLLEGE STUDENTS, TAPE IT ALL, AND SELL IT TO YOU!"
COCKTAL
GIRLS GONE NAUGHTY!
"FOR ONLY $19.95 PLUS SHIPPING AND HANDLING!"
"AND, GIRLS, DON'T FORGET, IF YOU THINK YOU HAVE WHAT IT TAKES, AND YOU CAN GO NAUGHTY, SIGN UP ON THE WEBSITE TO COME TO THE NAUGHTIEST PARTY ON EARTH!"
SPONSORED BY FLAMBUCA FLAMIN' SHOTS.

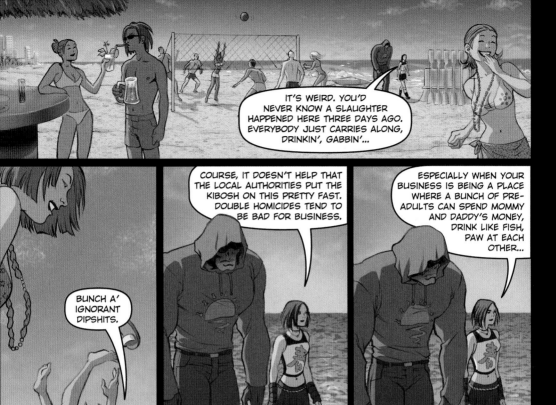

IT'S WEIRD. YOU'D NEVER KNOW A SLAUGHTER HAPPENED HERE THREE DAYS AGO. EVERYBODY JUST CARRIES ALONG, DRINKIN', GABBIN'...

COURSE, IT DOESN'T HELP THAT THE LOCAL AUTHORITIES PUT THE KIBOSH ON THIS PRETTY FAST. DOUBLE HOMICIDES TEND TO BE BAD FOR BUSINESS.

BUNCH A' IGNORANT DIPSHITS.

ESPECIALLY WHEN YOUR BUSINESS IS BEING A PLACE WHERE A BUNCH OF PRE-ADULTS CAN SPEND MOMMY AND DADDY'S MONEY, DRINK LIKE FISH, PAW AT EACH OTHER...

...AND NOT HAVE A CARE IN THE WORLD.

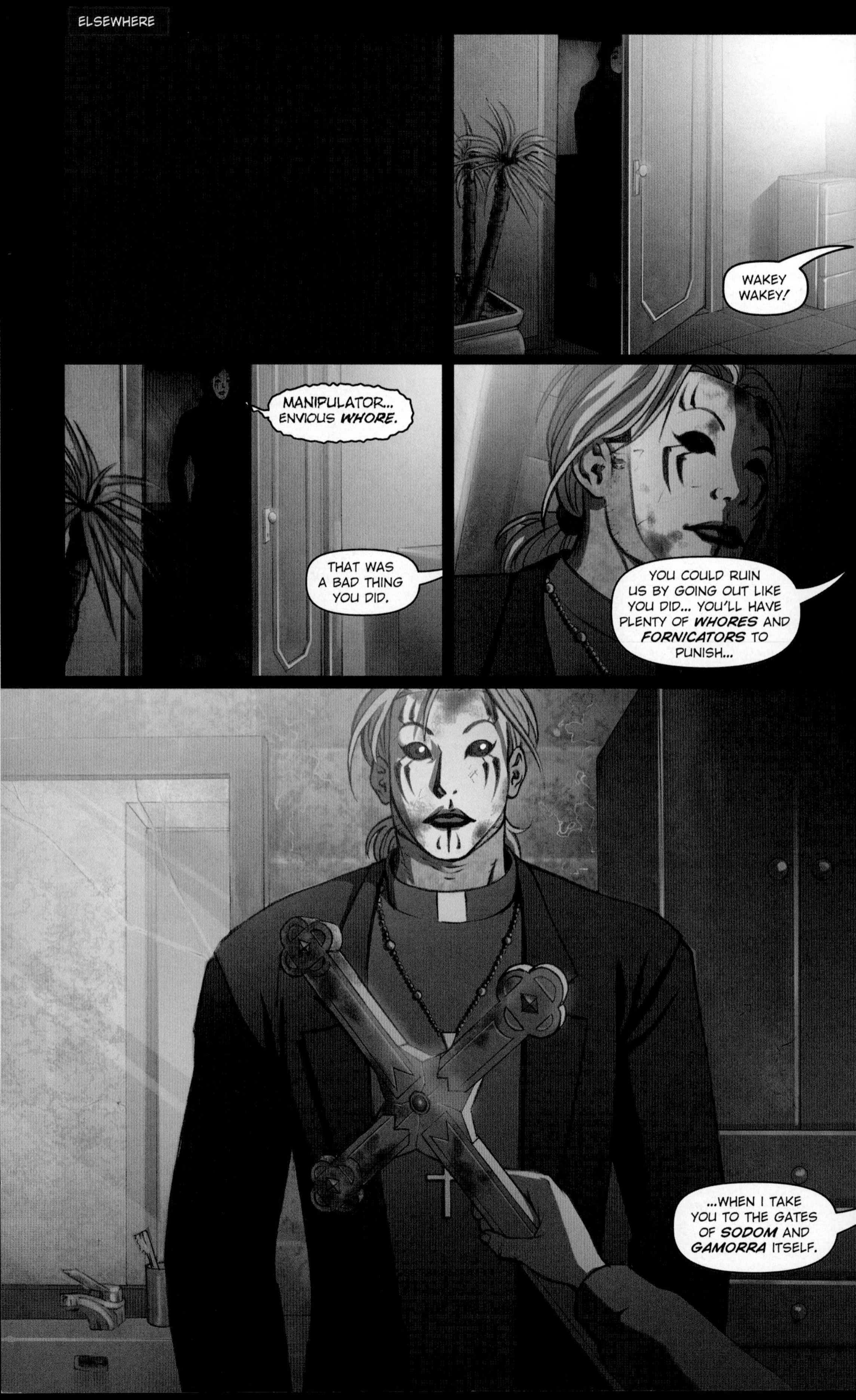
ELSEWHERE
WAKEY WAKEY!
MANIPULATOR... ENVIOUS WHORE.
THAT WAS A BAD THING YOU DID.
YOU COULD RUIN US BY GOING OUT LIKE YOU DID... YOU'LL HAVE PLENTY OF WHORES AND FORNICATORS TO PUNISH...
...WHEN I TAKE YOU TO THE GATES OF SODOM AND GAMORRA ITSELF.

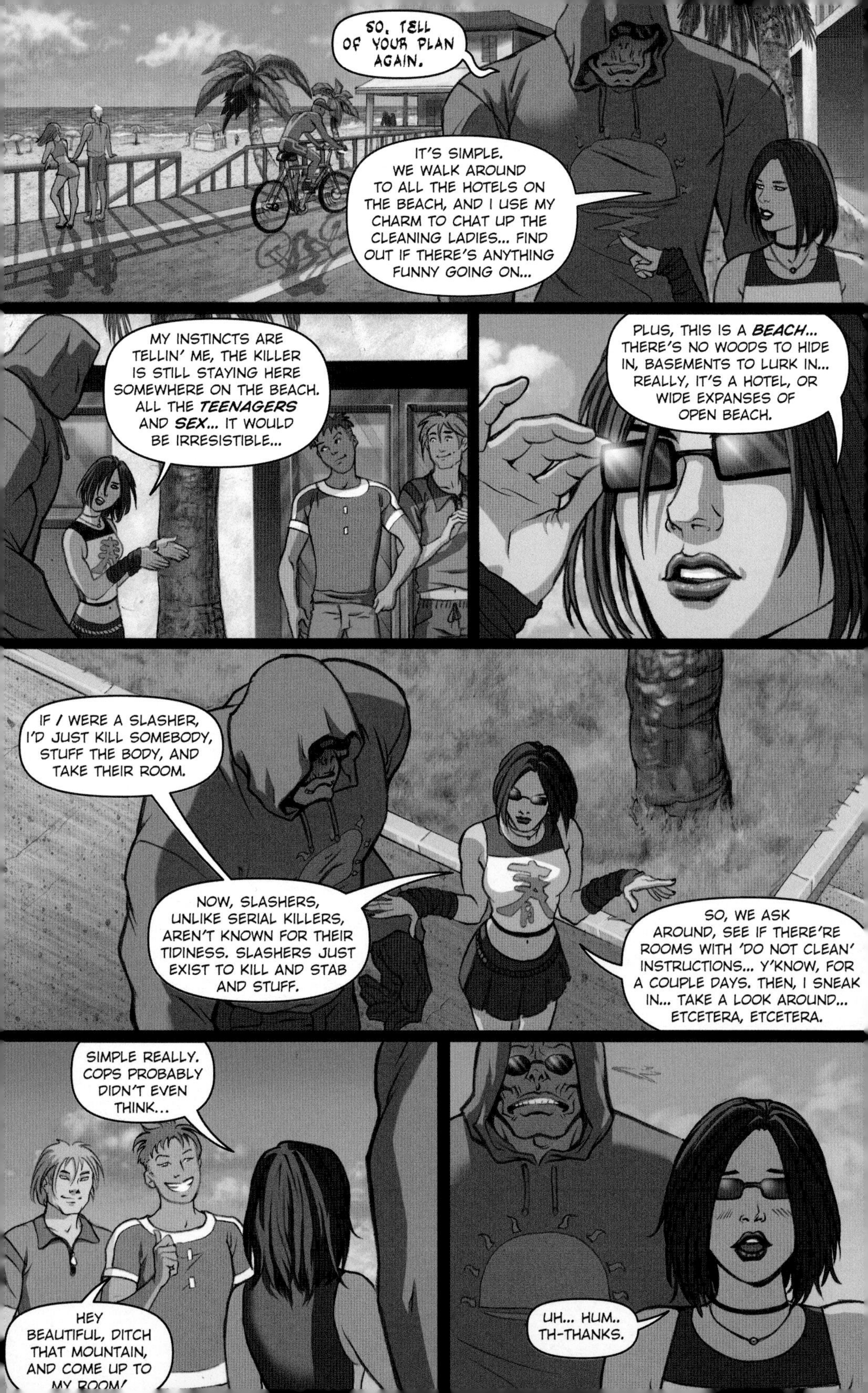
SO, TELL OF YOUR PLAN AGAIN.
IT'S SIMPLE. WE WALK AROUND TO ALL THE HOTELS ON THE BEACH, AND I USE MY CHARM TO CHAT UP THE CLEANING LADIES... FIND OUT IF THERE'S ANYTHING FUNNY GOING ON...
MY INSTINCTS ARE TELLIN' ME, THE KILLER IS STILL STAYING HERE SOMEWHERE ON THE BEACH. ALL THE *TEENAGERS* AND *SEX*... IT WOULD BE IRRESISTIBLE...
PLUS, THIS IS A *BEACH*... THERE'S NO WOODS TO HIDE IN, BASEMENTS TO LURK IN... REALLY, IT'S A HOTEL, OR WIDE EXPANSES OF OPEN BEACH.
IF *I* WERE A SLASHER, I'D JUST KILL SOMEBODY, STUFF THE BODY, AND TAKE THEIR ROOM.
NOW, SLASHERS, UNLIKE SERIAL KILLERS, AREN'T KNOWN FOR THEIR TIDINESS. SLASHERS JUST EXIST TO KILL AND STAB AND STUFF.
SO, WE ASK AROUND, SEE IF THERE'RE ROOMS WITH 'DO NOT CLEAN' INSTRUCTIONS... Y'KNOW, FOR A COUPLE DAYS. THEN, I SNEAK IN... TAKE A LOOK AROUND... ETCETERA, ETCETERA.
SIMPLE REALLY. COPS PROBABLY DIDN'T EVEN THINK...
HEY BEAUTIFUL, DITCH THAT MOUNTAIN, AND COME UP TO MY ROOM!
UH... HUM.. TH-THANKS.

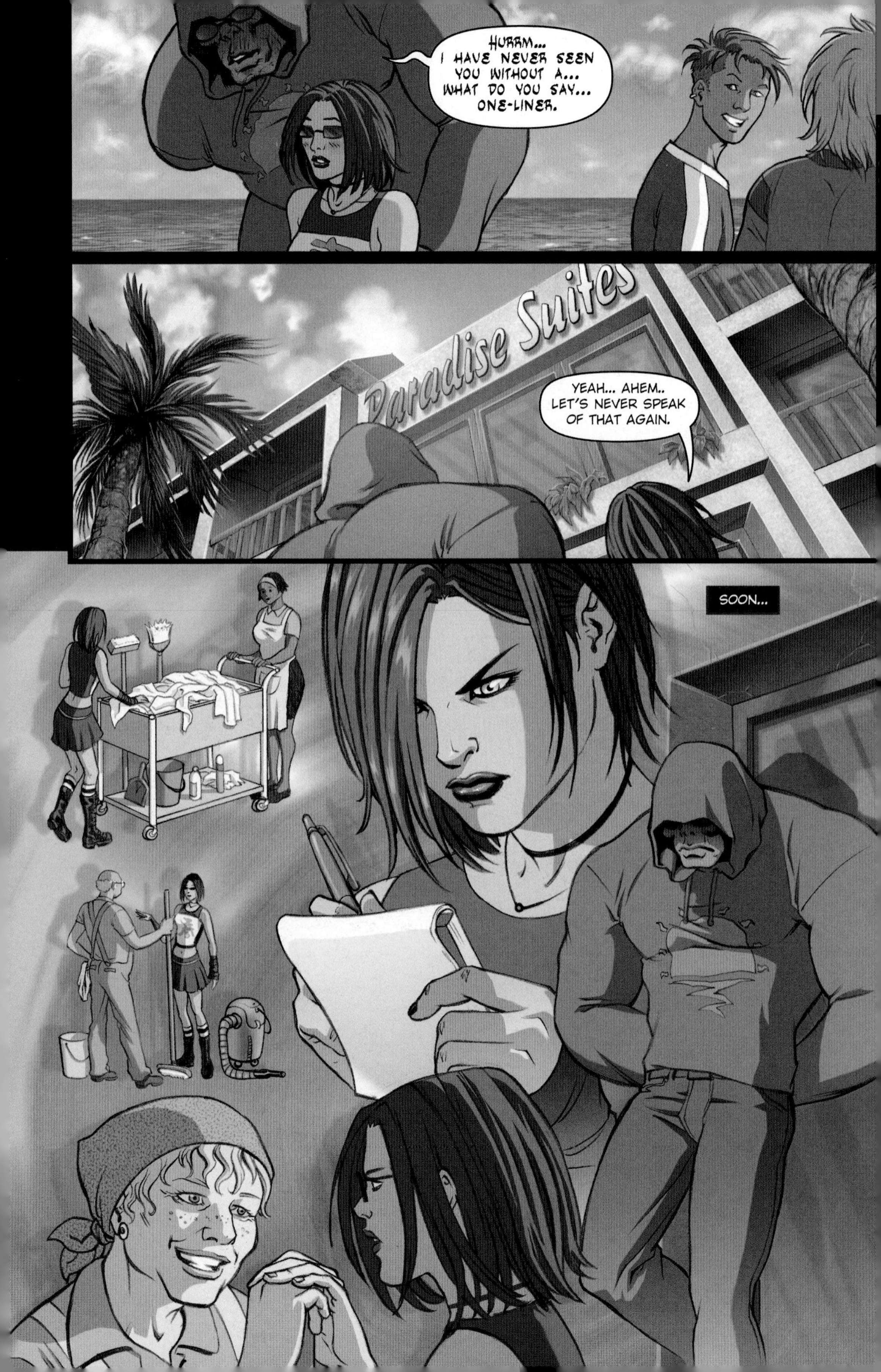
HURRM... I HAVE NEVER SEEN YOU WITHOUT A... WHAT DO YOU SAY... ONE-LINER.
Paradise Suites
YEAH... AHEM.. LET'S NEVER SPEAK OF THAT AGAIN.
SOON...

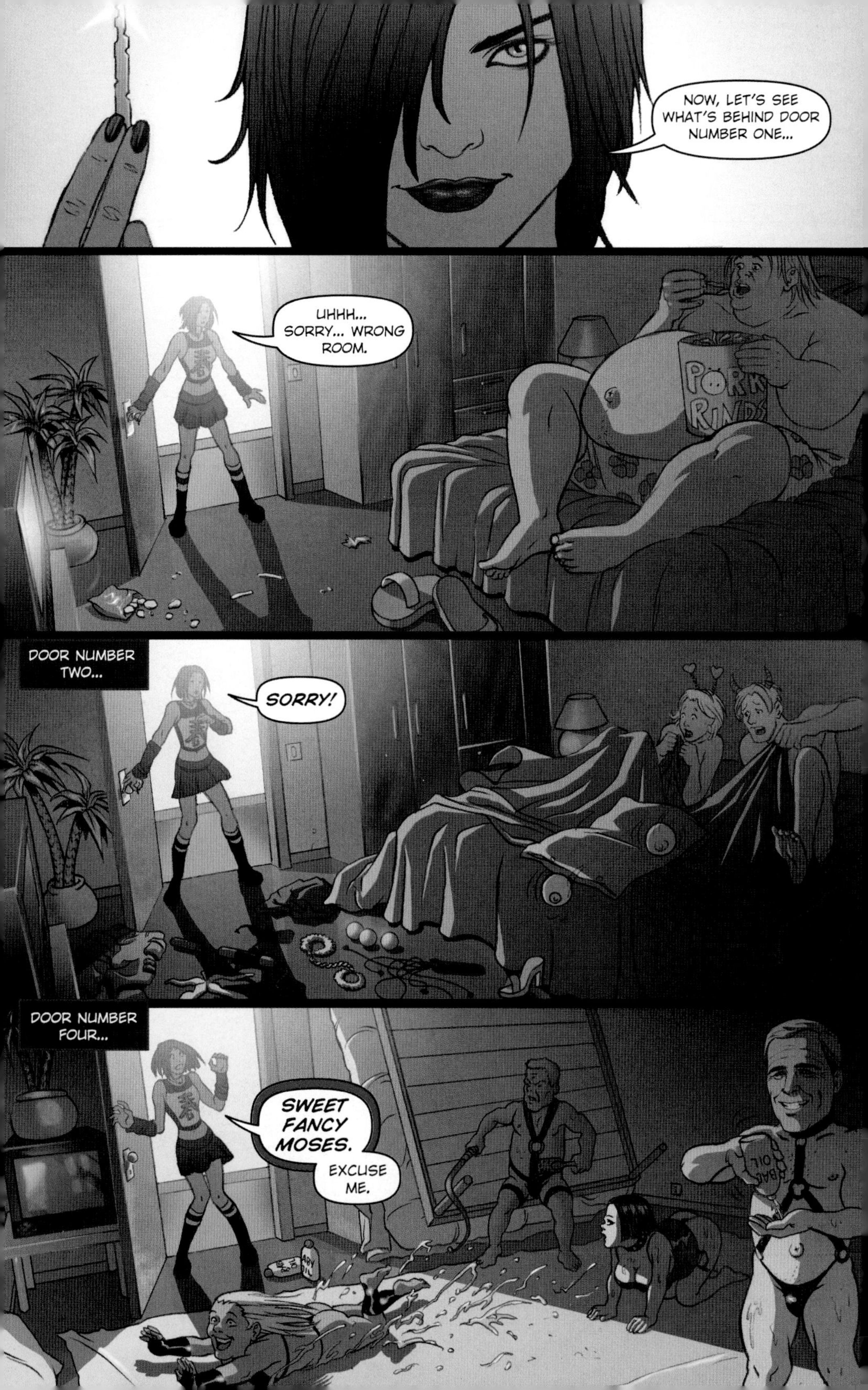
NOW, LET'S SEE WHAT'S BEHIND DOOR NUMBER ONE...
UHHH... SORRY... WRONG ROOM.
DOOR NUMBER TWO...
SORRY!
DOOR NUMBER FOUR...
SWEET FANCY MOSES.
EXCUSE ME.

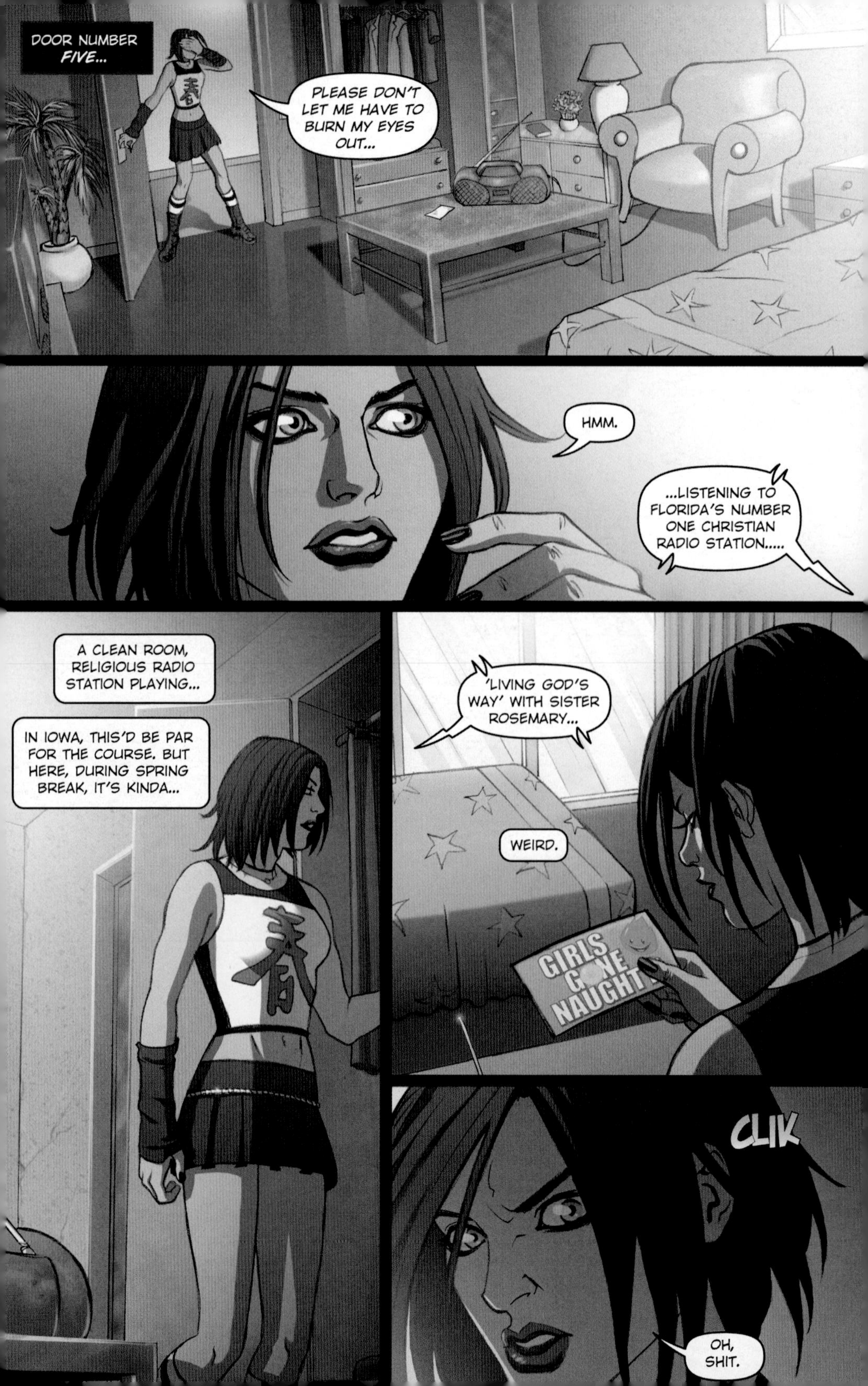
DOOR NUMBER FIVE...
PLEASE DON'T LET ME HAVE TO BURN MY EYES OUT...
HMM.
...LISTENING TO FLORIDA'S NUMBER ONE CHRISTIAN RADIO STATION.....
A CLEAN ROOM, RELIGIOUS RADIO STATION PLAYING...
IN IOWA, THIS'D BE PAR FOR THE COURSE. BUT HERE, DURING SPRING BREAK, IT'S KINDA...
'LIVING GOD'S WAY' WITH SISTER ROSEMARY...
WEIRD.
GIRLS GONE NAUGHTY
CLIK
OH, SHIT.

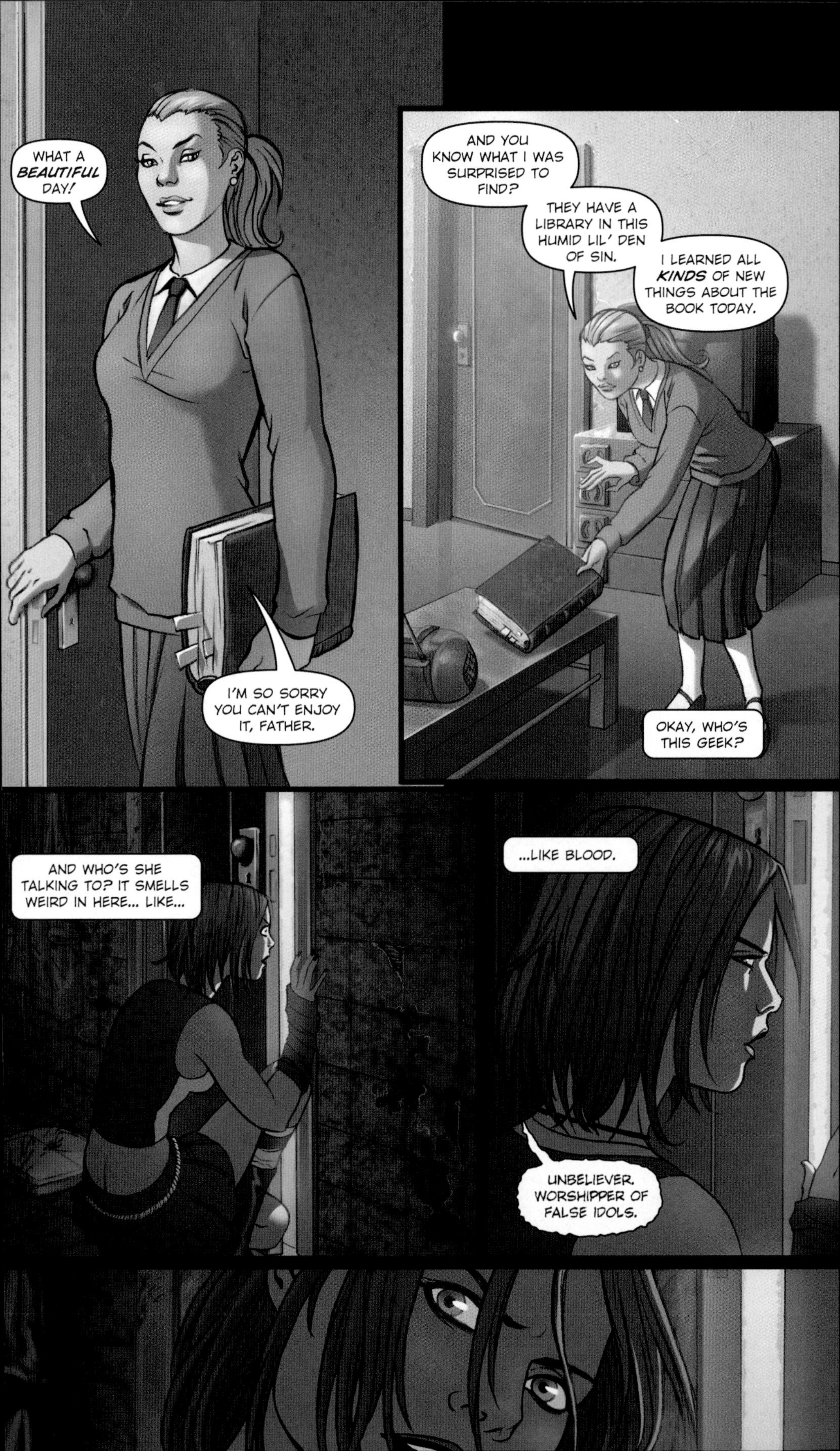
WHAT A *BEAUTIFUL* DAY!
I'M SO SORRY YOU CAN'T ENJOY IT, FATHER.
AND YOU KNOW WHAT I WAS SURPRISED TO FIND?
THEY HAVE A LIBRARY IN THIS HUMID LIL' DEN OF SIN.
I LEARNED ALL *KINDS* OF NEW THINGS ABOUT THE BOOK TODAY.
OKAY, WHO'S THIS GEEK?
AND WHO'S SHE TALKING TO? IT SMELLS WEIRD IN HERE... LIKE...
...LIKE BLOOD.
UNBELIEVER. WORSHIPPER OF FALSE IDOLS.

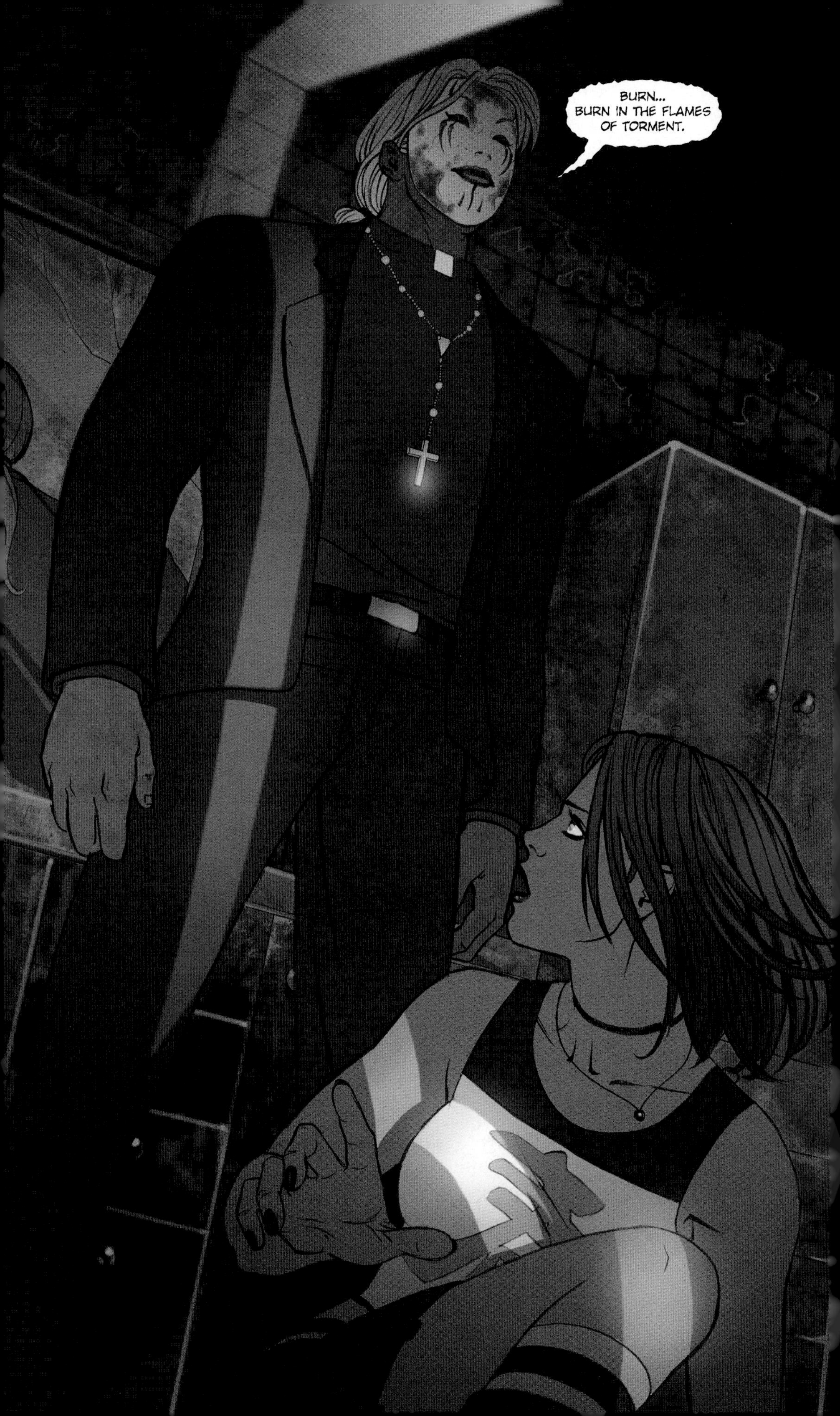
BURN... BURN IN THE FLAMES OF TORMENT.

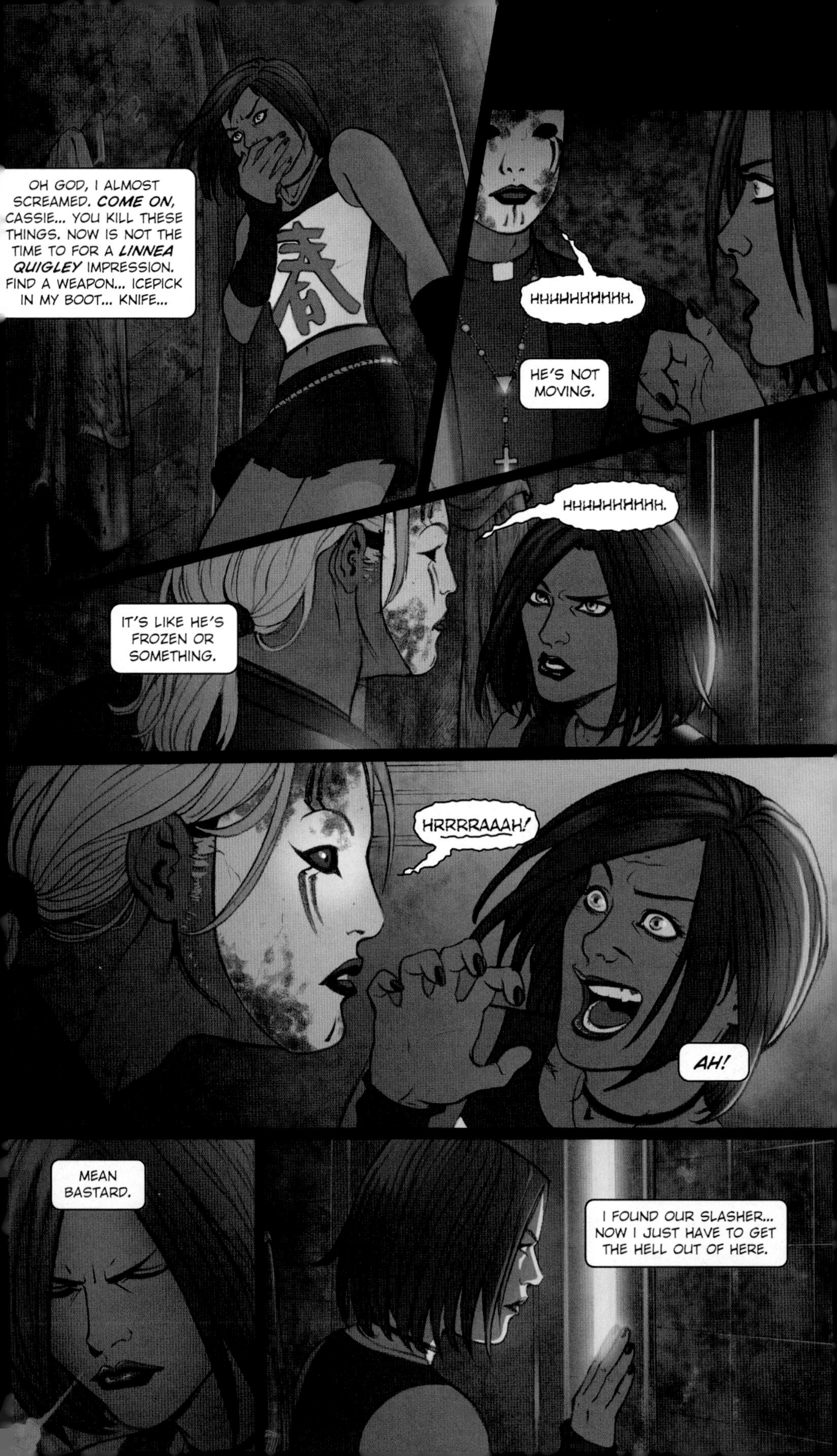
OH GOD, I ALMOST SCREAMED. **COME ON,** CASSIE... YOU KILL THESE THINGS. NOW IS NOT THE TIME TO FOR A ***LINNEA QUIGLEY*** IMPRESSION. FIND A WEAPON... ICEPICK IN MY BOOT... KNIFE...
春
HHHHHHHHHH.
HE'S NOT MOVING.
HHHHHHHHHH.
IT'S LIKE HE'S FROZEN OR SOMETHING.
HRRRRAAAH!
AH!
MEAN BASTARD.
I FOUND OUR SLASHER... NOW I JUST HAVE TO GET THE HELL OUT OF HERE.

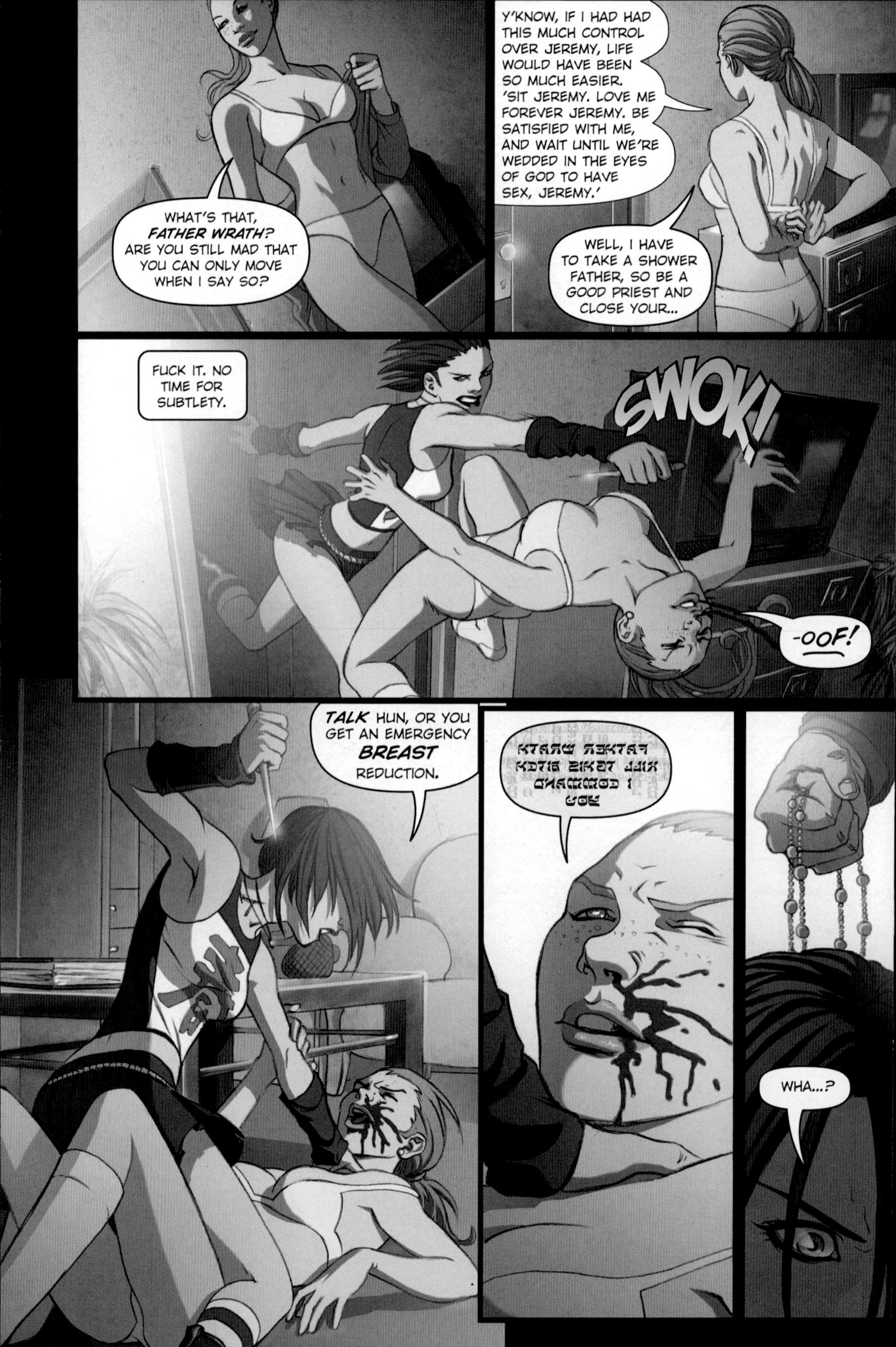
WHAT'S THAT, FATHER WRATH? ARE YOU STILL MAD THAT YOU CAN ONLY MOVE WHEN I SAY SO?
Y'KNOW, IF I HAD HAD THIS MUCH CONTROL OVER JEREMY, LIFE WOULD HAVE BEEN SO MUCH EASIER. 'SIT JEREMY. LOVE ME FOREVER JEREMY. BE SATISFIED WITH ME, AND WAIT UNTIL WE'RE WEDDED IN THE EYES OF GOD TO HAVE SEX, JEREMY.'
WELL, I HAVE TO TAKE A SHOWER FATHER, SO BE A GOOD PRIEST AND CLOSE YOUR...
FUCK IT. NO TIME FOR SUBTLETY.
SWOK!
-OOF!
TALK HUN, OR YOU GET AN EMERGENCY BREAST REDUCTION.
WHA...?

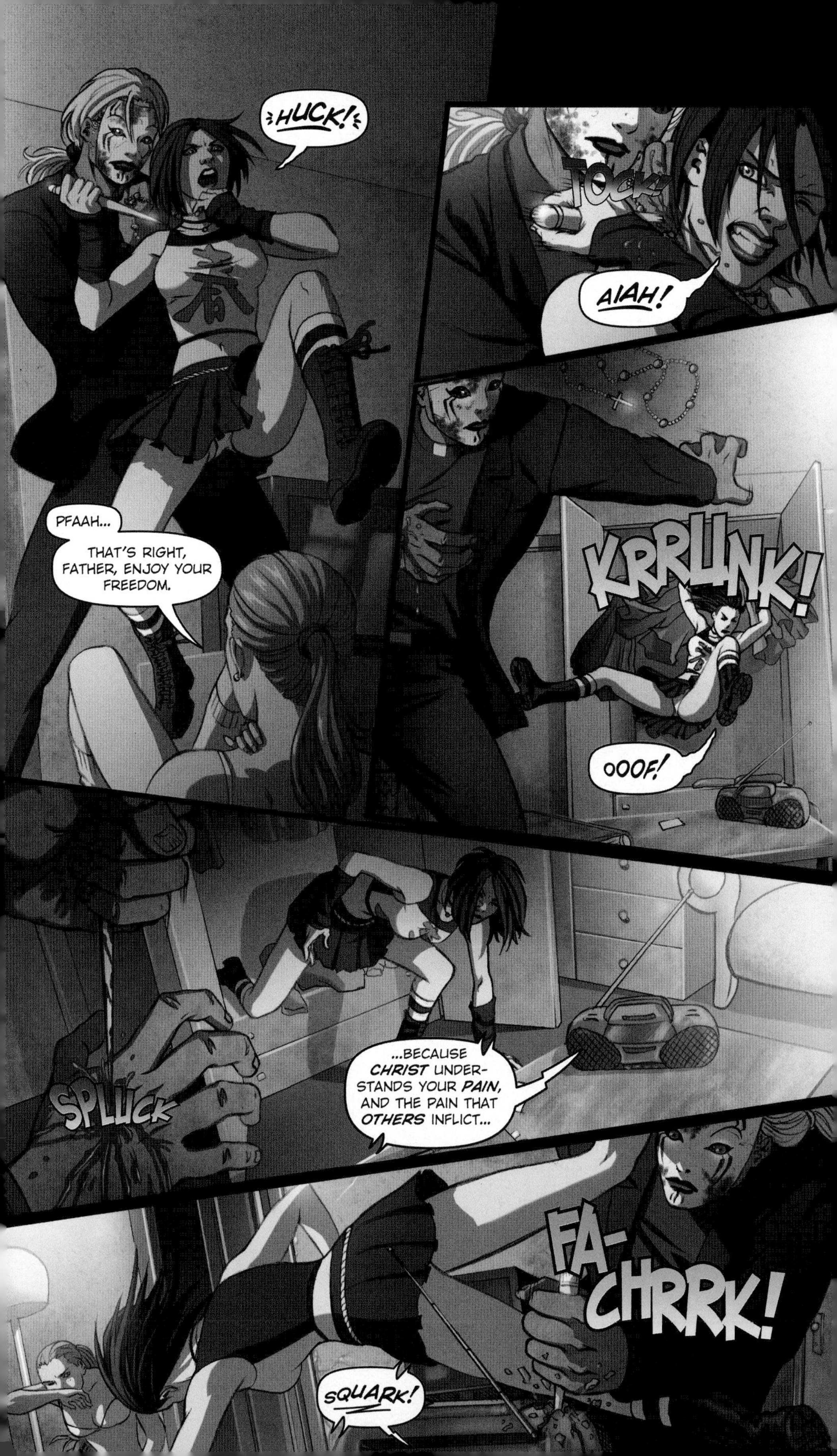
HUCK!
TOCK!
AIAH!
PFAAH...
THAT'S RIGHT, FATHER, ENJOY YOUR FREEDOM.
KRRUNK!
OOOF!
SPLUCK
...BECAUSE CHRIST UNDER-STANDS YOUR PAIN, AND THE PAIN THAT OTHERS INFLICT...
FA-CHRRK!
SQUARK!

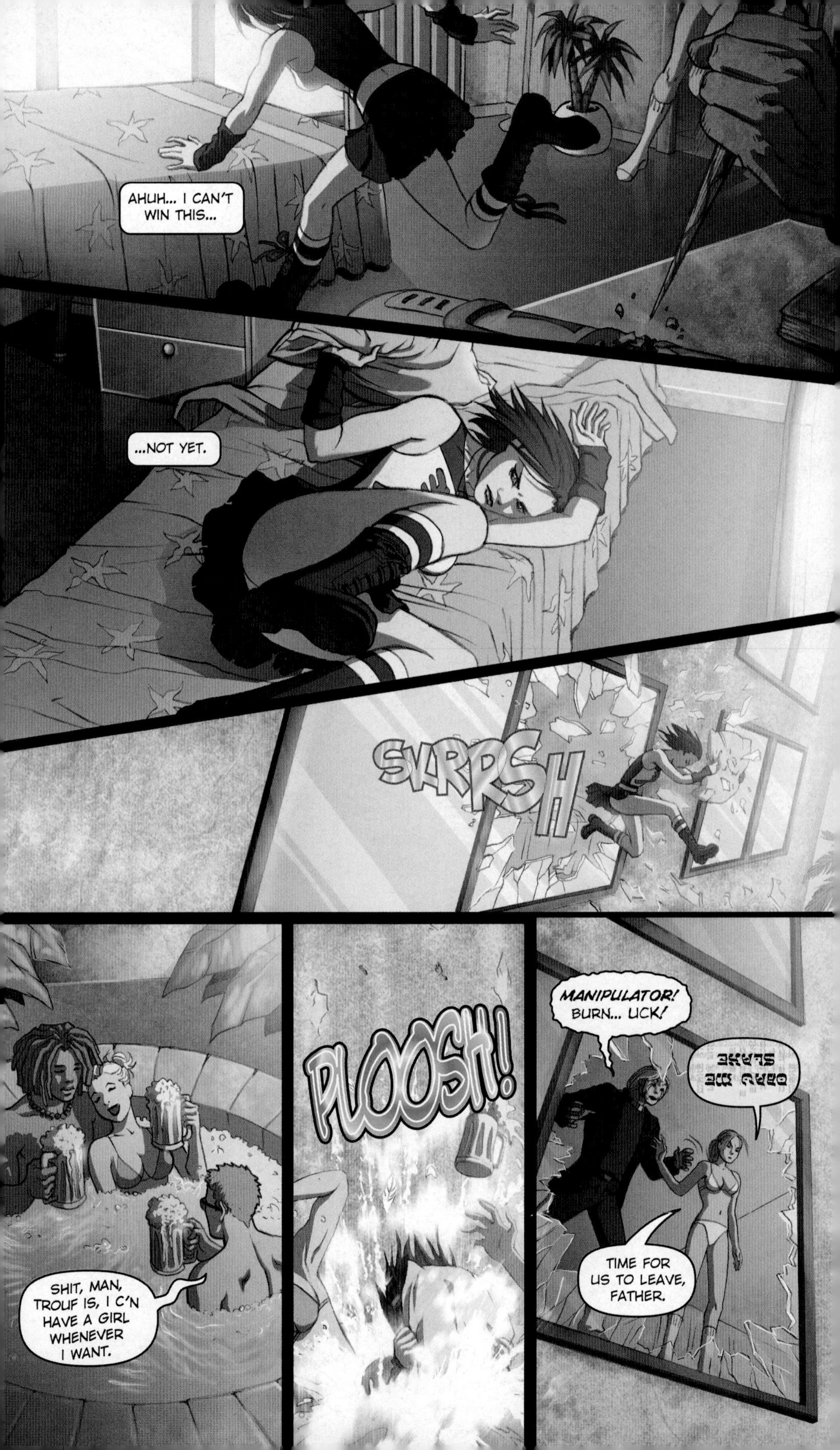
AHUH... I CAN'T WIN THIS...
...NOT YET.
SKRRSH
SHIT, MAN, TROUF IS, I C'N HAVE A GIRL WHENEVER I WANT.
PLOOSH!
MANIPULATOR! BURN... UCK!
TIME FOR US TO LEAVE, FATHER.

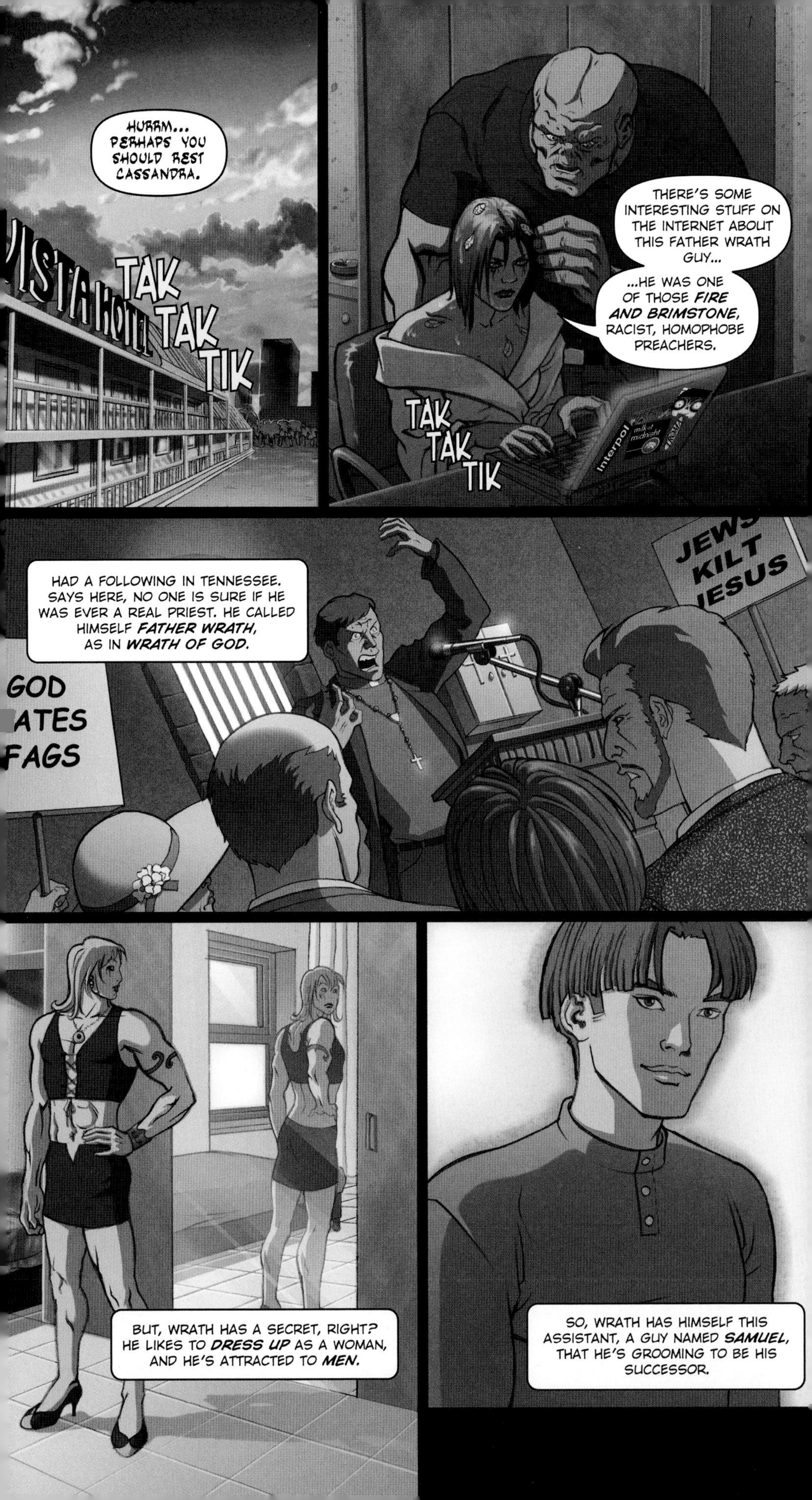
HURRM... PERHAPS YOU SHOULD REST CASSANDRA.
VISTA HOTEL
TAK TAK TIK
THERE'S SOME INTERESTING STUFF ON THE INTERNET ABOUT THIS FATHER WRATH GUY...
...HE WAS ONE OF THOSE FIRE AND BRIMSTONE, RACIST, HOMOPHOBE PREACHERS.
TAK TAK TIK
interpol
HAD A FOLLOWING IN TENNESSEE. SAYS HERE, NO ONE IS SURE IF HE WAS EVER A REAL PRIEST. HE CALLED HIMSELF FATHER WRATH, AS IN WRATH OF GOD.
GOD ATES FAGS
KILT JESUS
BUT, WRATH HAS A SECRET, RIGHT? HE LIKES TO DRESS UP AS A WOMAN, AND HE'S ATTRACTED TO MEN.
SO, WRATH HAS HIMSELF THIS ASSISTANT, A GUY NAMED SAMUEL, THAT HE'S GROOMING TO BE HIS SUCCESSOR.

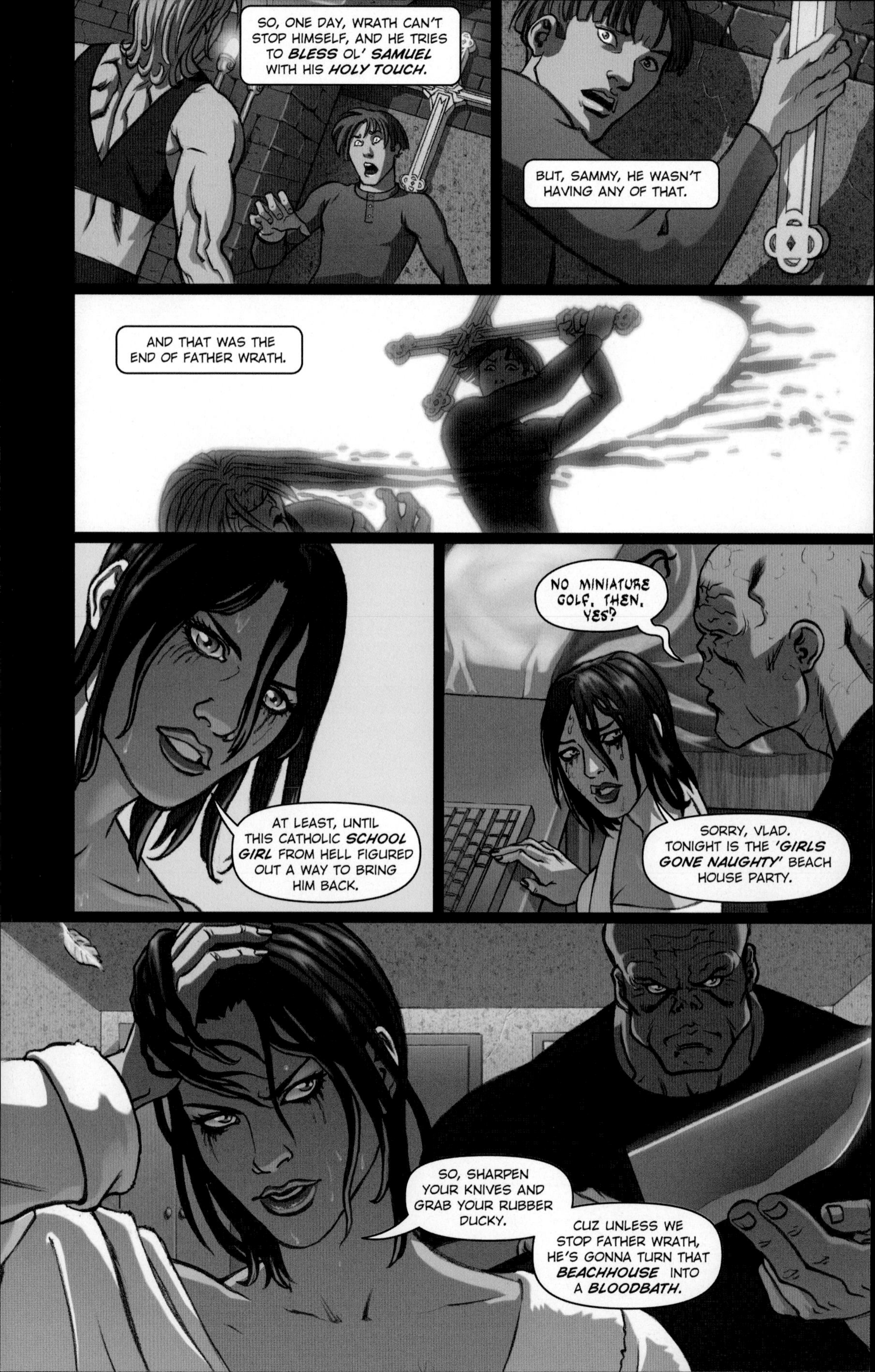
SO, ONE DAY, WRATH CAN'T STOP HIMSELF, AND HE TRIES TO BLESS OL' SAMUEL WITH HIS HOLY TOUCH.
BUT, SAMMY, HE WASN'T HAVING ANY OF THAT.
AND THAT WAS THE END OF FATHER WRATH.
AT LEAST, UNTIL THIS CATHOLIC SCHOOL GIRL FROM HELL FIGURED OUT A WAY TO BRING HIM BACK.
NO MINIATURE GOLF, THEN, YES?
SORRY, VLAD. TONIGHT IS THE 'GIRLS GONE NAUGHTY' BEACH HOUSE PARTY.
SO, SHARPEN YOUR KNIVES AND GRAB YOUR RUBBER DUCKY.
CUZ UNLESS WE STOP FATHER WRATH, HE'S GONNA TURN THAT BEACHHOUSE INTO A BLOODBATH.

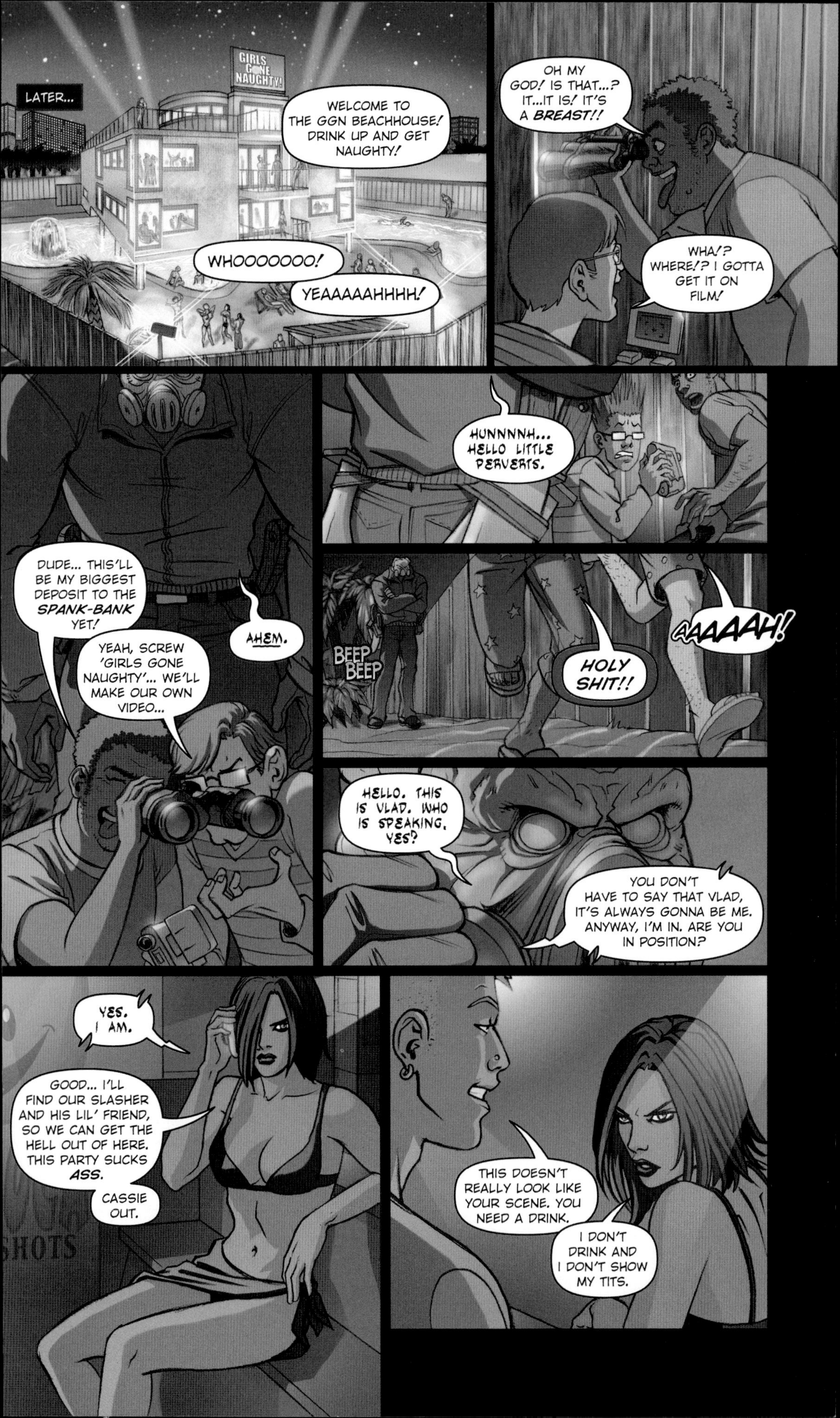
LATER...
GIRLS GONE NAUGHTY!
WELCOME TO THE GGN BEACHHOUSE! DRINK UP AND GET NAUGHTY!
WHOOOOOOO!
YEAAAAAHHHH!
OH MY GOD! IS THAT...? IT...IT IS! IT'S A BREAST!!
WHA!? WHERE!? I GOTTA GET IT ON FILM!
DUDE... THIS'LL BE MY BIGGEST DEPOSIT TO THE SPANK-BANK YET!
YEAH, SCREW 'GIRLS GONE NAUGHTY'... WE'LL MAKE OUR OWN VIDEO...
AHEM.
HUNNNNH... HELLO LITTLE PERVERTS.
HOLY SHIT!!
AAAAAH!
BEEP BEEP
HELLO. THIS IS VLAD. WHO IS SPEAKING, YES?
YOU DON'T HAVE TO SAY THAT VLAD, IT'S ALWAYS GONNA BE ME. ANYWAY, I'M IN. ARE YOU IN POSITION?
YES. I AM.
GOOD... I'LL FIND OUR SLASHER AND HIS LIL' FRIEND, SO WE CAN GET THE HELL OUT OF HERE. THIS PARTY SUCKS ASS.
CASSIE OUT.
SHOTS
THIS DOESN'T REALLY LOOK LIKE YOUR SCENE. YOU NEED A DRINK.
I DON'T DRINK AND I DON'T SHOW MY TITS.

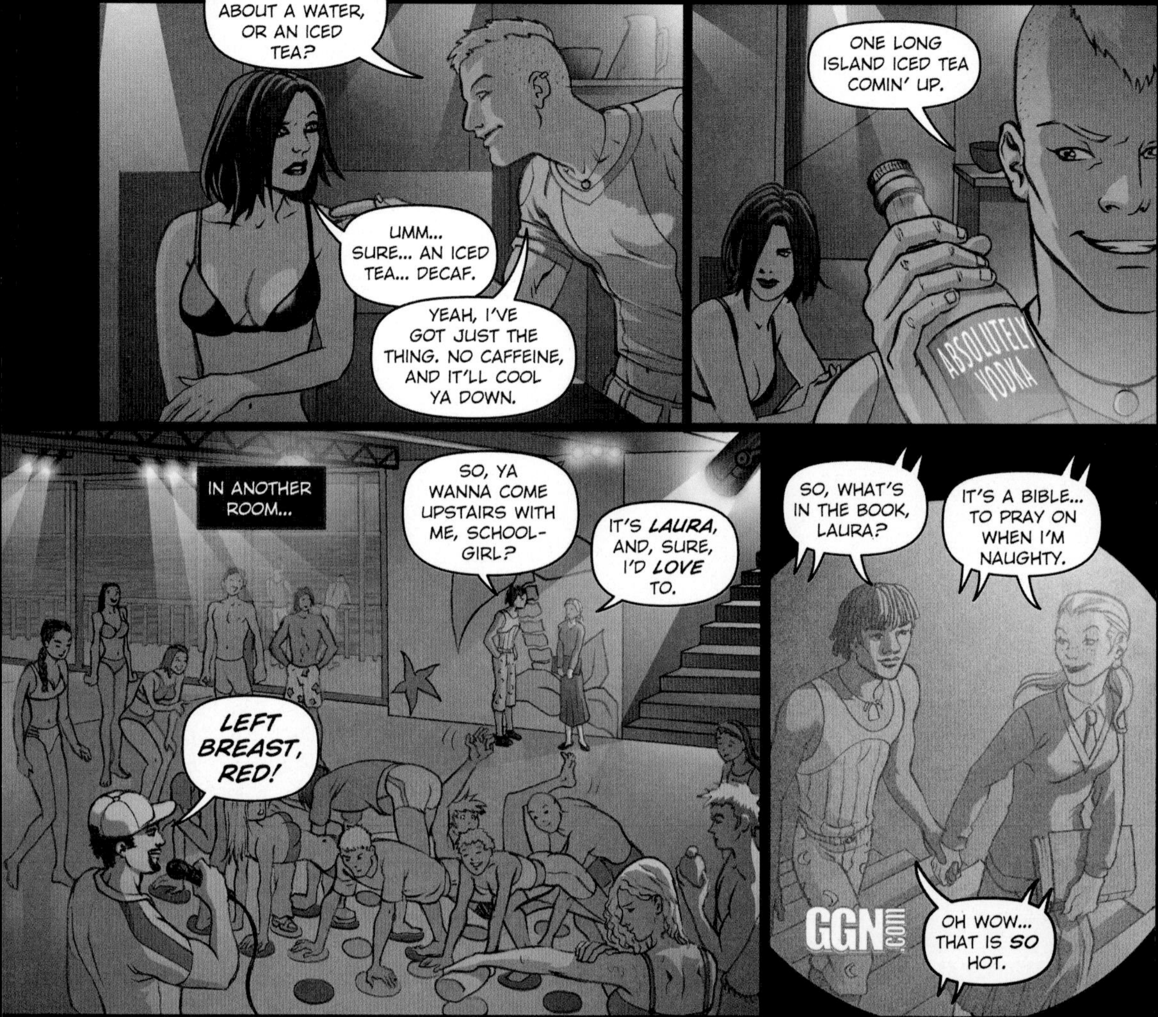
NAH, NOTHIN' LIKE THAT. HOW ABOUT A WATER, OR AN ICED TEA?
UMM... SURE... AN ICED TEA... DECAF.
YEAH, I'VE GOT JUST THE THING. NO CAFFEINE, AND IT'LL COOL YA DOWN.
ONE LONG ISLAND ICED TEA COMIN' UP.
ABSOLUTELY VODKA
IN ANOTHER ROOM...
SO, YA WANNA COME UPSTAIRS WITH ME, SCHOOL-GIRL?
IT'S *LAURA*, AND, SURE, I'D *LOVE* TO.
LEFT BREAST, RED!
SO, WHAT'S IN THE BOOK, LAURA?
IT'S A BIBLE... TO PRAY ON WHEN I'M NAUGHTY.
OH WOW... THAT IS *SO* HOT.

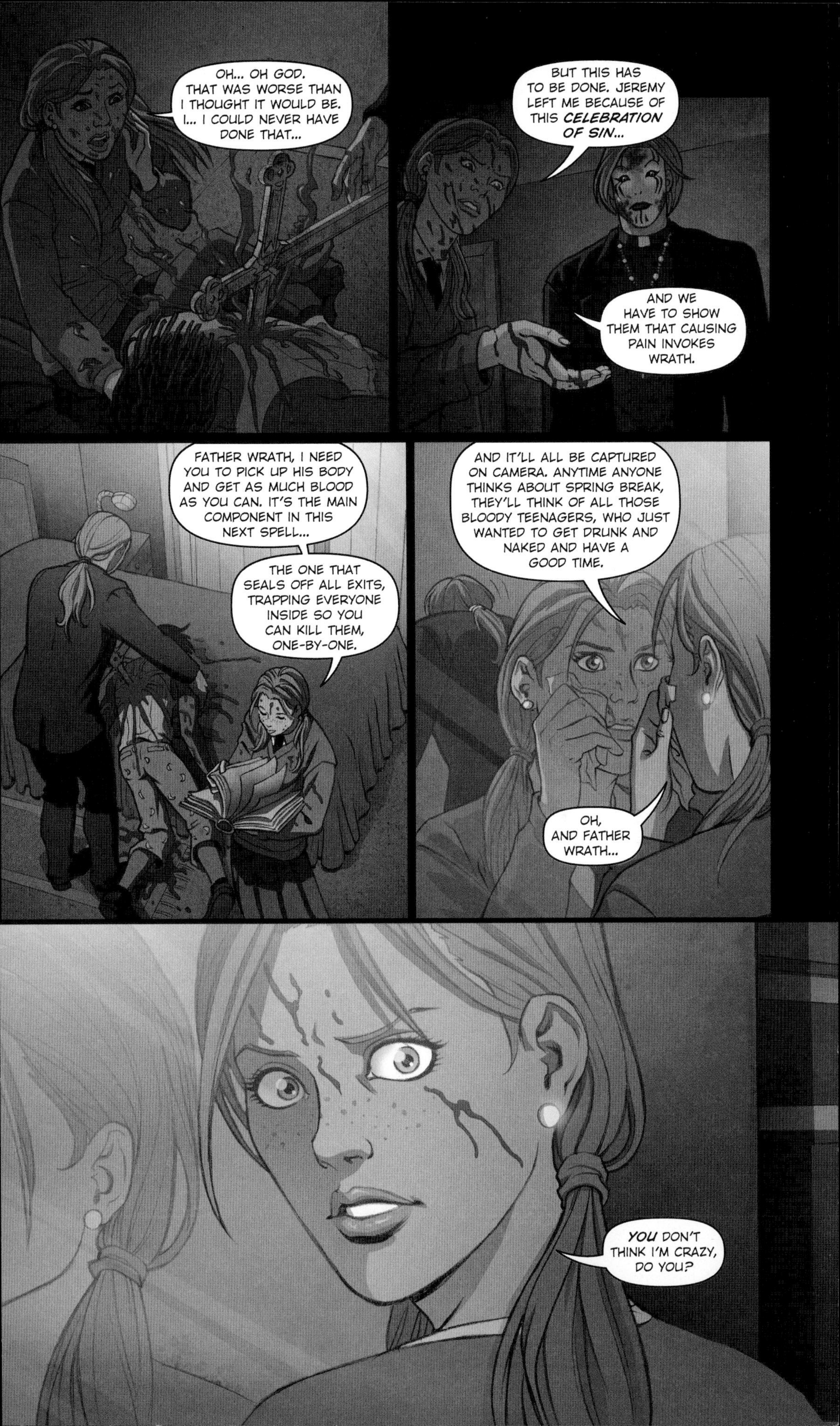
OH... OH GOD. THAT WAS WORSE THAN I THOUGHT IT WOULD BE. I... I COULD NEVER HAVE DONE THAT...
BUT THIS HAS TO BE DONE. JEREMY LEFT ME BECAUSE OF THIS *CELEBRATION OF SIN*...
AND WE HAVE TO SHOW THEM THAT CAUSING PAIN INVOKES WRATH.
FATHER WRATH, I NEED YOU TO PICK UP HIS BODY AND GET AS MUCH BLOOD AS YOU CAN. IT'S THE MAIN COMPONENT IN THIS NEXT SPELL...
THE ONE THAT SEALS OFF ALL EXITS, TRAPPING EVERYONE INSIDE SO YOU CAN KILL THEM, ONE-BY-ONE.
AND IT'LL ALL BE CAPTURED ON CAMERA. ANYTIME ANYONE THINKS ABOUT SPRING BREAK, THEY'LL THINK OF ALL THOSE BLOODY TEENAGERS, WHO JUST WANTED TO GET DRUNK AND NAKED AND HAVE A GOOD TIME.
OH, AND FATHER WRATH...
YOU DON'T THINK I'M CRAZY, DO YOU?

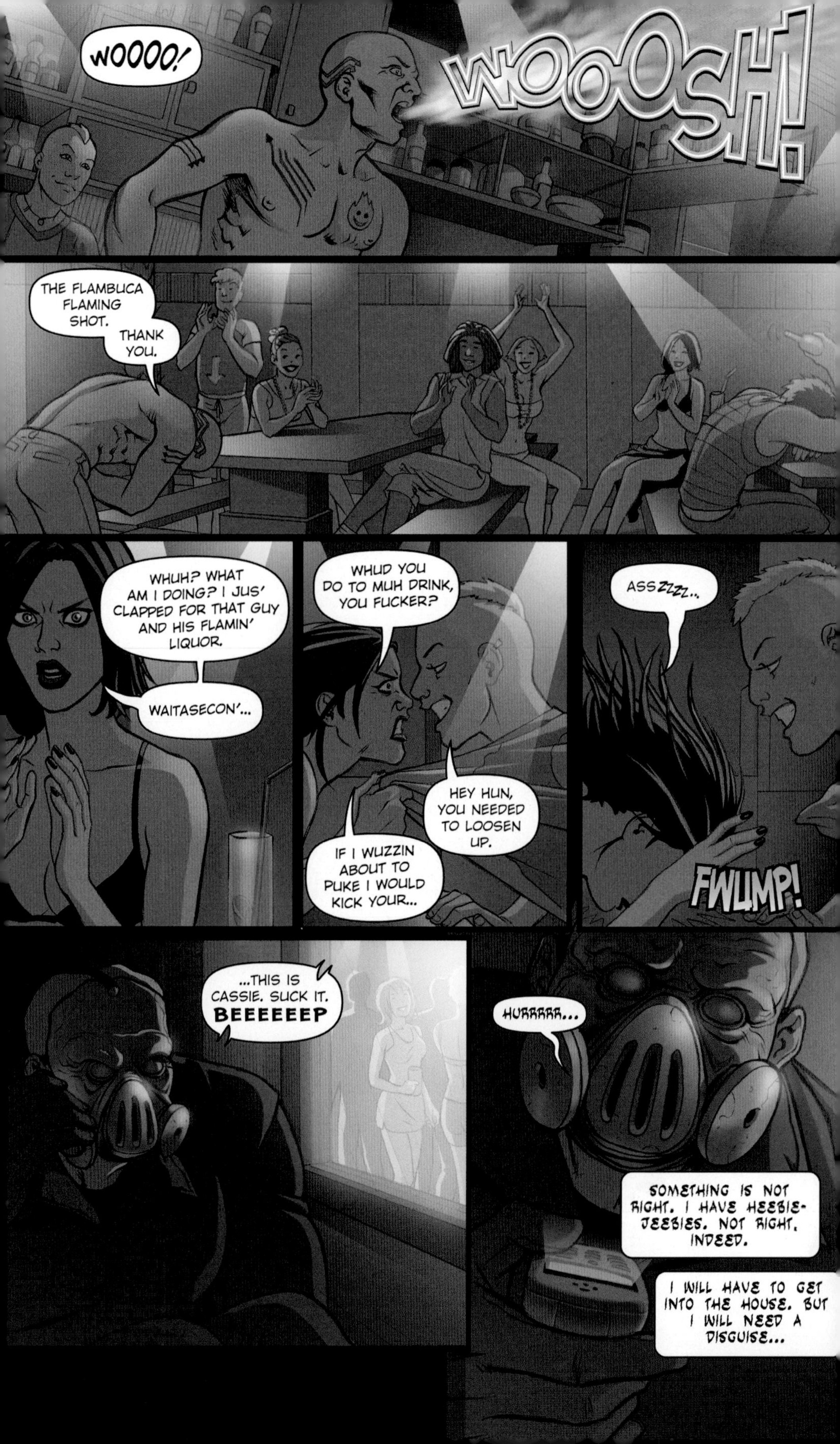
WOOOO!
WOOOSH!
THE FLAMBUCA FLAMING SHOT.
THANK YOU.
WHUH? WHAT AM I DOING? I JUS' CLAPPED FOR THAT GUY AND HIS FLAMIN' LIQUOR.
WAITASECON'...
WHUD YOU DO TO MUH DRINK, YOU FUCKER?
HEY HUN, YOU NEEDED TO LOOSEN UP.
IF I WUZZIN ABOUT TO PUKE I WOULD KICK YOUR...
ASSZZZZ...
FWUMP!
...THIS IS CASSIE. SUCK IT. BEEEEEEP
HURRRRR...
SOMETHING IS NOT RIGHT. I HAVE HEEBIE-JEEBIES. NOT RIGHT, INDEED.
I WILL HAVE TO GET INTO THE HOUSE. BUT I WILL NEED A DISGUISE...

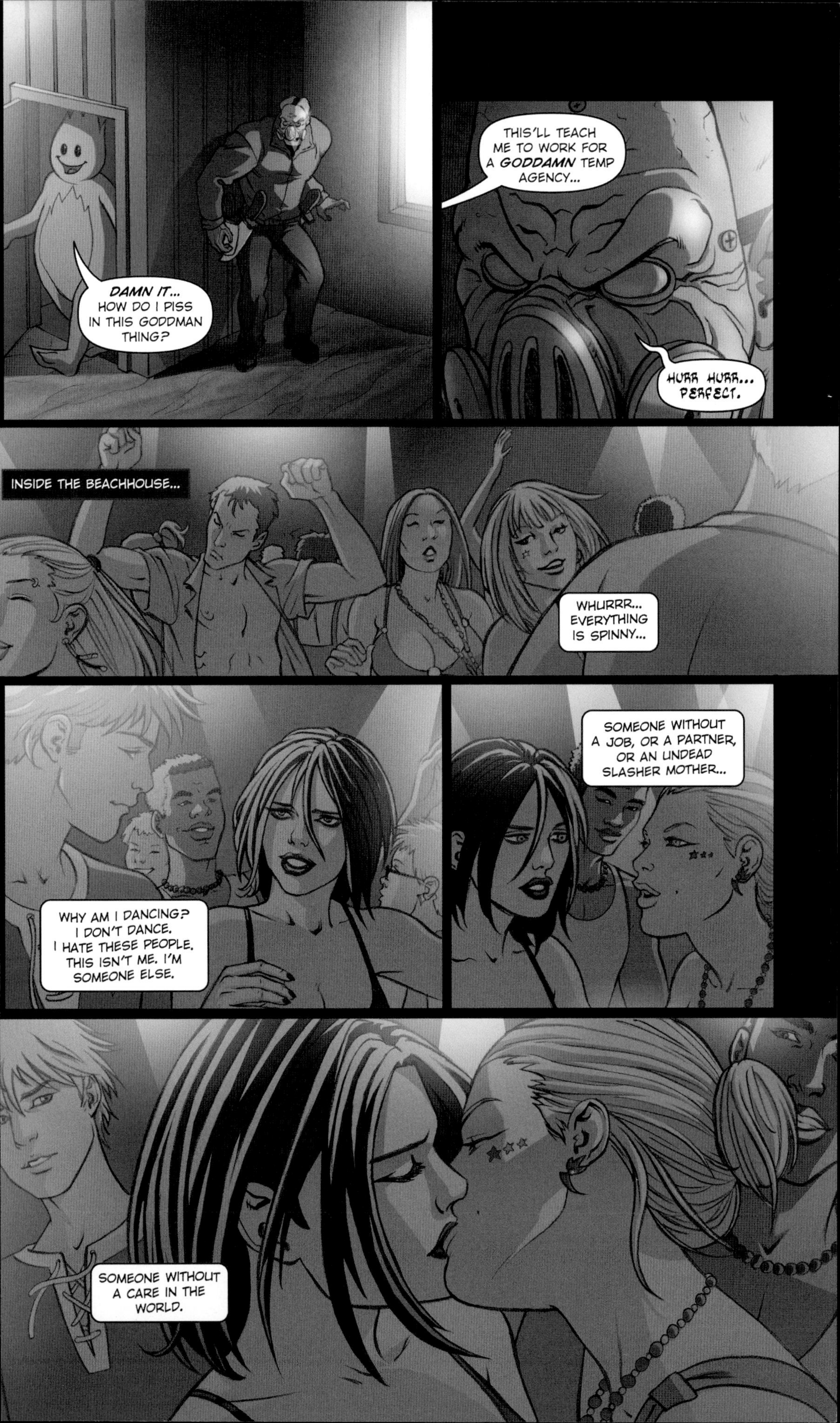
DAMN IT... HOW DO I PISS IN THIS GODDMAN THING?
THIS'LL TEACH ME TO WORK FOR A GODDAMN TEMP AGENCY...
HURR HURR... PERFECT.
INSIDE THE BEACHHOUSE...
WHURRR... EVERYTHING IS SPINNY...
WHY AM I DANCING? I DON'T DANCE. I HATE THESE PEOPLE. THIS ISN'T ME. I'M SOMEONE ELSE.
SOMEONE WITHOUT A JOB, OR A PARTNER, OR AN UNDEAD SLASHER MOTHER...
SOMEONE WITHOUT A CARE IN THE WORLD.

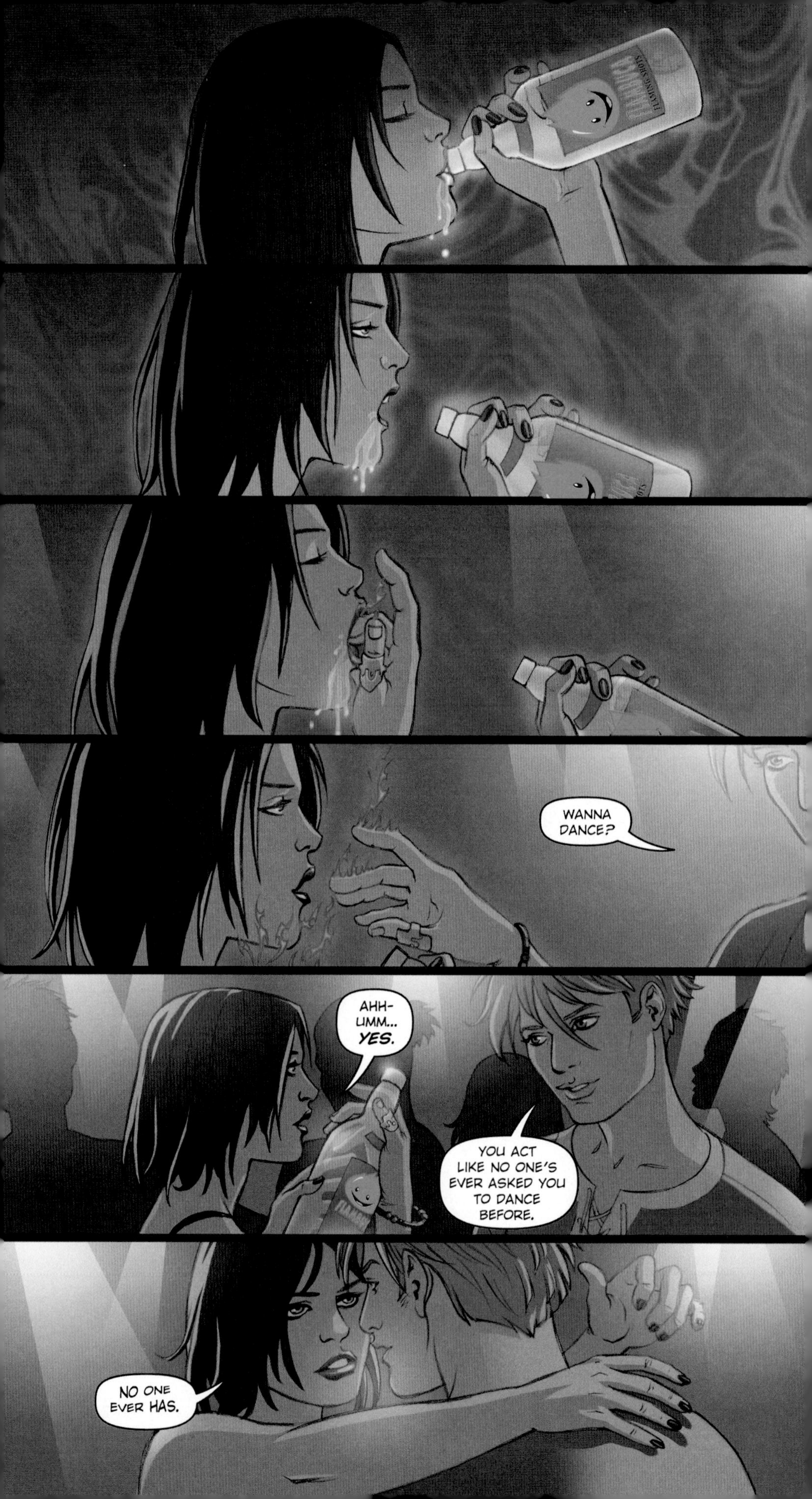
WANNA DANCE?
AHH-UMM... YES.
YOU ACT LIKE NO ONE'S EVER ASKED YOU TO DANCE BEFORE.
NO ONE EVER HAS.

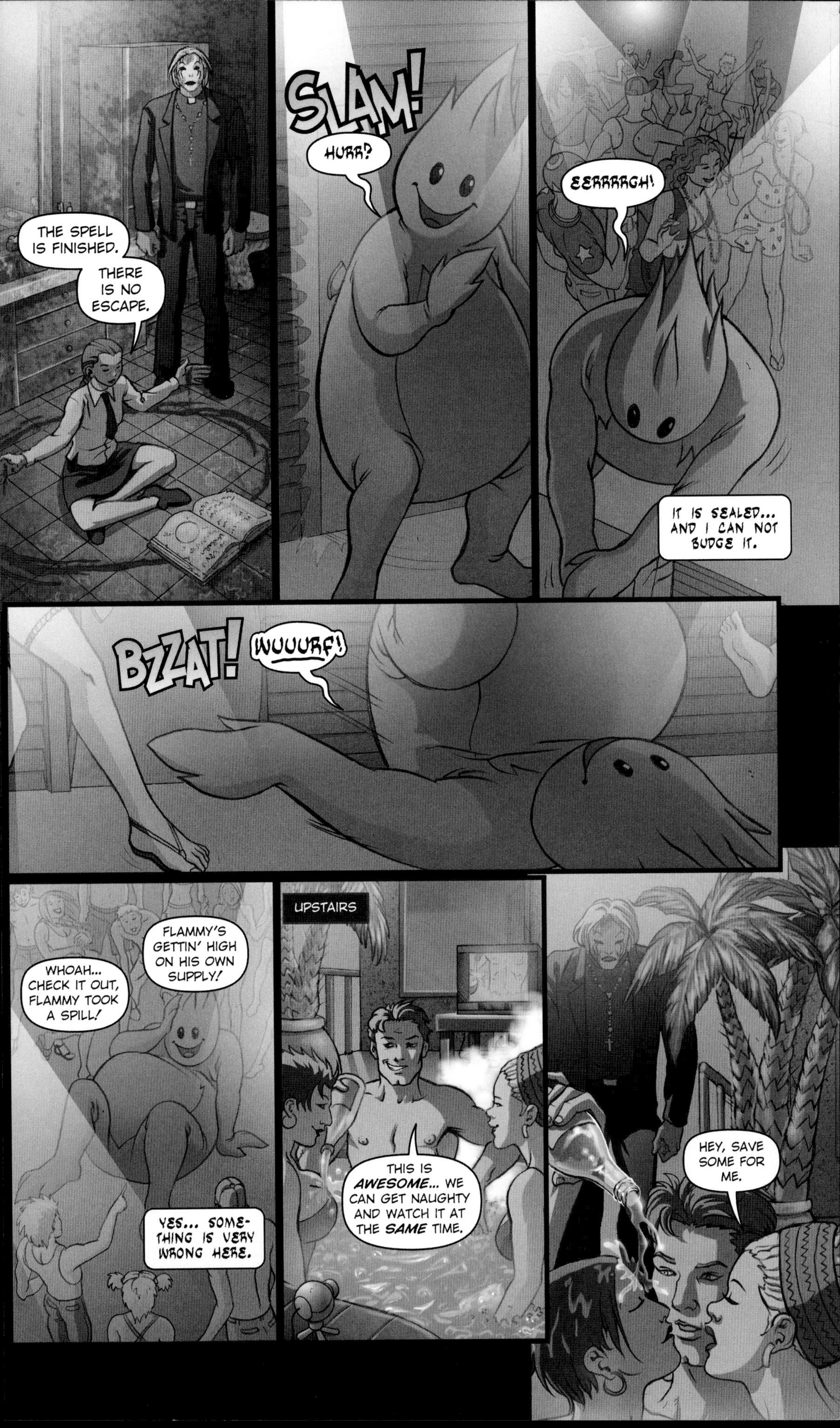
THE SPELL IS FINISHED.
THERE IS NO ESCAPE.
SLAM!
HURR?
EERRRRGH!
IT IS SEALED... AND I CAN NOT BUDGE IT.
BZZAT!
WUUURF!
WHOAH... CHECK IT OUT, FLAMMY TOOK A SPILL!
FLAMMY'S GETTIN' HIGH ON HIS OWN SUPPLY!
YES... SOMETHING IS VERY WRONG HERE.
UPSTAIRS
THIS IS AWESOME... WE CAN GET NAUGHTY AND WATCH IT AT THE SAME TIME.
HEY, SAVE SOME FOR ME.

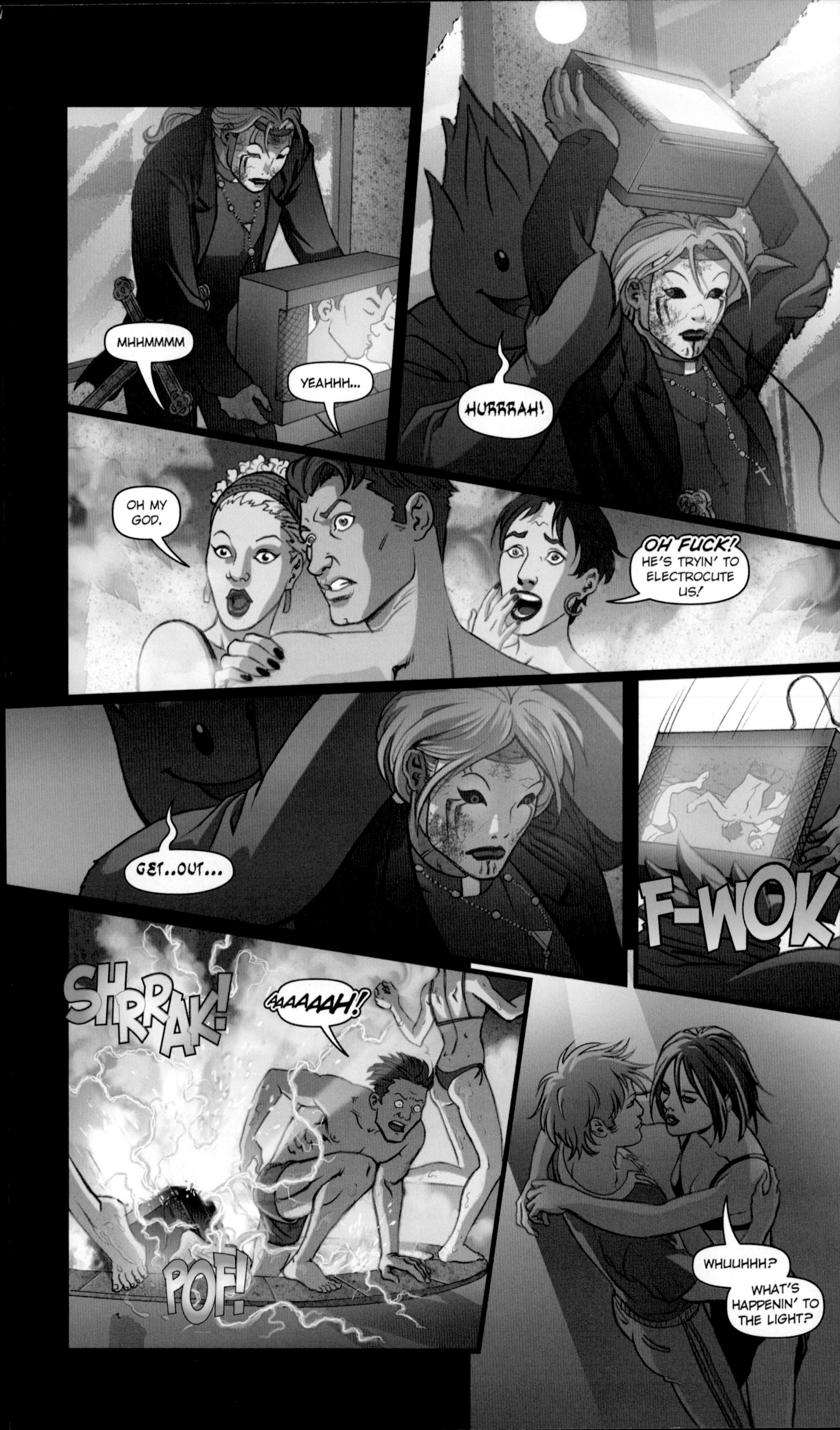
MHHMMMM
YEAHHH...
HURRRAH!
OH MY GOD.
OH FUCK! HE'S TRYIN' TO ELECTROCUTE US!
GET..OUT...
F-WOK
SHRRAK!
AAAAAAH!
POF!
WHUUHHH?
WHAT'S HAPPENIN' TO THE LIGHT?

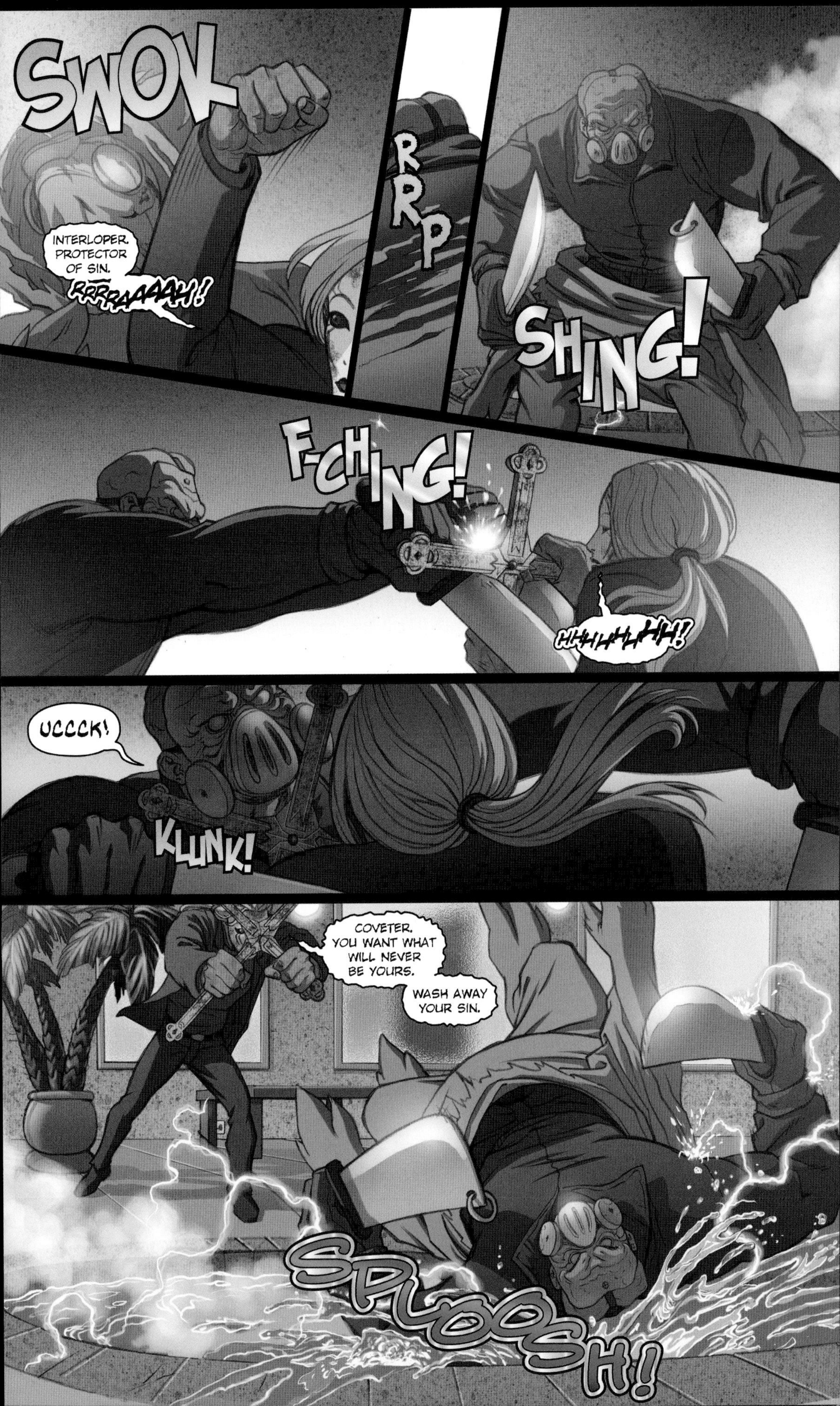
SWOK
INTERLOPER. PROTECTOR OF SIN.
RRRRAAAAH!
RRRP
SHING!
F-CHING!
HHHHHHH!
UCCCK!
KLUNK!
COVETER. YOU WANT WHAT WILL NEVER BE YOURS.
WASH AWAY YOUR SIN.
SPLOOSH!

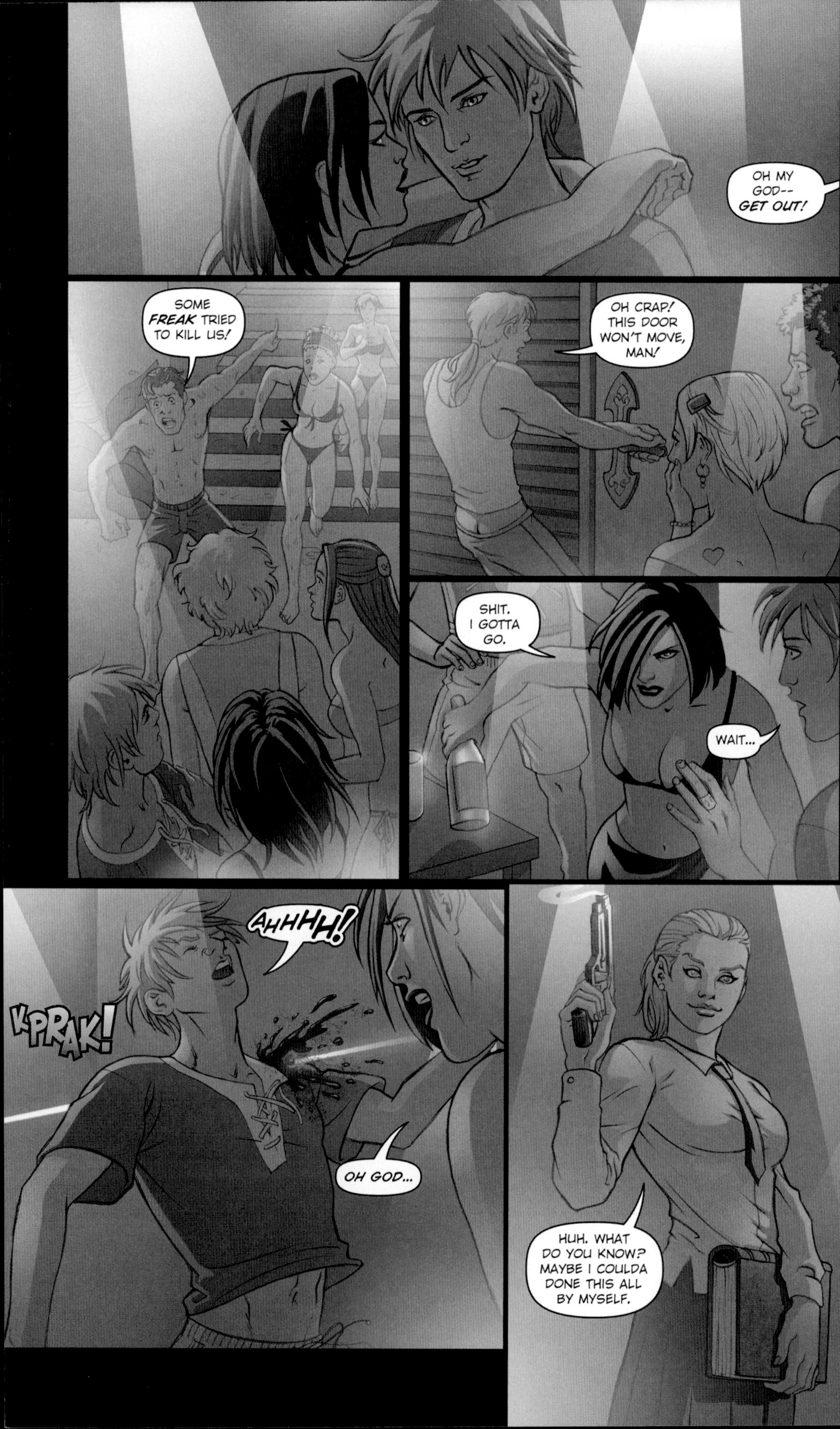
OH MY GOD-- GET OUT!
SOME FREAK TRIED TO KILL US!
OH CRAP! THIS DOOR WON'T MOVE, MAN!
SHIT. I GOTTA GO.
WAIT...
AHHHH!
KPRAK!
OH GOD...
HUH. WHAT DO YOU KNOW? MAYBE I COULDA DONE THIS ALL BY MYSELF.

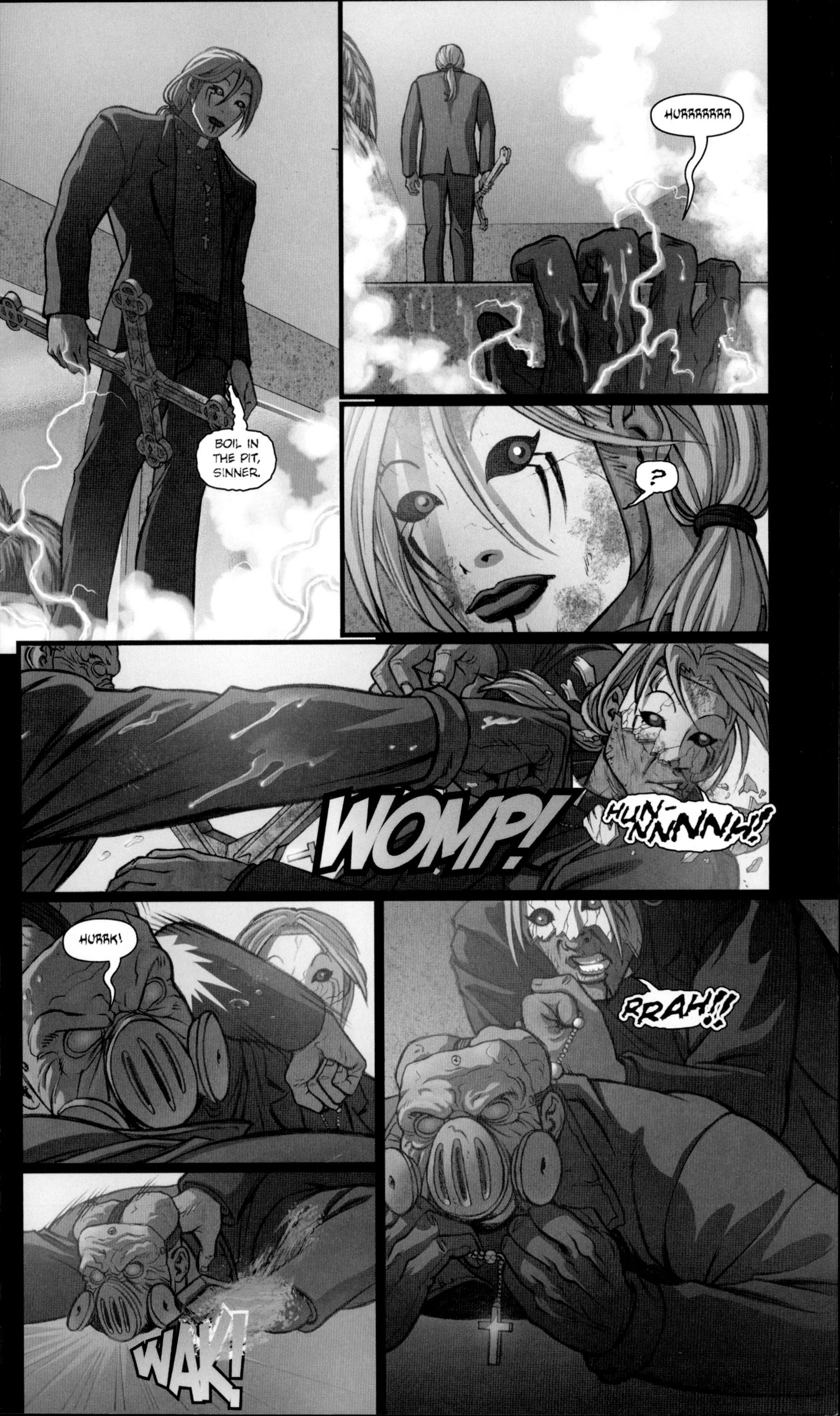
BOIL IN THE PIT, SINNER.
HURRRRRRRR
?
WOMP!
HUN-NNNNH!
HURRK!
WAK!
RRAH!!

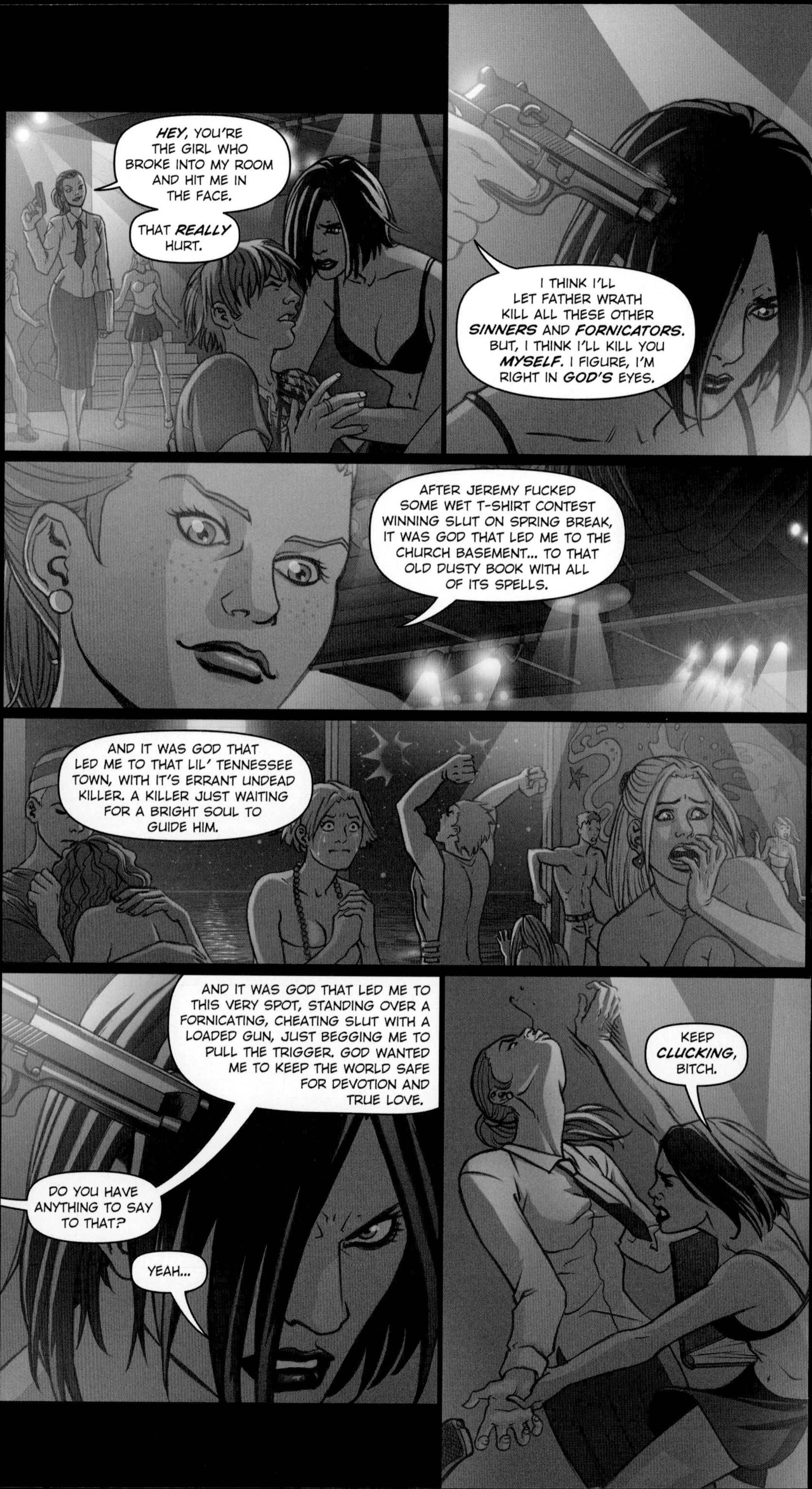
HEY, YOU'RE THE GIRL WHO BROKE INTO MY ROOM AND HIT ME IN THE FACE.
THAT REALLY HURT.
I THINK I'LL LET FATHER WRATH KILL ALL THESE OTHER SINNERS AND FORNICATORS. BUT, I THINK I'LL KILL YOU MYSELF. I FIGURE, I'M RIGHT IN GOD'S EYES.
AFTER JEREMY FUCKED SOME WET T-SHIRT CONTEST WINNING SLUT ON SPRING BREAK, IT WAS GOD THAT LED ME TO THE CHURCH BASEMENT... TO THAT OLD DUSTY BOOK WITH ALL OF ITS SPELLS.
AND IT WAS GOD THAT LED ME TO THAT LIL' TENNESSEE TOWN, WITH IT'S ERRANT UNDEAD KILLER. A KILLER JUST WAITING FOR A BRIGHT SOUL TO GUIDE HIM.
AND IT WAS GOD THAT LED ME TO THIS VERY SPOT, STANDING OVER A FORNICATING, CHEATING SLUT WITH A LOADED GUN, JUST BEGGING ME TO PULL THE TRIGGER. GOD WANTED ME TO KEEP THE WORLD SAFE FOR DEVOTION AND TRUE LOVE.
DO YOU HAVE ANYTHING TO SAY TO THAT?
YEAH...
KEEP CLUCKING, BITCH.

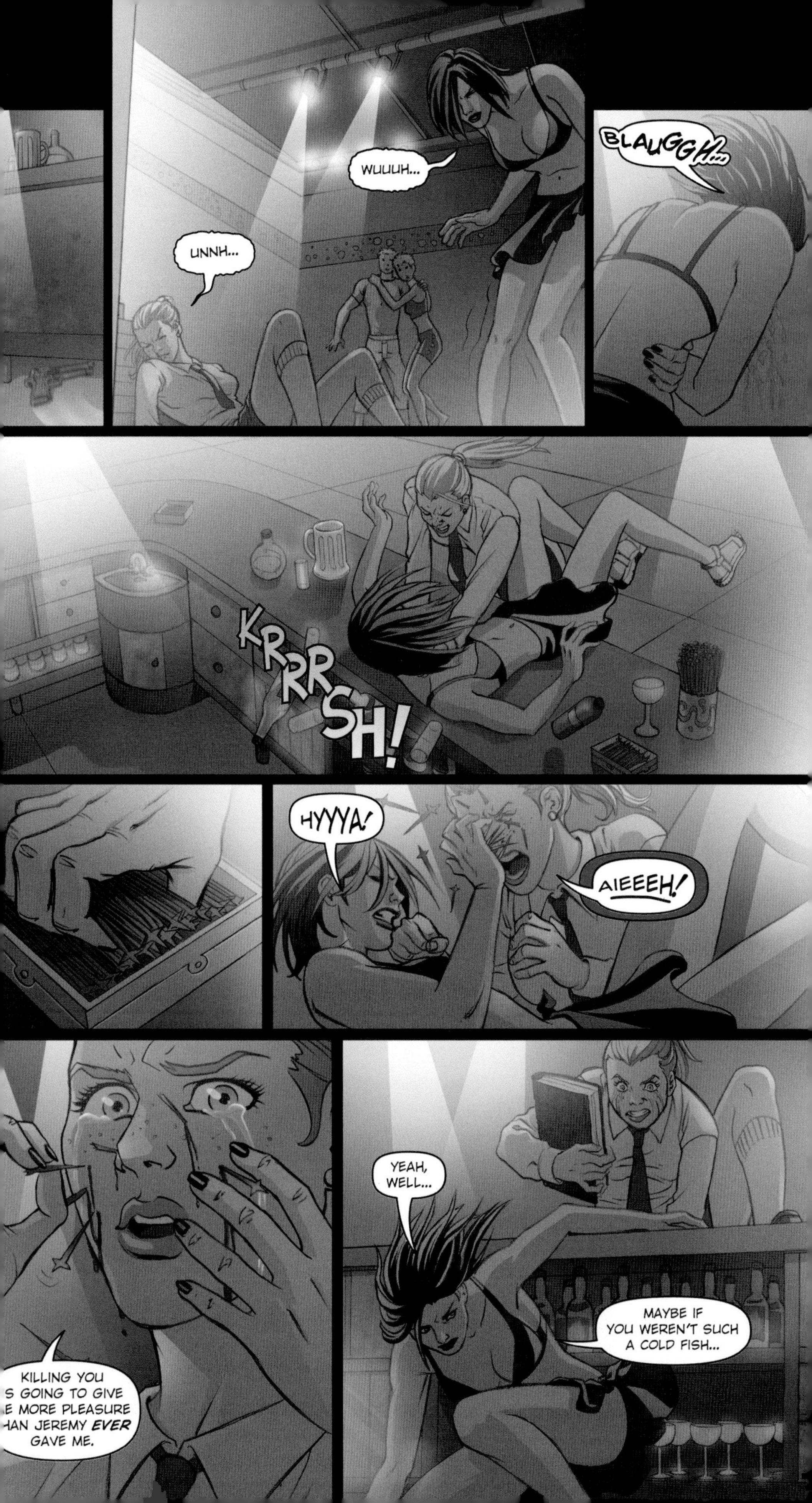

UNNH...
WUUUH...
BLAUGGH...
KRRRSH!
HYYYA!
AIEEEH!
KILLING YOU
S GOING TO GIVE
E MORE PLEASURE
HAN JEREMY EVER
GAVE ME.
YEAH, WELL...
MAYBE IF
YOU WEREN'T SUCH
A COLD FISH...

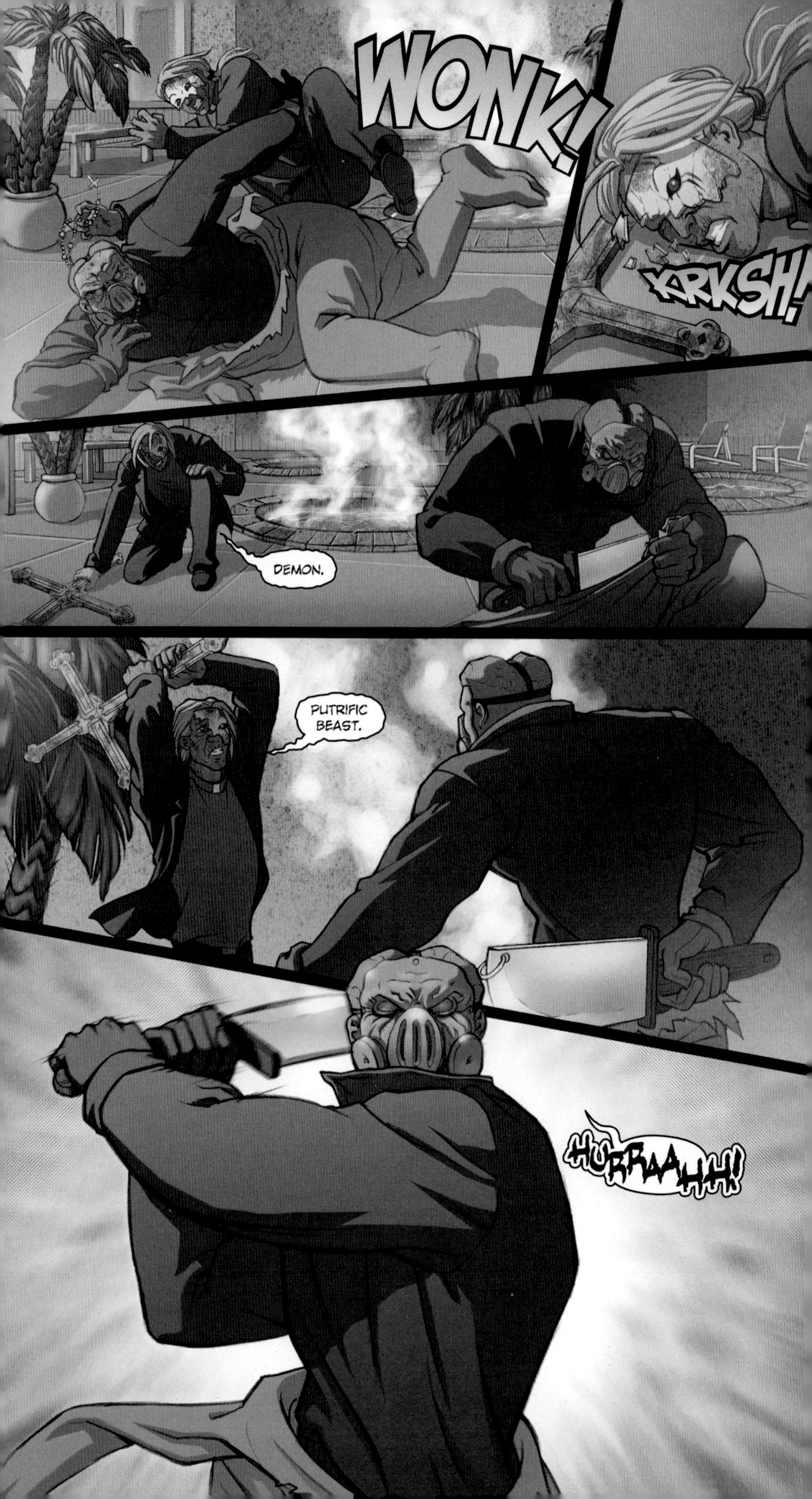
WONK!
KRKSH!
DEMON.
PUTRIFIC BEAST.
HURRAAHH!

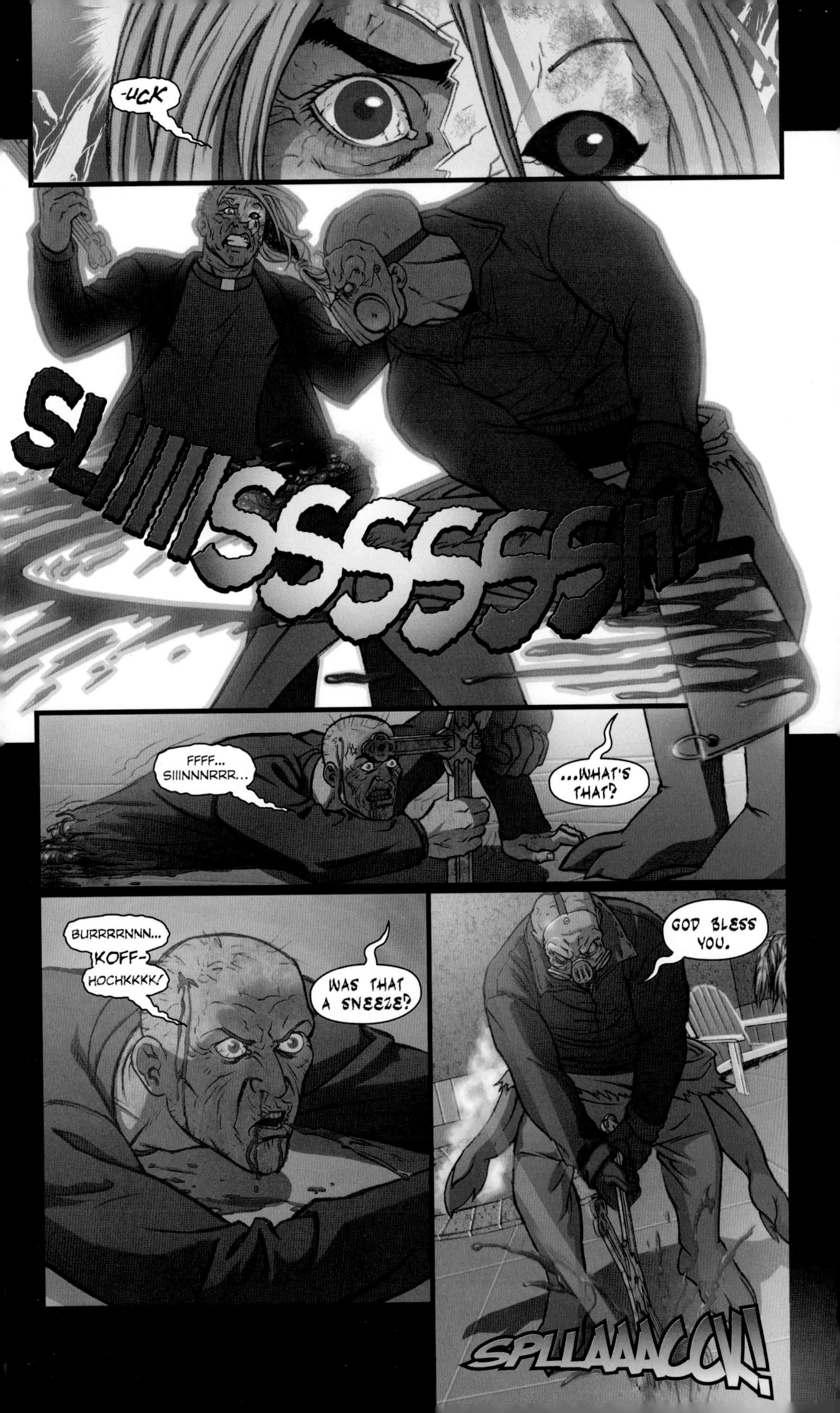
-UCK
SLIIIISSSSSSH!
FFFF... SIIINNNRRR...
...WHAT'S THAT?
BURRRRNNN... KOFF-HOCHKKKK!
WAS THAT A SNEEZE?
GOD BLESS YOU.
SPLLAAACCK!

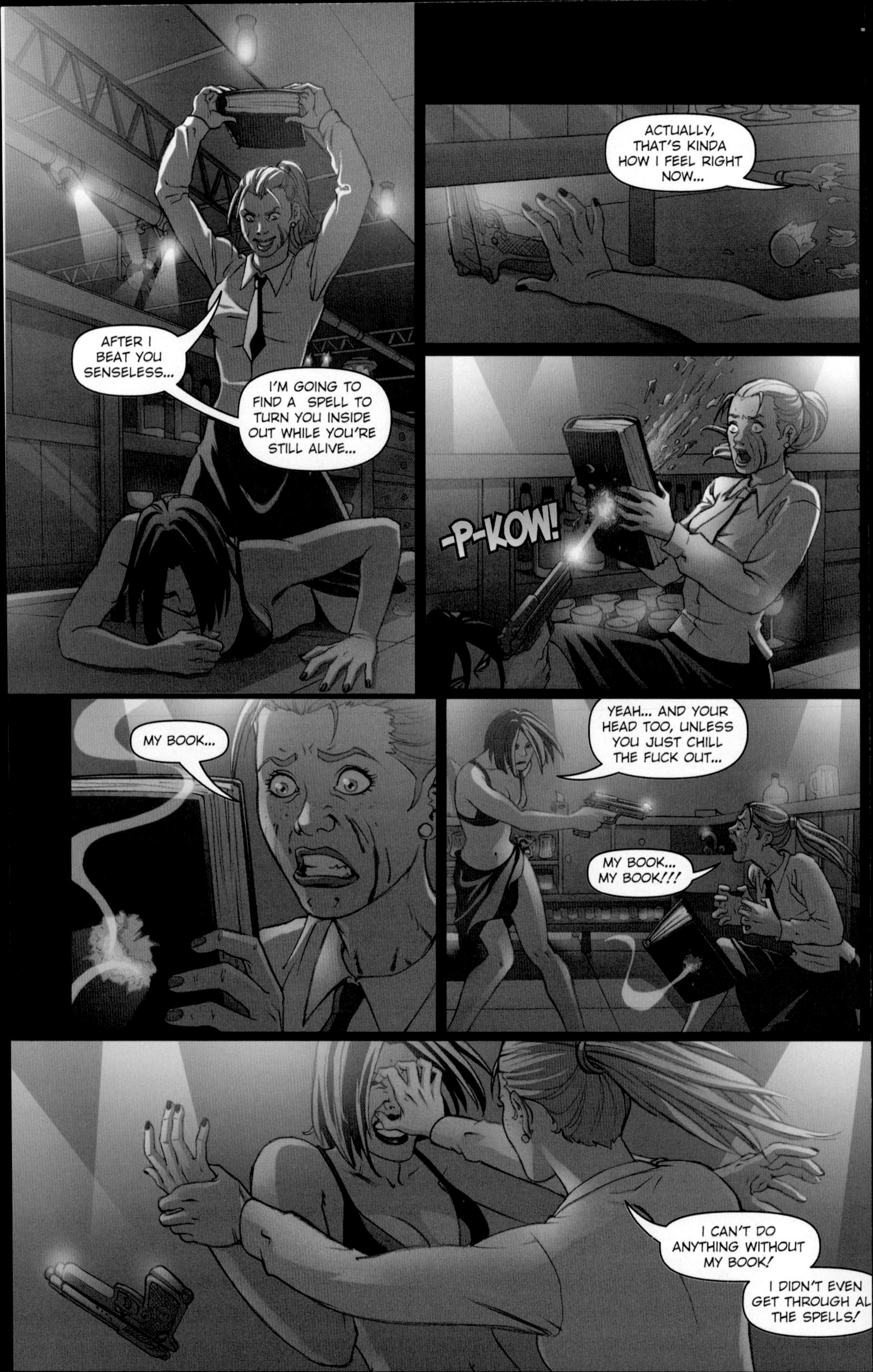
AFTER I BEAT YOU SENSELESS...
I'M GOING TO FIND A SPELL TO TURN YOU INSIDE OUT WHILE YOU'RE STILL ALIVE...
ACTUALLY, THAT'S KINDA HOW I FEEL RIGHT NOW...
-P-KOW!
MY BOOK...
YEAH... AND YOUR HEAD TOO, UNLESS YOU JUST CHILL THE FUCK OUT...
MY BOOK... MY BOOK!!!
I CAN'T DO ANYTHING WITHOUT MY BOOK!
I DIDN'T EVEN GET THROUGH AL THE SPELLS!

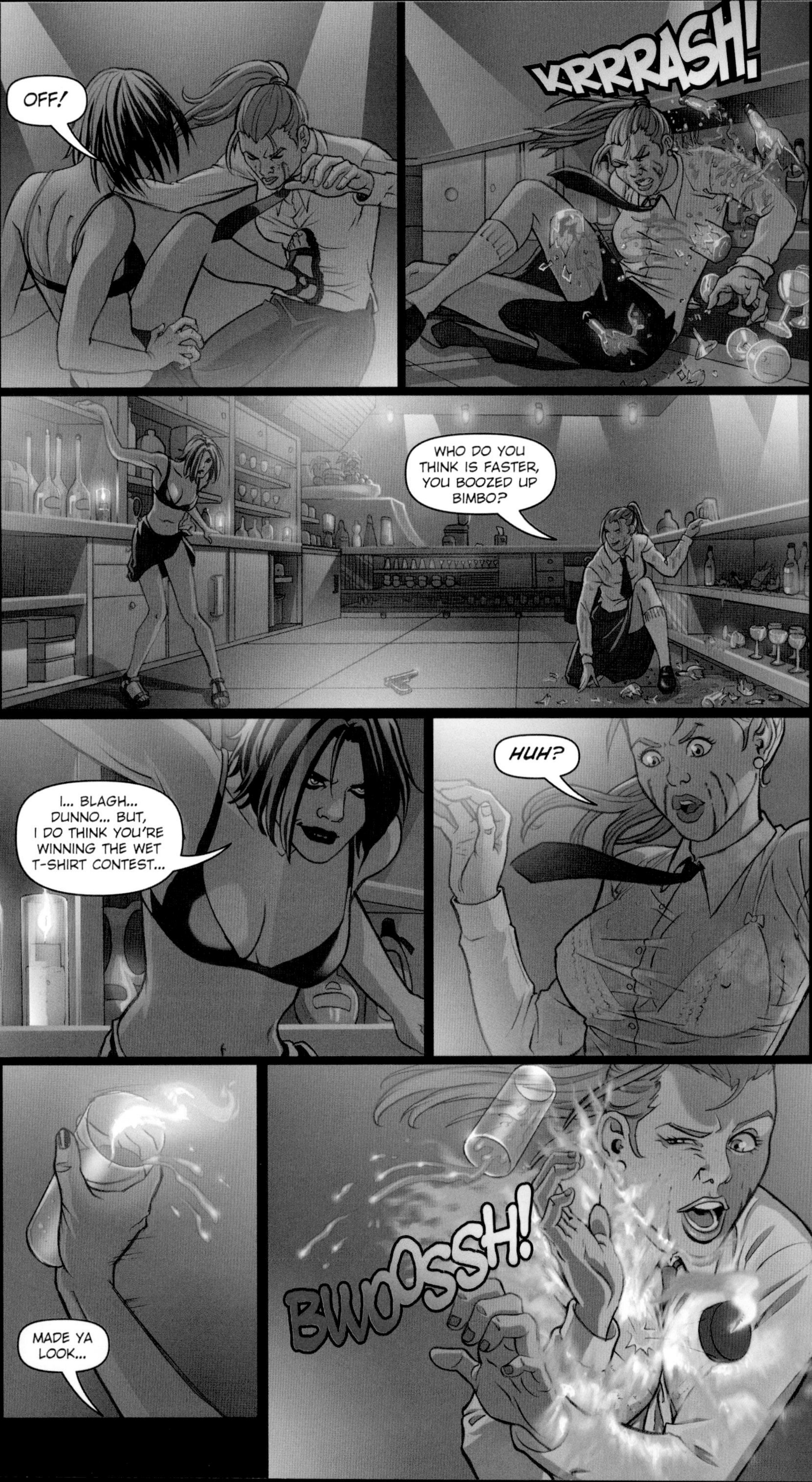
OFF!
KRRRASH!
WHO DO YOU THINK IS FASTER, YOU BOOZED UP BIMBO?
I... BLAGH... DUNNO... BUT, I DO THINK YOU'RE WINNING THE WET T-SHIRT CONTEST...
HUH?
MADE YA LOOK...
BWOOSSH!

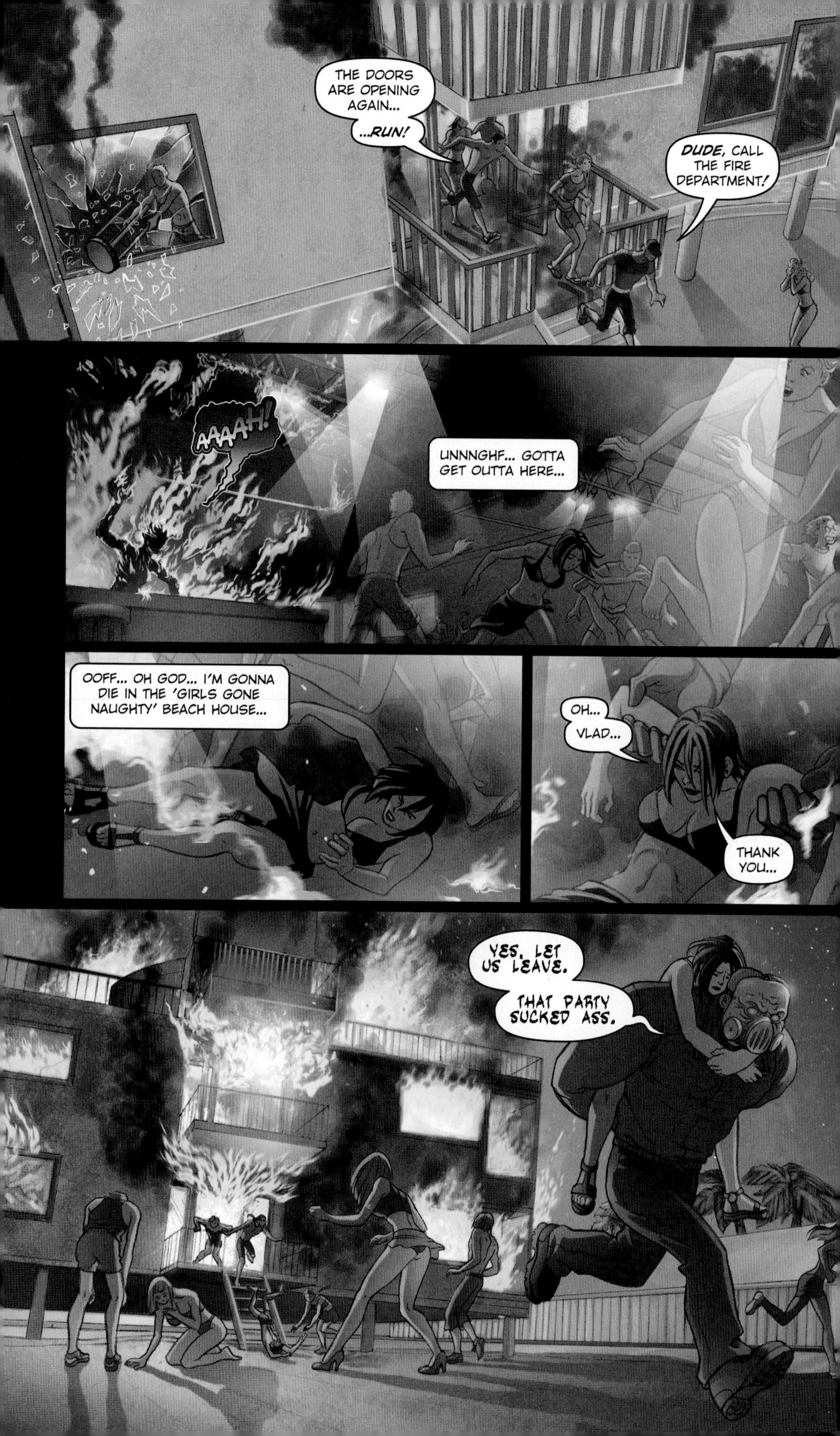
THE DOORS ARE OPENING AGAIN...
...RUN!
DUDE, CALL THE FIRE DEPARTMENT!
AAAAH!
UNNNGHF... GOTTA GET OUTTA HERE...
OOFF... OH GOD... I'M GONNA DIE IN THE 'GIRLS GONE NAUGHTY' BEACH HOUSE...
OH...
VLAD...
THANK YOU...
YES. LET US LEAVE.
THAT PARTY SUCKED ASS.

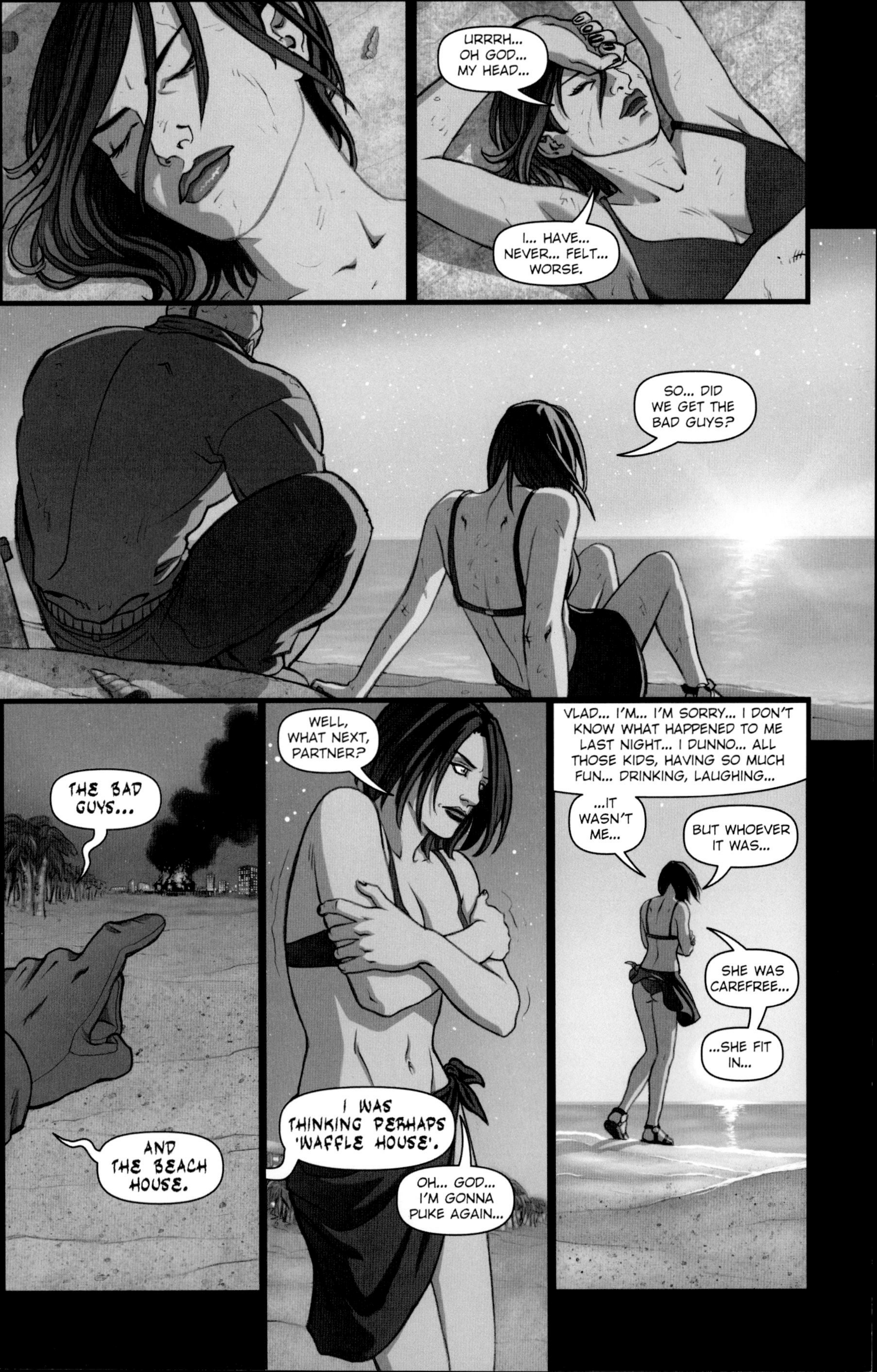
URRRH... OH GOD... MY HEAD...
I... HAVE... NEVER... FELT... WORSE.
SO... DID WE GET THE BAD GUYS?
THE BAD GUYS...
AND THE BEACH HOUSE.
WELL, WHAT NEXT, PARTNER?
I WAS THINKING PERHAPS 'WAFFLE HOUSE'.
OH... GOD... I'M GONNA PUKE AGAIN...
VLAD... I'M... I'M SORRY... I DON'T KNOW WHAT HAPPENED TO ME LAST NIGHT... I DUNNO... ALL THOSE KIDS, HAVING SO MUCH FUN... DRINKING, LAUGHING...
...IT WASN'T ME...
BUT WHOEVER IT WAS...
SHE WAS CAREFREE...
...SHE FIT IN...

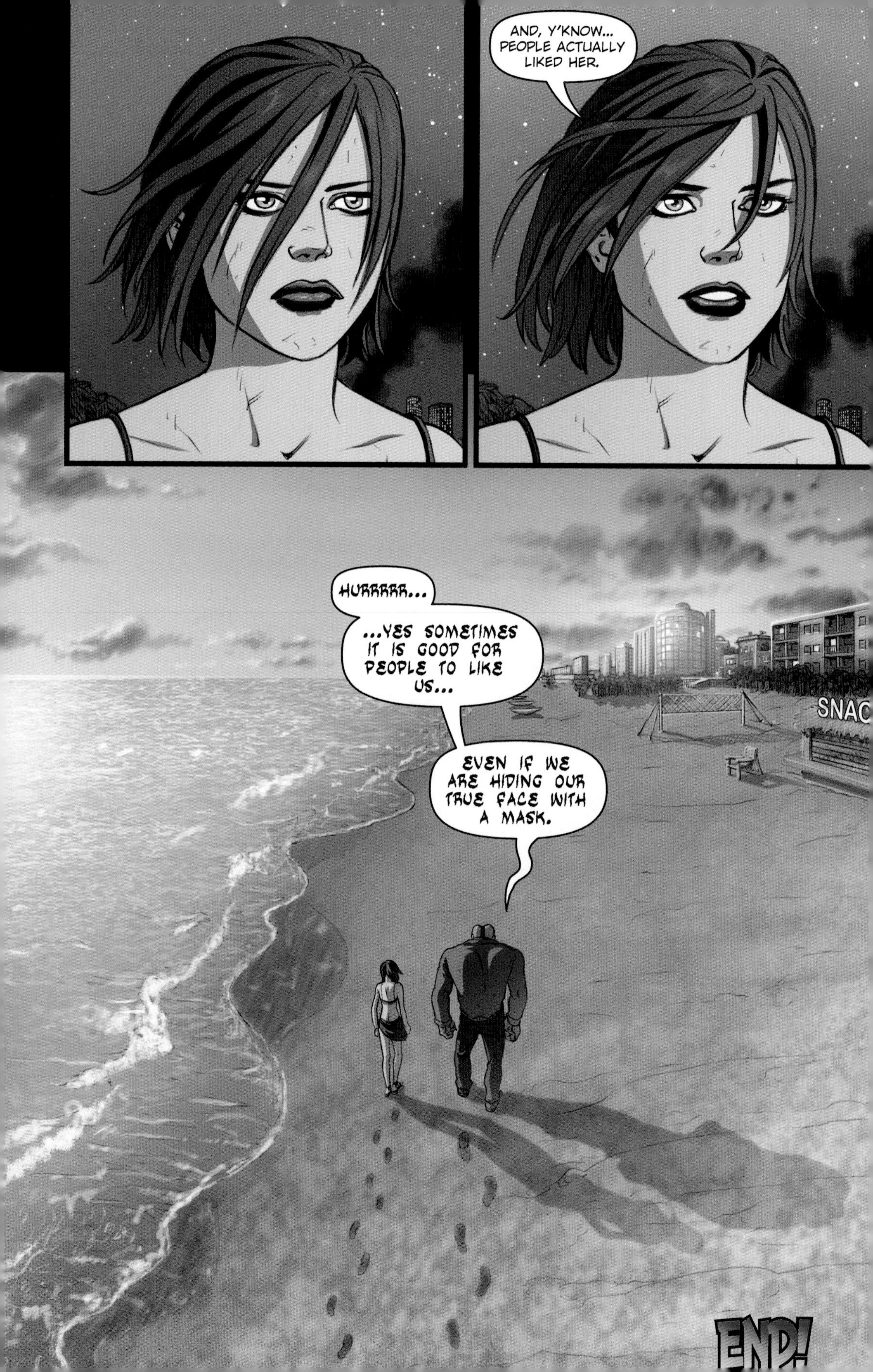
AND, Y'KNOW... PEOPLE ACTUALLY LIKED HER.
HURRRRR...
...YES SOMETIMES IT IS GOOD FOR PEOPLE TO LIKE US...
EVEN IF WE ARE HIDING OUR TRUE FACE WITH A MASK.
SNAC
END!

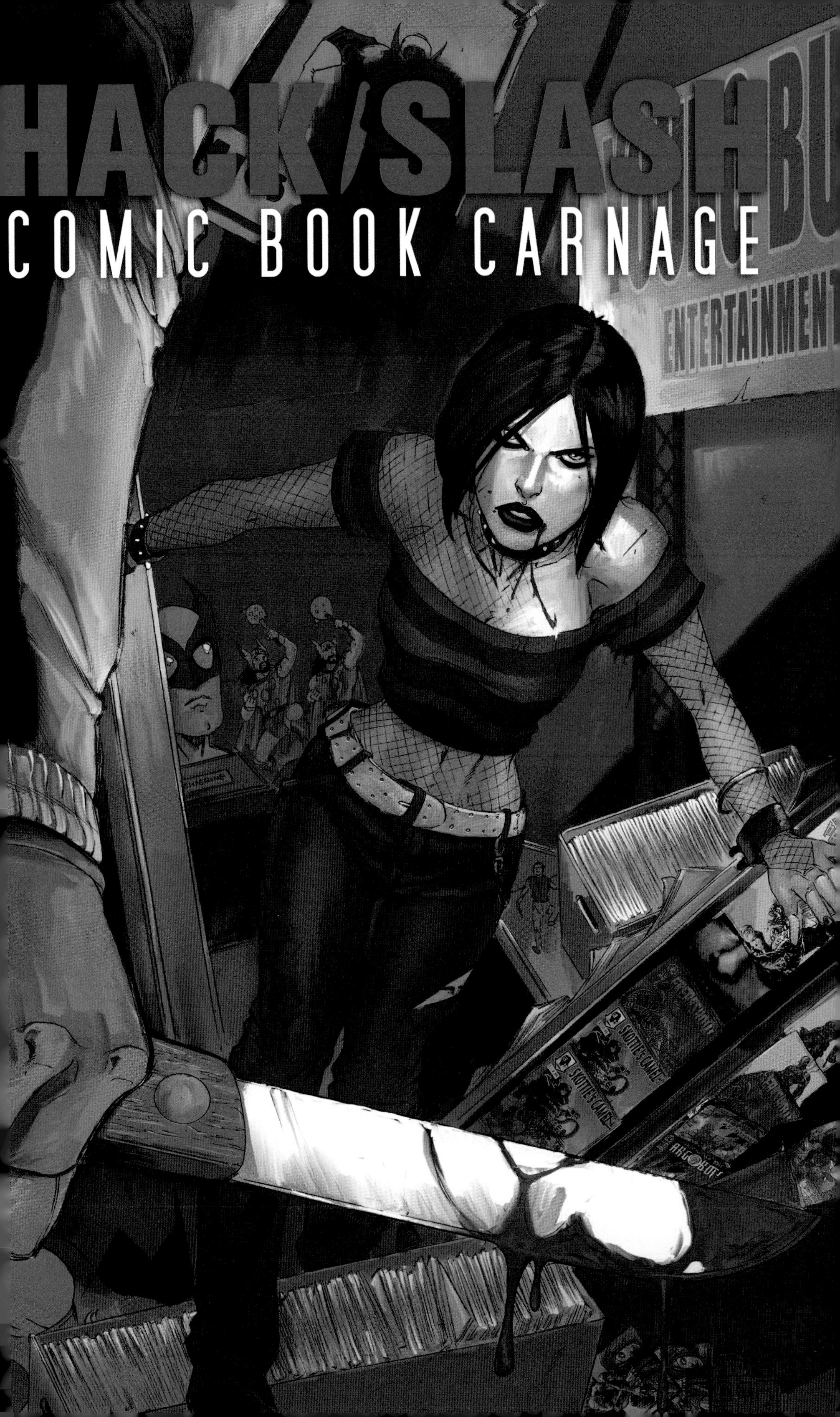
HACK/SLASH
COMIC BOOK CARNAGE
ENTERTAINMENT

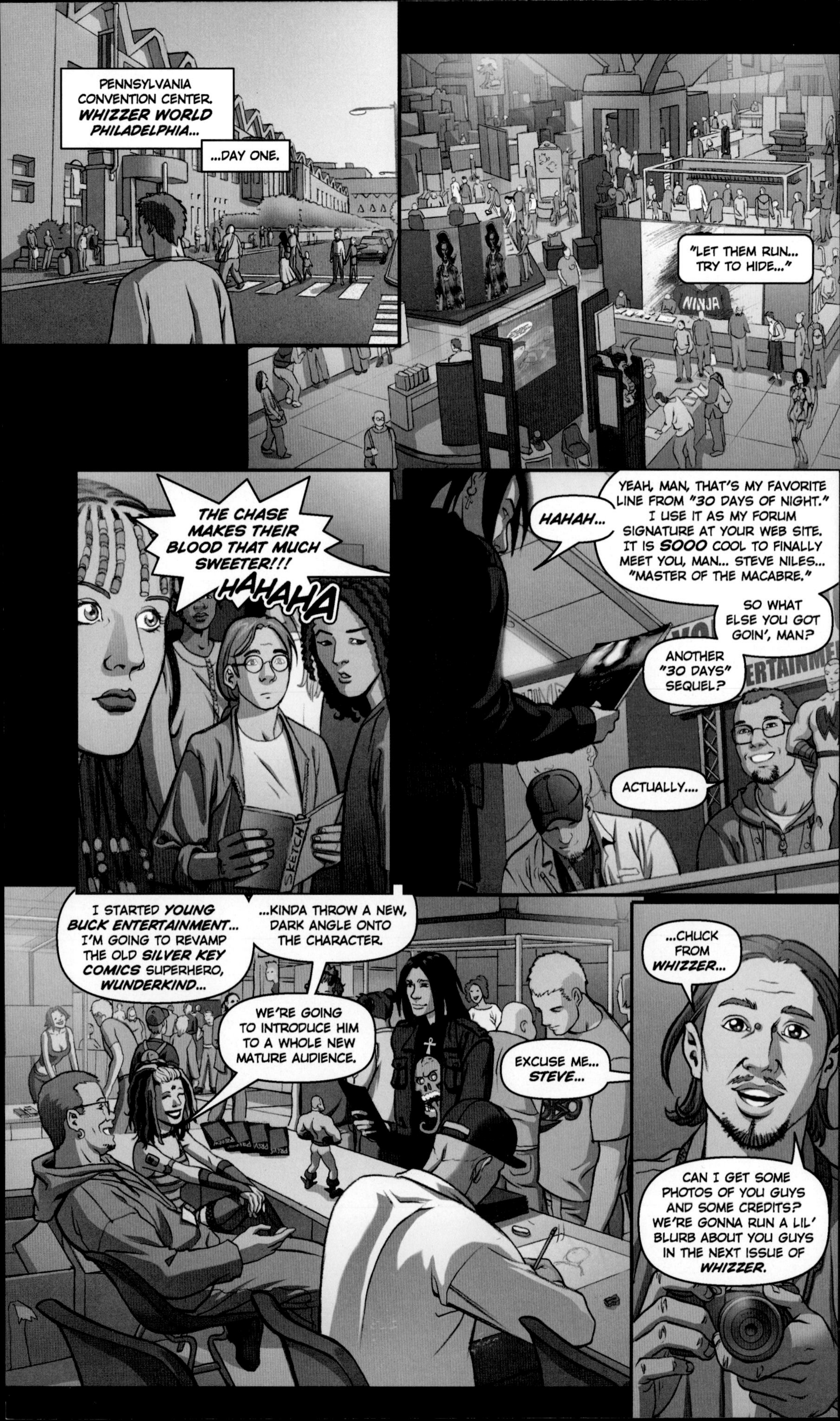
PENNSYLVANIA CONVENTION CENTER. *WHIZZER WORLD PHILADELPHIA...*
...DAY ONE.
"LET THEM RUN... TRY TO HIDE..."
NINJA
THE CHASE MAKES THEIR BLOOD THAT MUCH SWEETER!!!
HAHAHA
SKETCH
HAHAH...
YEAH, MAN, THAT'S MY FAVORITE LINE FROM "30 DAYS OF NIGHT." I USE IT AS MY FORUM SIGNATURE AT YOUR WEB SITE. IT IS *SOOO* COOL TO FINALLY MEET YOU, MAN... STEVE NILES... "MASTER OF THE MACABRE."
SO WHAT ELSE YOU GOT GOIN', MAN?
ANOTHER "30 DAYS" SEQUEL?
ACTUALLY....
I STARTED *YOUNG BUCK ENTERTAINMENT*... I'M GOING TO REVAMP THE OLD *SILVER KEY COMICS* SUPERHERO, *WUNDERKIND*...
...KINDA THROW A NEW, DARK ANGLE ONTO THE CHARACTER.
WE'RE GOING TO INTRODUCE HIM TO A WHOLE NEW MATURE AUDIENCE.
EXCUSE ME... *STEVE*...
...CHUCK FROM *WHIZZER*...
CAN I GET SOME PHOTOS OF YOU GUYS AND SOME CREDITS? WE'RE GONNA RUN A LIL' BLURB ABOUT YOU GUYS IN THE NEXT ISSUE OF *WHIZZER*.

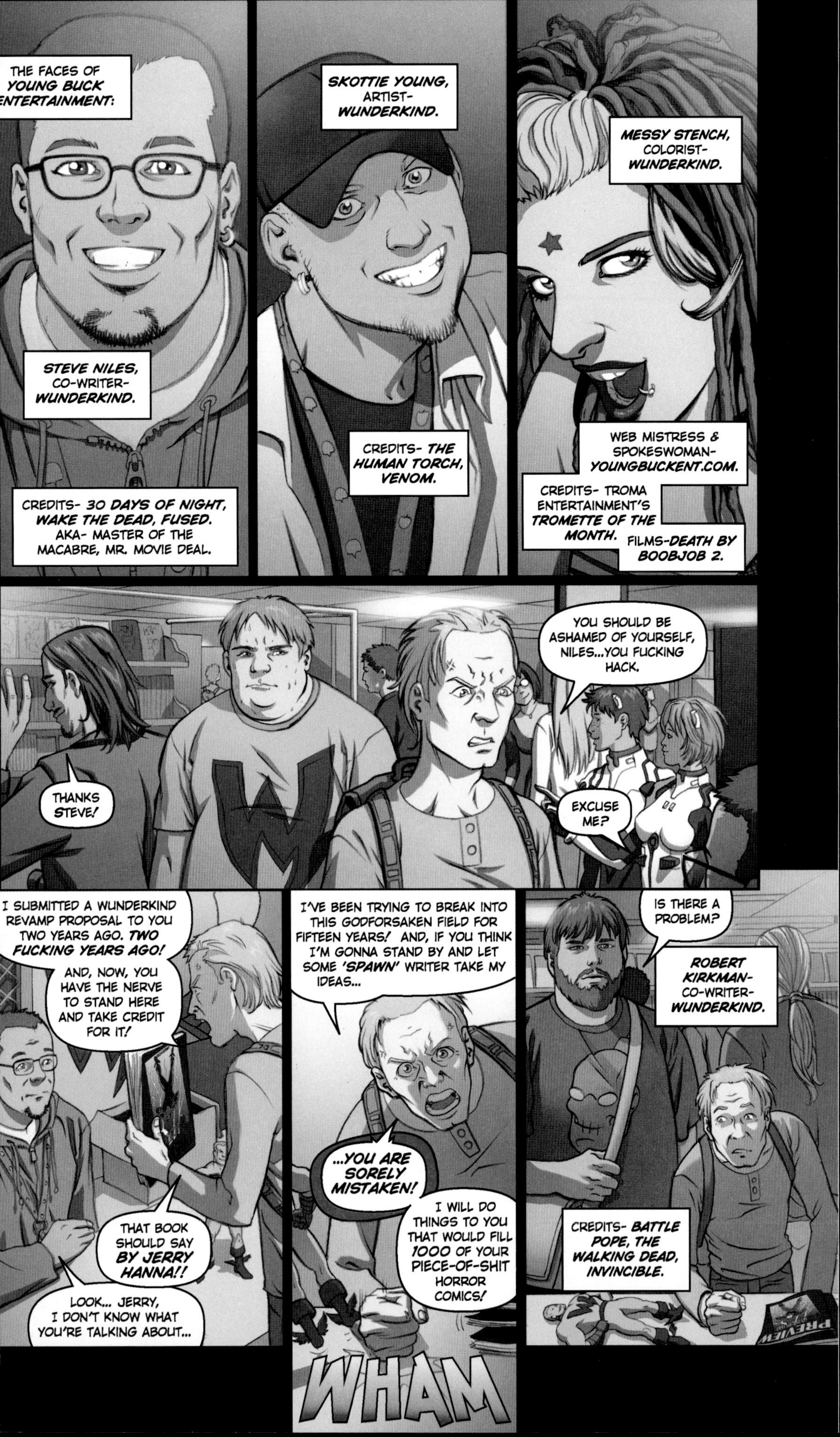
THE FACES OF YOUNG BUCK ENTERTAINMENT:
STEVE NILES, CO-WRITER-WUNDERKIND.
CREDITS- 30 DAYS OF NIGHT, WAKE THE DEAD, FUSED. AKA- MASTER OF THE MACABRE, MR. MOVIE DEAL.
SKOTTIE YOUNG, ARTIST-WUNDERKIND.
CREDITS- THE HUMAN TORCH, VENOM.
MESSY STENCH, COLORIST-WUNDERKIND.
WEB MISTRESS & SPOKESWOMAN-YOUNGBUCKENT.COM.
CREDITS- TROMA ENTERTAINMENT'S TROMETTE OF THE MONTH.
FILMS-DEATH BY BOOBJOB 2.
THANKS STEVE!
YOU SHOULD BE ASHAMED OF YOURSELF, NILES...YOU FUCKING HACK.
EXCUSE ME?
I SUBMITTED A WUNDERKIND REVAMP PROPOSAL TO YOU TWO YEARS AGO. TWO FUCKING YEARS AGO!
AND, NOW, YOU HAVE THE NERVE TO STAND HERE AND TAKE CREDIT FOR IT!
THAT BOOK SHOULD SAY BY JERRY HANNA!!
LOOK... JERRY, I DON'T KNOW WHAT YOU'RE TALKING ABOUT...
I'VE BEEN TRYING TO BREAK INTO THIS GODFORSAKEN FIELD FOR FIFTEEN YEARS! AND, IF YOU THINK I'M GONNA STAND BY AND LET SOME 'SPAWN' WRITER TAKE MY IDEAS...
...YOU ARE SORELY MISTAKEN!
I WILL DO THINGS TO YOU THAT WOULD FILL 1000 OF YOUR PIECE-OF-SHIT HORROR COMICS!
WHAM
IS THERE A PROBLEM?
ROBERT KIRKMAN-CO-WRITER-WUNDERKIND.
CREDITS- BATTLE POPE, THE WALKING DEAD, INVINCIBLE.
PREVIEW

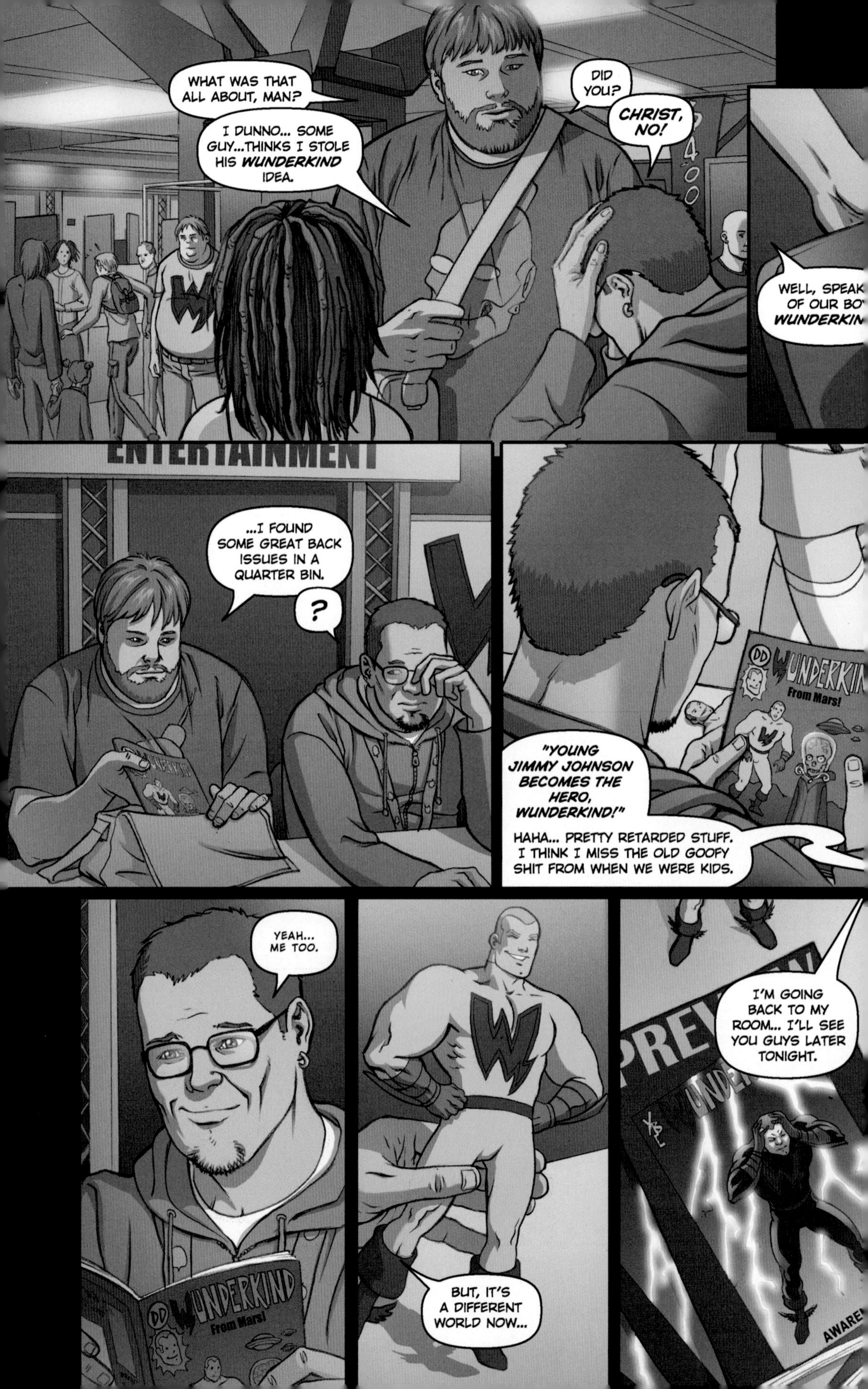
WHAT WAS THAT ALL ABOUT, MAN?
I DUNNO... SOME GUY...THINKS I STOLE HIS WUNDERKIND IDEA.
DID YOU?
CHRIST, NO!
WELL, SPEAK OF OUR BOY WUNDERKIN
ENTERTAINMENT
...I FOUND SOME GREAT BACK ISSUES IN A QUARTER BIN.
?
WUNDERKIND From Mars!
"YOUNG JIMMY JOHNSON BECOMES THE HERO, WUNDERKIND!"
HAHA... PRETTY RETARDED STUFF. I THINK I MISS THE OLD GOOFY SHIT FROM WHEN WE WERE KIDS.
YEAH... ME TOO.
WUNDERKIND From Mars!
BUT, IT'S A DIFFERENT WORLD NOW...
I'M GOING BACK TO MY ROOM... I'LL SEE YOU GUYS LATER TONIGHT.

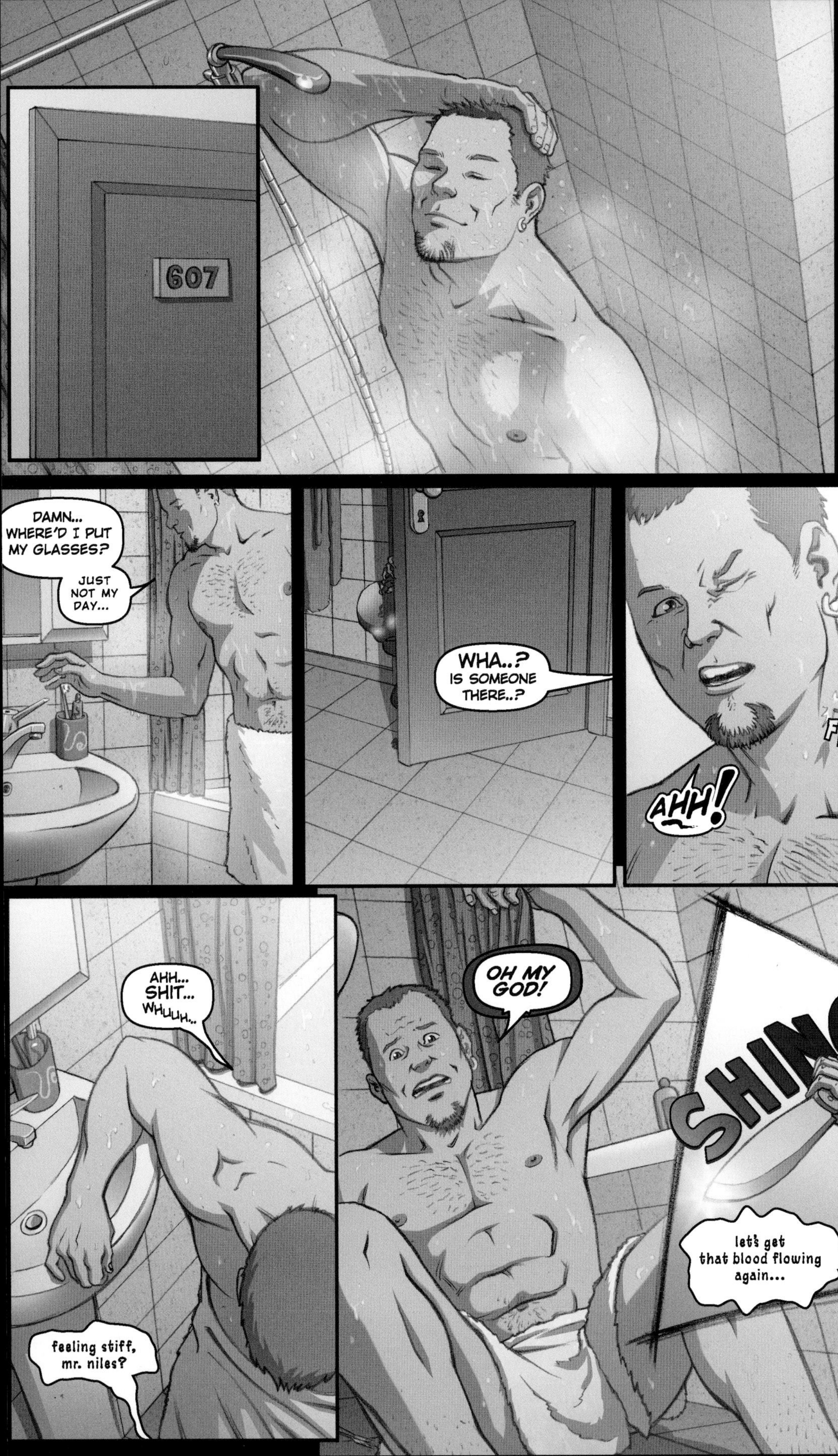
607
DAMN... WHERE'D I PUT MY GLASSES?
JUST NOT MY DAY...
WHA..? IS SOMEONE THERE..?
FWIT!
AHH!
AHH... SHIT... WHUUH...
feeling stiff, mr. niles?
OH MY GOD!
SHING
let's get that blood flowing again...

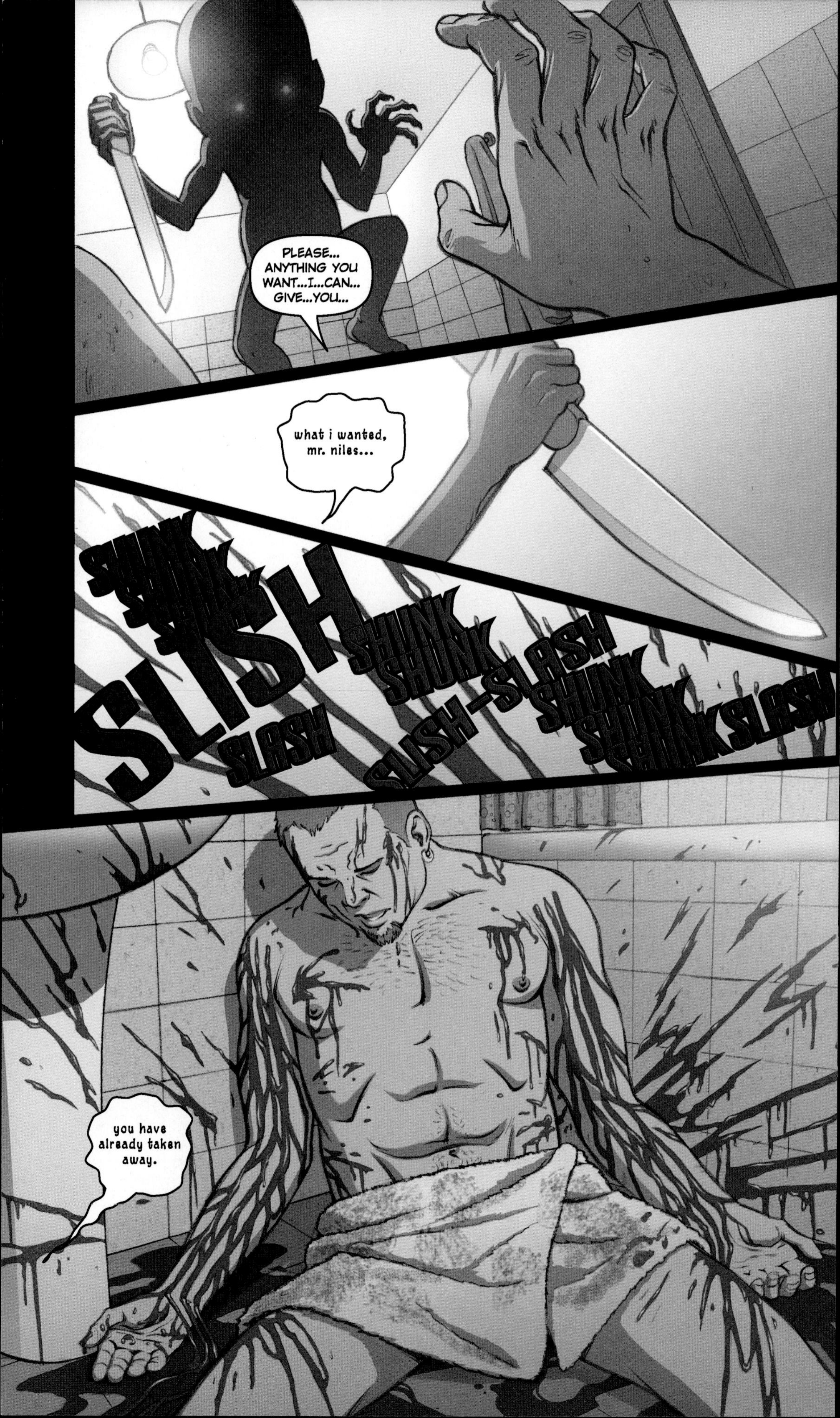
PLEASE... ANYTHING YOU WANT...I...CAN... GIVE...YOU...
what i wanted, mr. niles...
SHUNK SHUNK SHUNK
SLISH
SLASH
SHUNK SHUNK
SLISH-SLASH
SHUNK SHUNK SHUNKSLASH
you have already taken away.

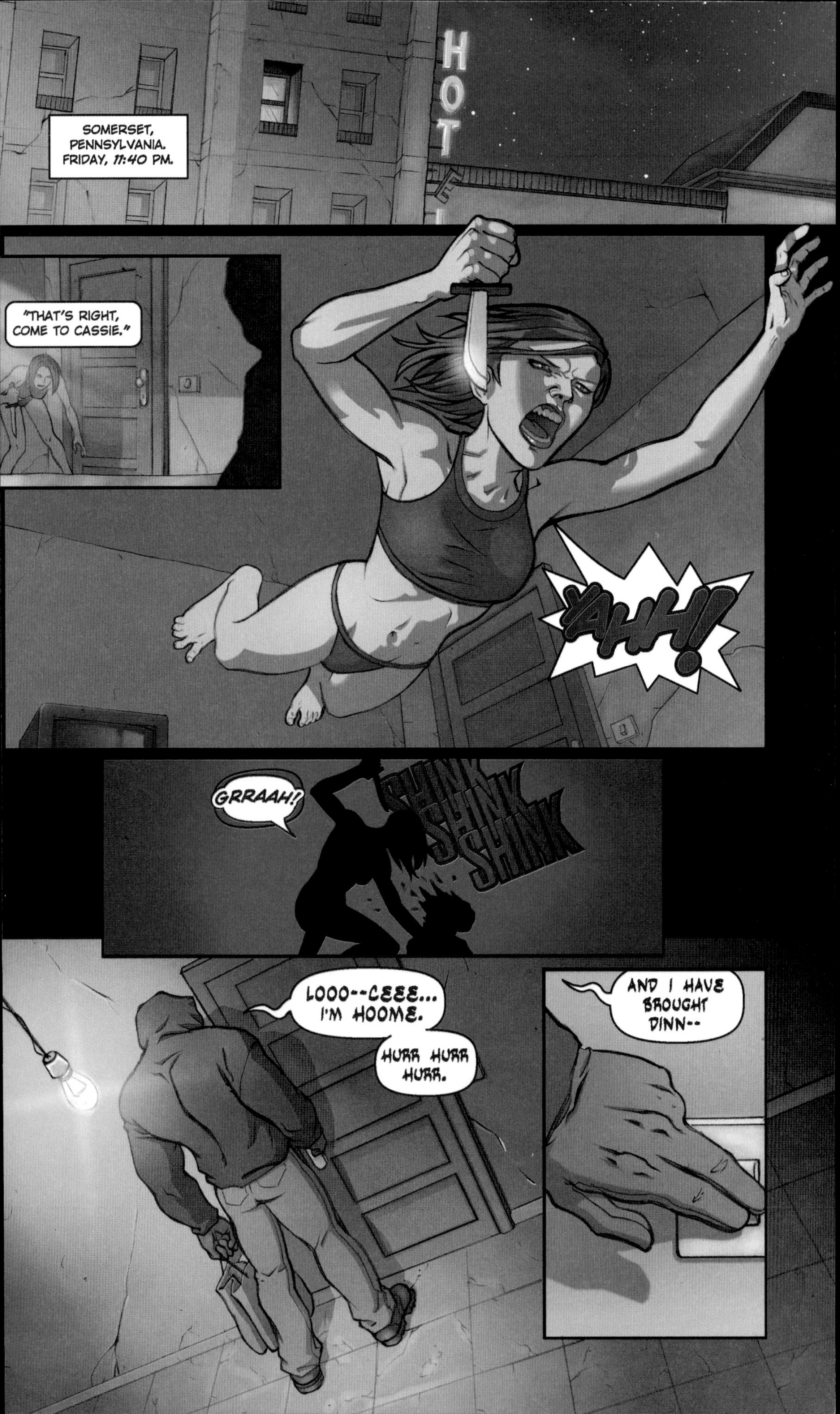
SOMERSET, PENNSYLVANIA. FRIDAY, 11:40 PM.
HOT
"THAT'S RIGHT, COME TO CASSIE."
YAHH!
GRRAAH!
SHINK SHINK SHINK
LOOO--CEEE... I'M HOOME.
HURR HURR HURR.
AND I HAVE BROUGHT DINN--

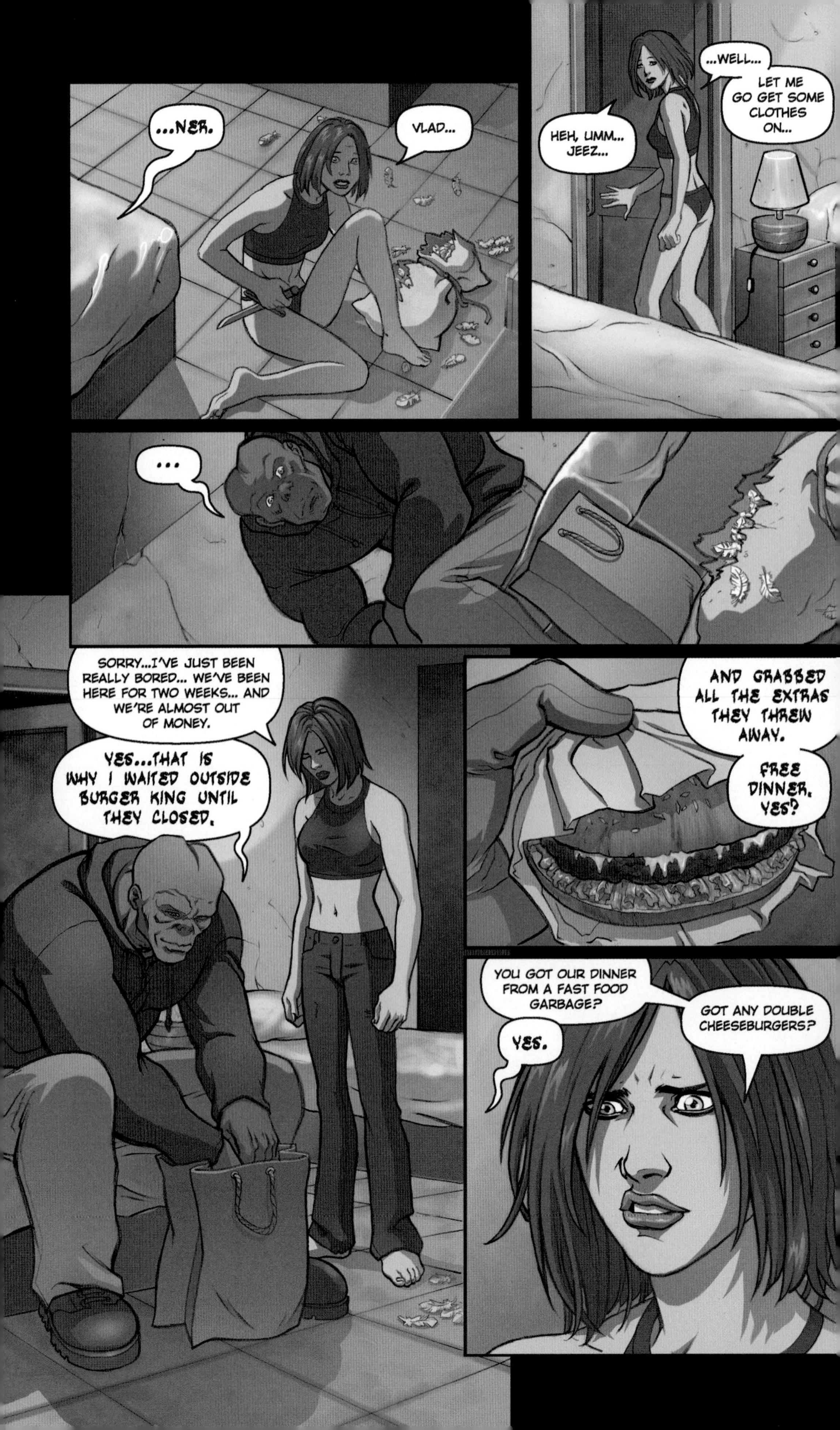
...NER.
VLAD...
HEH, UMM... JEEZ...
...WELL...
LET ME GO GET SOME CLOTHES ON...
...
SORRY...I'VE JUST BEEN REALLY BORED... WE'VE BEEN HERE FOR TWO WEEKS... AND WE'RE ALMOST OUT OF MONEY.
YES...THAT IS WHY I WAITED OUTSIDE BURGER KING UNTIL THEY CLOSED.
AND GRABBED ALL THE EXTRAS THEY THREW AWAY.
FREE DINNER, YES?
YOU GOT OUR DINNER FROM A FAST FOOD GARBAGE?
YES.
GOT ANY DOUBLE CHEESEBURGERS?

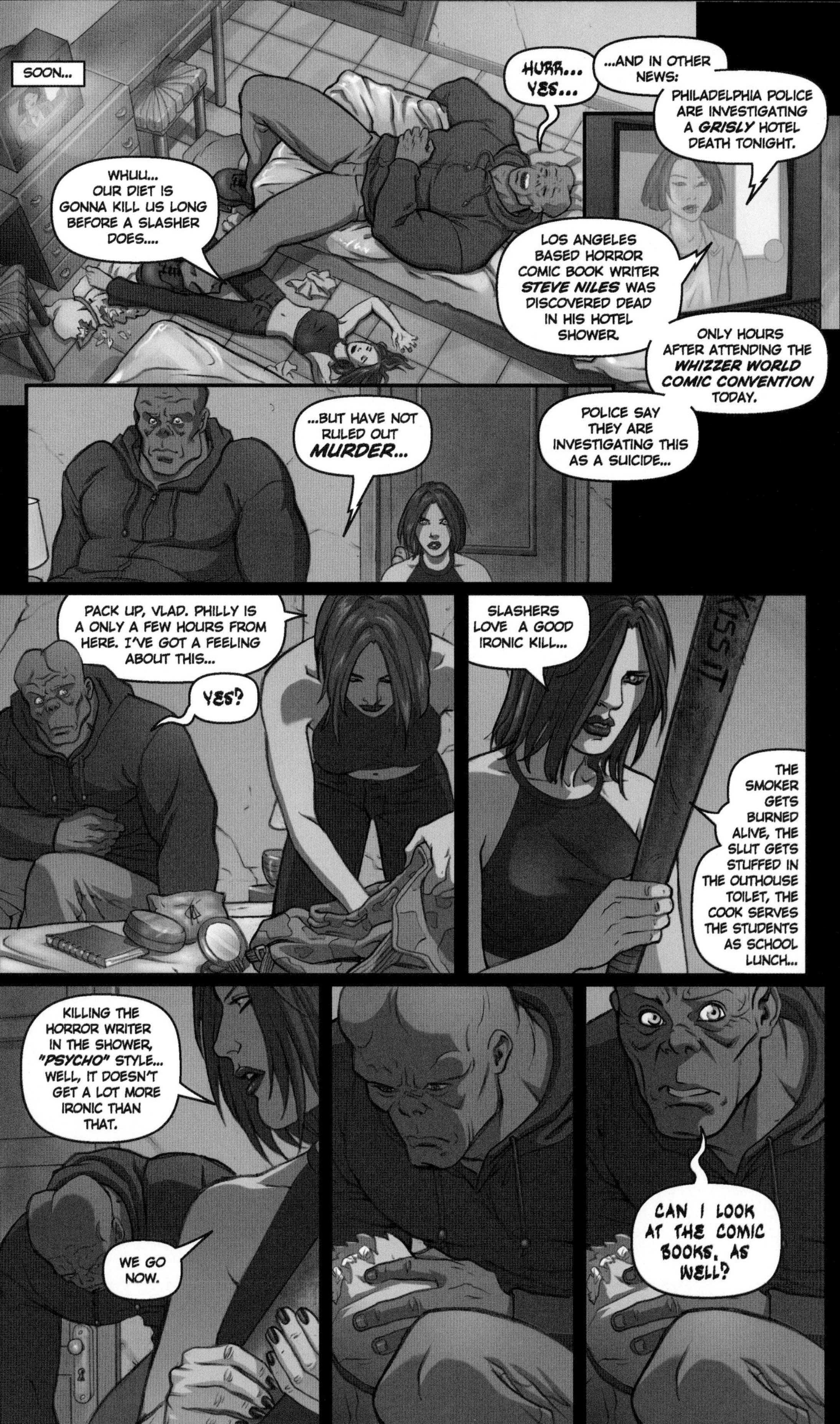
SOON...
WHUU... OUR DIET IS GONNA KILL US LONG BEFORE A SLASHER DOES....
HURR... YES...
...AND IN OTHER NEWS:
PHILADELPHIA POLICE ARE INVESTIGATING A GRISLY HOTEL DEATH TONIGHT.
LOS ANGELES BASED HORROR COMIC BOOK WRITER STEVE NILES WAS DISCOVERED DEAD IN HIS HOTEL SHOWER.
ONLY HOURS AFTER ATTENDING THE WHIZZER WORLD COMIC CONVENTION TODAY.
POLICE SAY THEY ARE INVESTIGATING THIS AS A SUICIDE...
...BUT HAVE NOT RULED OUT MURDER...
PACK UP, VLAD. PHILLY IS A ONLY A FEW HOURS FROM HERE. I'VE GOT A FEELING ABOUT THIS...
YES?
SLASHERS LOVE A GOOD IRONIC KILL...
THE SMOKER GETS BURNED ALIVE, THE SLUT GETS STUFFED IN THE OUTHOUSE TOILET, THE COOK SERVES THE STUDENTS AS SCHOOL LUNCH...
KILLING THE HORROR WRITER IN THE SHOWER, "PSYCHO" STYLE... WELL, IT DOESN'T GET A LOT MORE IRONIC THAN THAT.
WE GO NOW.
CAN I LOOK AT THE COMIC BOOKS, AS WELL?

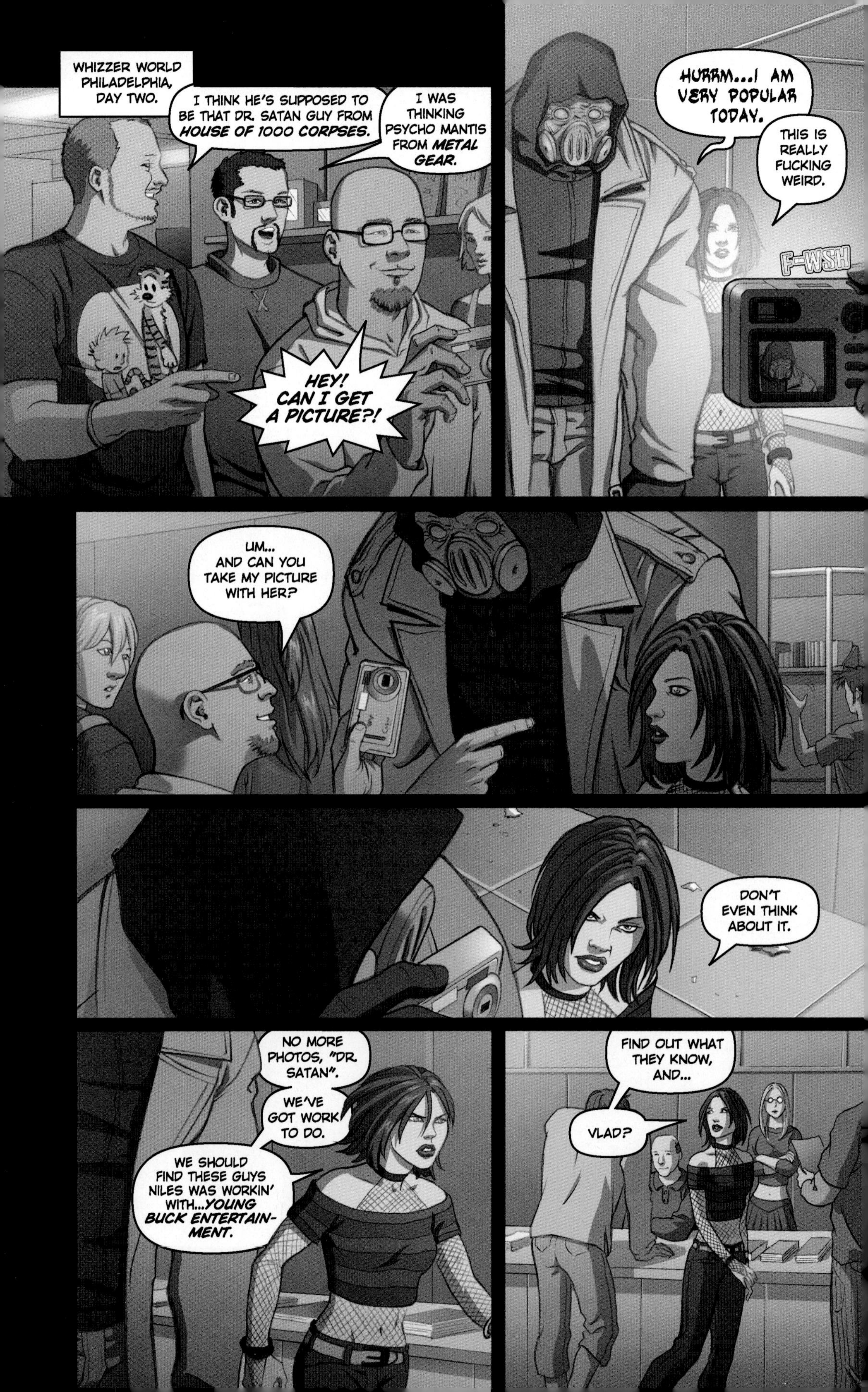
WHIZZER WORLD PHILADELPHIA, DAY TWO.
I THINK HE'S SUPPOSED TO BE THAT DR. SATAN GUY FROM *HOUSE OF 1000 CORPSES.*
I WAS THINKING PSYCHO MANTIS FROM *METAL GEAR.*
HEY! CAN I GET A PICTURE?!
HURRM...I AM VERY POPULAR TODAY.
THIS IS REALLY FUCKING WEIRD.
F-WSH
UM... AND CAN YOU TAKE MY PICTURE WITH HER?
DON'T EVEN THINK ABOUT IT.
NO MORE PHOTOS, "DR. SATAN".
WE'VE GOT WORK TO DO.
WE SHOULD FIND THESE GUYS NILES WAS WORKIN' WITH...*YOUNG BUCK ENTERTAIN-MENT.*
FIND OUT WHAT THEY KNOW, AND...
VLAD?

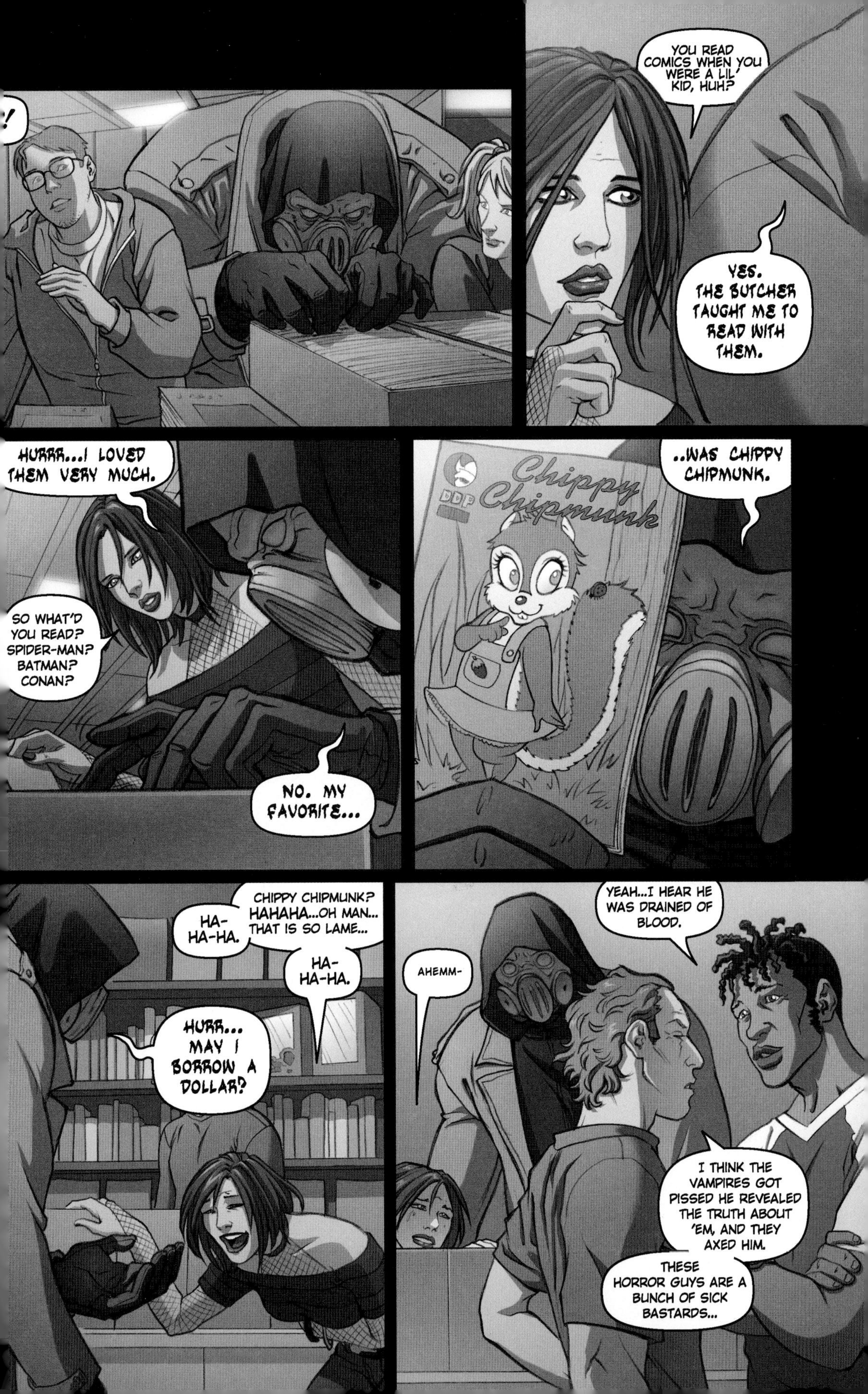
!
YOU READ COMICS WHEN YOU WERE A LIL' KID, HUH?
YES. THE BUTCHER TAUGHT ME TO READ WITH THEM.
HURRR...I LOVED THEM VERY MUCH.
SO WHAT'D YOU READ? SPIDER-MAN? BATMAN? CONAN?
NO. MY FAVORITE...
..WAS CHIPPY CHIPMUNK.
Chippy Chipmunk
DDP
HA-HA-HA.
CHIPPY CHIPMUNK? HAHAHA...OH MAN... THAT IS SO LAME...
HA-HA-HA.
HURR... MAY I BORROW A DOLLAR?
AHEMM-
YEAH...I HEAR HE WAS DRAINED OF BLOOD.
I THINK THE VAMPIRES GOT PISSED HE REVEALED THE TRUTH ABOUT 'EM, AND THEY AXED HIM.
THESE HORROR GUYS ARE A BUNCH OF SICK BASTARDS...

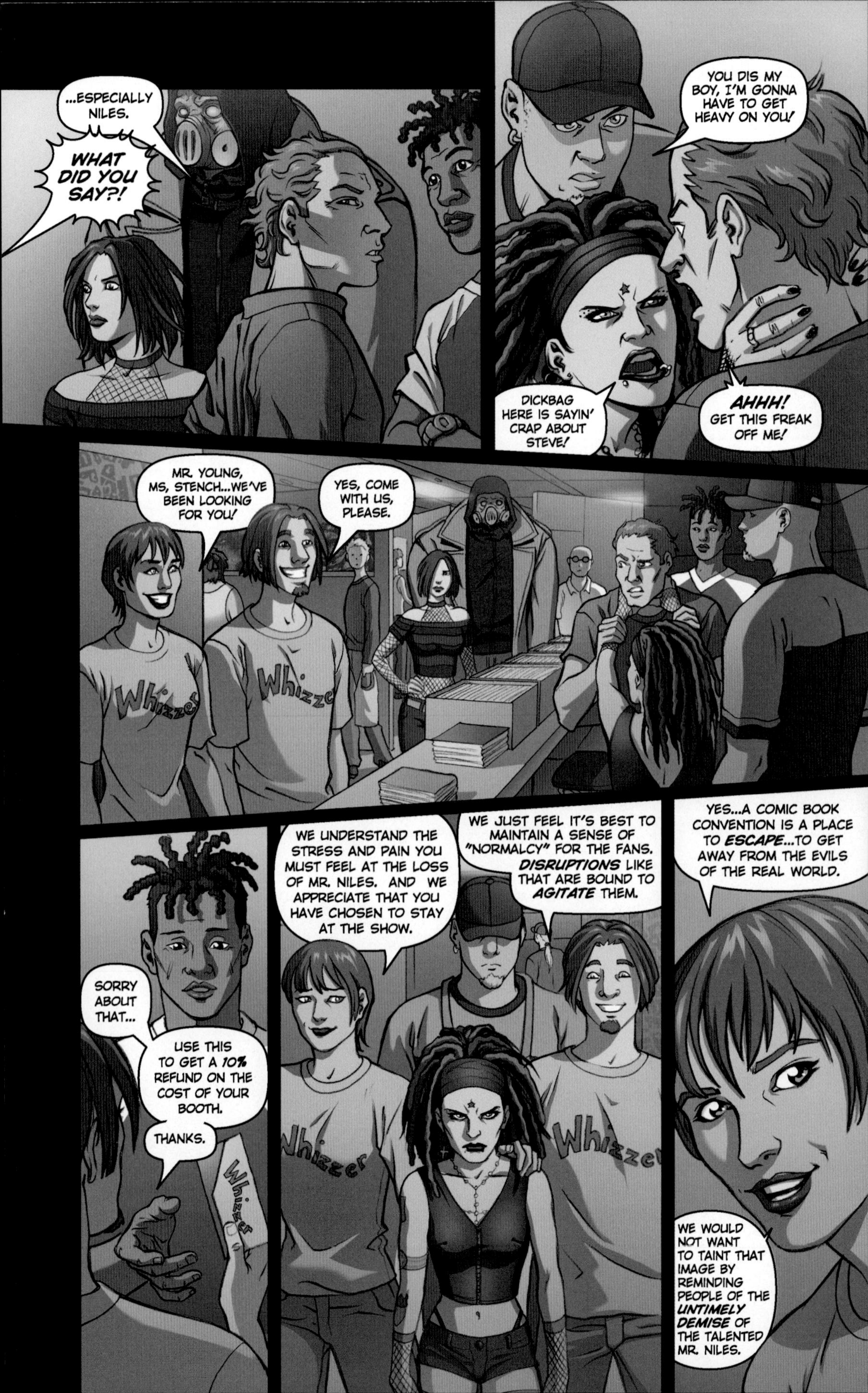
...ESPECIALLY NILES.
WHAT DID YOU SAY?!
YOU DIS MY BOY, I'M GONNA HAVE TO GET HEAVY ON YOU!
DICKBAG HERE IS SAYIN' CRAP ABOUT STEVE!
AHHH! GET THIS FREAK OFF ME!
MR. YOUNG, MS, STENCH...WE'VE BEEN LOOKING FOR YOU!
YES, COME WITH US, PLEASE.
Whizzer
SORRY ABOUT THAT...
USE THIS TO GET A 10% REFUND ON THE COST OF YOUR BOOTH.
THANKS.
WE UNDERSTAND THE STRESS AND PAIN YOU MUST FEEL AT THE LOSS OF MR. NILES. AND WE APPRECIATE THAT YOU HAVE CHOSEN TO STAY AT THE SHOW.
WE JUST FEEL IT'S BEST TO MAINTAIN A SENSE OF "NORMALCY" FOR THE FANS. DISRUPTIONS LIKE THAT ARE BOUND TO AGITATE THEM.
YES...A COMIC BOOK CONVENTION IS A PLACE TO ESCAPE...TO GET AWAY FROM THE EVILS OF THE REAL WORLD.
WE WOULD NOT WANT TO TAINT THAT IMAGE BY REMINDING PEOPLE OF THE UNTIMELY DEMISE OF THE TALENTED MR. NILES.

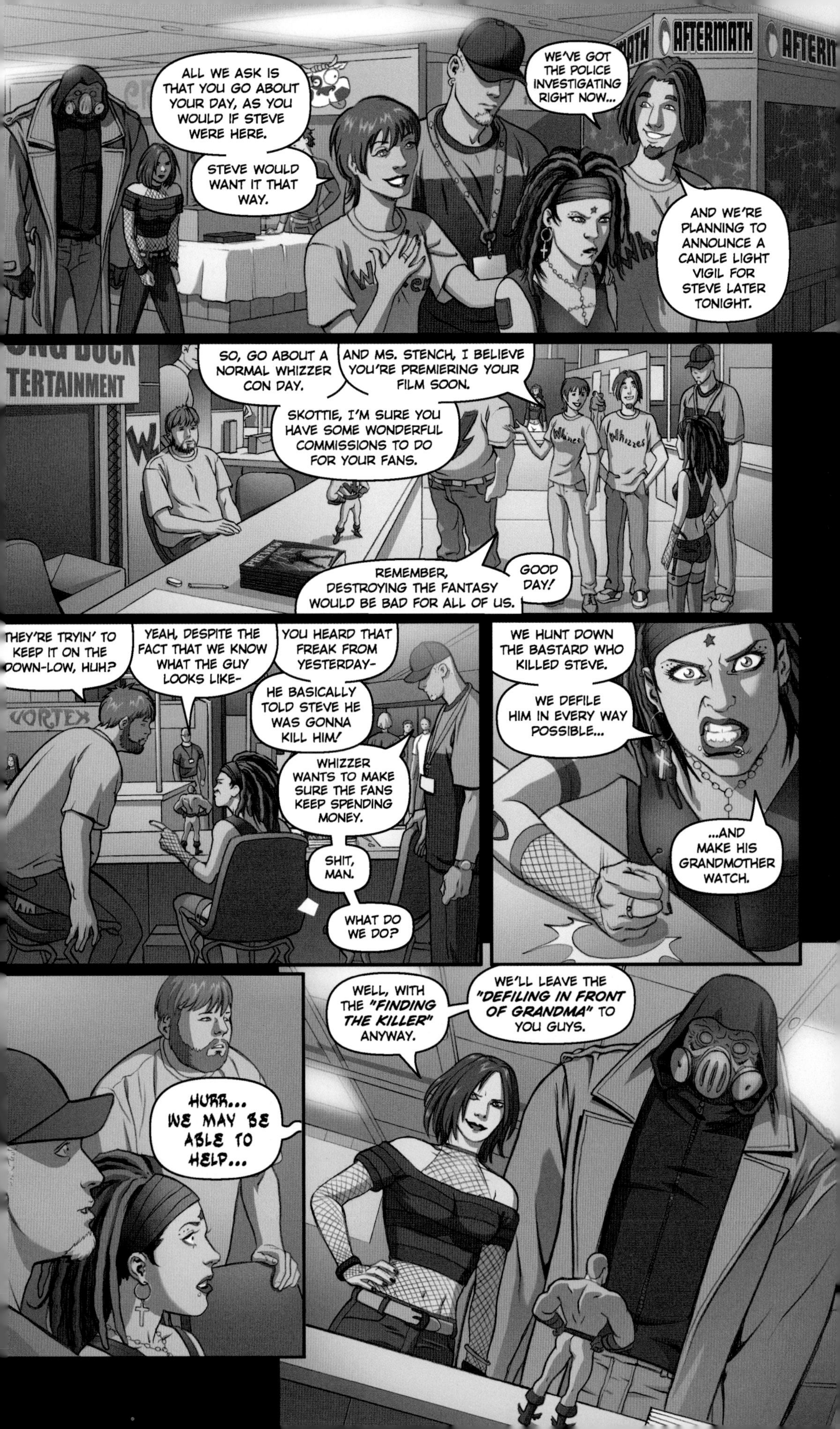
ALL WE ASK IS THAT YOU GO ABOUT YOUR DAY, AS YOU WOULD IF STEVE WERE HERE.
STEVE WOULD WANT IT THAT WAY.
WE'VE GOT THE POLICE INVESTIGATING RIGHT NOW...
AND WE'RE PLANNING TO ANNOUNCE A CANDLE LIGHT VIGIL FOR STEVE LATER TONIGHT.
AFTERMATH
TERTAINMENT
SO, GO ABOUT A NORMAL WHIZZER CON DAY.
AND MS. STENCH, I BELIEVE YOU'RE PREMIERING YOUR FILM SOON.
SKOTTIE, I'M SURE YOU HAVE SOME WONDERFUL COMMISSIONS TO DO FOR YOUR FANS.
REMEMBER, DESTROYING THE FANTASY WOULD BE BAD FOR ALL OF US.
GOOD DAY!
THEY'RE TRYIN' TO KEEP IT ON THE DOWN-LOW, HUH?
YEAH, DESPITE THE FACT THAT WE KNOW WHAT THE GUY LOOKS LIKE-
YOU HEARD THAT FREAK FROM YESTERDAY-
HE BASICALLY TOLD STEVE HE WAS GONNA KILL HIM!
WHIZZER WANTS TO MAKE SURE THE FANS KEEP SPENDING MONEY.
SHIT, MAN.
WHAT DO WE DO?
VORTEX
WE HUNT DOWN THE BASTARD WHO KILLED STEVE.
WE DEFILE HIM IN EVERY WAY POSSIBLE...
...AND MAKE HIS GRANDMOTHER WATCH.
HURR... WE MAY BE ABLE TO HELP...
WELL, WITH THE "FINDING THE KILLER" ANYWAY.
WE'LL LEAVE THE "DEFILING IN FRONT OF GRANDMA" TO YOU GUYS.

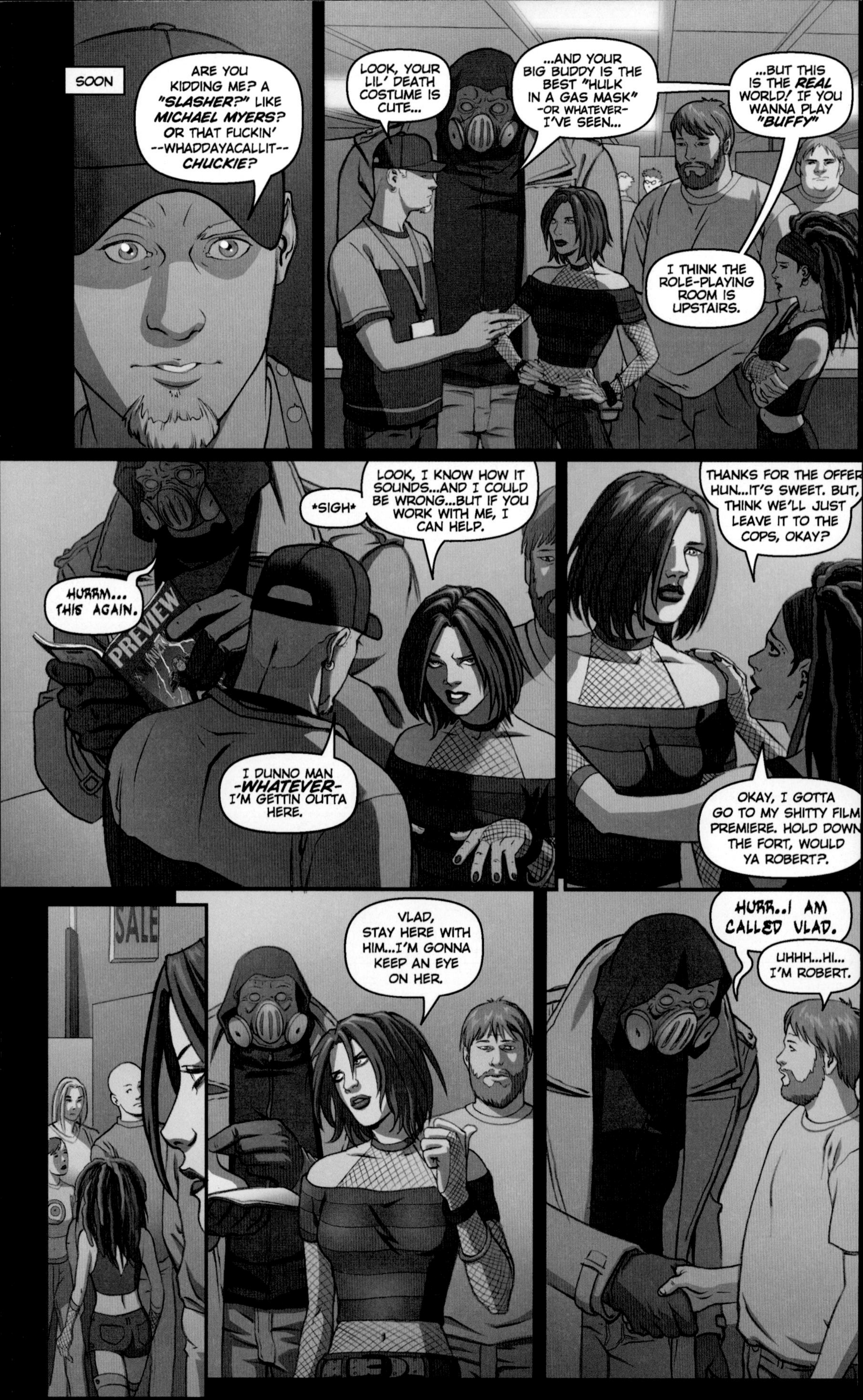
SOON
ARE YOU KIDDING ME? A "SLASHER?" LIKE MICHAEL MYERS? OR THAT FUCKIN' --WHADDAYACALLIT-- CHUCKIE?
LOOK, YOUR LIL' DEATH COSTUME IS CUTE...
...AND YOUR BIG BUDDY IS THE BEST "HULK IN A GAS MASK" -OR WHATEVER- I'VE SEEN...
...BUT THIS IS THE REAL WORLD! IF YOU WANNA PLAY "BUFFY"
I THINK THE ROLE-PLAYING ROOM IS UPSTAIRS.
SIGH
LOOK, I KNOW HOW IT SOUNDS...AND I COULD BE WRONG...BUT IF YOU WORK WITH ME, I CAN HELP.
HURRM... THIS AGAIN.
PREVIEW
I DUNNO MAN -WHATEVER- I'M GETTIN OUTTA HERE.
THANKS FOR THE OFFER HUN...IT'S SWEET. BUT, THINK WE'LL JUST LEAVE IT TO THE COPS, OKAY?
OKAY, I GOTTA GO TO MY SHITTY FILM PREMIERE. HOLD DOWN THE FORT, WOULD YA ROBERT?.
SALE
VLAD, STAY HERE WITH HIM...I'M GONNA KEEP AN EYE ON HER.
HURR..I AM CALLED VLAD.
UHHH...HI... I'M ROBERT.

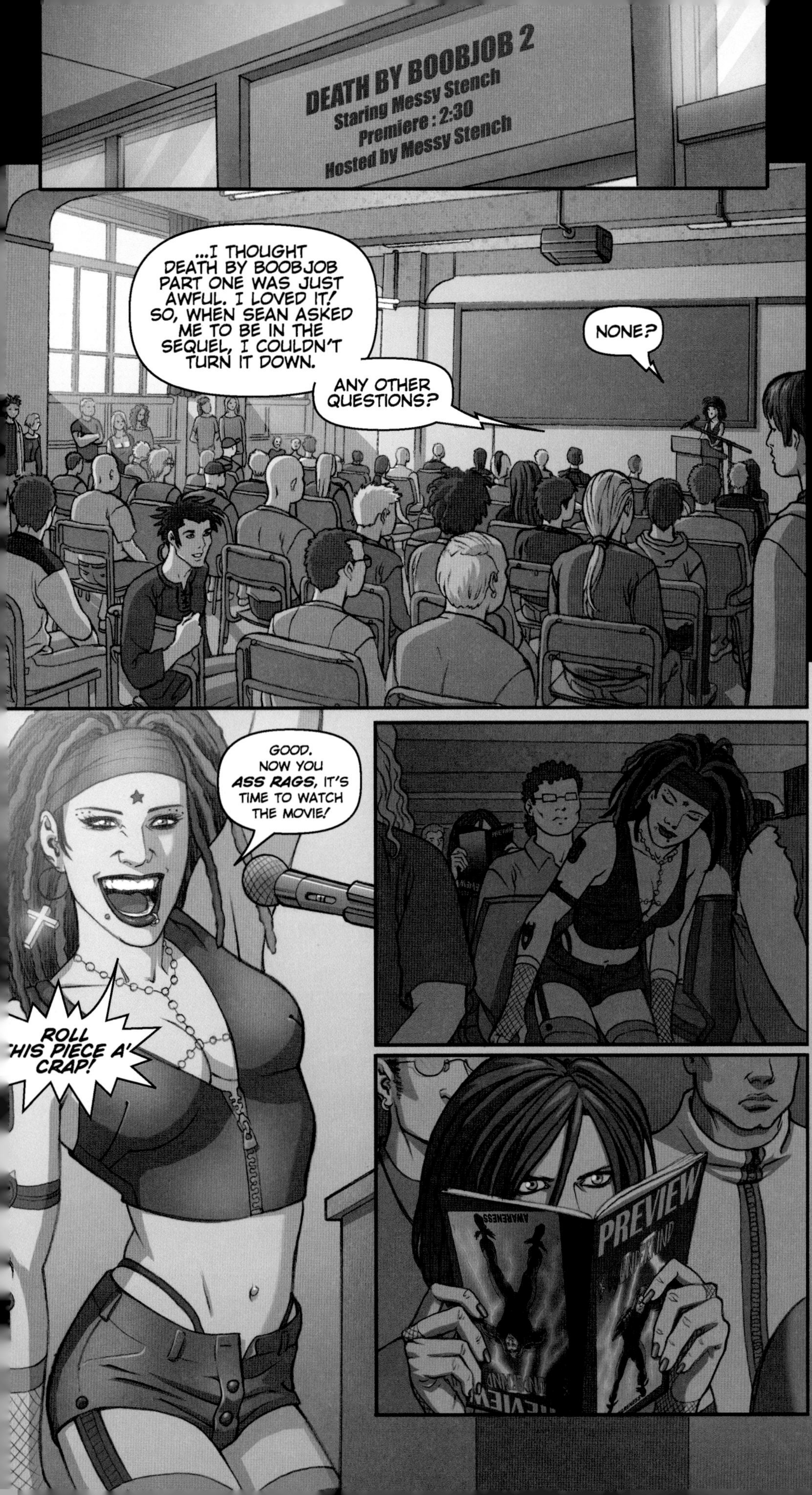
DEATH BY BOOBJOB 2
Staring Messy Stench
Premiere : 2:30
Hosted by Messy Stench
...I THOUGHT DEATH BY BOOBJOB PART ONE WAS JUST AWFUL. I LOVED IT! SO, WHEN SEAN ASKED ME TO BE IN THE SEQUEL, I COULDN'T TURN IT DOWN.
ANY OTHER QUESTIONS?
NONE?
GOOD. NOW YOU ASS RAGS, IT'S TIME TO WATCH THE MOVIE!
ROLL THIS PIECE A' CRAP!
PREVIEW
AWARENESS

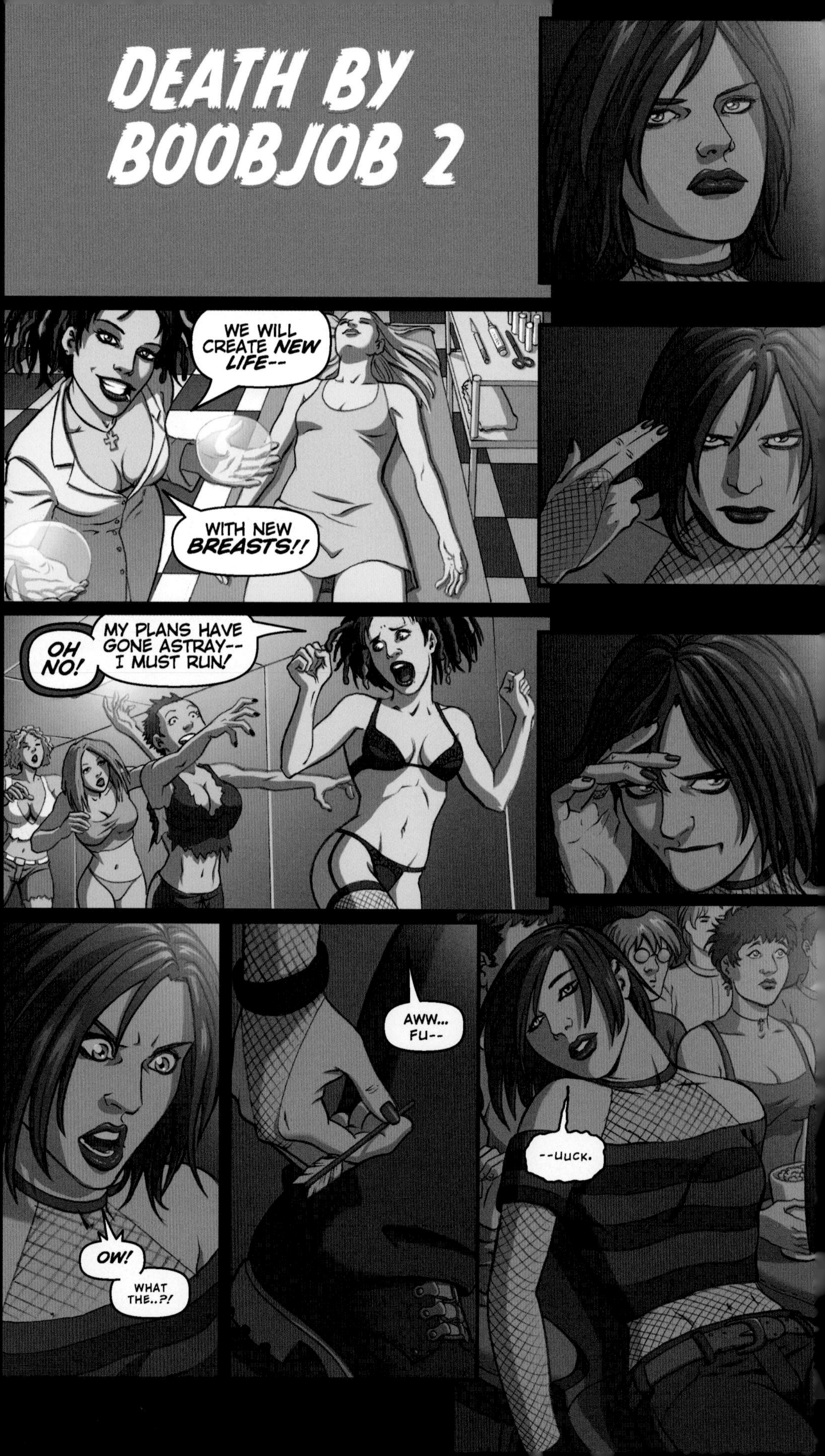
DEATH BY BOOBJOB 2
WE WILL CREATE NEW LIFE--
WITH NEW BREASTS!!
OH NO!
MY PLANS HAVE GONE ASTRAY-- I MUST RUN!
OW!
WHAT THE..?!
AWW... FU--
--UUCK.

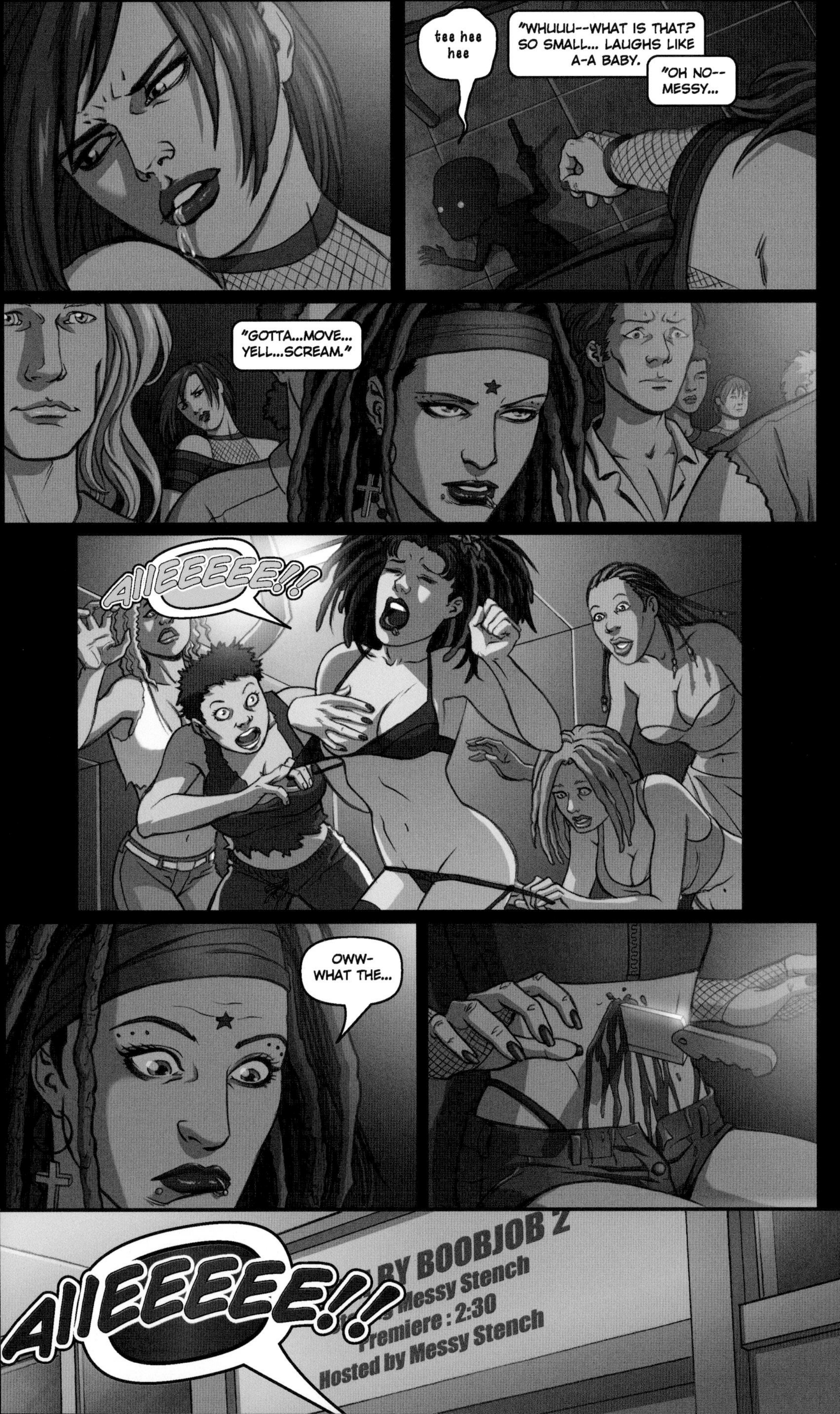
tee hee hee
"WHUUU--WHAT IS THAT? SO SMALL... LAUGHS LIKE A-A BABY.
"OH NO--MESSY...
"GOTTA...MOVE... YELL...SCREAM."
AIIEEEEEE!!!
OWW-WHAT THE...
AIIEEEEEE!!!
BY BOOBJOB 2
Messy Stench
Premiere : 2:30
Hosted by Messy Stench

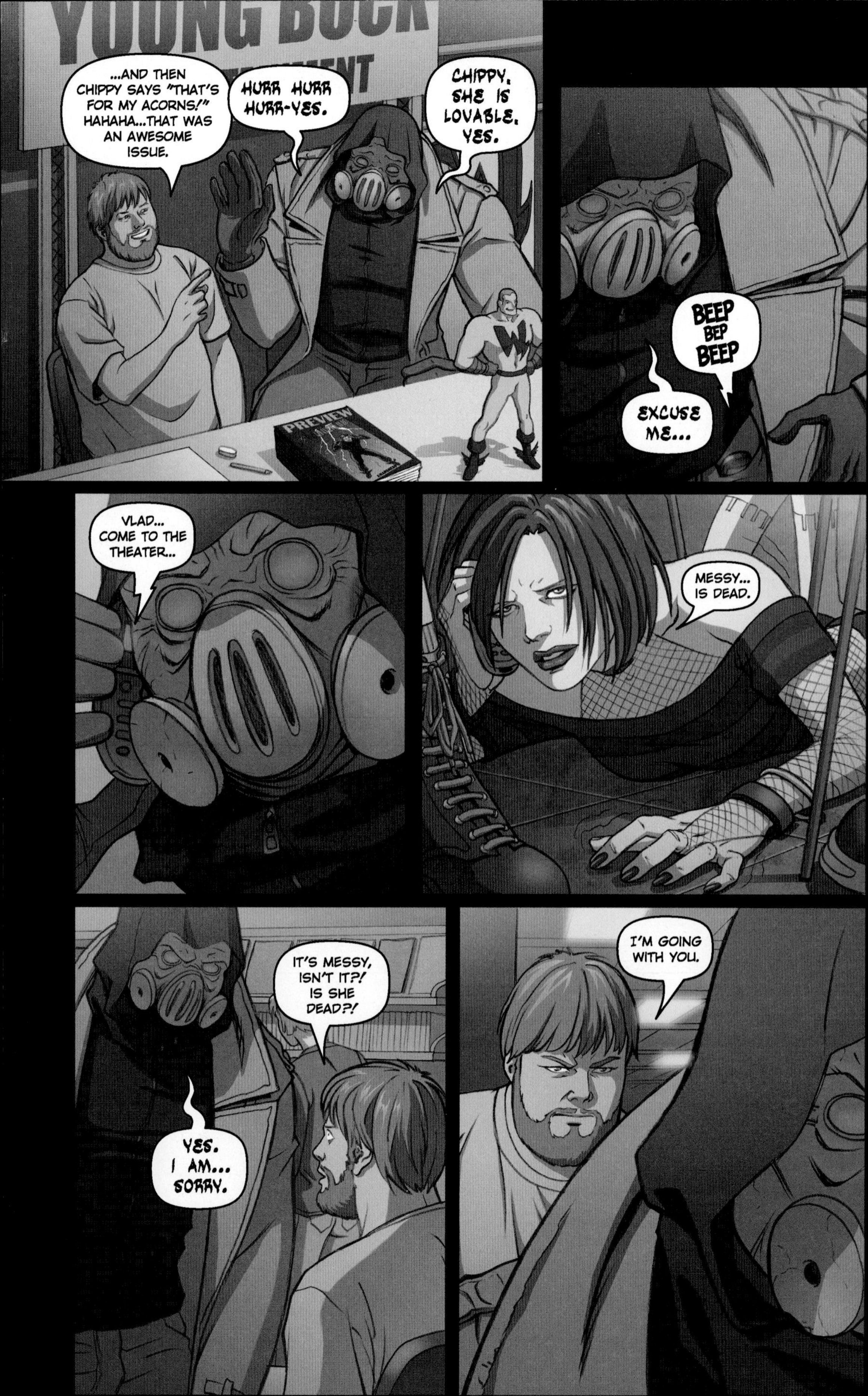
YOUNG BUCK
...AND THEN CHIPPY SAYS "THAT'S FOR MY ACORNS!" HAHAHA...THAT WAS AN AWESOME ISSUE.
HURR HURR HURR-YES.
CHIPPY. SHE IS LOVABLE. YES.
PREVIEW
BEEP BEP BEEP
EXCUSE ME...
VLAD... COME TO THE THEATER...
MESSY... IS DEAD.
IT'S MESSY, ISN'T IT?! IS SHE DEAD?!
YES. I AM... SORRY.
I'M GOING WITH YOU.

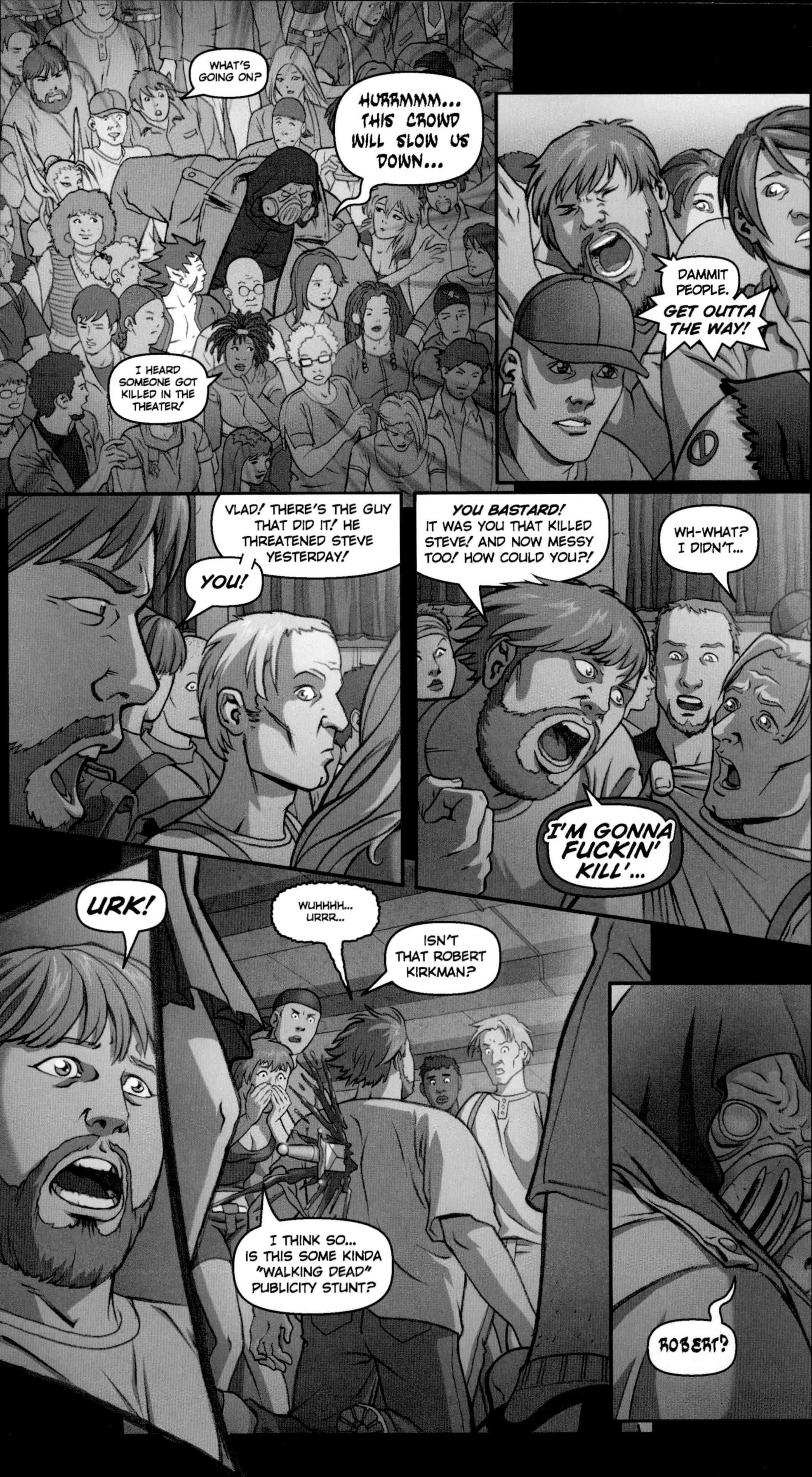

WHAT'S GOING ON?
HURRMMM... THIS CROWD WILL SLOW US DOWN...
I HEARD SOMEONE GOT KILLED IN THE THEATER!
DAMMIT PEOPLE. GET OUTTA THE WAY!
VLAD! THERE'S THE GUY THAT DID IT! HE THREATENED STEVE YESTERDAY!
YOU!
YOU BASTARD! IT WAS YOU THAT KILLED STEVE! AND NOW MESSY TOO! HOW COULD YOU?!
WH-WHAT? I DIDN'T...
I'M GONNA FUCKIN' KILL'...
URK!
WUHHHH... URRR...
ISN'T THAT ROBERT KIRKMAN?
I THINK SO... IS THIS SOME KINDA "WALKING DEAD" PUBLICITY STUNT?
ROBERT?

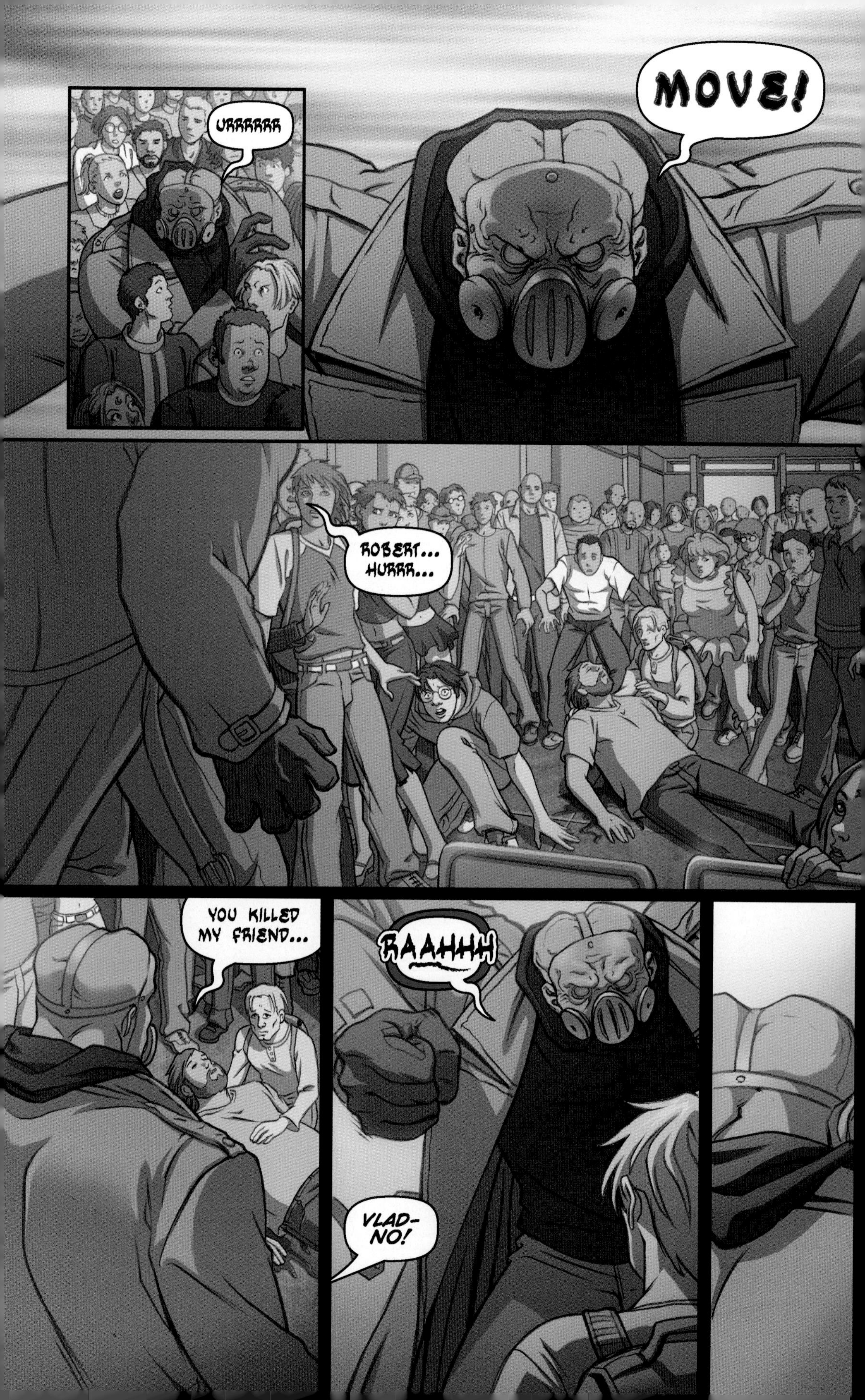

URRRRRR
MOVE!
ROBERT... HURRR...
YOU KILLED MY FRIEND...
RAAHHH
VLAD- NO!

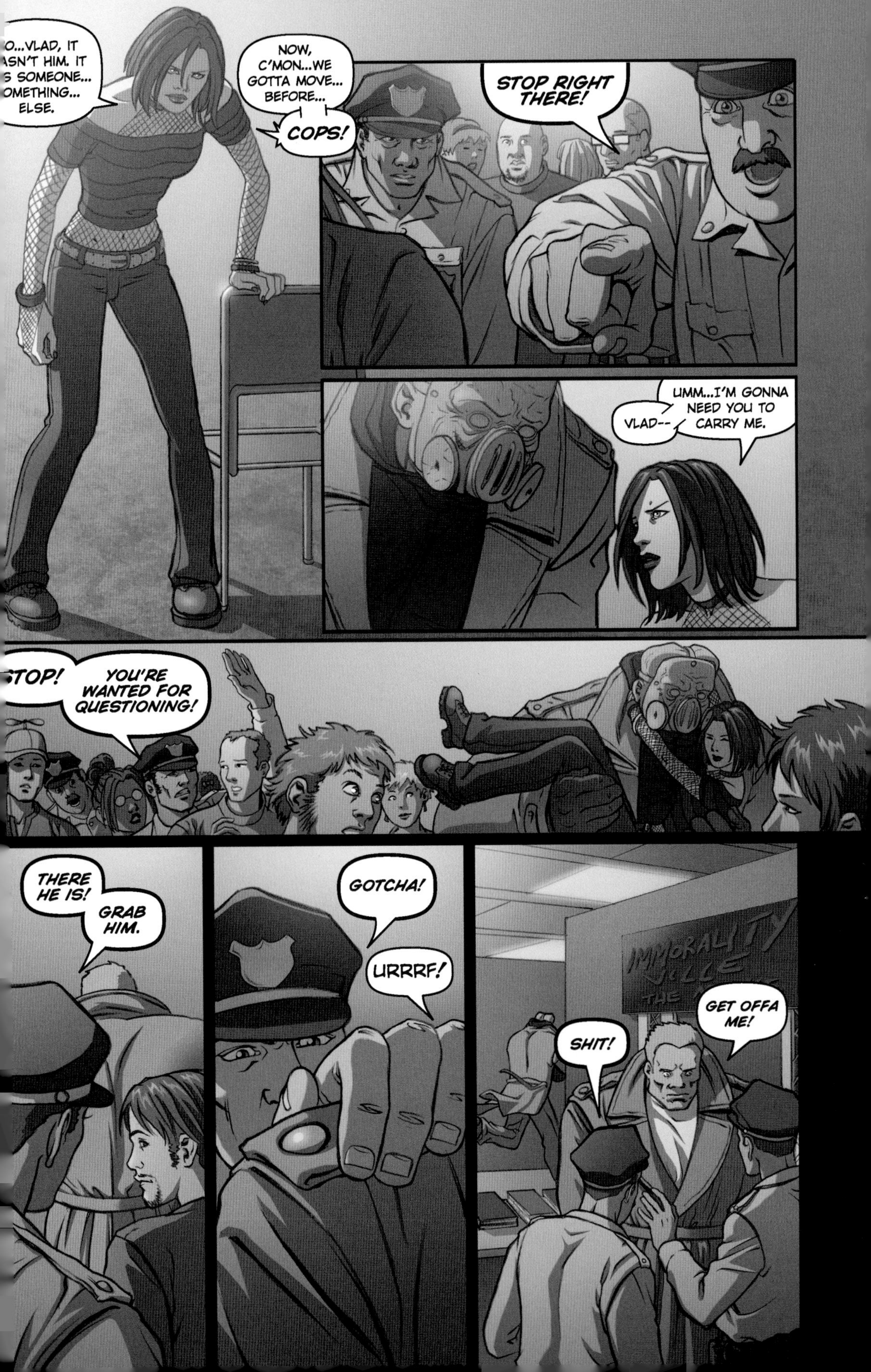
O...VLAD, IT
ASN'T HIM. IT
S SOMEONE...
OMETHING...
ELSE.
NOW, C'MON...WE GOTTA MOVE... BEFORE...
COPS!
STOP RIGHT THERE!
UMM...I'M GONNA NEED YOU TO
VLAD--
CARRY ME.
STOP!
YOU'RE WANTED FOR QUESTIONING!
THERE HE IS!
GRAB HIM.
GOTCHA!
URRRF!
IMMORALITY VILLE
SHIT!
GET OFFA ME!

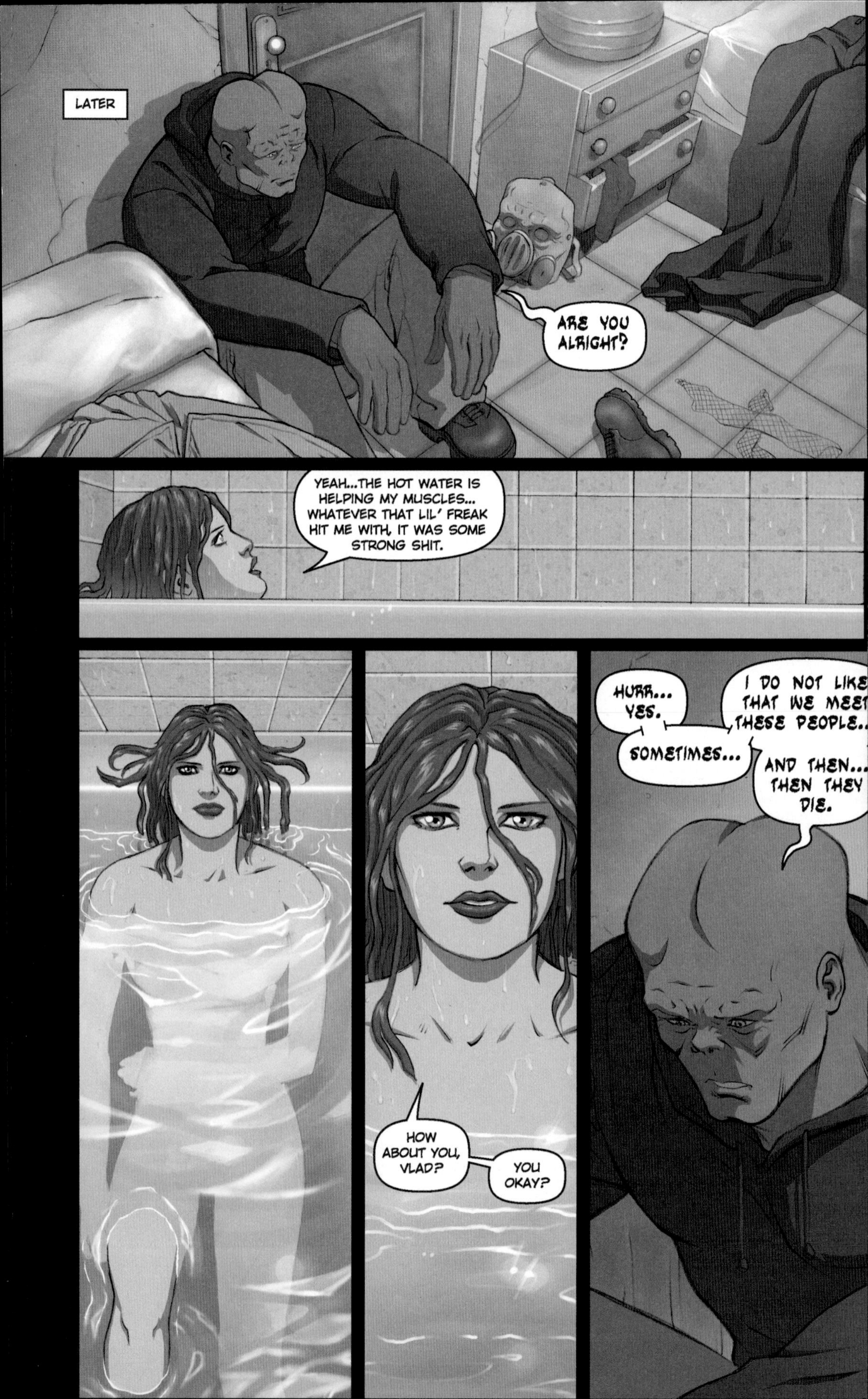
LATER
ARE YOU ALRIGHT?
YEAH...THE HOT WATER IS HELPING MY MUSCLES... WHATEVER THAT LIL' FREAK HIT ME WITH, IT WAS SOME STRONG SHIT.
HOW ABOUT YOU, VLAD?
YOU OKAY?
HURR... YES.
SOMETIMES...
I DO NOT LIKE THAT WE MEET THESE PEOPLE...
AND THEN... THEN THEY DIE.

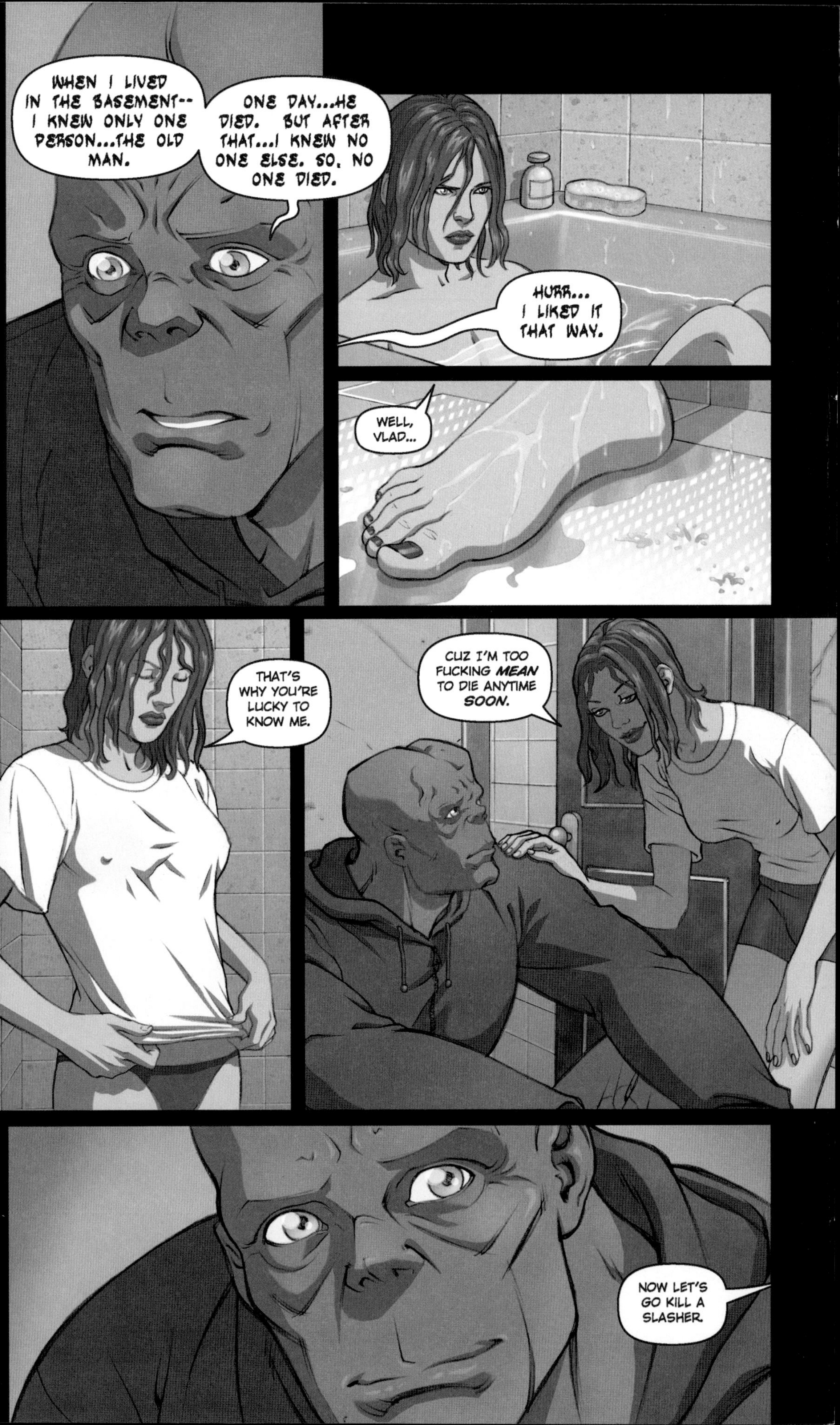
WHEN I LIVED IN THE BASEMENT-- I KNEW ONLY ONE PERSON...THE OLD MAN.
ONE DAY...HE DIED. BUT AFTER THAT...I KNEW NO ONE ELSE. SO, NO ONE DIED.
HURR... I LIKED IT THAT WAY.
WELL, VLAD...
THAT'S WHY YOU'RE LUCKY TO KNOW ME.
CUZ I'M TOO FUCKING *MEAN* TO DIE ANYTIME *SOON*.
NOW LET'S GO KILL A SLASHER.

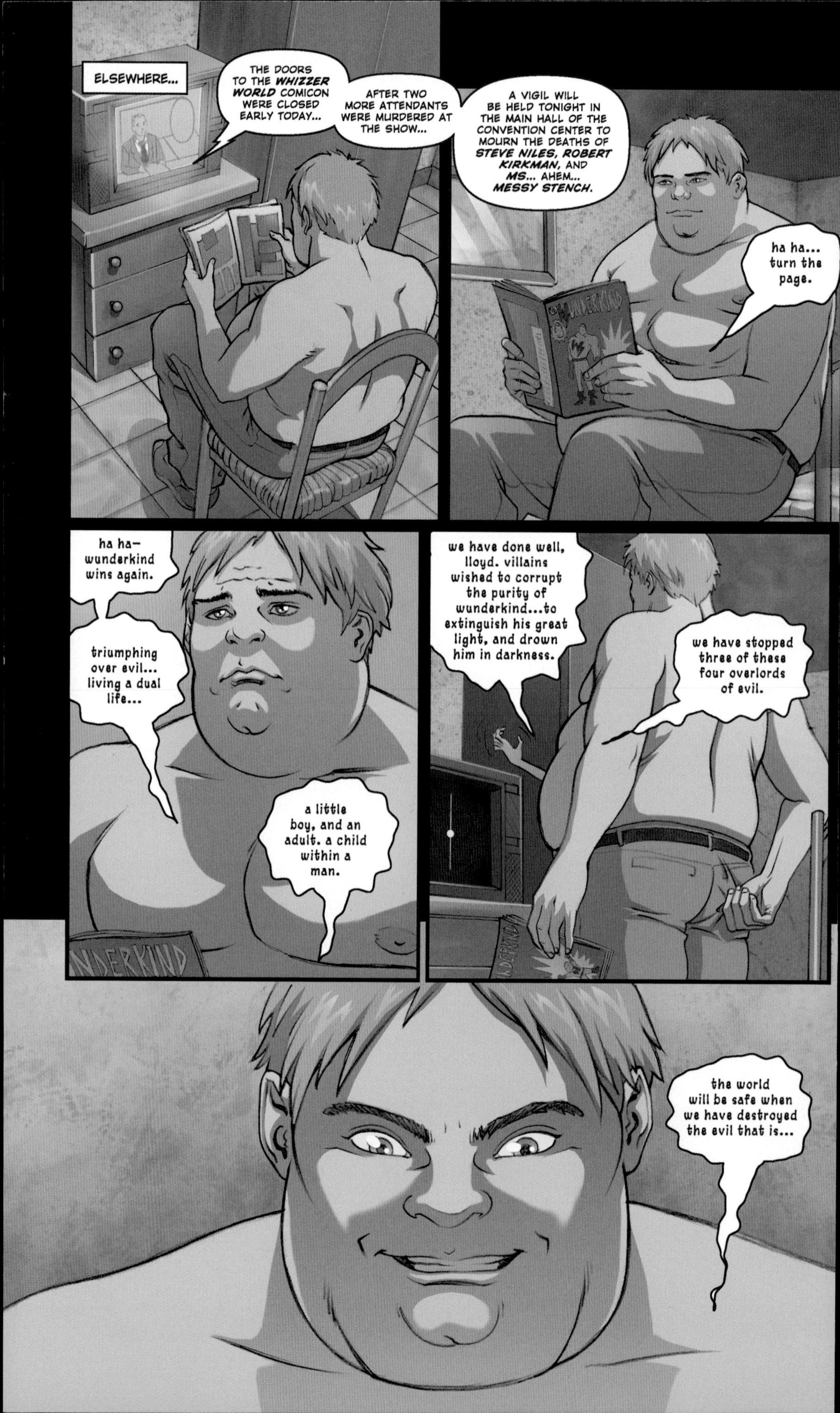
ELSEWHERE...
THE DOORS TO THE WHIZZER WORLD COMICON WERE CLOSED EARLY TODAY...
AFTER TWO MORE ATTENDANTS WERE MURDERED AT THE SHOW...
A VIGIL WILL BE HELD TONIGHT IN THE MAIN HALL OF THE CONVENTION CENTER TO MOURN THE DEATHS OF STEVE NILES, ROBERT KIRKMAN, AND MS... AHEM... MESSY STENCH.
WUNDERKIND
ha ha... turn the page.
ha ha— wunderkind wins again.
triumphing over evil... living a dual life...
a little boy, and an adult. a child within a man.
NDERKIND
we have done well, lloyd. villains wished to corrupt the purity of wunderkind...to extinguish his great light, and drown him in darkness.
we have stopped three of these four overlords of evil.
the world will be safe when we have destroyed the evil that is...

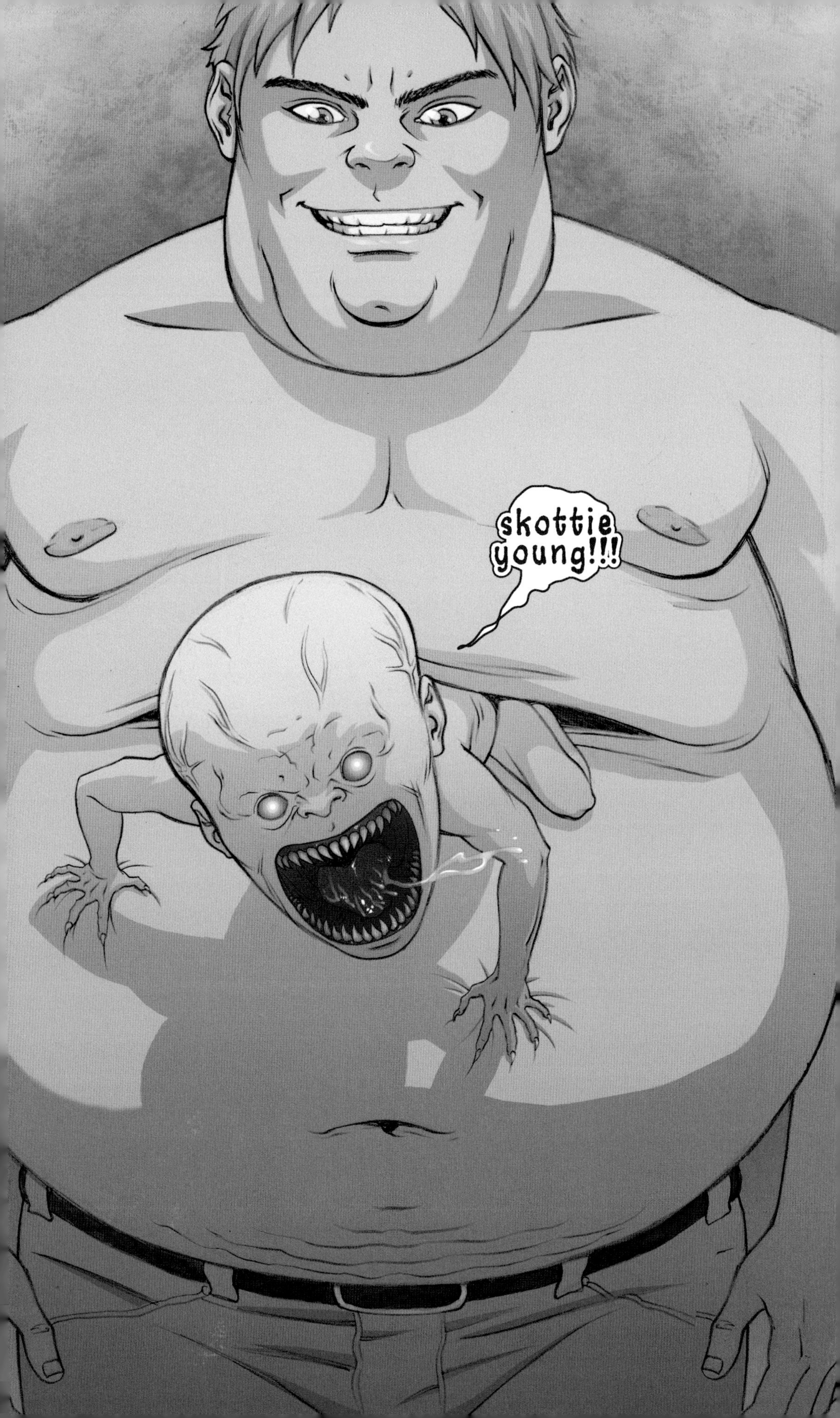
skottie young!!!

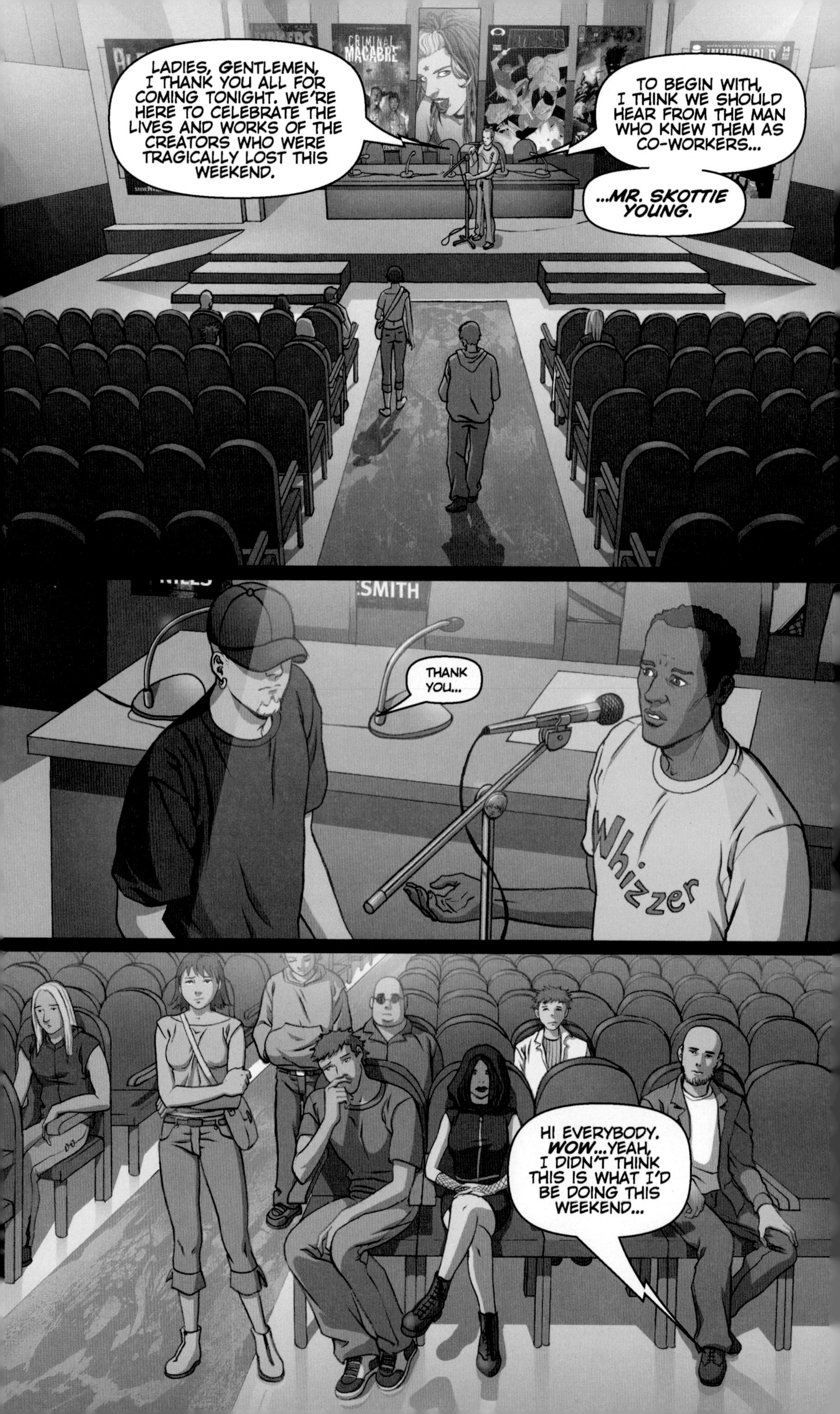

LADIES, GENTLEMEN, I THANK YOU ALL FOR COMING TONIGHT. WE'RE HERE TO CELEBRATE THE LIVES AND WORKS OF THE CREATORS WHO WERE TRAGICALLY LOST THIS WEEKEND.
TO BEGIN WITH, I THINK WE SHOULD HEAR FROM THE MAN WHO KNEW THEM AS CO-WORKERS...
...MR. SKOTTIE YOUNG.
CRIMINAL MACABRE
SMITH
THANK YOU...
Whizzer
HI EVERYBODY. WOW...YEAH, I DIDN'T THINK THIS IS WHAT I'D BE DOING THIS WEEKEND...

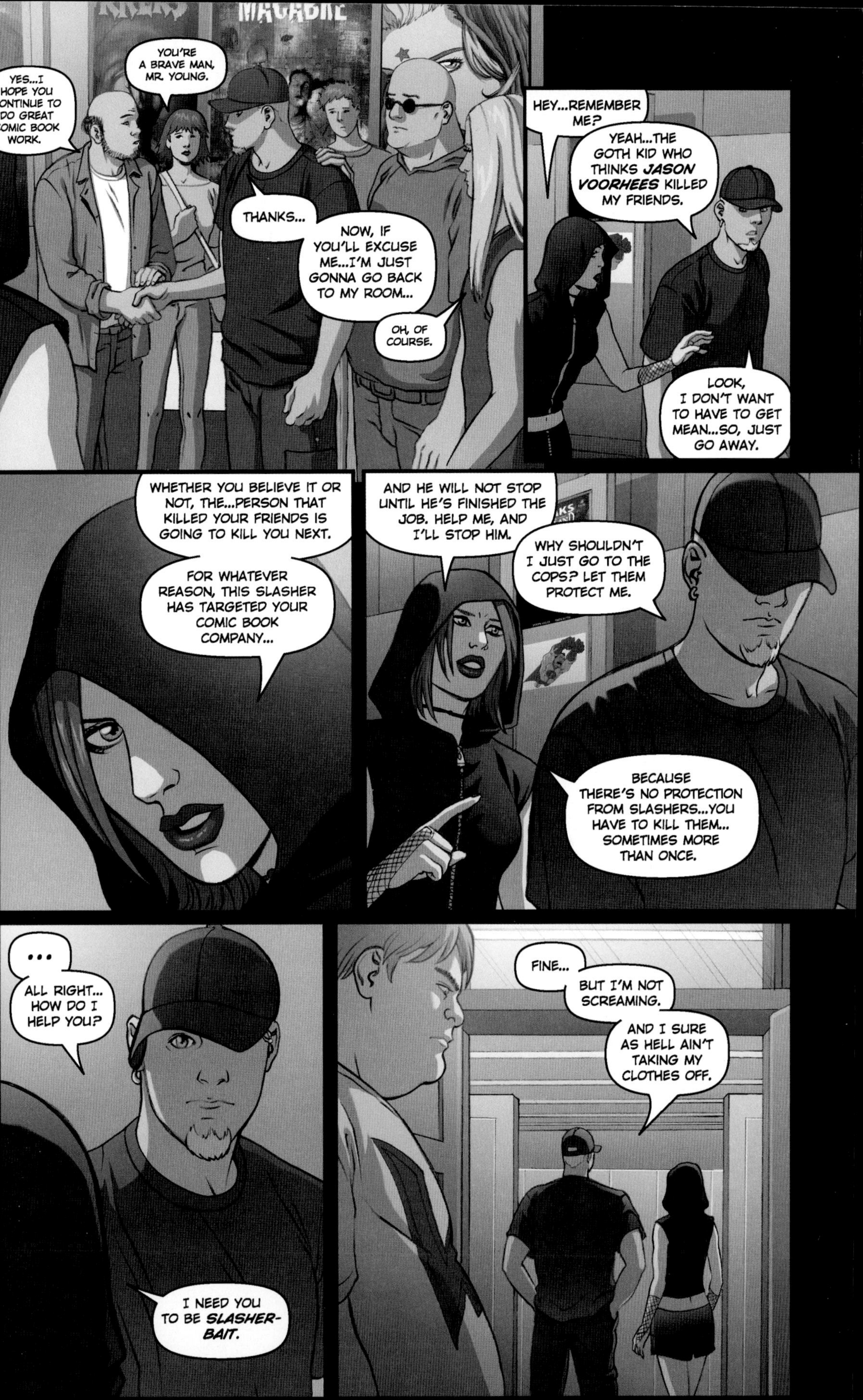
MACABRE
YES...I HOPE YOU CONTINUE TO DO GREAT COMIC BOOK WORK.
YOU'RE A BRAVE MAN, MR. YOUNG.
THANKS...
NOW, IF YOU'LL EXCUSE ME...I'M JUST GONNA GO BACK TO MY ROOM...
OH, OF COURSE.
HEY...REMEMBER ME?
YEAH...THE GOTH KID WHO THINKS JASON VOORHEES KILLED MY FRIENDS.
LOOK, I DON'T WANT TO HAVE TO GET MEAN...SO, JUST GO AWAY.
WHETHER YOU BELIEVE IT OR NOT, THE...PERSON THAT KILLED YOUR FRIENDS IS GOING TO KILL YOU NEXT.
FOR WHATEVER REASON, THIS SLASHER HAS TARGETED YOUR COMIC BOOK COMPANY...
AND HE WILL NOT STOP UNTIL HE'S FINISHED THE JOB. HELP ME, AND I'LL STOP HIM.
WHY SHOULDN'T I JUST GO TO THE COPS? LET THEM PROTECT ME.
BECAUSE THERE'S NO PROTECTION FROM SLASHERS...YOU HAVE TO KILL THEM... SOMETIMES MORE THAN ONCE.
...
ALL RIGHT... HOW DO I HELP YOU?
I NEED YOU TO BE SLASHER-BAIT.
FINE...
BUT I'M NOT SCREAMING.
AND I SURE AS HELL AIN'T TAKING MY CLOTHES OFF.

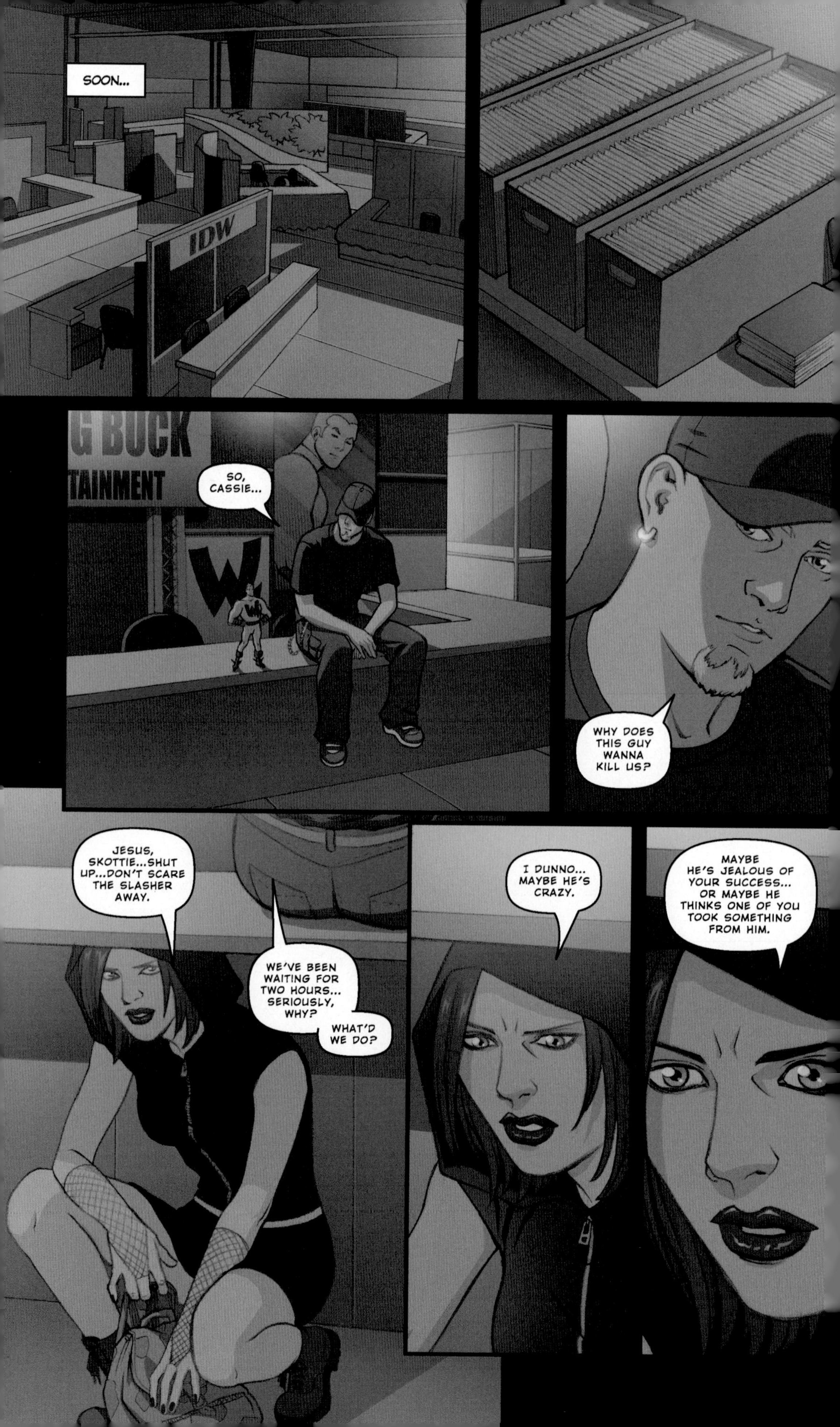
SOON...
IDW
G BUCK
TAINMENT
SO, CASSIE...
WHY DOES THIS GUY WANNA KILL US?
JESUS, SKOTTIE...SHUT UP...DON'T SCARE THE SLASHER AWAY.
WE'VE BEEN WAITING FOR TWO HOURS... SERIOUSLY, WHY?
WHAT'D WE DO?
I DUNNO... MAYBE HE'S CRAZY.
MAYBE HE'S JEALOUS OF YOUR SUCCESS... OR MAYBE HE THINKS ONE OF YOU TOOK SOMETHING FROM HIM.

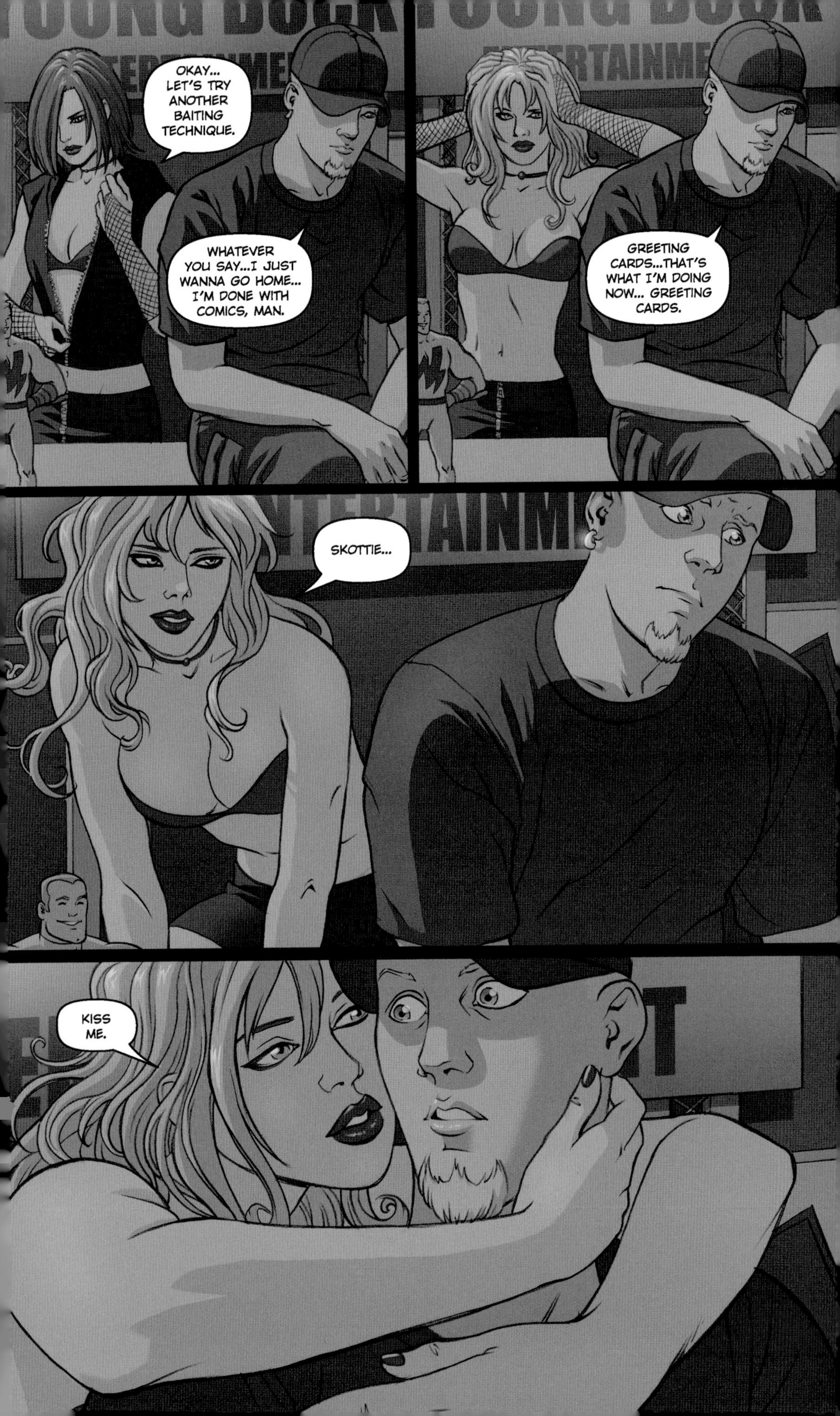
OKAY... LET'S TRY ANOTHER BAITING TECHNIQUE.
WHATEVER YOU SAY...I JUST WANNA GO HOME... I'M DONE WITH COMICS, MAN.
GREETING CARDS...THAT'S WHAT I'M DOING NOW... GREETING CARDS.
SKOTTIE...
KISS ME.

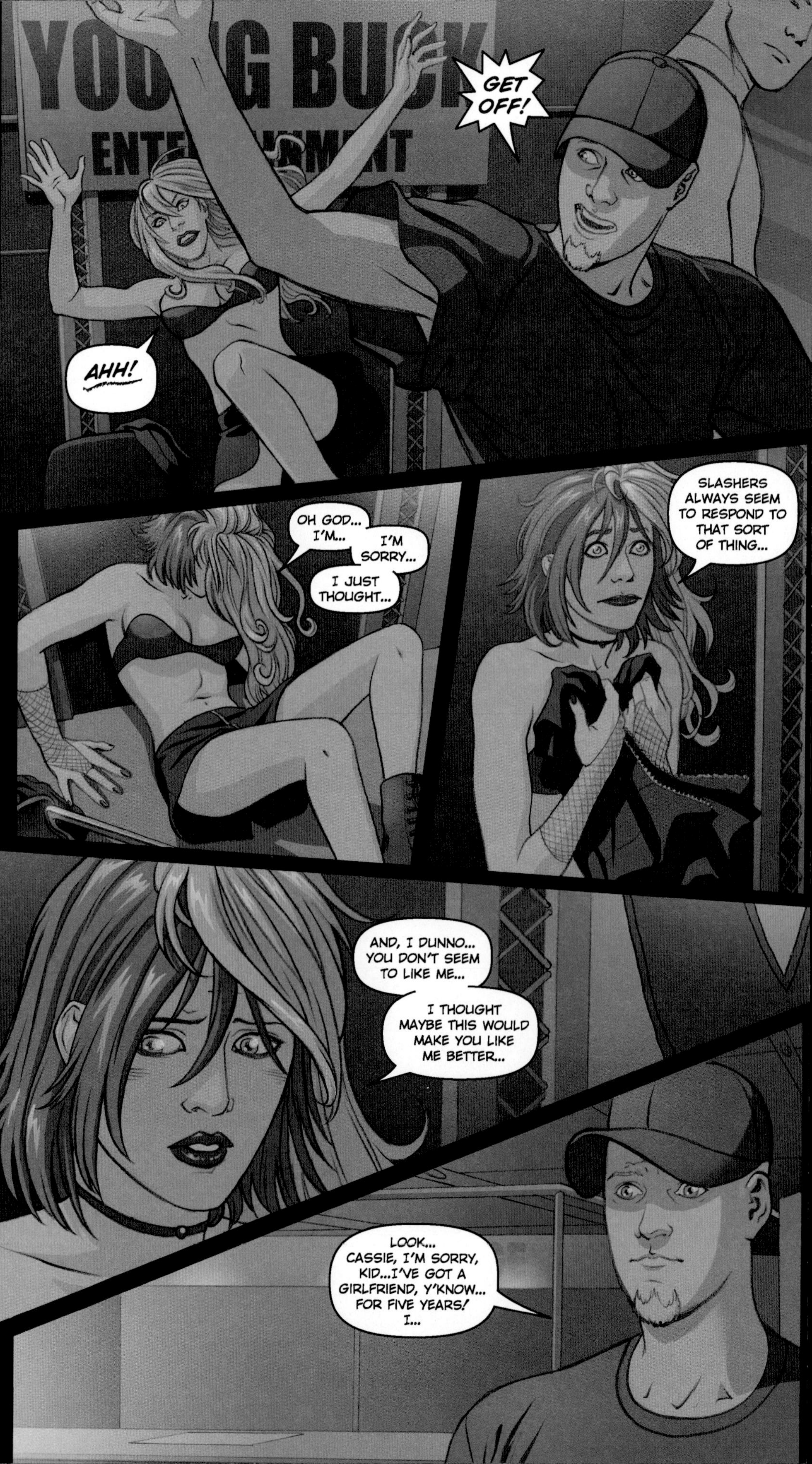
YOUNG BUCK ENTERTAINMENT
GET OFF!
AHH!
OH GOD... I'M...
I'M SORRY...
I JUST THOUGHT...
SLASHERS ALWAYS SEEM TO RESPOND TO THAT SORT OF THING...
AND, I DUNNO... YOU DON'T SEEM TO LIKE ME...
I THOUGHT MAYBE THIS WOULD MAKE YOU LIKE ME BETTER...
LOOK... CASSIE, I'M SORRY, KID...I'VE GOT A GIRLFRIEND, Y'KNOW... FOR FIVE YEARS! I...

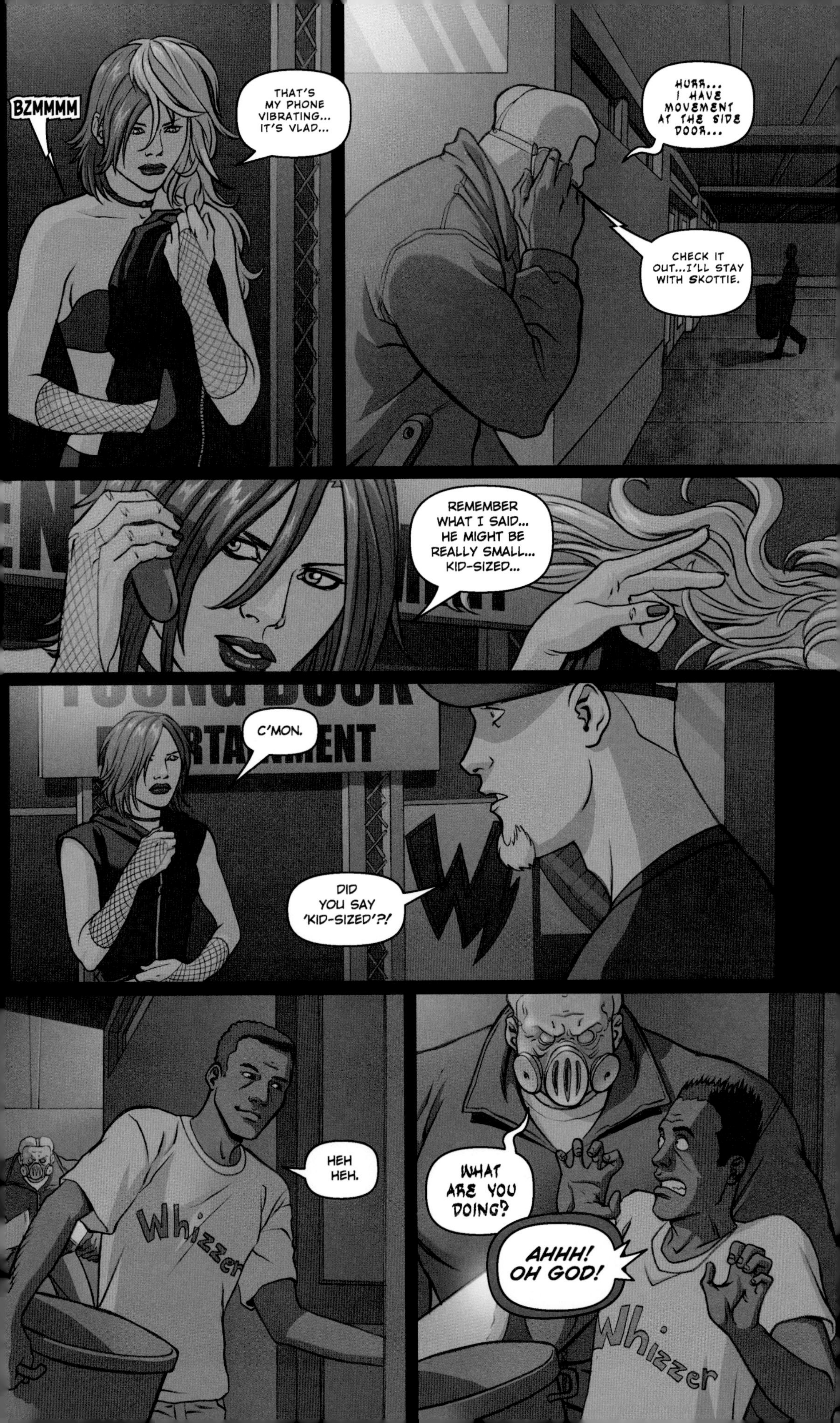
BZMMMM
THAT'S MY PHONE VIBRATING... IT'S VLAD...
HURR... I HAVE MOVEMENT AT THE SIDE DOOR...
CHECK IT OUT...I'LL STAY WITH SKOTTIE.
REMEMBER WHAT I SAID... HE MIGHT BE REALLY SMALL... KID-SIZED...
C'MON.
DID YOU SAY 'KID-SIZED'?!
HEH HEH.
WHAT ARE YOU DOING?
AHHH! OH GOD!

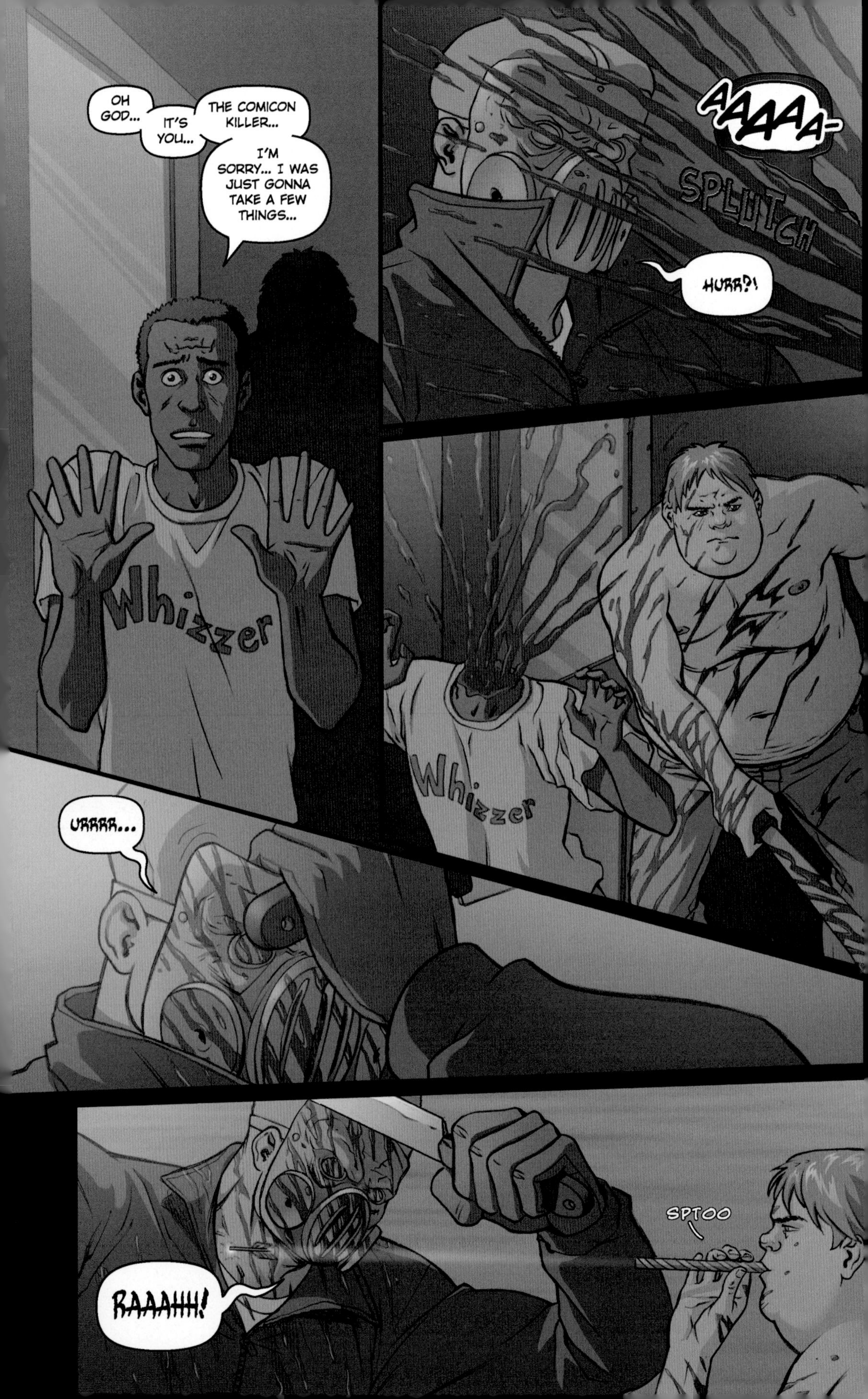
OH GOD...
IT'S YOU...
THE COMICON KILLER...
I'M SORRY... I WAS JUST GONNA TAKE A FEW THINGS...
Whizzer
AAAAA-
SPLUTCH
HURR?!
Whizzer
URRRR...
SPTOO
RAAAHH!

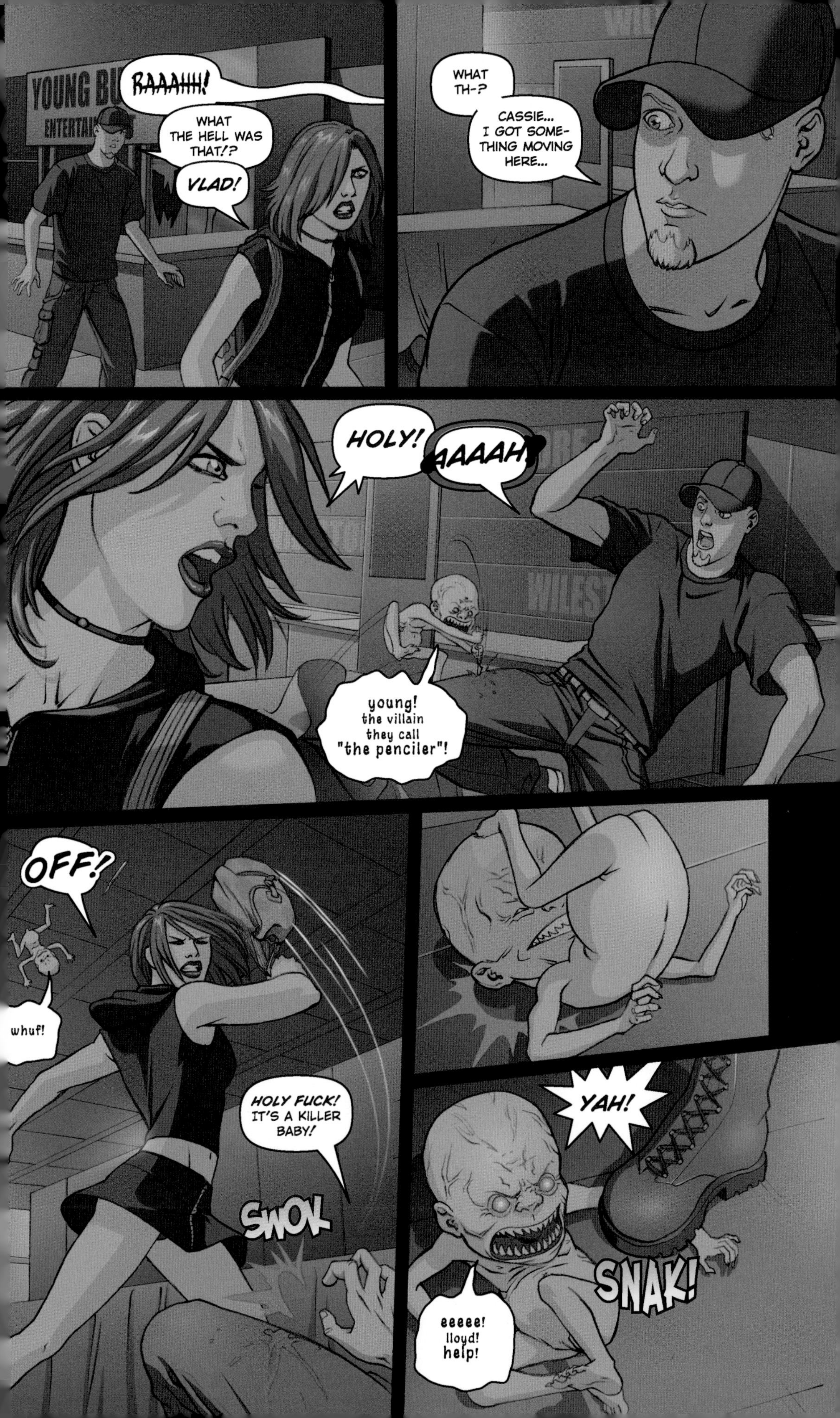
YOUNG BU
ENTERTAI
RAAAHHH!
WHAT THE HELL WAS THAT!?
VLAD!
WHAT TH-?
CASSIE... I GOT SOME-THING MOVING HERE...
HOLY!
AAAAH!
WILES
young! the villain they call "the penciler"!
OFF!
whuf!
HOLY FUCK! IT'S A KILLER BABY!
SWOK
YAH!
SNAK!
eeeee! lloyd! help!

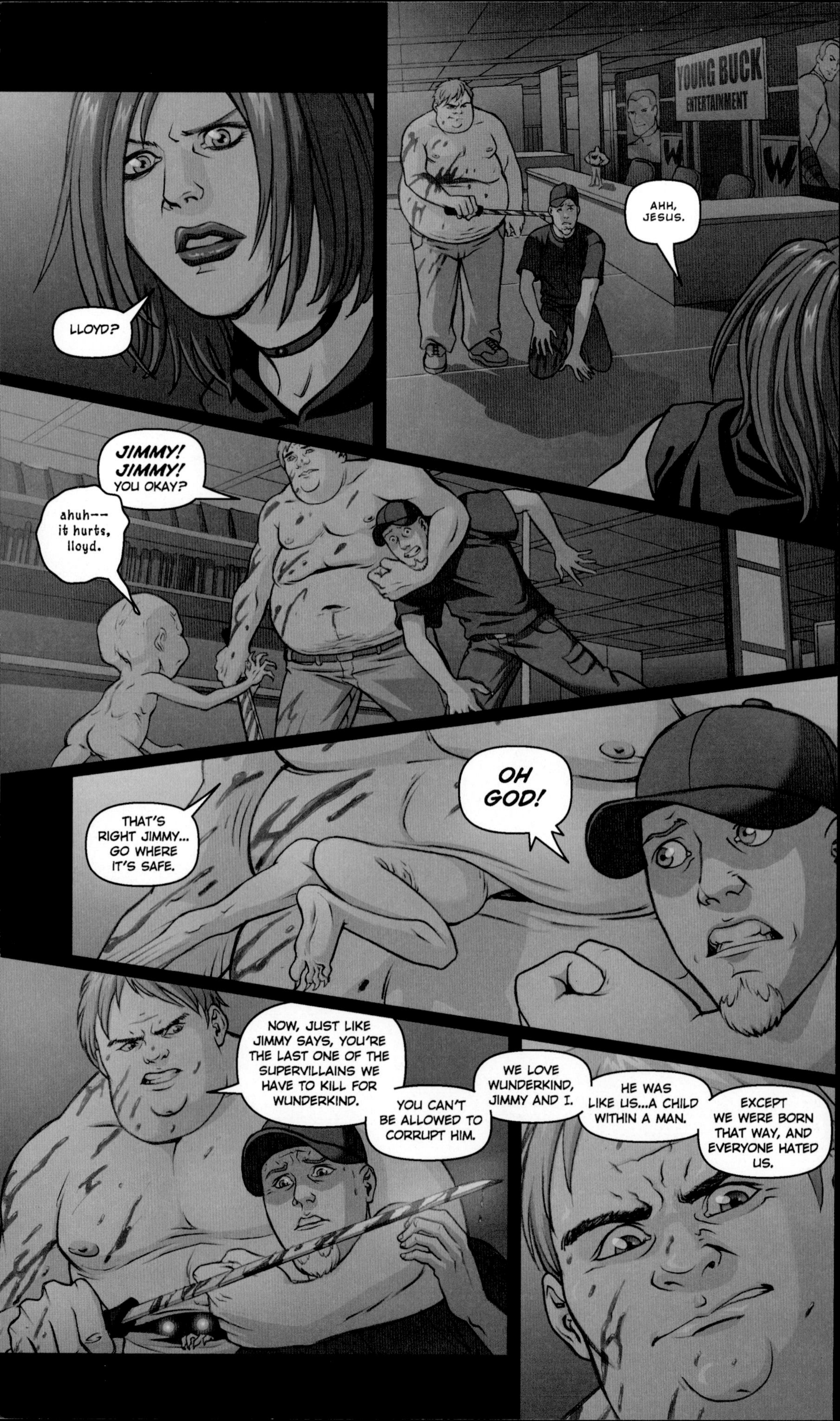

LLOYD?
YOUNG BUCK ENTERTAINMENT
AHH, JESUS.
JIMMY! JIMMY! YOU OKAY?
ahuh-- it hurts, lloyd.
THAT'S RIGHT JIMMY... GO WHERE IT'S SAFE.
OH GOD!
NOW, JUST LIKE JIMMY SAYS, YOU'RE THE LAST ONE OF THE SUPERVILLAINS WE HAVE TO KILL FOR WUNDERKIND.
YOU CAN'T BE ALLOWED TO CORRUPT HIM.
WE LOVE WUNDERKIND, JIMMY AND I.
HE WAS LIKE US...A CHILD WITHIN A MAN.
EXCEPT WE WERE BORN THAT WAY, AND EVERYONE HATED US.

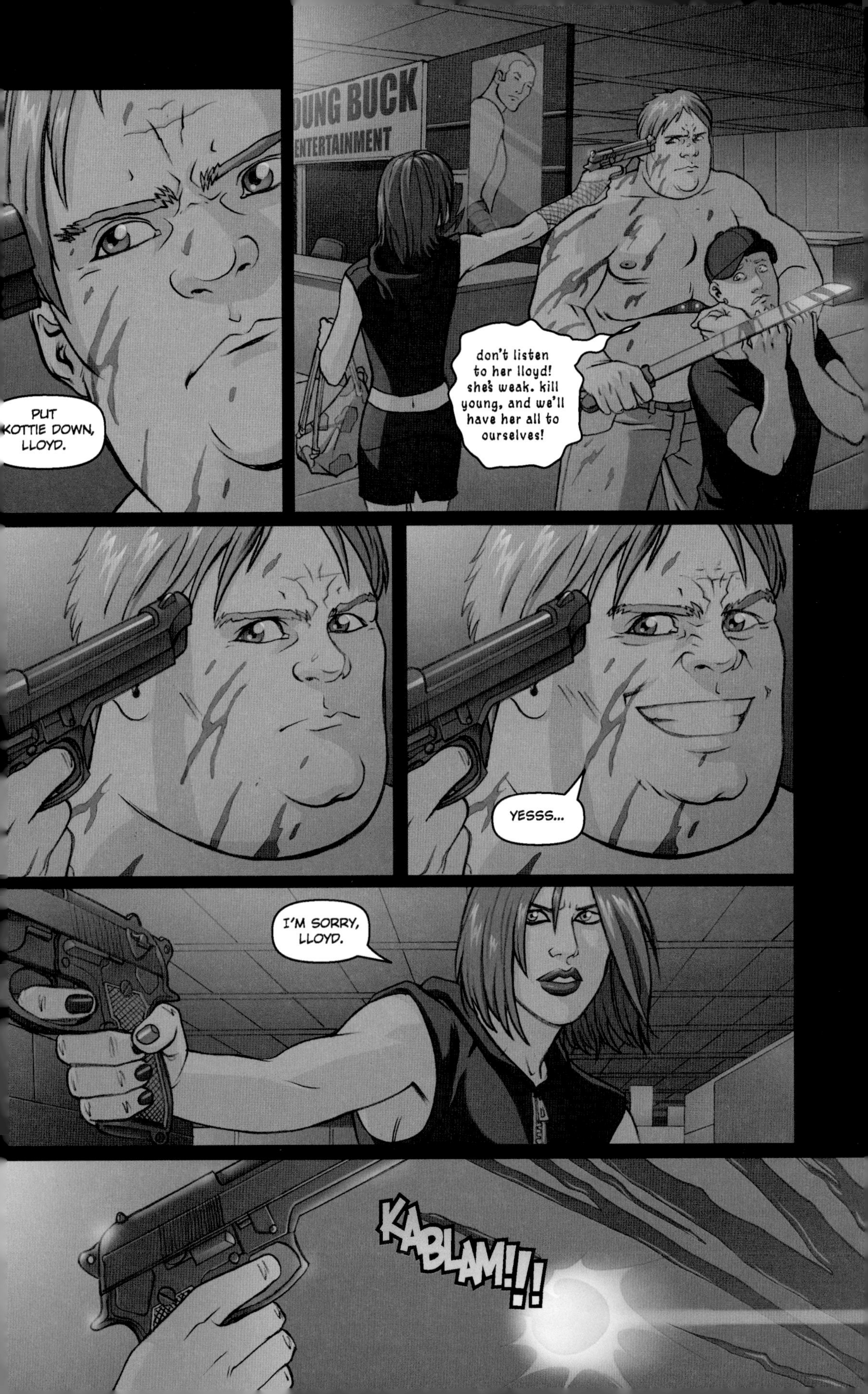

OUNG BUCK
ENTERTAINMENT
PUT KOTTIE DOWN, LLOYD.
don't listen to her lloyd! she's weak. kill young, and we'll have her all to ourselves!
YESSS...
I'M SORRY, LLOYD.
KABLAM!!!

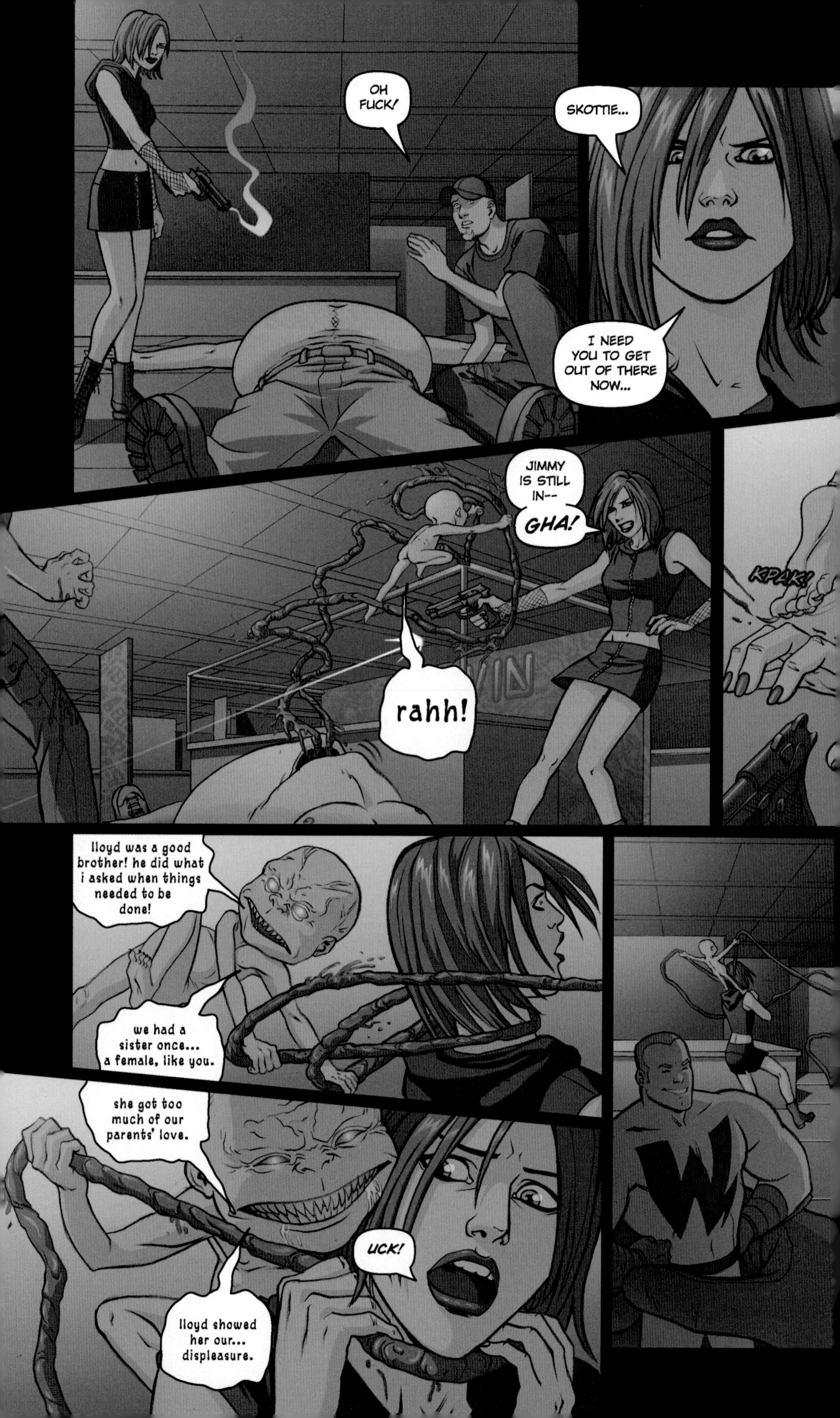

OH FUCK!
SKOTTIE...
I NEED YOU TO GET OUT OF THERE NOW...
JIMMY IS STILL IN--
GHA!
rahh!
KPAK!
lloyd was a good brother! he did what i asked when things needed to be done!
we had a sister once... a female, like you.
she got too much of our parents' love.
UCK!
lloyd showed her our... displeasure.

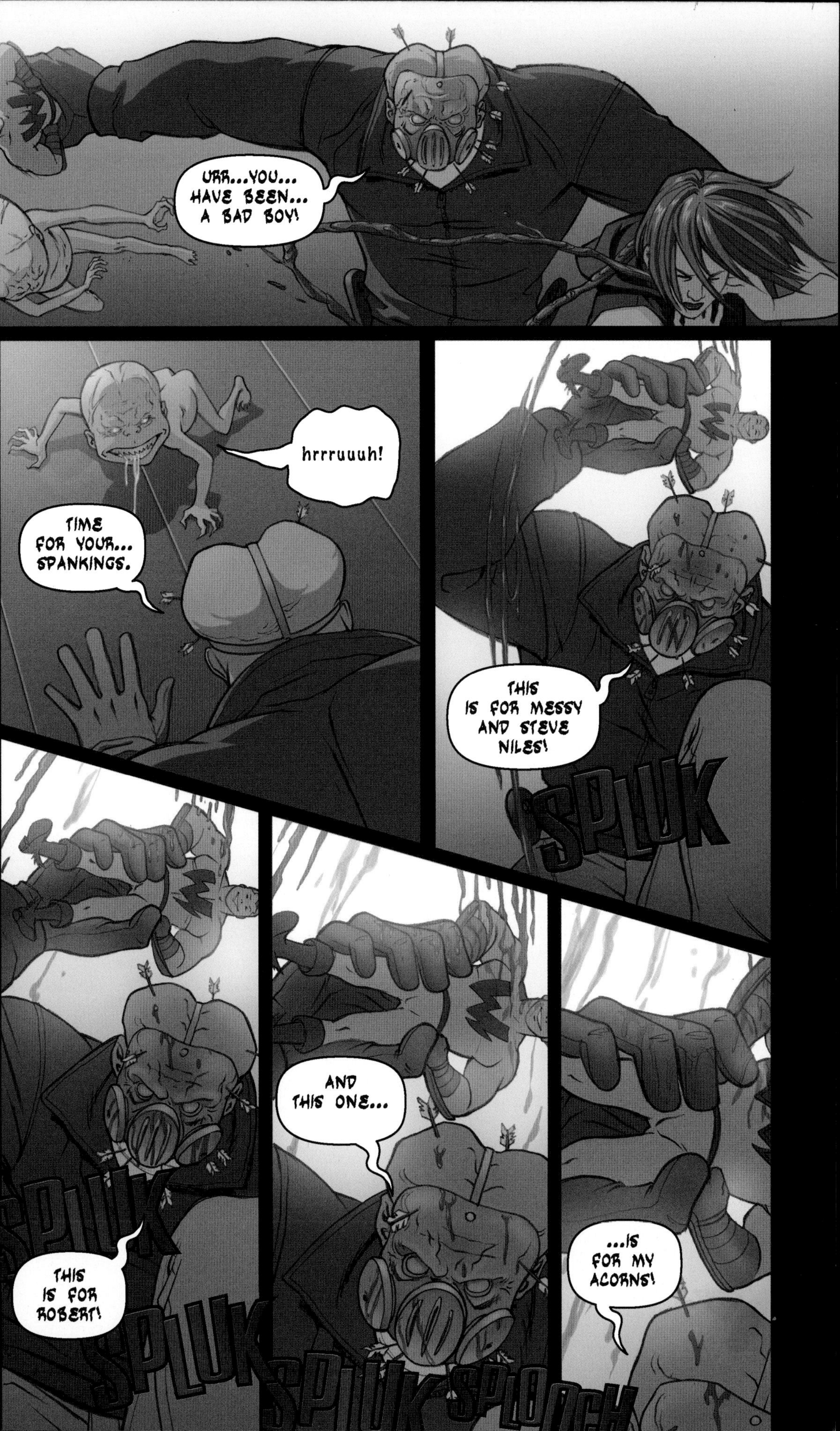
URR...YOU...
HAVE BEEN...
A BAD BOY!
hrrruuuh!
TIME
FOR YOUR...
SPANKINGS.
THIS
IS FOR MESSY
AND STEVE
NILES!
SPLUK
SPLUK
THIS
IS FOR
ROBERT!
SPLUK
AND
THIS ONE...
SPLUK
...IS
FOR MY
ACORNS!
SPLOOCH

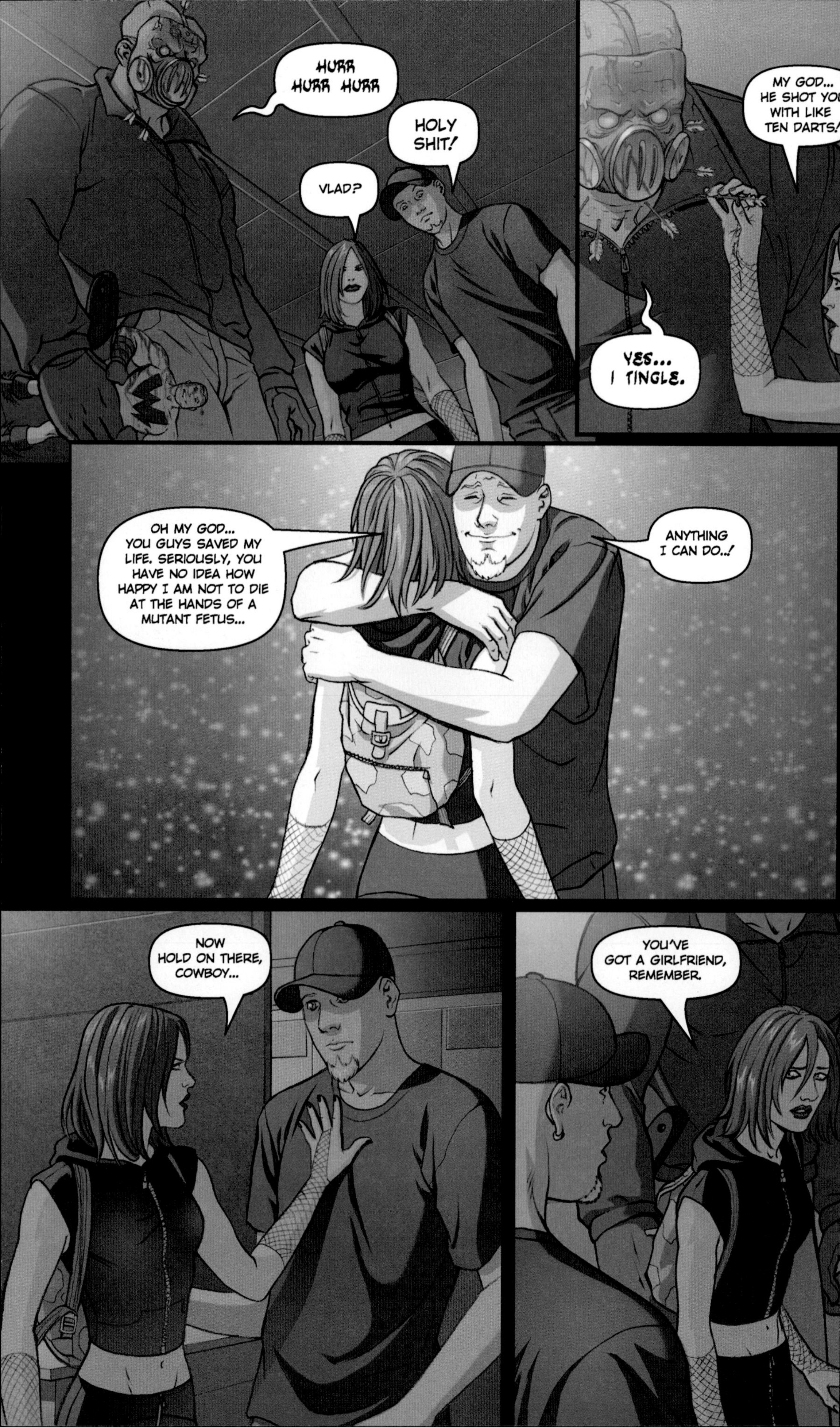
HURR HURR HURR
VLAD?
HOLY SHIT!
MY GOD... HE SHOT YOU WITH LIKE TEN DARTS!
YES... I TINGLE.
OH MY GOD... YOU GUYS SAVED MY LIFE. SERIOUSLY, YOU HAVE NO IDEA HOW HAPPY I AM NOT TO DIE AT THE HANDS OF A MUTANT FETUS...
ANYTHING I CAN DO..!
NOW HOLD ON THERE, COWBOY...
YOU'VE GOT A GIRLFRIEND, REMEMBER.

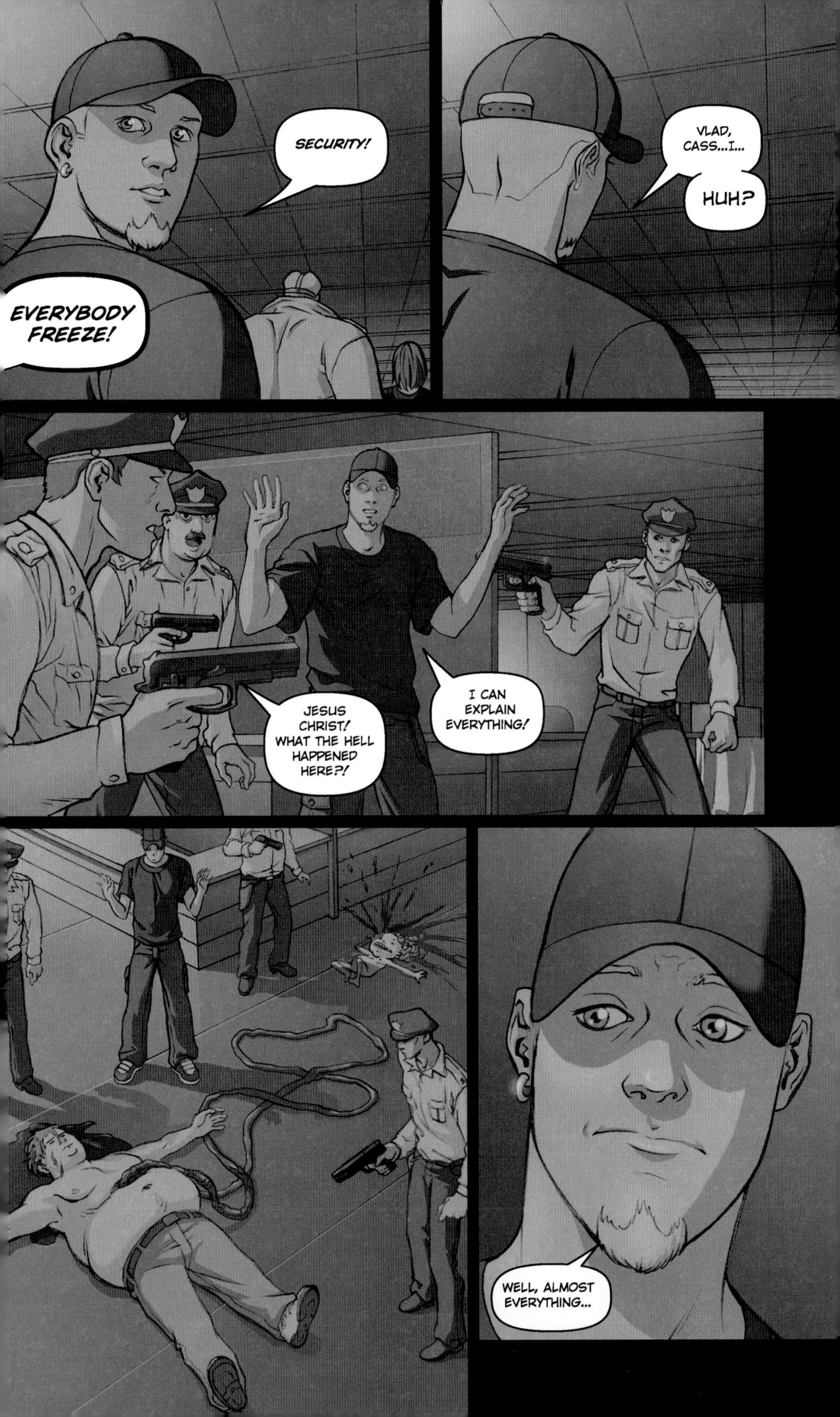
SECURITY!
EVERYBODY FREEZE!
VLAD, CASS...I...
HUH?
JESUS CHRIST! WHAT THE HELL HAPPENED HERE?!
I CAN EXPLAIN EVERYTHING!
WELL, ALMOST EVERYTHING...

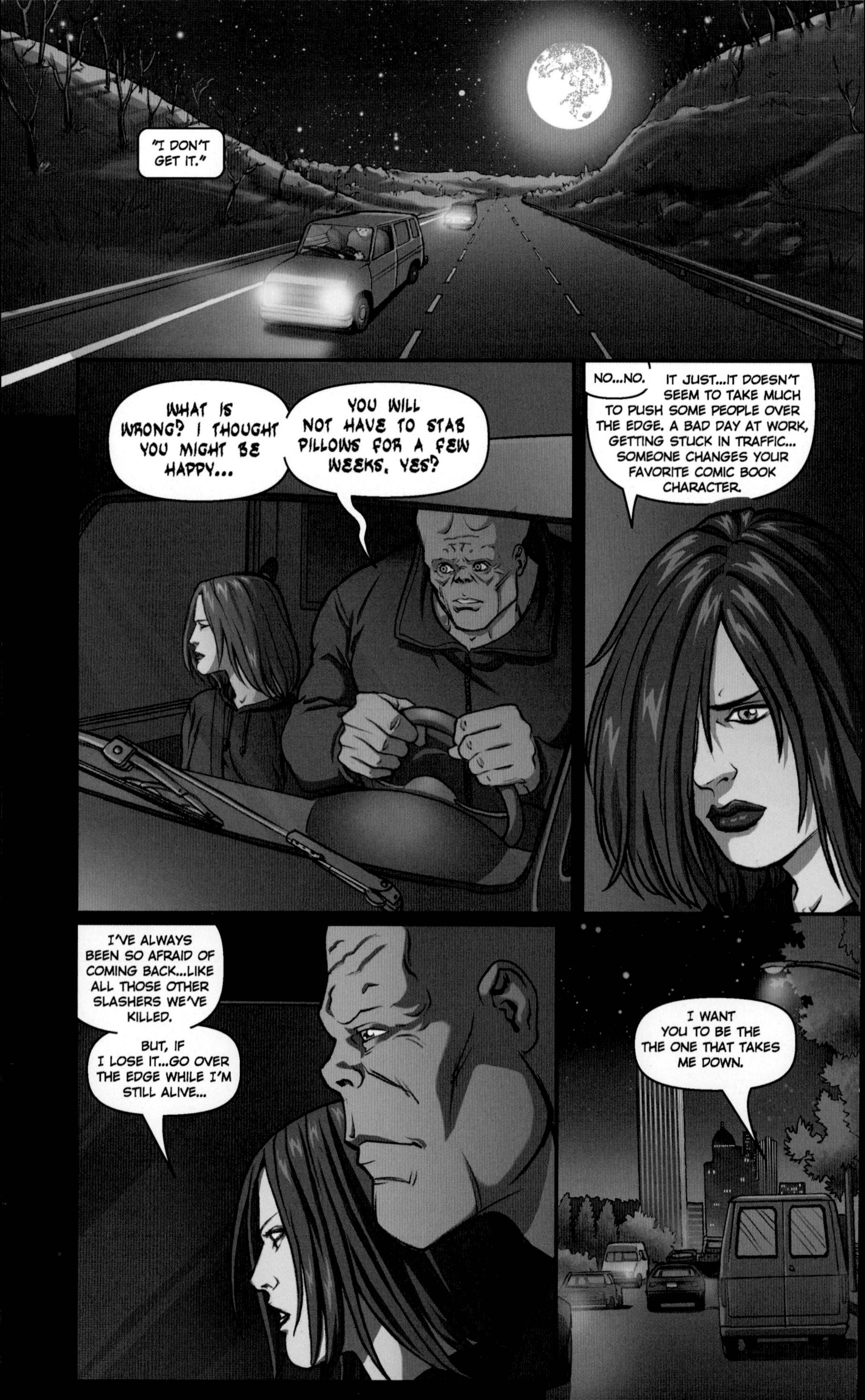
"I DON'T GET IT."
WHAT IS WRONG? I THOUGHT YOU MIGHT BE HAPPY...
YOU WILL NOT HAVE TO STAB PILLOWS FOR A FEW WEEKS, YES?
NO...NO.
IT JUST...IT DOESN'T SEEM TO TAKE MUCH TO PUSH SOME PEOPLE OVER THE EDGE. A BAD DAY AT WORK, GETTING STUCK IN TRAFFIC... SOMEONE CHANGES YOUR FAVORITE COMIC BOOK CHARACTER.
I'VE ALWAYS BEEN SO AFRAID OF COMING BACK...LIKE ALL THOSE OTHER SLASHERS WE'VE KILLED.
BUT, IF I LOSE IT...GO OVER THE EDGE WHILE I'M STILL ALIVE...
I WANT YOU TO BE THE THE ONE THAT TAKES ME DOWN.

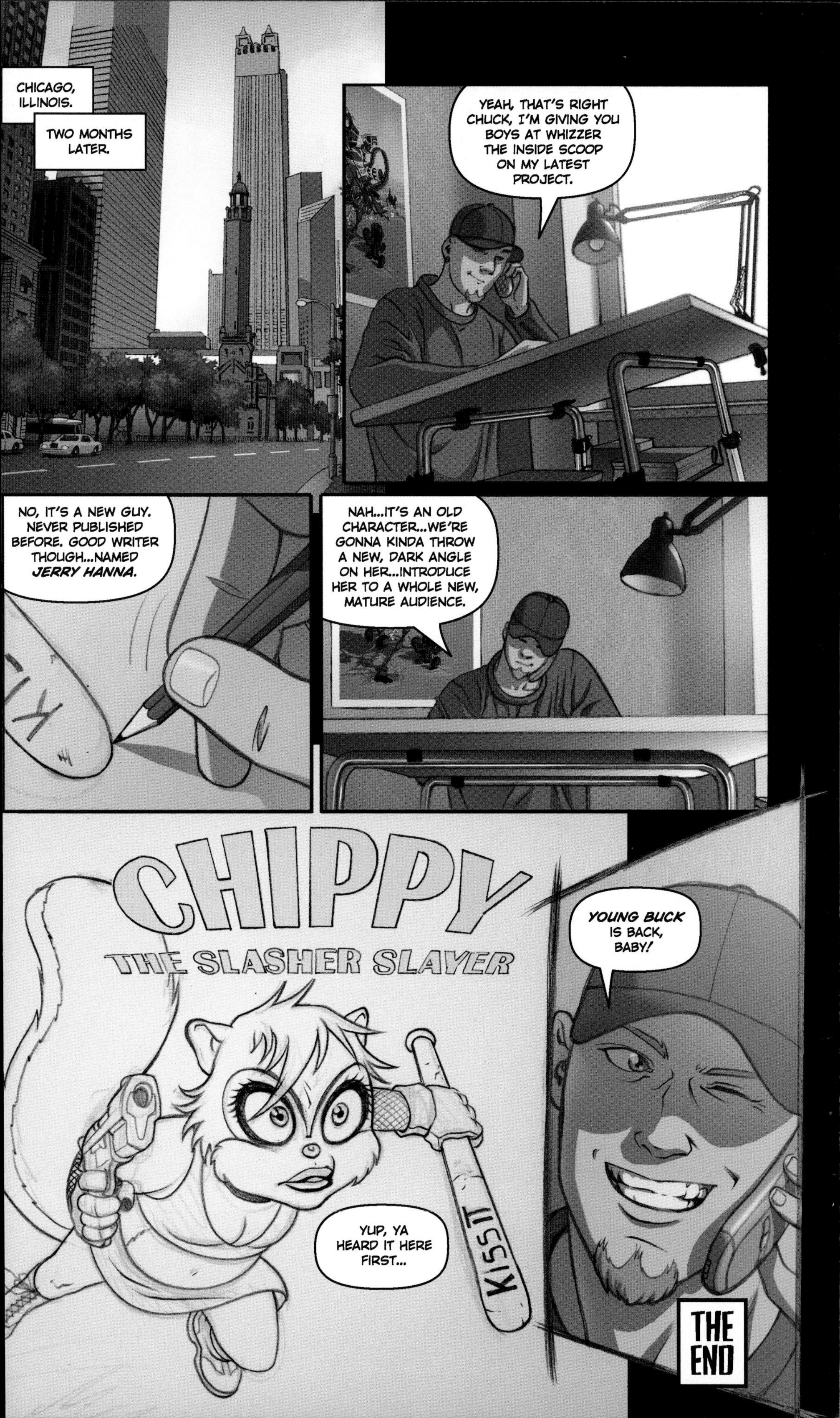
CHICAGO, ILLINOIS.
TWO MONTHS LATER.
YEAH, THAT'S RIGHT CHUCK, I'M GIVING YOU BOYS AT WHIZZER THE INSIDE SCOOP ON MY LATEST PROJECT.
NO, IT'S A NEW GUY. NEVER PUBLISHED BEFORE. GOOD WRITER THOUGH...NAMED *JERRY HANNA.*
NAH...IT'S AN OLD CHARACTER...WE'RE GONNA KINDA THROW A NEW, DARK ANGLE ON HER...INTRODUCE HER TO A WHOLE NEW, MATURE AUDIENCE.
CHIPPY
THE SLASHER SLAYER
YUP, YA HEARD IT HERE FIRST...
KISS IT
YOUNG BUCK IS BACK, BABY!
THE END

SLASHING THROUGH THE SNOW

WRITTEN BY
TIM SEELEY
DRAWN BY
MIKE O'SULLIVAN
PAINTED BY
STEVE SEELEY
TITLE ILLUSTRATION BY SEAN DOVE

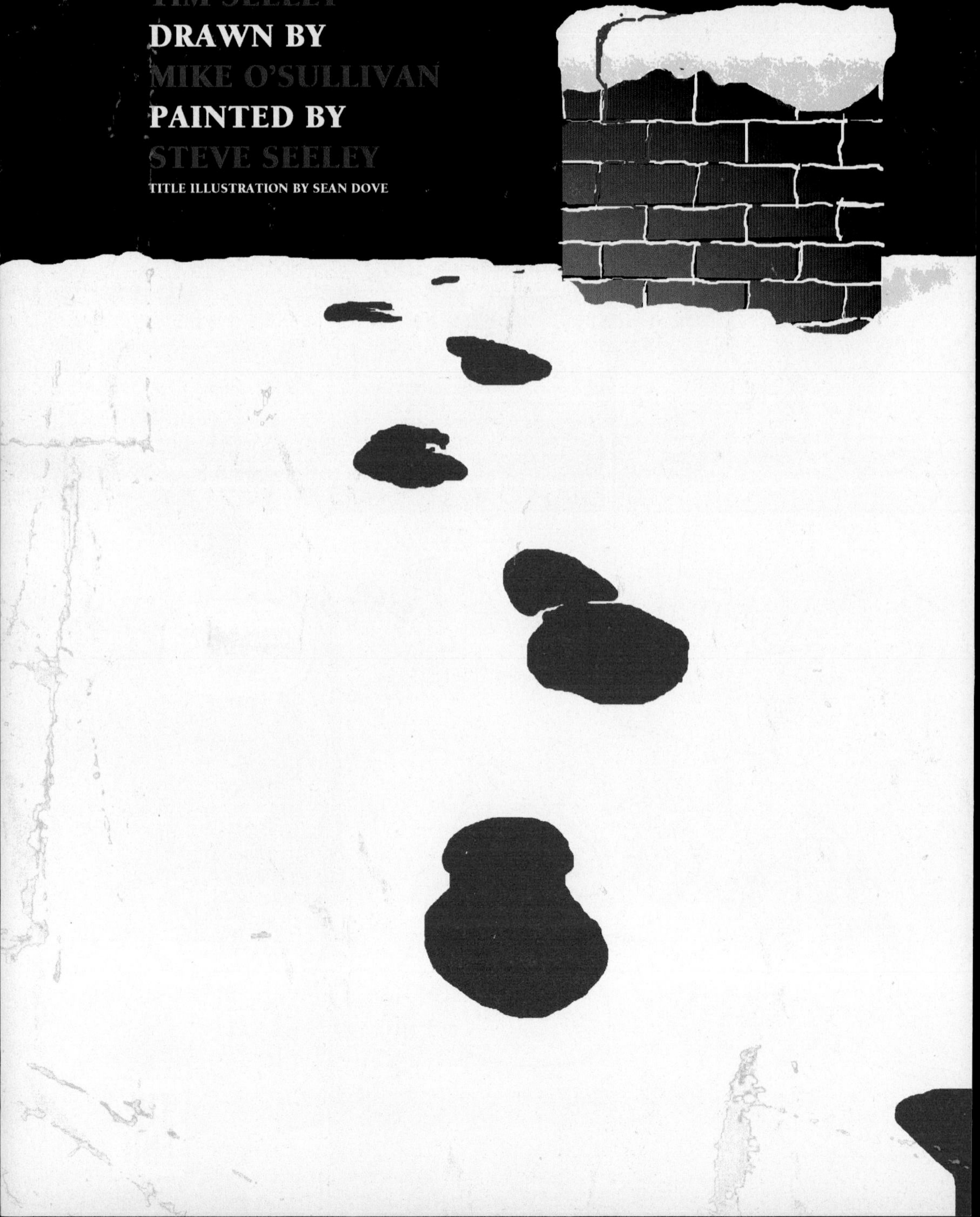

'Twas the night before Christmas,
And a killer did creep,
Preparing for murder,
As the children did sleep.

His name was Rudolph,
And he hated Christmas so.
He peered through the window,
As he brushed off the snow.

Inside, a tree, presents, and lights.
He's had this home long in his sights.
So perfect, so cheery,
The rage filled his pores.
This perfect little family
Never locked their doors.

'Dressed in his Santa suit,
Rudolph excitedly shook.
He gave the antlers strapped to his hand
One last, loving look.

"Soon you'll taste flesh!"
Rudolph said with a grin.
"We'll punish their greed,
The worst Deadly Sin!"

Yes, that's Rudolph's motivation,
Pretty weak, I admit.
But he's a slasher, okay?!
Crazy...BATSHIT!!

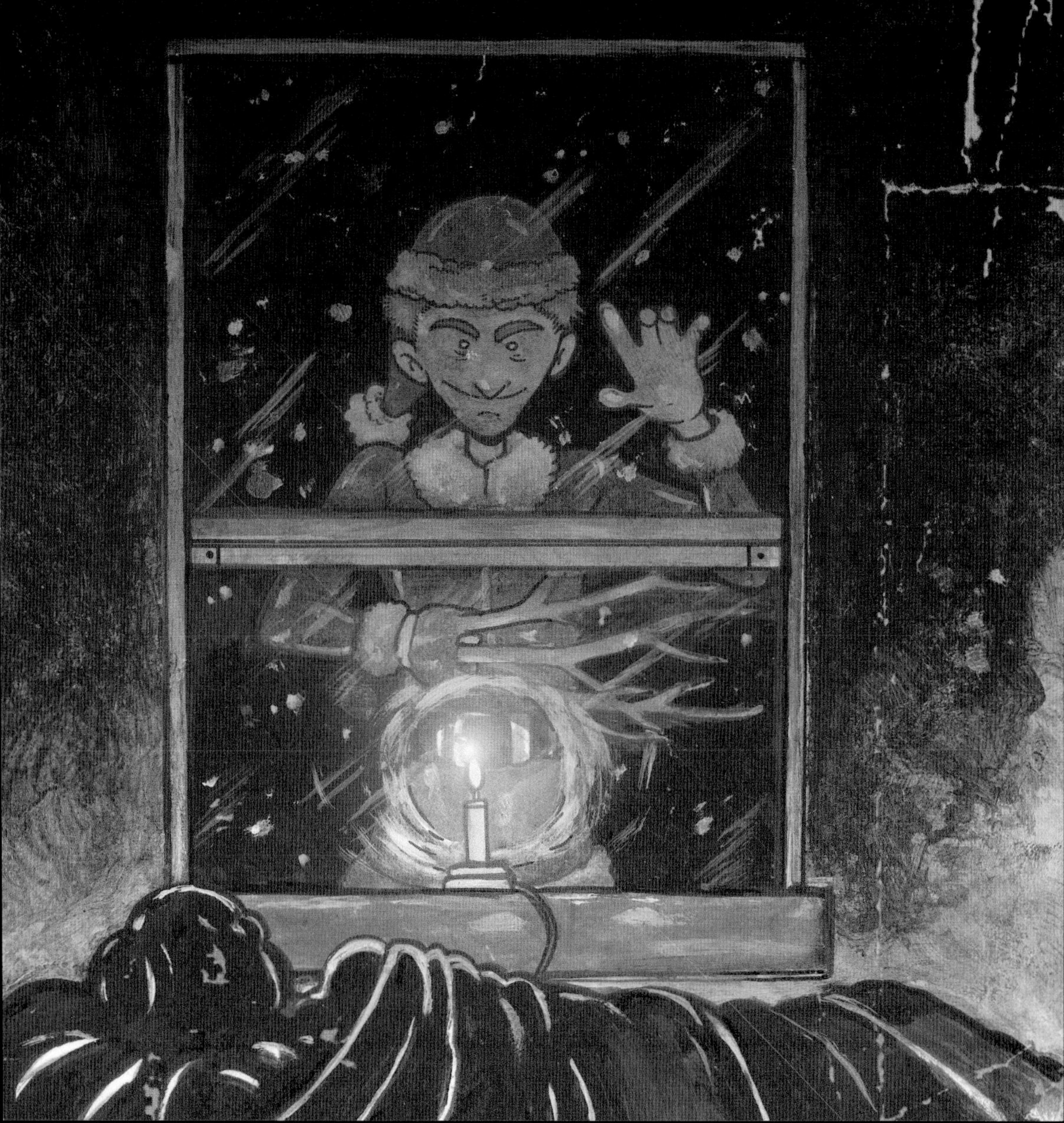

Rudolph crept through the twinkling lit gray
His first kill of the season
Merely seconds away.

There's room for the child,
The young of the litter.
He'll stick his antlers through
This greedy little critter.

He pulled back the covers
To unwrap his tiny gift,
When a handgun popped up,
Rudolph'd been stiffed!

"Ho ho ho, motherfucker," said a young woman, s
"What's going on?" said Rudolph.

"Not this year, and not this crime
Damn, it's annoying to have to fucking rhyme
This goth teen, she'd stop his spree!
He slashed her hand with his antlers,
And away he did flee.

ck down the stairs, he ran
o flee this awful trap.
e bumped into a huge shape,
undled in gift wrap.

ormally a gift so big could hardly be bad.
ut it is if you're a slasher,
nd the gift's name is Vlad.

ad tore open the paper, and shreds did fly!
Merry Christmas, Mr. Slasher!
ime for you to die!"

Rudolph dodged the cleavers
That nearly bisected his head.
He wished he wasn't a killer,
Perhaps a librarian, instead.

Seeing a way out,
Rudolph used his head.
He clambered up the chimney,
And got stuck there instead.

Maybe a little disappointed,
Cassie and Vlad saw their slasher was stuck.
The first killer they hadn't killed.
Why Rudolph, what luck!

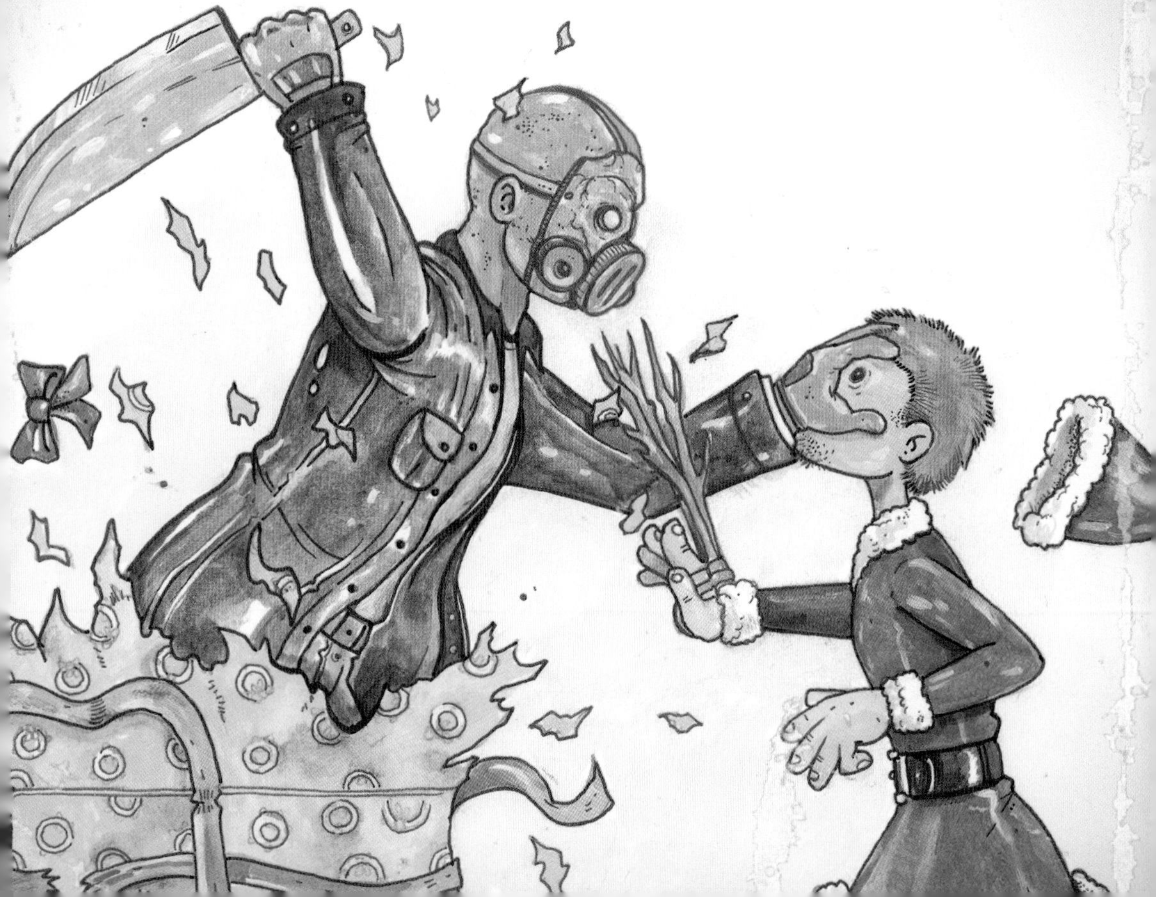

The family came back
To open presents 'round the tree.
They'd let their house be bait
For merely a modest fee.

The police came to grab Rudolph
And take him off to jail.
His Christmas gift would be iron bars,
Not fruitcake or bail.

Cassie and Vlad snuck off into the night,
Dark as the river Styx.
Their prize some cookies
And some Tom N' Jerry mix.

As they munched on sugar
And filled up their tummies,
Cassie gave Vlad a gift,
"Vocabulary for Dummies."

It's Christmas for Slasher hunte
To Cassie, a new bright, shiny
To replace her old one
That smelled of dead cat.

Cassie, who hates mushy,
Said, "We got killers to slay.
Our first holiday slasher!
Can't wait for Valentine's Day!"

End.

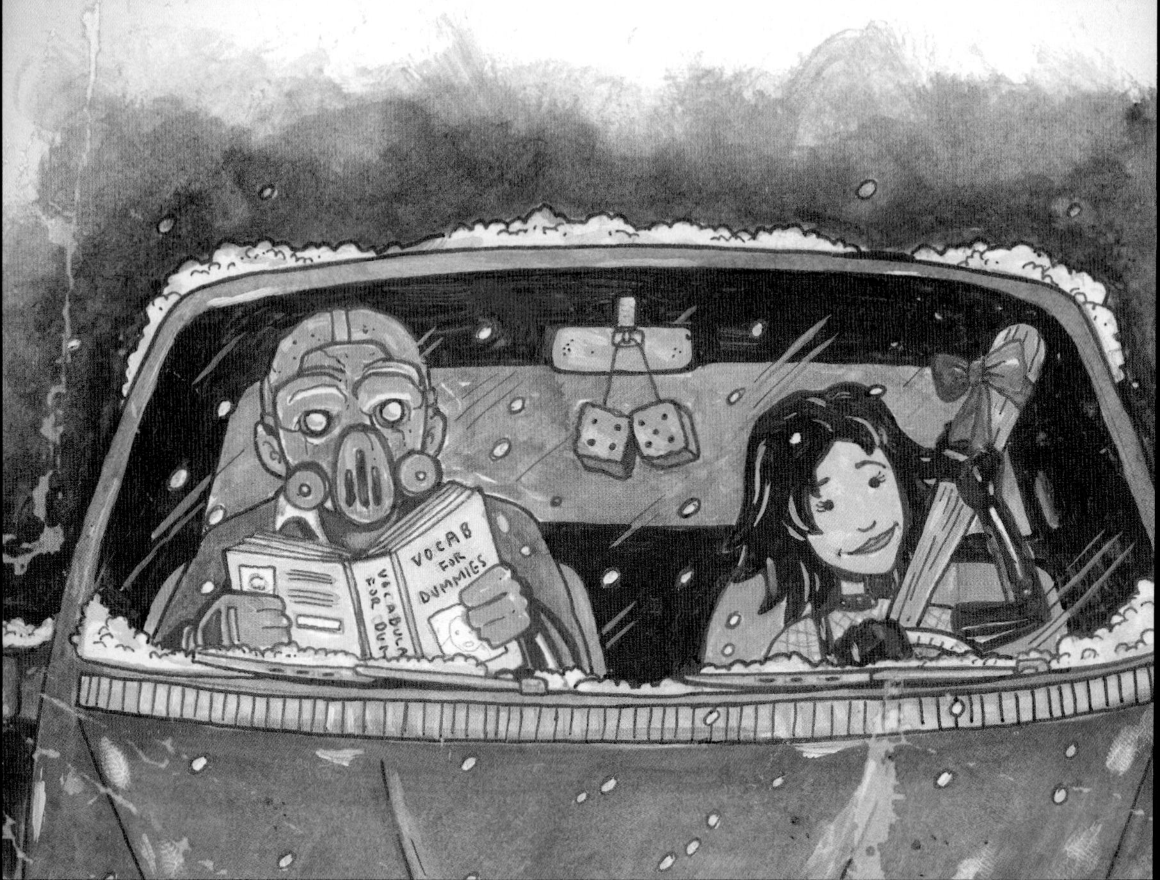
VOCAB FOR DUMMIES

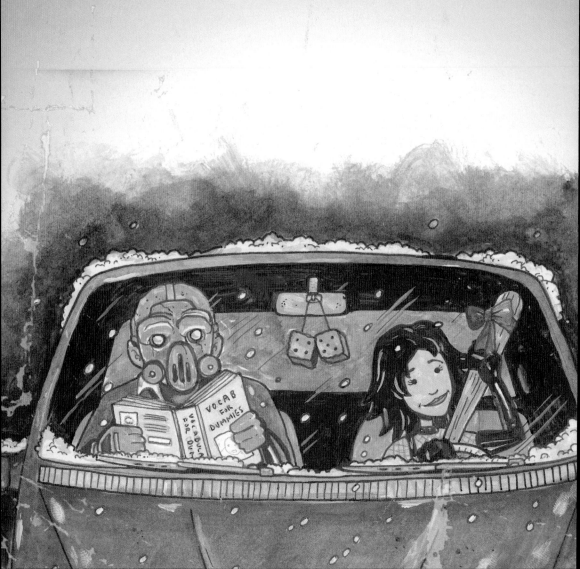

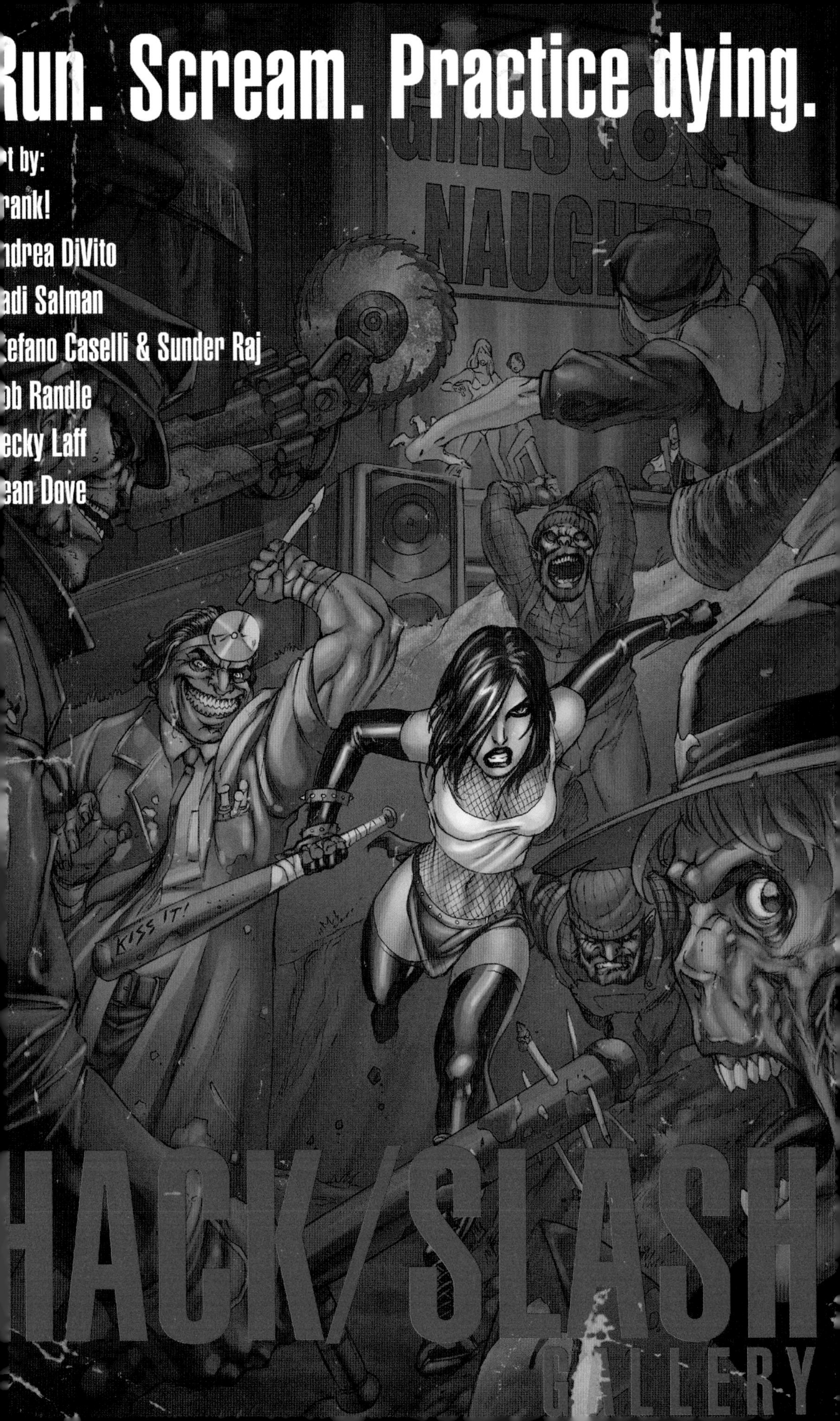
Run. Scream. Practice dying.
t by:
rank!
ndrea DiVito
adi Salman
efano Caselli & Sunder Raj
ob Randle
ecky Laff
ean Dove
KISS IT!
HACK/SLASH
GALLERY

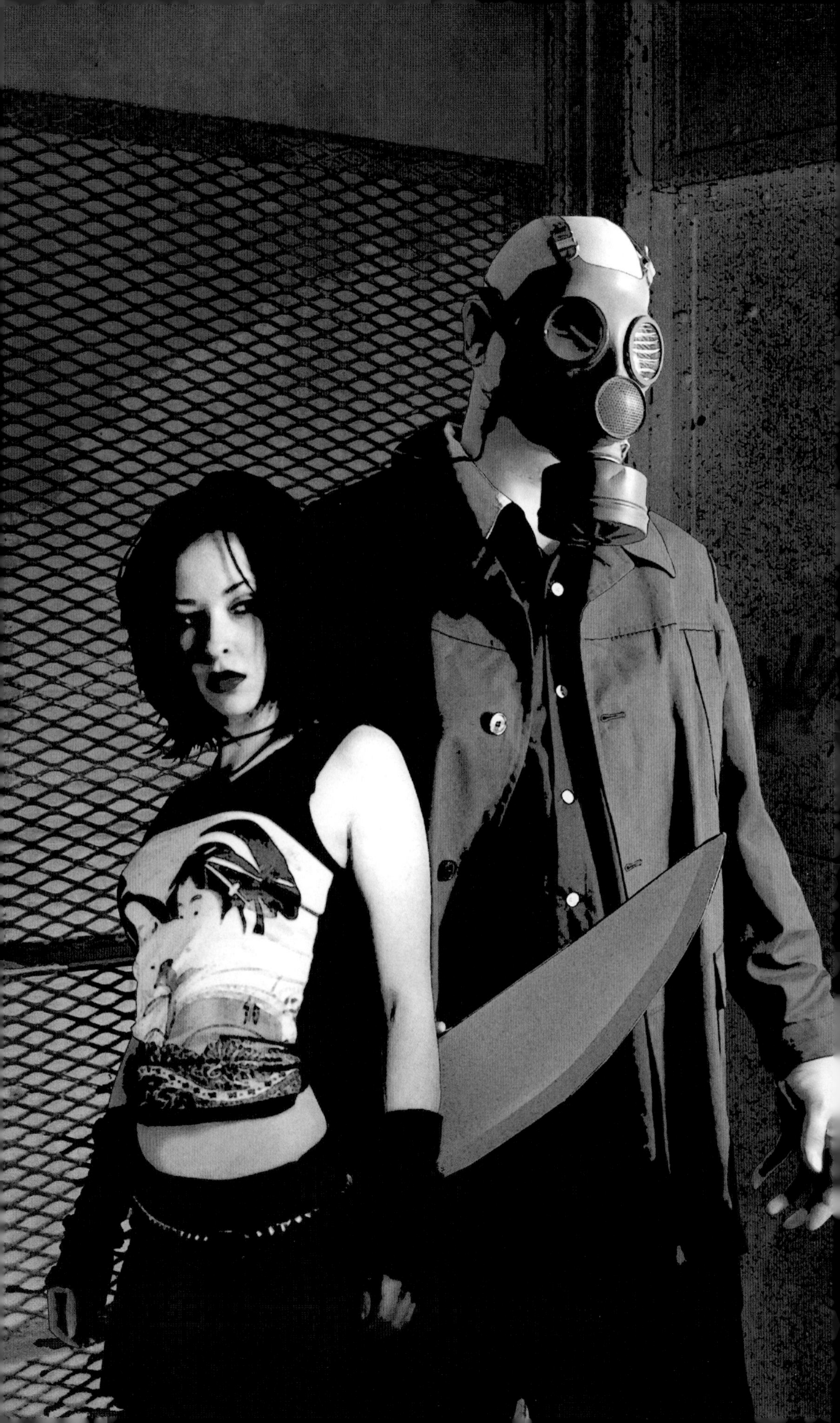

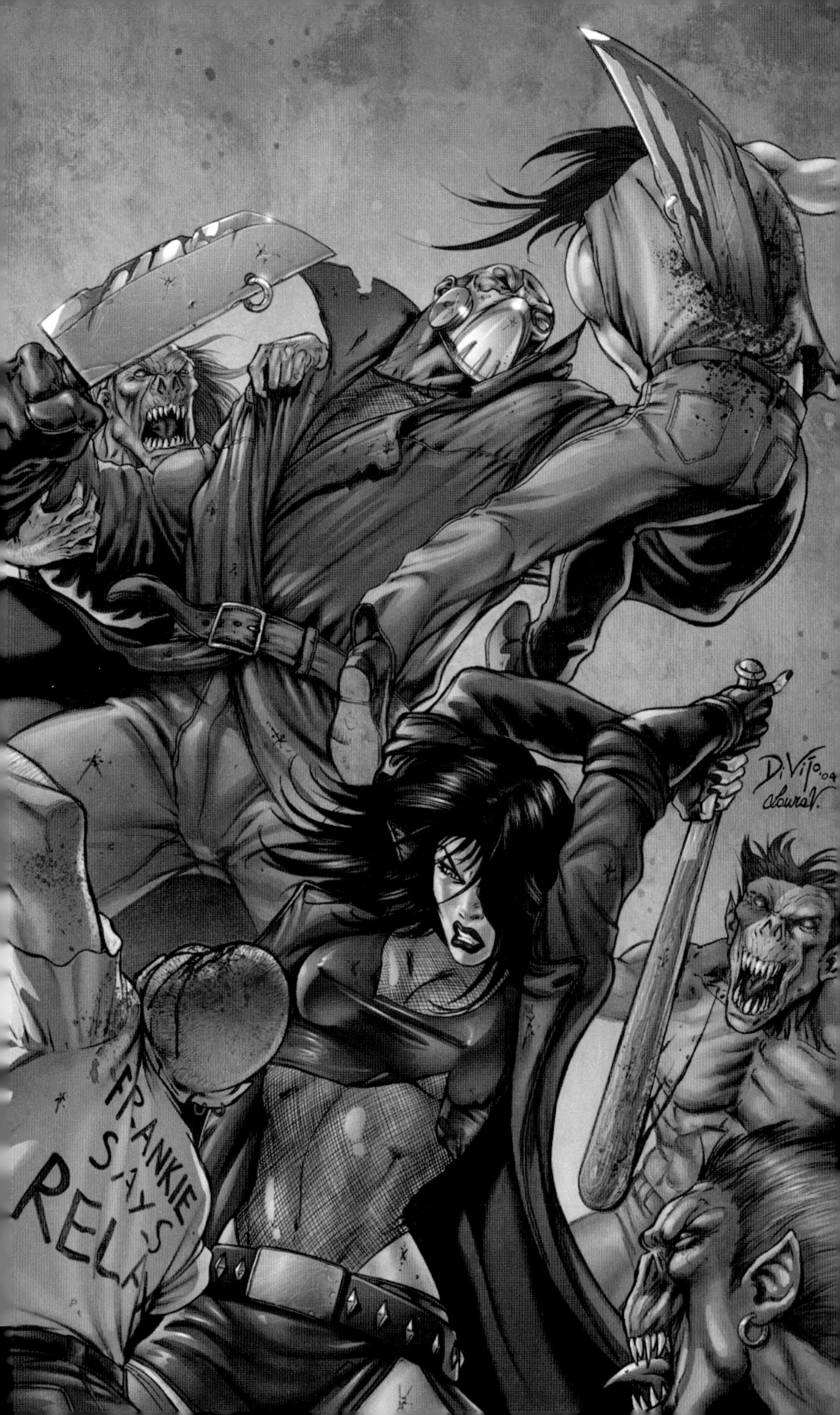
FRANKIE
SAYS
RELA

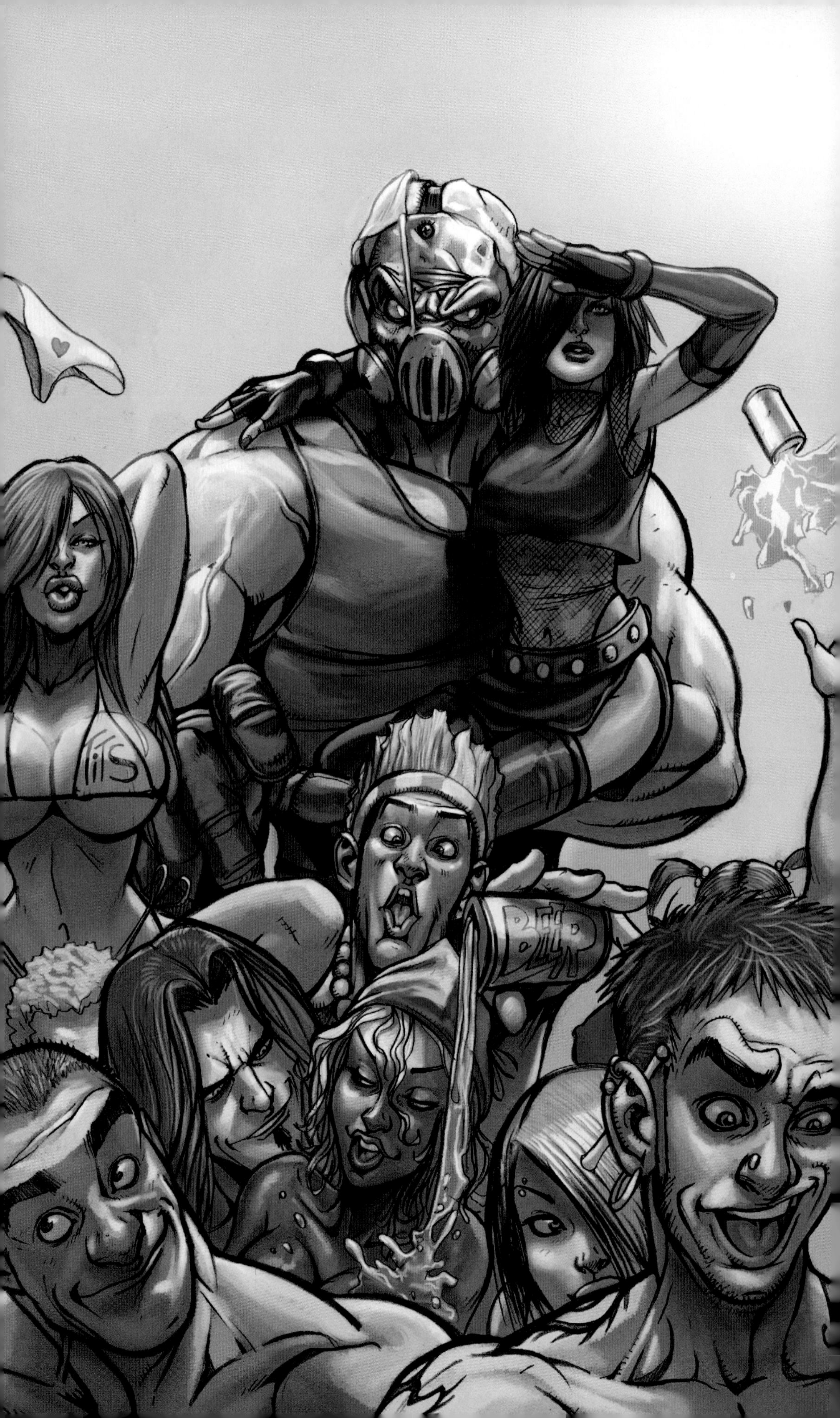
TITS
BEER

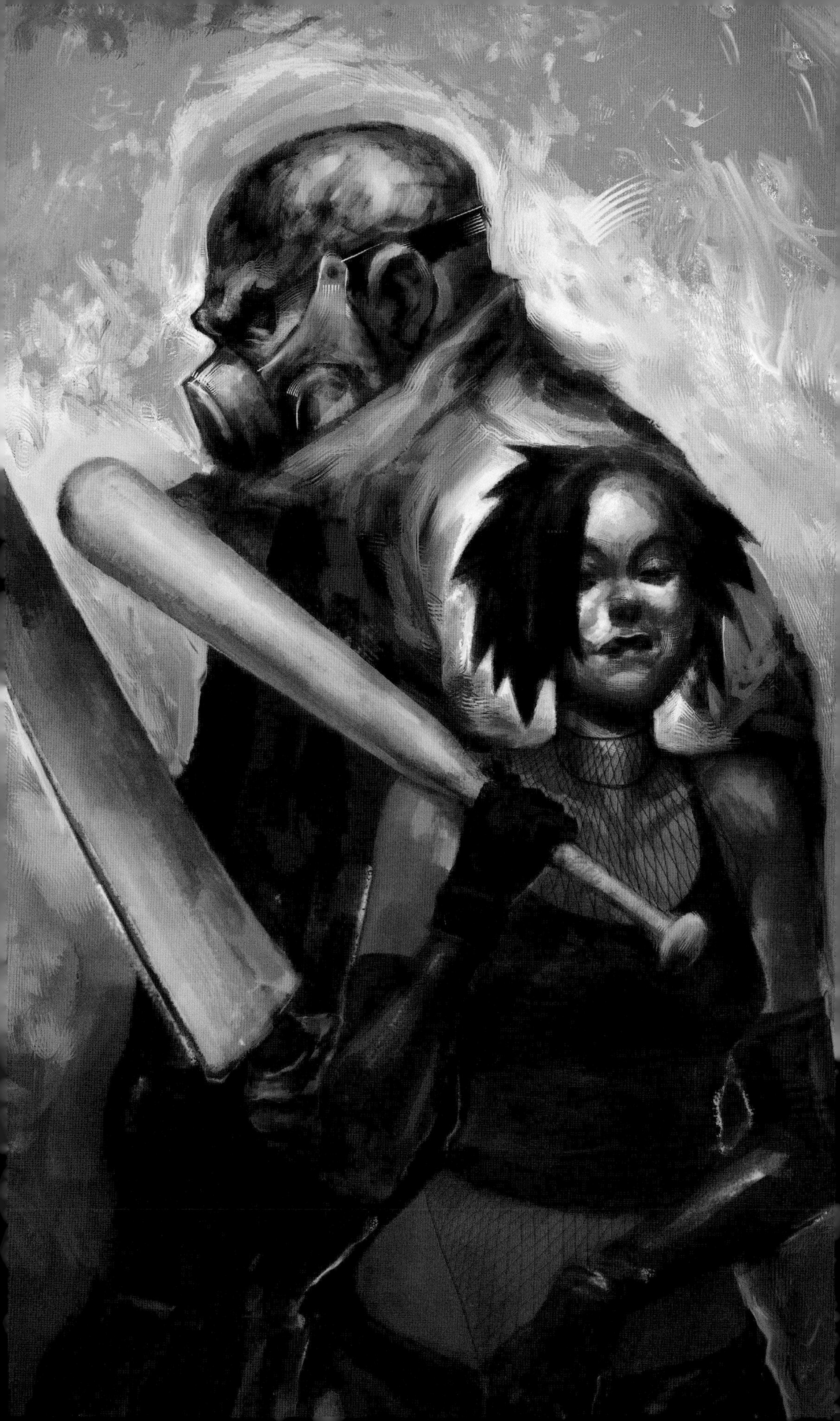

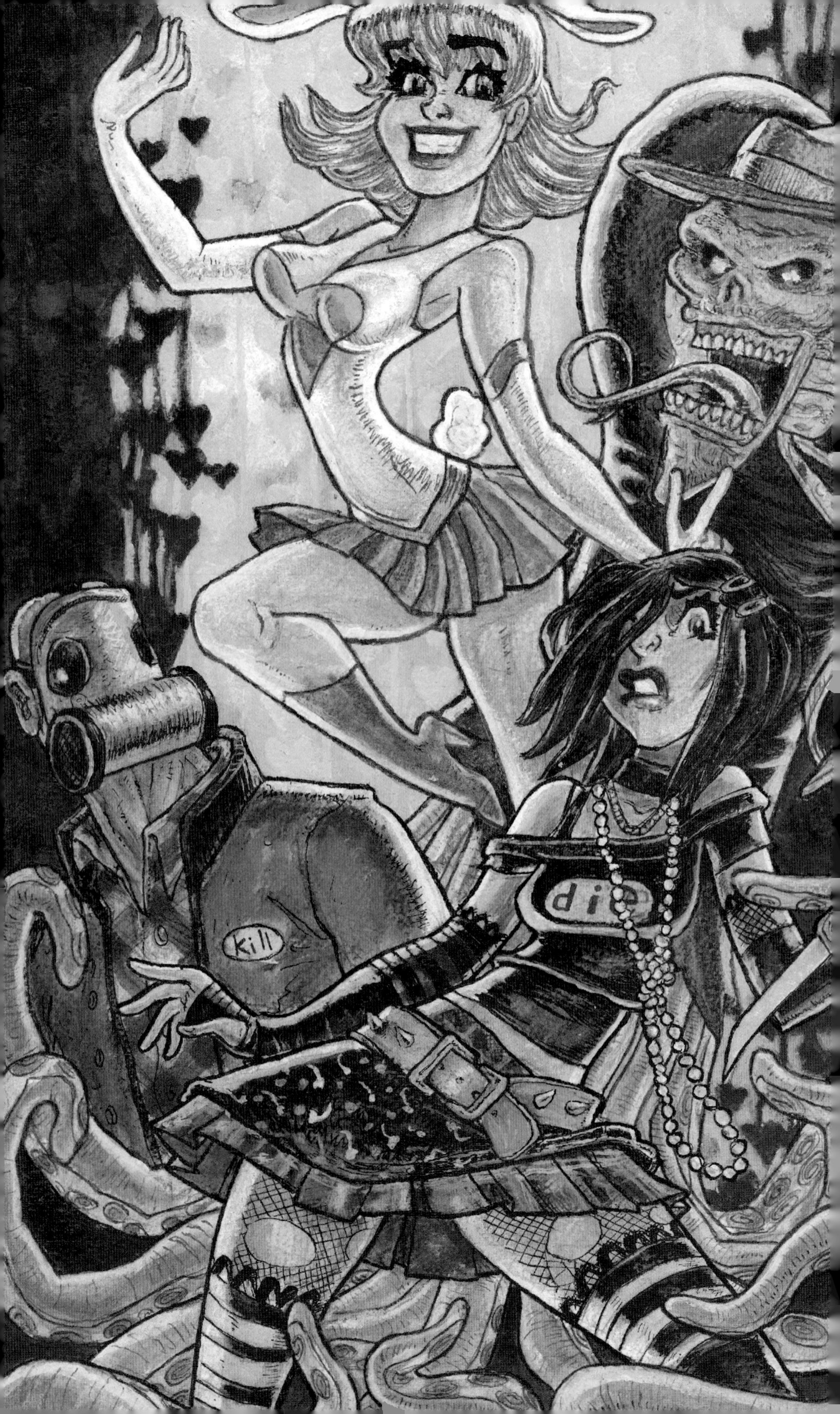
die
kill

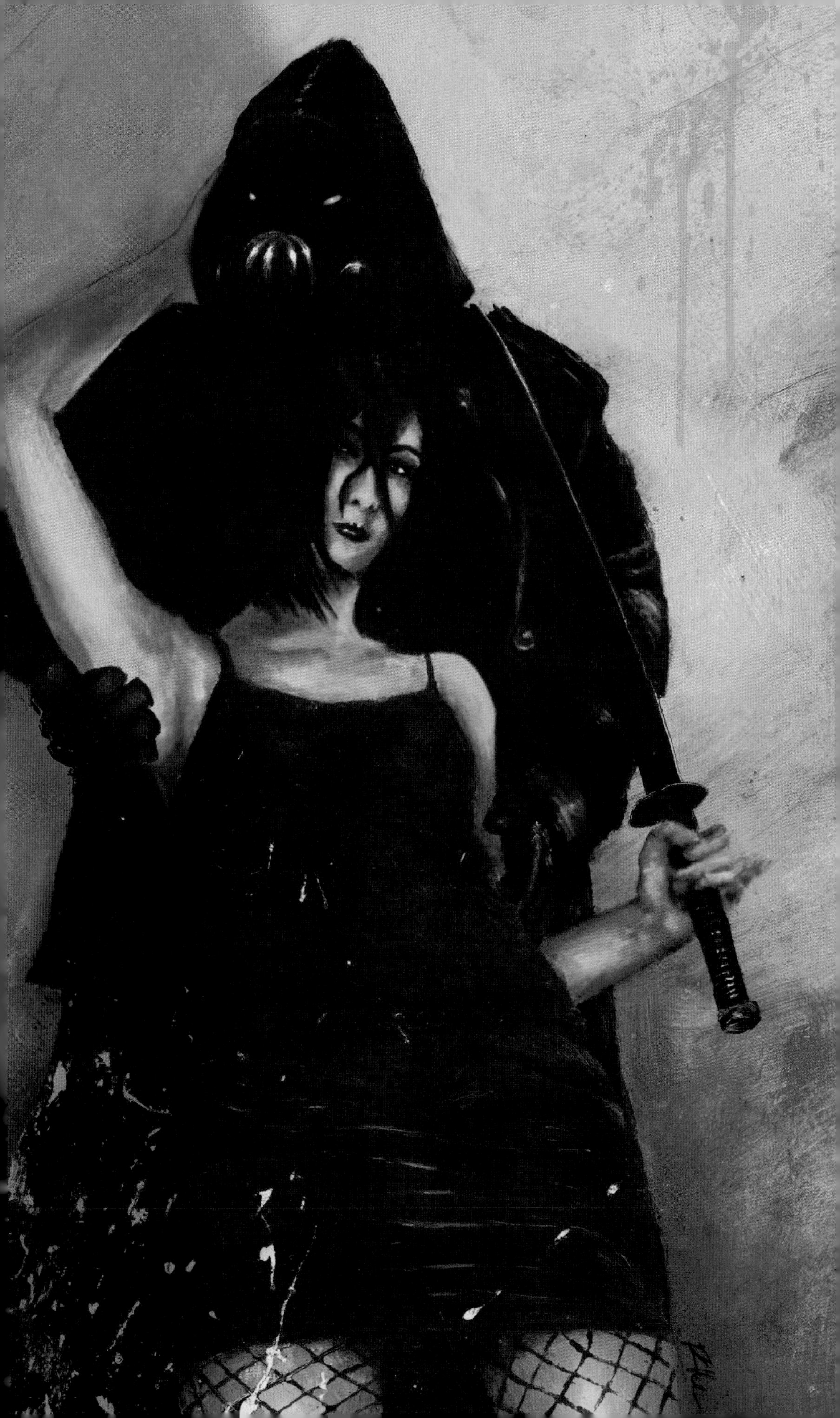

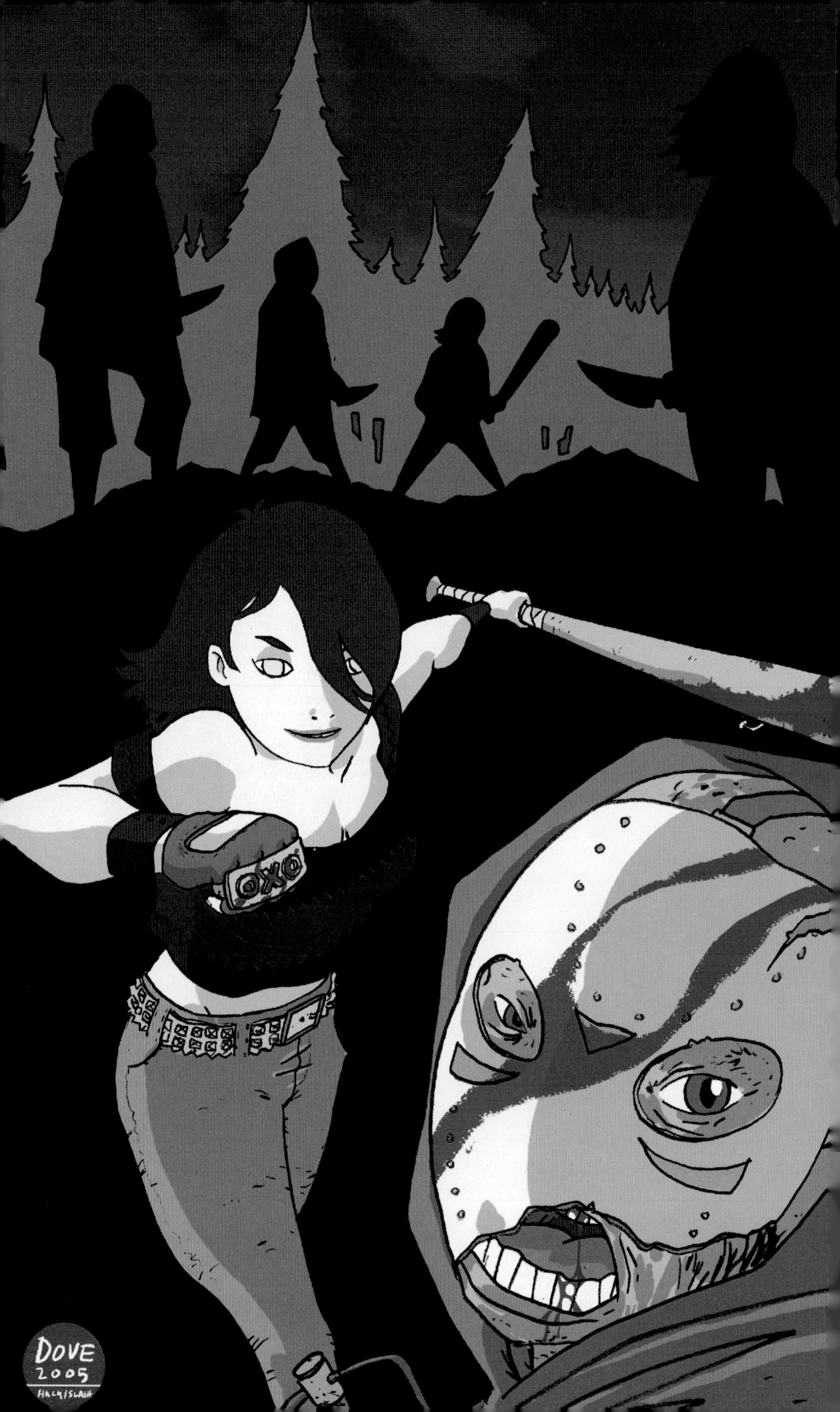
OXO
DOVE
2005
HACK/SLASH

Who will survive

and who will clean up after them?

HACK/SLASH

SKETCHBOOK

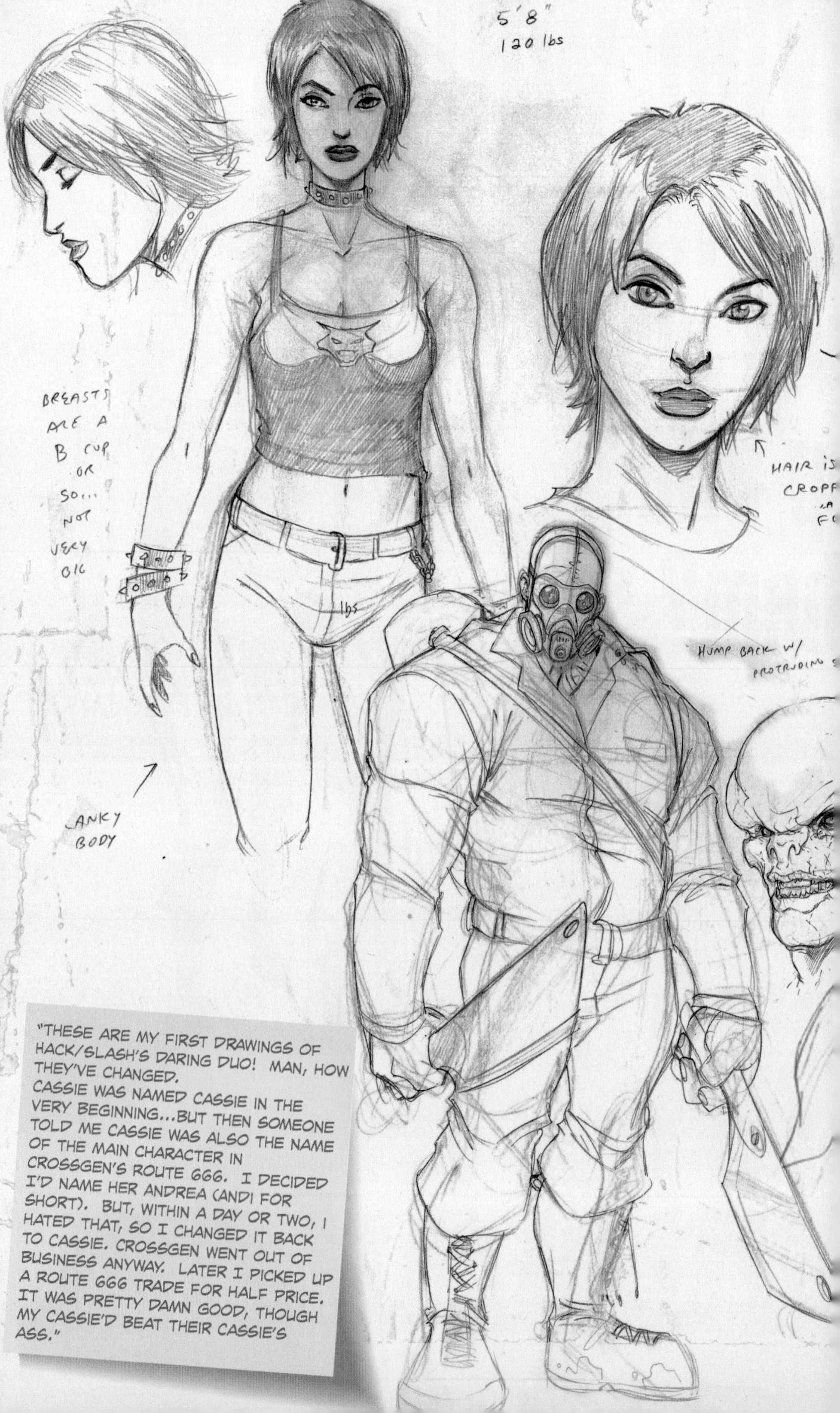
5'8"
120 lbs
BREASTS ARE A B CUP OR SO... NOT VERY BIG
lbs
LANKY BODY
HAIR IS
HUMP BACK W/

"THESE ARE MY FIRST DRAWINGS OF HACK/SLASH'S DARING DUO! MAN, HOW THEY'VE CHANGED.
CASSIE WAS NAMED CASSIE IN THE VERY BEGINNING...BUT THEN SOMEONE TOLD ME CASSIE WAS ALSO THE NAME OF THE MAIN CHARACTER IN CROSSGEN'S ROUTE 666. I DECIDED I'D NAME HER ANDREA (ANDI FOR SHORT). BUT, WITHIN A DAY OR TWO, I HATED THAT, SO I CHANGED IT BACK TO CASSIE. CROSSGEN WENT OUT OF BUSINESS ANYWAY. LATER I PICKED UP A ROUTE 666 TRADE FOR HALF PRICE. IT WAS PRETTY DAMN GOOD, THOUGH MY CASSIE'D BEAT THEIR CASSIE'S ASS."

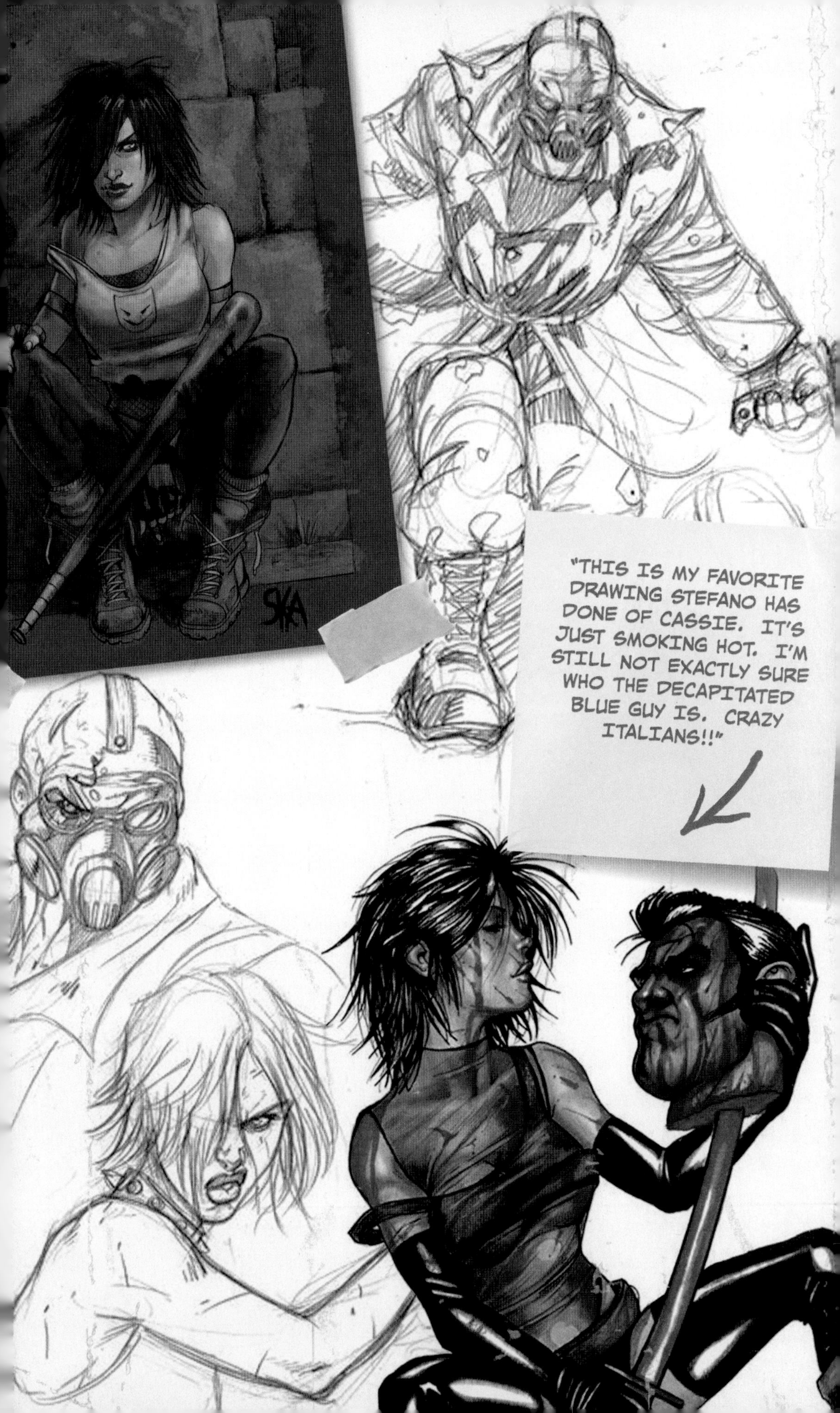
SKA
"THIS IS MY FAVORITE DRAWING STEFANO HAS DONE OF CASSIE. IT'S JUST SMOKING HOT. I'M STILL NOT EXACTLY SURE WHO THE DECAPITATED BLUE GUY IS. CRAZY ITALIANS!!"

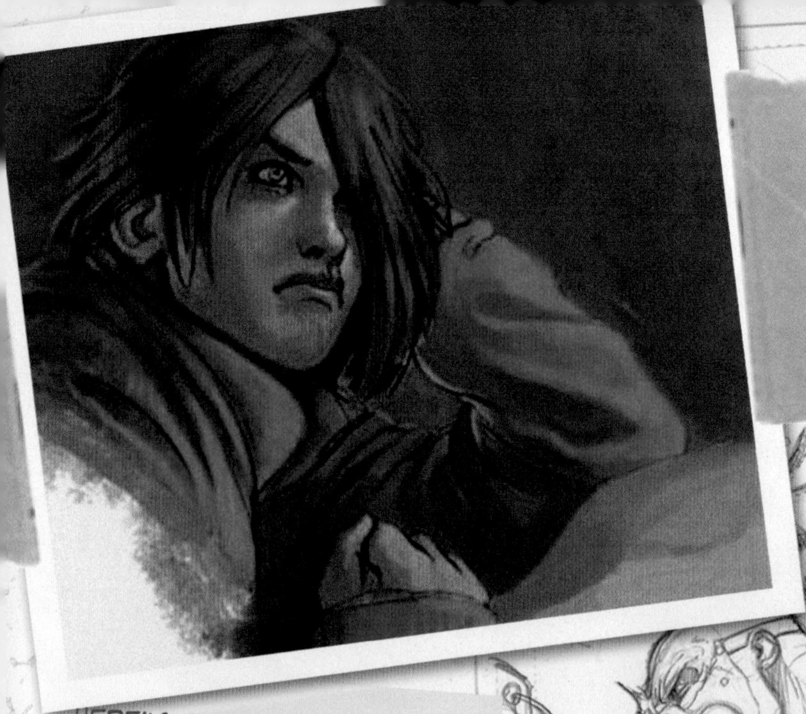

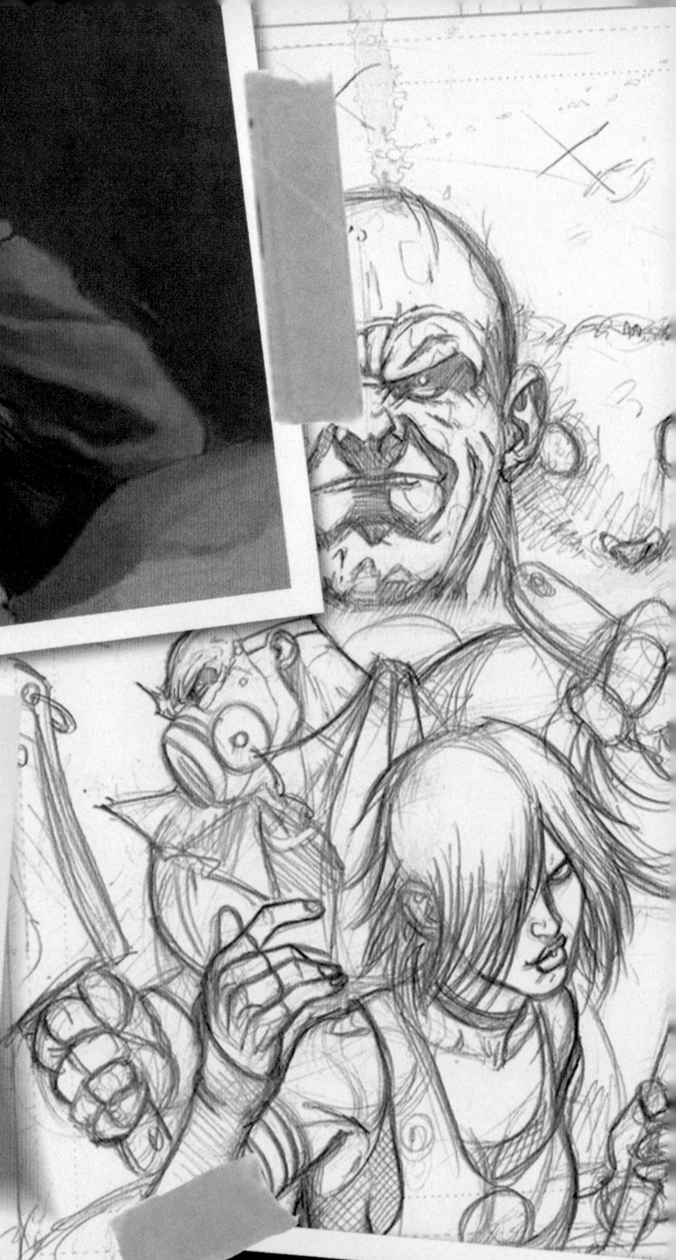

HERE'IS A SKETCH FOR A SLASHER THAT HASEN'T APPEARED YET. HEH, THE RABBIT GIRL WAS ACTUALLY THE ORIGINAL SLASHER IN AN EARLY DRAFT OF"GIRLS GONE DEAD." DANIEL ALTER (MY MOVIE AGENT GUY) AND JOSH BLAYLOCK REALLY HATED THE BUNNY GIRL IDEA. IT JUST GOES TO SHOW YA, FIRST IDEAS AREN'T ALWAYS THE BEST IDEAS! "

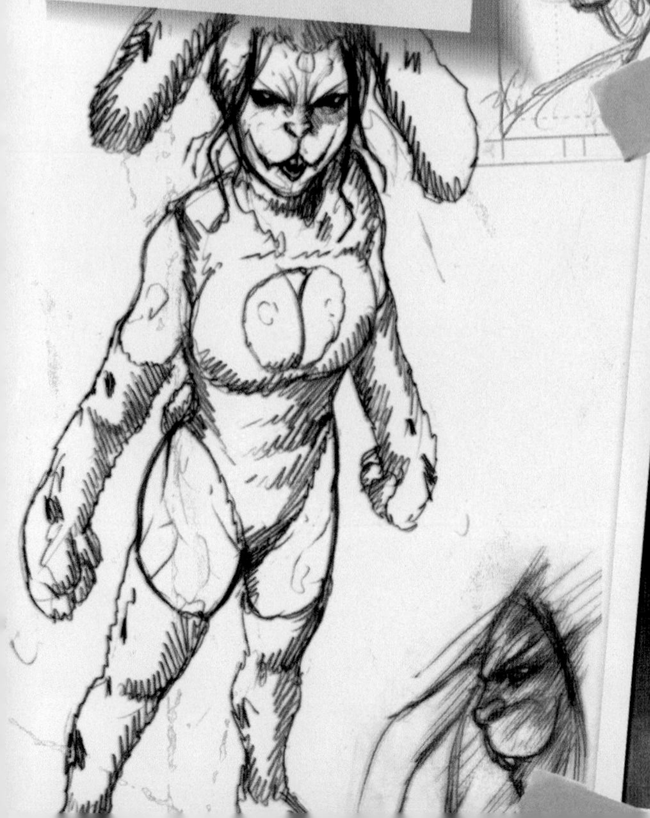

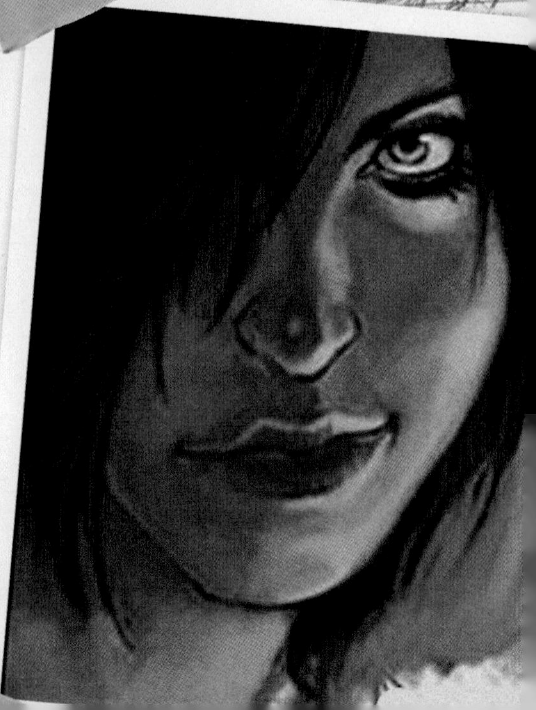

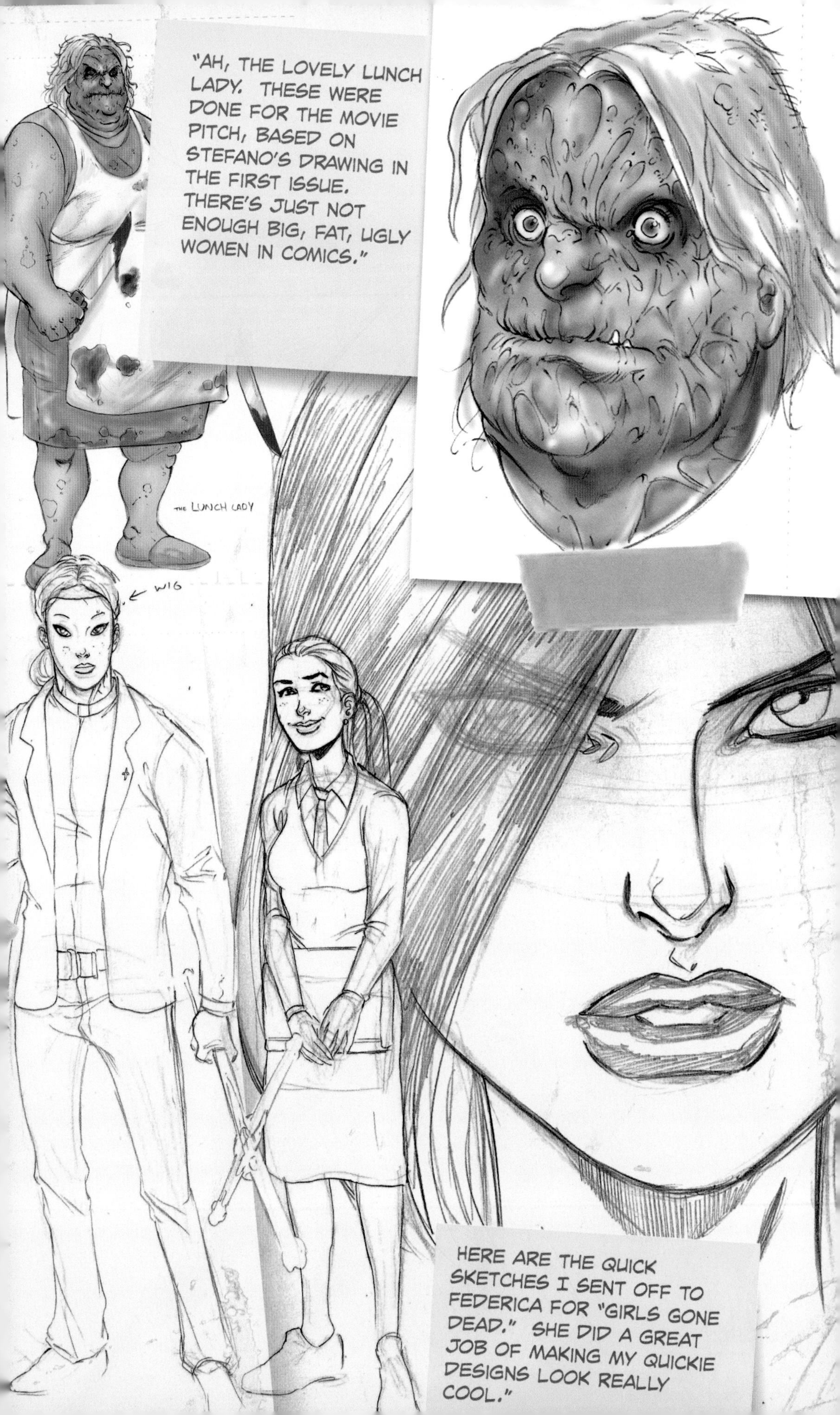
"AH, THE LOVELY LUNCH LADY. THESE WERE DONE FOR THE MOVIE PITCH, BASED ON STEFANO'S DRAWING IN THE FIRST ISSUE. THERE'S JUST NOT ENOUGH BIG, FAT, UGLY WOMEN IN COMICS."
THE LUNCH LADY
WIG
HERE ARE THE QUICK SKETCHES I SENT OFF TO FEDERICA FOR "GIRLS GONE DEAD." SHE DID A GREAT JOB OF MAKING MY QUICKIE DESIGNS LOOK REALLY COOL."

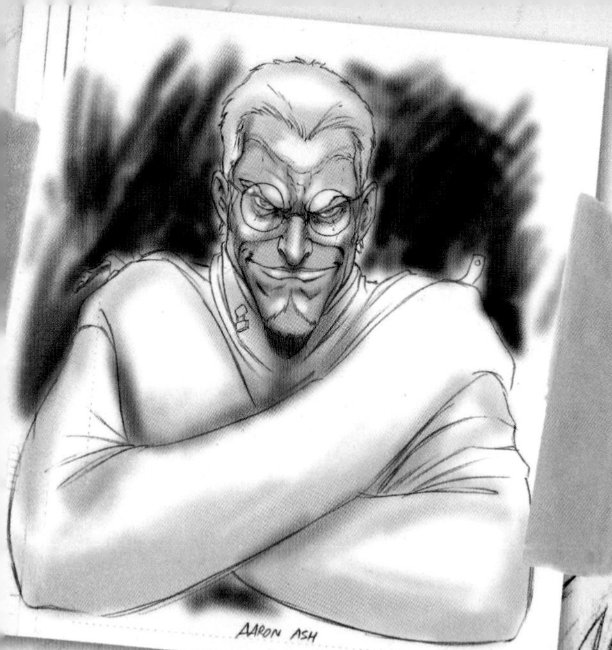
AARON ASH

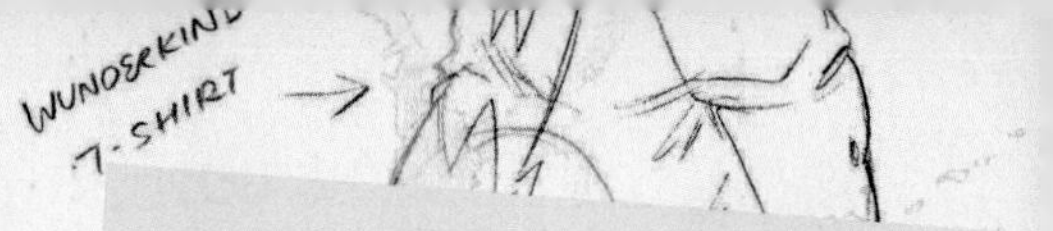
WUNDERKIND
T-SHIRT

"MY ORIGINAL DESIGNS FOR THE GROSSEST SLASHER I'LL EVER COME UP WITH. LOOKING BACK, IT'S KIND OF FUNNY THAT I NEVER THOUGHT "HMM...MAYBE THIS IS JUST A LITTLE TOO DEMENTED.

ALSO, THESE ARE TWO CHARACTERS DONE FOR THE MOVIE PITCH THAT HAVEN'T MADE IT INTO THE COMIC. BY THE TIME THEY MAKE ITINTO THE BOOK, THEY'LL PROBABLY GET A COMPLETE OVERHAUL.""

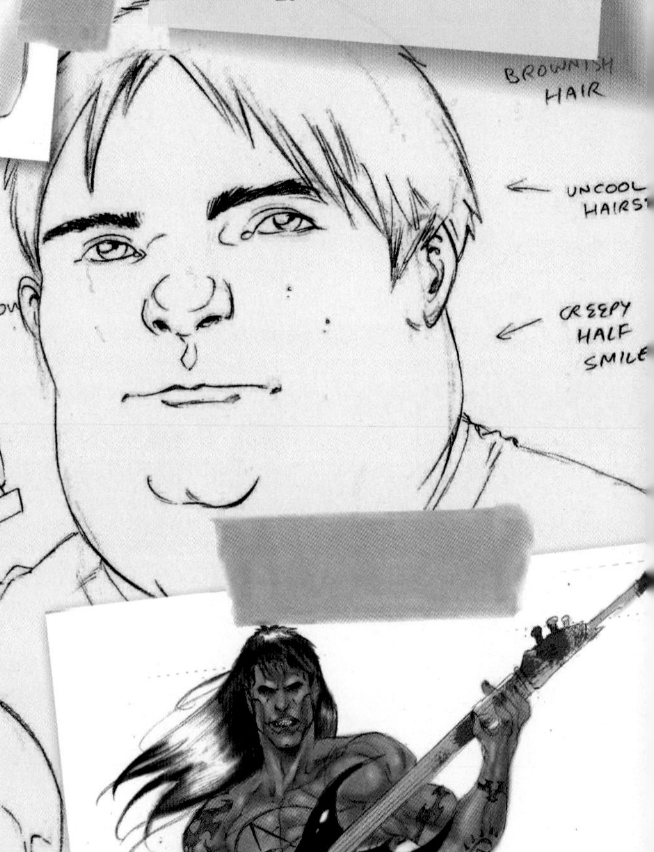
BROWNISH
HAIR
UNCOOL
HAIRS
CREEPY
HALF
SMILE

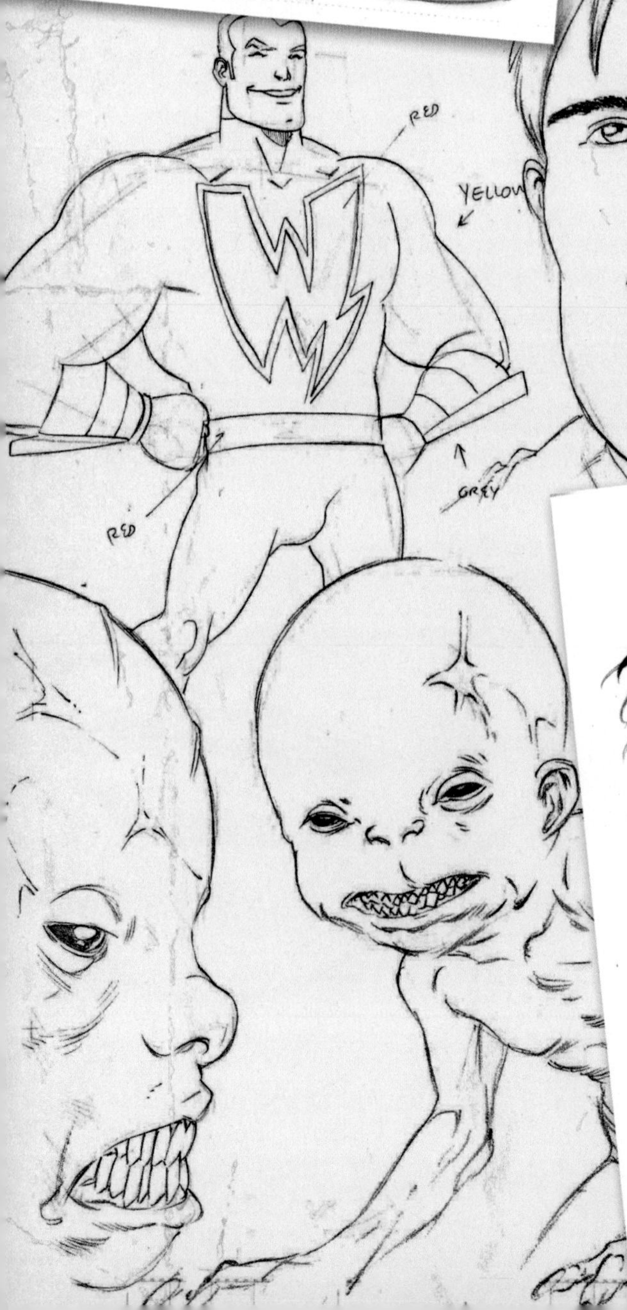
RED
YELLOW
GREY
RED

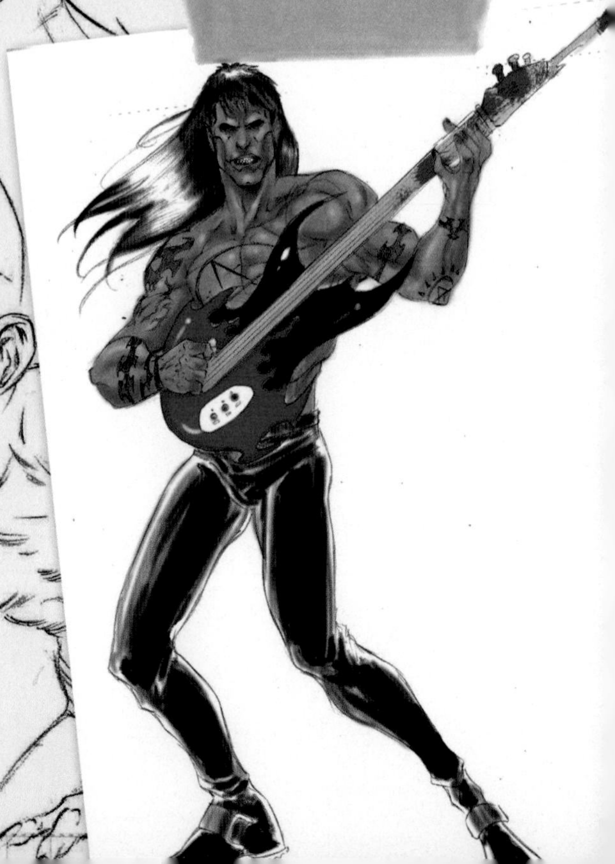

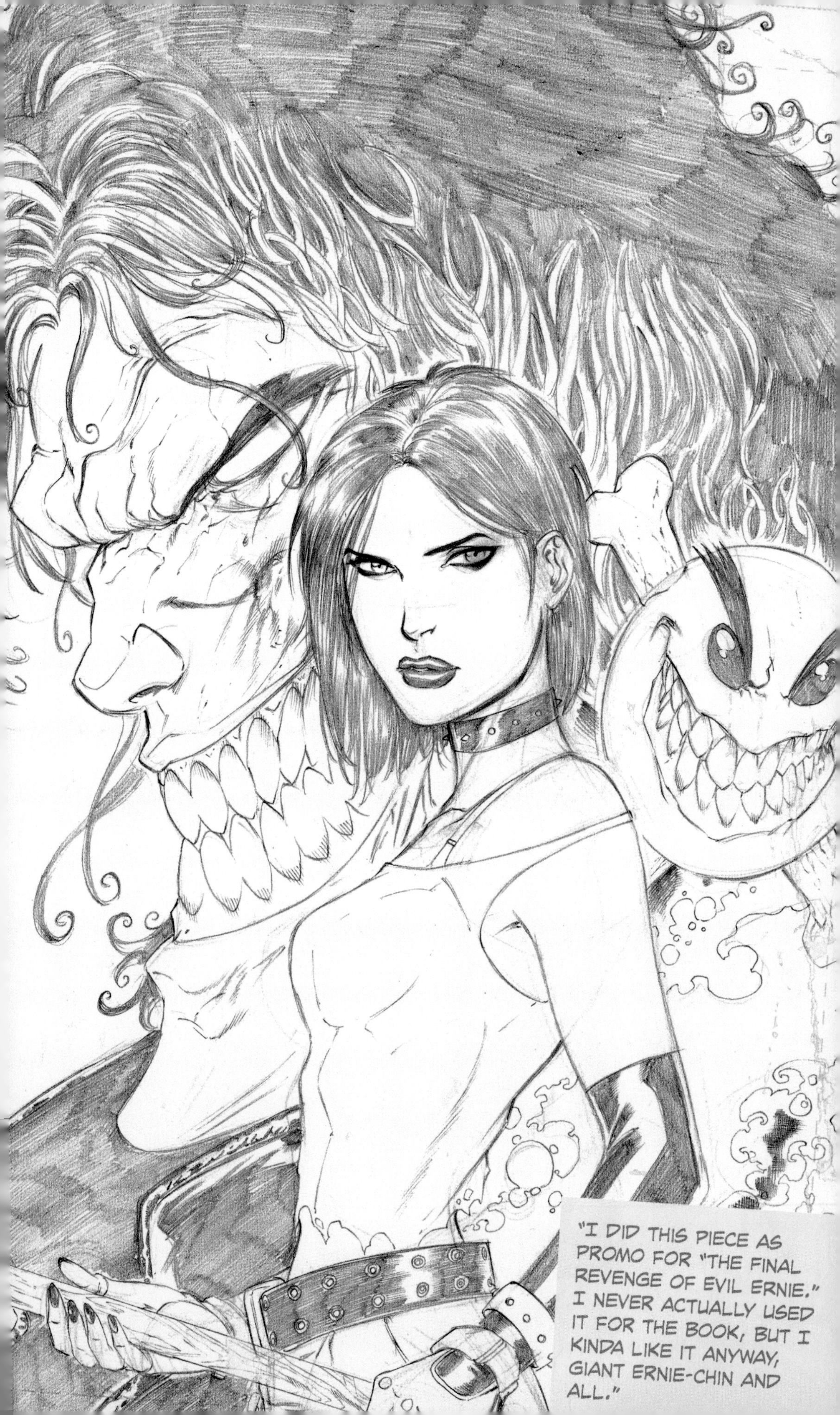

"I DID THIS PIECE AS PROMO FOR "THE FINAL REVENGE OF EVIL ERNIE." I NEVER ACTUALLY USED IT FOR THE BOOK, BUT I KINDA LIKE IT ANYWAY, GIANT ERNIE-CHIN AND ALL."

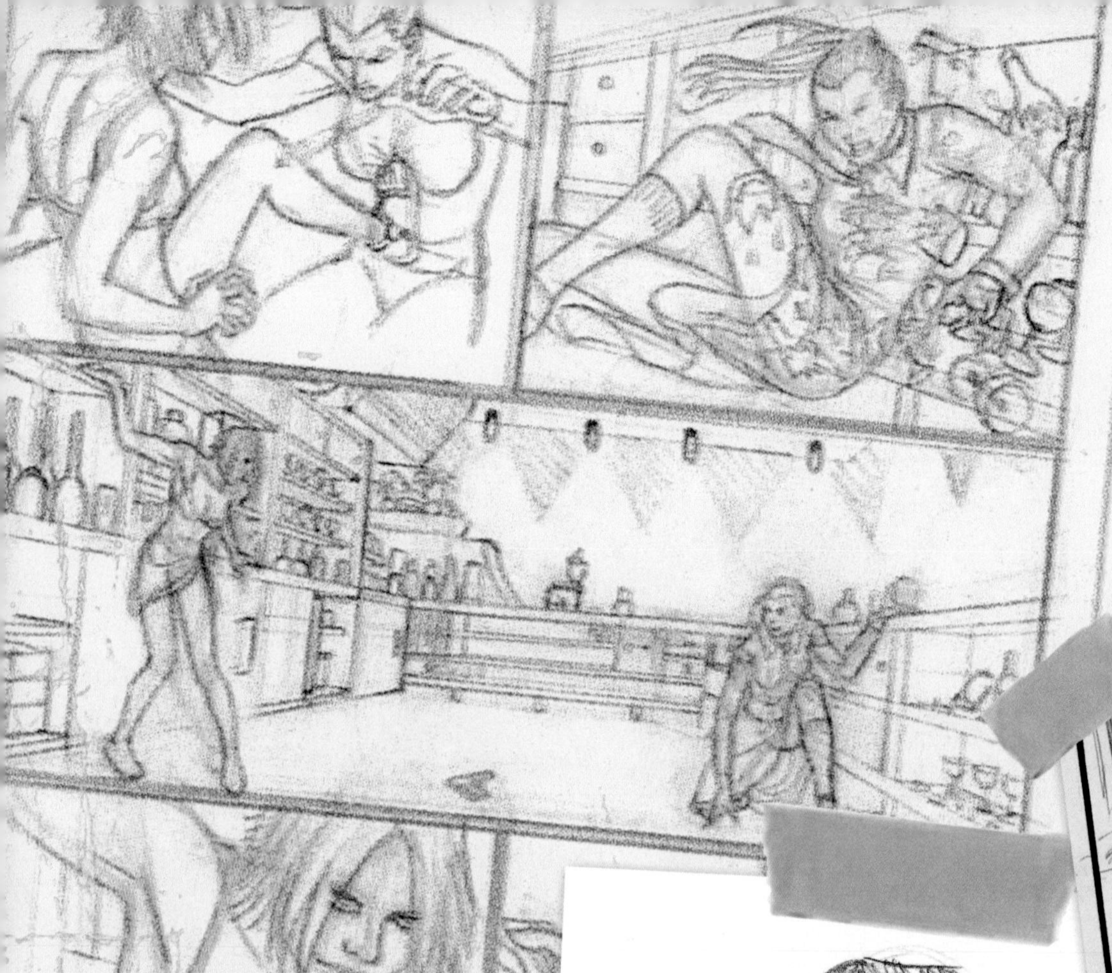

FEDE DID THIS GREAT PIECE FOR AN ITALIAN "FANZINE" CALLED KILLERS. I LOVE THAT CASSIE POSE!"

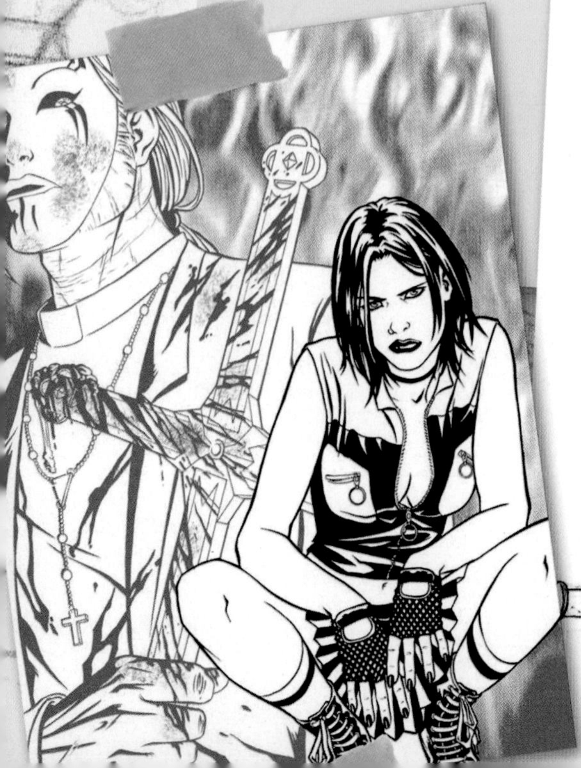

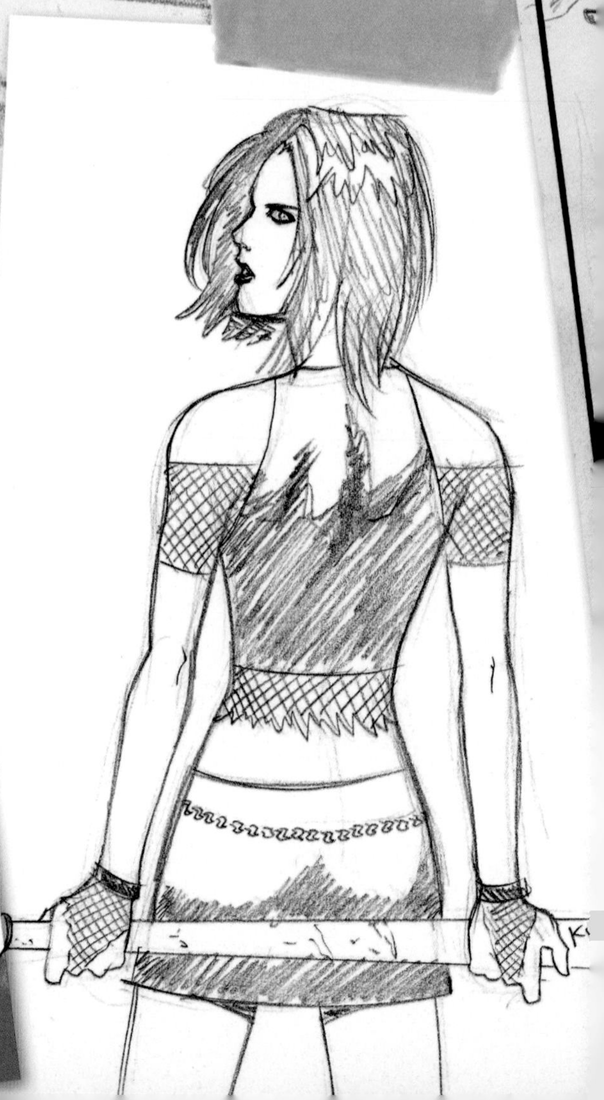

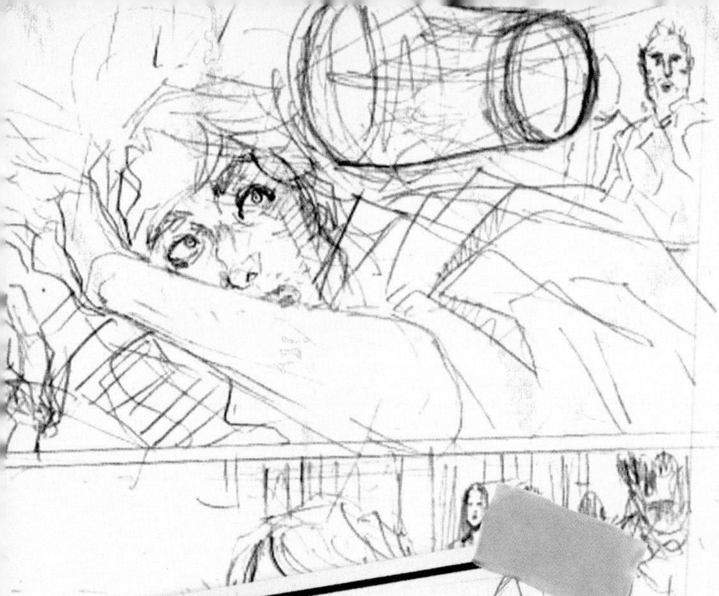

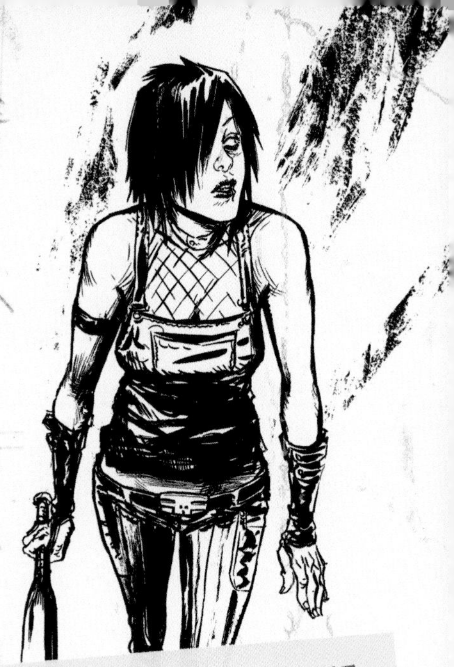

AADI SENT THIS TO SHOW ME THE STYLE HE'D BE USING FOR THE BOOK, AND TO SHOW HIS VERSION OF THE CHARACTERS. I LOVED IT. I HAD HIM CHANGE VLAD'S MASK TO THE FULL-FACE, GOGGLEY ONE."

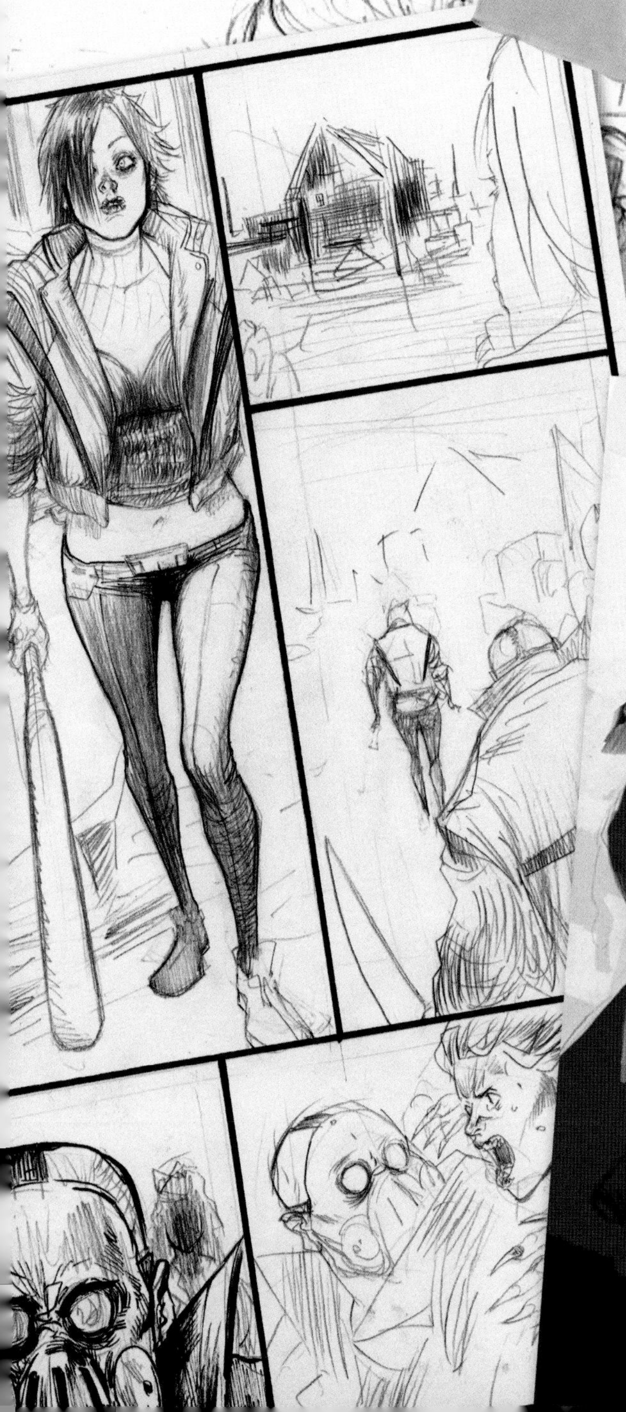

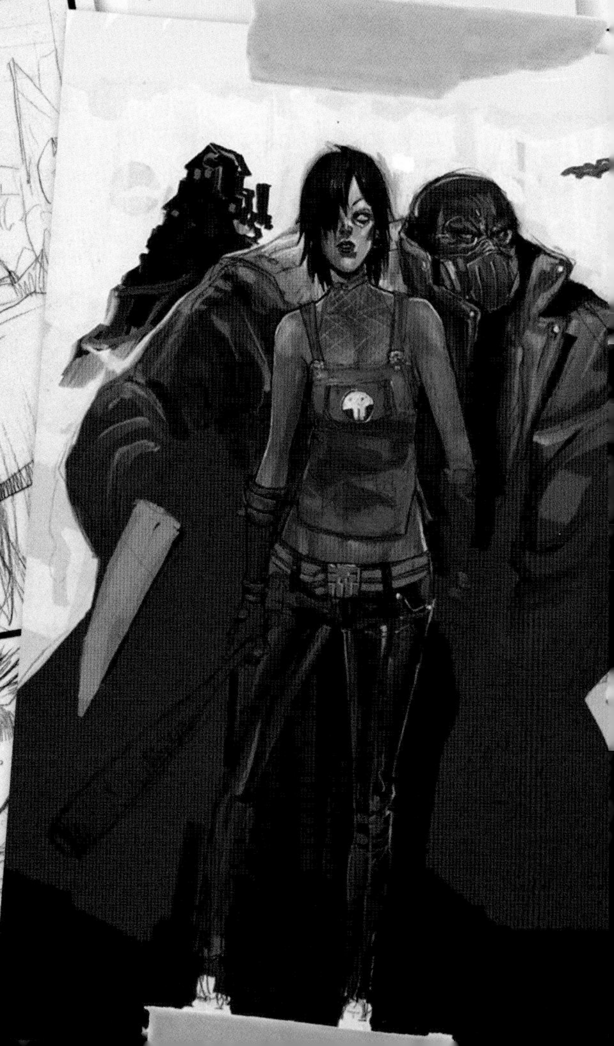

I first met Sandra Kammerer at a convention in 2003. I had an instant crush on her, but, alas, with her being far-away in Florida, and me being a big nerd, we could never date. But, we did keep in touch, and when I came up with the Hack/Slash book, my initial Cassie designs were based on Sanny. We decided to do an alt. over for GGD, so I had Crank! use photos of Sandra modeling as Cassie. It turned out bad-ass.. here's some of the other photos, that are just too hot to go to waste....

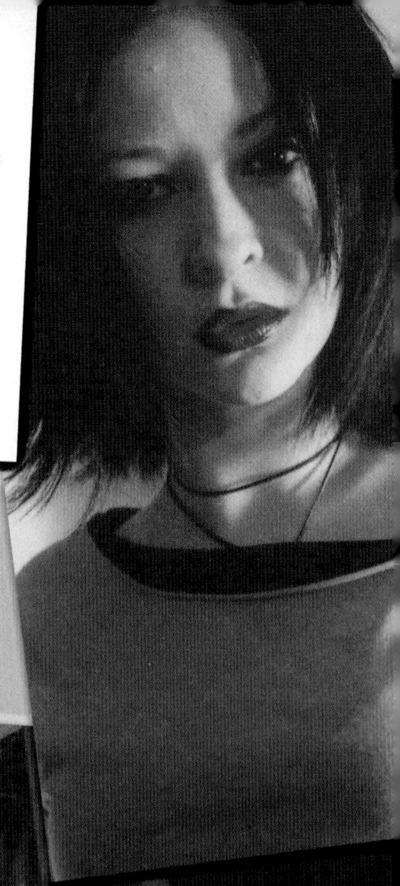

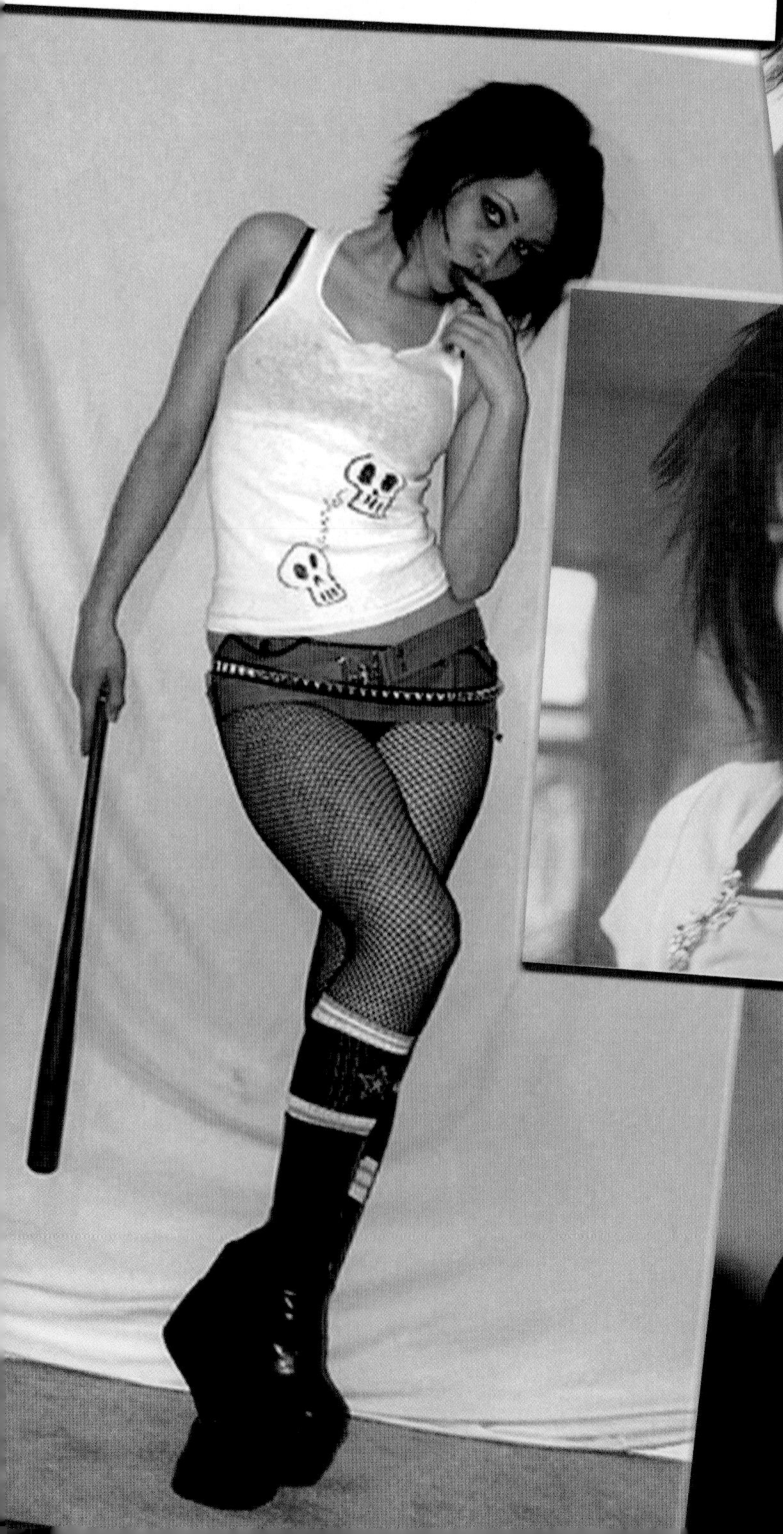

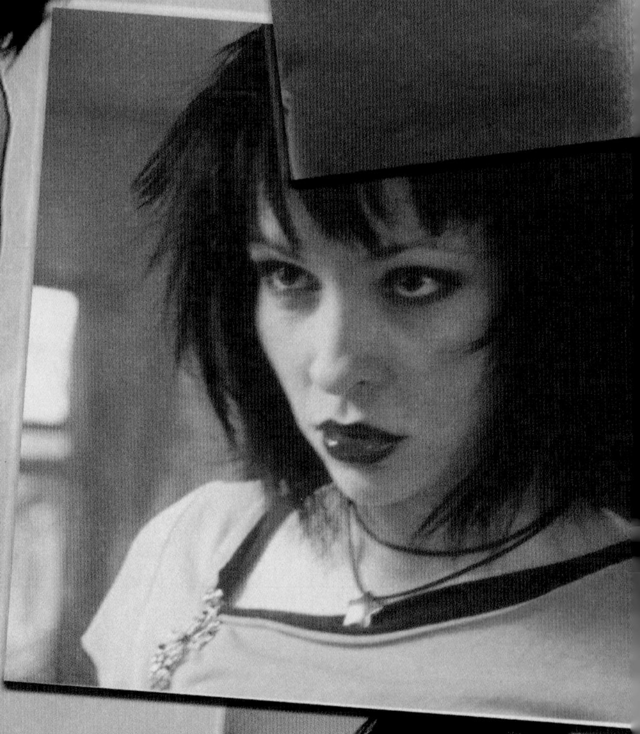

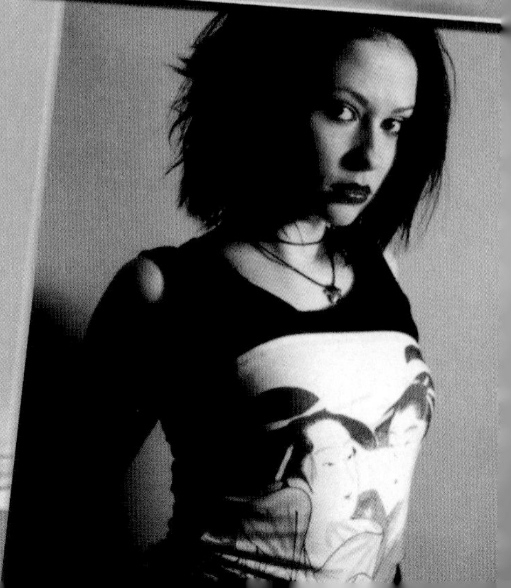

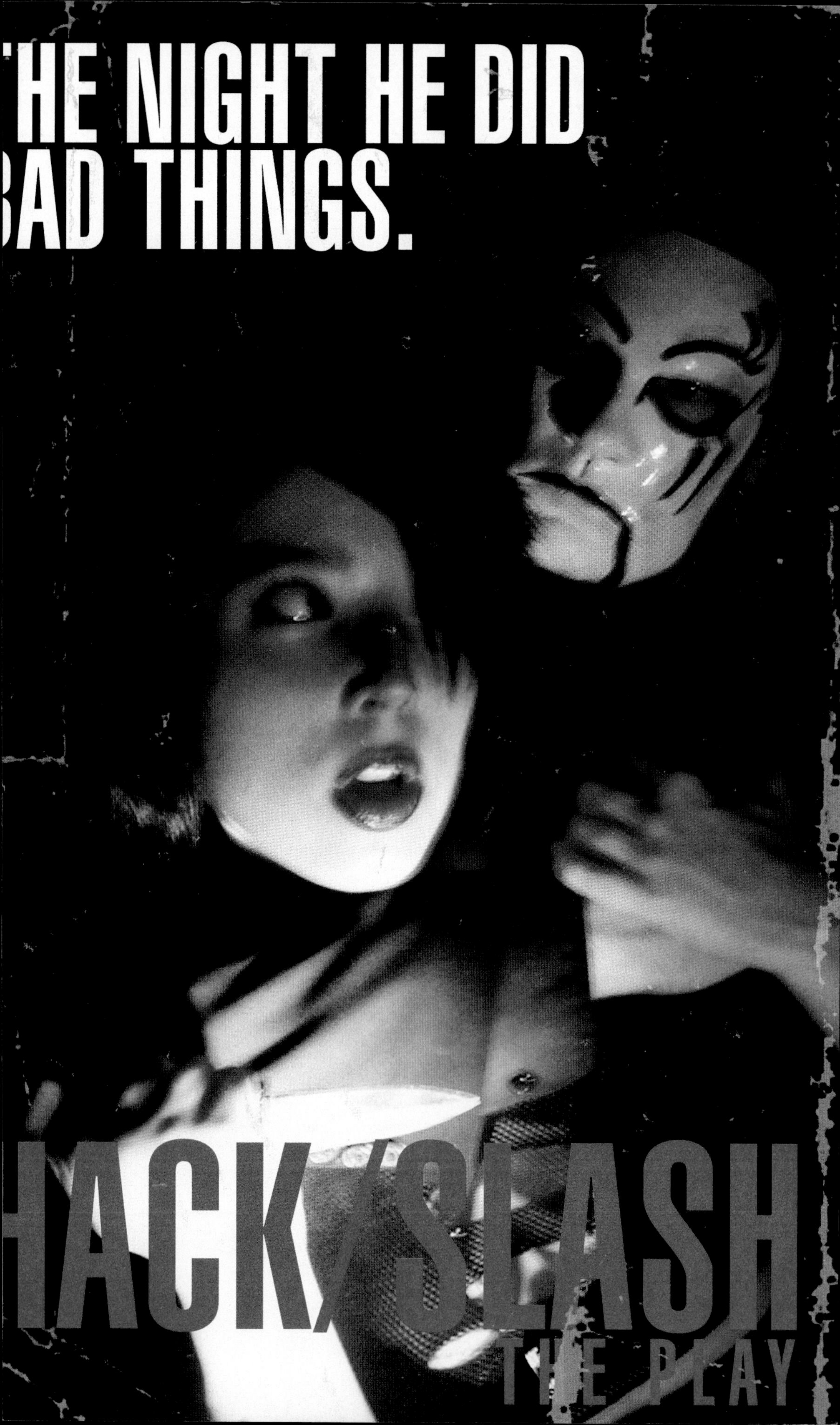
HE NIGHT HE DID
AD THINGS.
ACK/SLASH
THE PLAY

IN 2005, HACK/SLASH BECAME A PLAY, PERFORMED BY THE NEW MILLENNIUM THEATRE COMPANY (WWW.NMTCHICAGO.ORG). AUDIENCES DELIGHTED TO THE LIVE ANTICS OF VLAD, CASSIE, AND HALF-CLOTHED CO-EDS, AS WELL AS GOUTS OF GOOD OL' FASHIONED STAGE BLOOD.

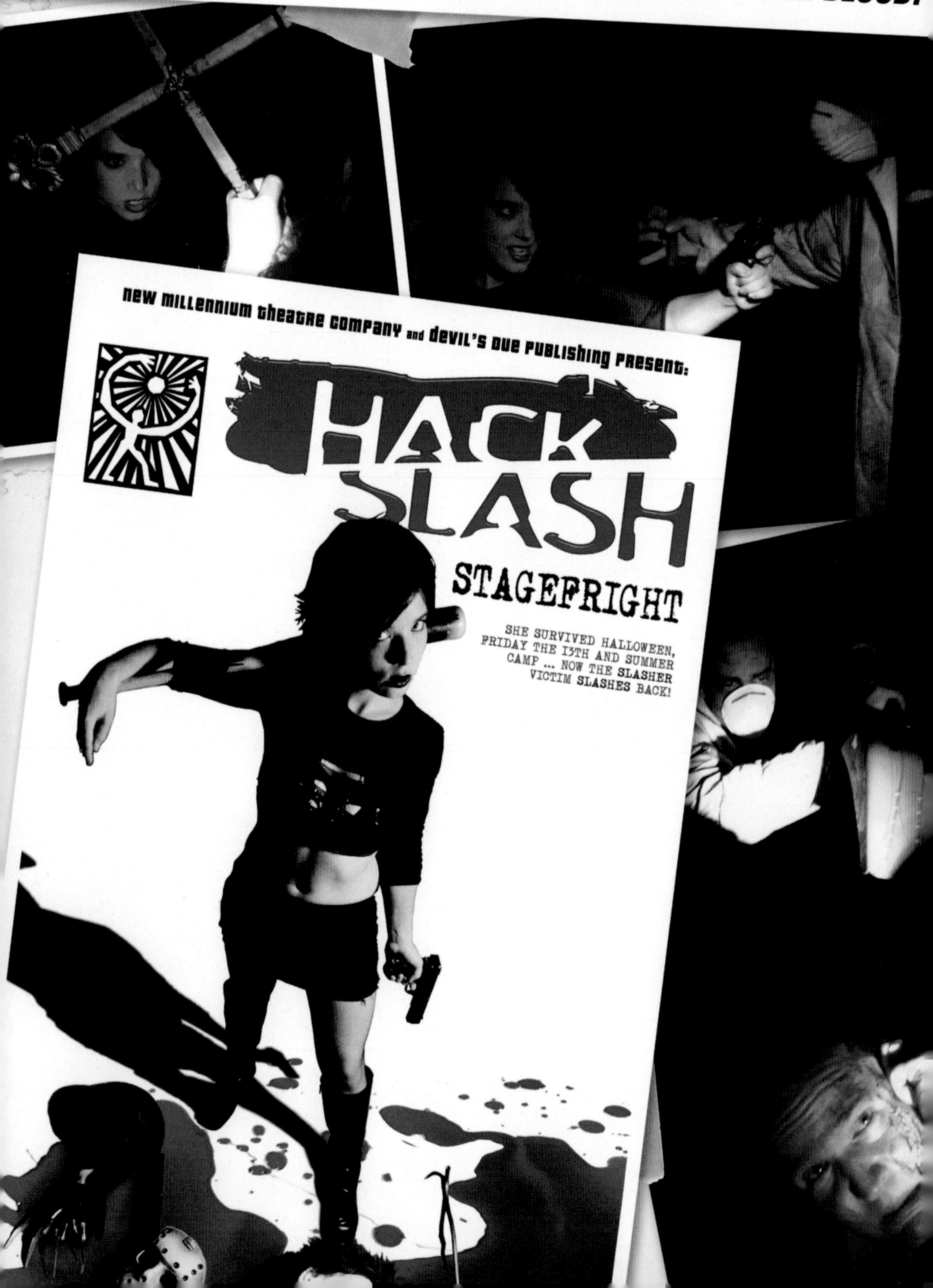
new millennium theatre company and devil's due publishing present:
HACK SLASH
STAGEFRIGHT
SHE SURVIVED HALLOWEEN, FRIDAY THE 13TH AND SUMMER CAMP ... NOW THE SLASHER VICTIM SLASHES BACK!

CAST:

CASSIE HACK: STEFANI BISHOP
VLAD: ADAM MACK
TODD/JOSH: DON ALSAFI
KYLE/ANNOUNCER/ROD: GUY SCHINGOETHE
LISA/MISSY: JENNA SCHMIDT
DANA/CHRISSY: ELLEN DOMONOKOS
JESS/MELANIE/SISSY: JENNY MYERS
DAN/MATT/NERD 2/NELSON: MATT RUSSELL
SHERIFF/FATHER WRATH: JASON BONE
LAURA LOCKE/WAITRESS: GINA FERENZI
BOBBY BRUNSWICK/NERD 1/PEPE: PAUL CZARNOWSKI

INTERVIEW WITH DIRECTOR CHAD WISE

QUICK, CHAD! FAVORITE SLASHER MOVIE?!
SCREAM. DEFINITELY. SURE ITS UNIQUENESS HAS BEEN REDUCED BY THE ONSLAUGHT OF PALE IMITATIONS (EVEN WITHIN ITS OWN SERIES) BUT THE ORIGINAL WAS JUST A HIP NEW WAY TO BE SCARED.

WHY HACK/SLASH: THE PLAY? SHOULDN'T YOU BE DOING WEST SIDE STORY OR GLASS MENAGERIE?
I PROBABLY SHOULD. MY COLLEGE THEATRE PROFESSORS PROBABLY THINK I SHOULD. BUT WHERE'S THE FUN IN DOING WHAT YOU 'SHOULD' ALL THE TIME? THIS REALLY ISN'T NEW GROUND FOR ME. YOU WON'T FIND ANYTHING ON MY RESUME YOU WERE FORCED TO READ IN HIGH SCHOOL. YOU WILL FIND THINGS LIKE 'MIYAGI! A KARATE KID MUSICAL', 'I KNOW WHAT YOU DID LAST SHERMER' AND 'EVIL DEAD! THE MUSICAL'. HACK/SLASH IS JUST THE NATURAL PROGRESSION.

WHAT'S YOUR THEATRE CREDS?
I HAVE A DEGREE IN THEATRE EDUCATION WHICH I'VE NEVER DIRECTLY USED (THERE'S NO WAY I COULD HAVE DONE 'EVIL DEAD!' IN A HIGH SCHOOL). SO I STARTED A THEATRE COMPANY WHERE I COULD PRODUCE THE KINDS OF SHOWS I WOULD WANT TO SEE. SEVEN YEARS AND (ONLY) ONE THREAT OF LITIGATION LATER, HERE I AM.

WHAT'S THE GOAL OF THE NEW MILLENNIUM THEATRE COMPANY? ARE THESE GOALS SIMILAR TO THOSE OF NOMI (ELIZABETH BERKLEY) IN SHOWGIRLS?
NOMI MALONE HAD A DREAM. TO BE IN THE BIG SHOW. TO BE APPRECIATED FOR HER TALENTS REGARDLESS OF HER LESS THAN STELLAR ORIGINS.

NMTC IS THE SAME IN A LOT OF WAYS. WE STARTED WITH NOTHING (THE $900 I MOVED TO CHICAGO WITH) AND HAVE SUPPORTED OURSELVES FROM TICKET SALES ALONE FOR SEVEN YEARS. WE ARE, TO SOME EXTENT, LOOKED DOWN UPON BY THE 'LEGTIMATE' THEATER COMMUNITY THAT THINKS A PLAY CAN'T BE GOOD UNLESS AT LEAST ONE CHARACTER'S LIFE IS RADICALLY ALTERED TO THE POINT THAT THEY END UP CRYING ON THE FLOOR IN THE FETAL POSITION. WE, TOO, RELUCTANTLY ICE OUR NIPPLES.

OUR GOAL, FIRST AND FOREMOST (LIKE NOMI) IS TO ENTERTAIN, BE THE BEST WE CAN POSSIBLY BE AT WHAT WE DO AND HAVE A GREAT TIME DOING IT. AND IF, BY DOING MORE POP-CULTURE BASED, NON-TRADITIONAL SHOWS, WE CAN GET PEOPLE OUT TO EXPE-RIENCE LIVE THEATRE WHO HAVEN'T SEEN A PLAY SINCE THEY WERE FORCED TO IN HIGH SCHOOL, THEN MAYBE MY EDUCATION DEGREE WASN'T JUST A RUSE TO KEEP ME IN COLLEGE FOR 6.5 YEARS AFTER ALL.

AND WE TOO STRUGGLE TO ESCAPE FROM ROBERT DAVI'S OPPRESSIVE HOLD ON OUR LIVES.

WHAT'S THE SIMILARITIES OF THEATRE AND COMIC BOOKS? DIFFERENCES? CAN THEY MEET IN THE MIDDLE?
BOTH MEDIUMS, AT THEIR CORE, ARE VISUAL STORYTELLING VEHICLES. SEELEY'S COMIC BOOK SCRIPTS ARE VERY SIMILAR TO A STAGE SCRIPT OR SCREENPLAY (EXCEPT FOR THE PRISON-G.E.D. GRAMMAR AND OVERUSE OF THE WORD 'LIL'). AND FEDERICA & SUNDER COULD BE CALLED THE DIRECTORS. THE DIFFERENCE COMES IN THE UNPREDICTABILITY OF THE LIVE THEATRE EXPERIENCE. YOU KNOW THAT EVERY TIME YOU OPEN UP 'WATCHMEN' YOU'RE GONNA FIND THE SAME ART AND THE SAME DIALOGUE. SURE, YOU MAY DISCOVER ASPECTS OR JOKES YOU NEVER CAUGHT BEFORE... BUT THEY WERE THERE. NO TWO PERFORMANCES OF 'EVIL DEAD! THE MUSICAL' WERE EXACTLY THE SAME. THAT'S THE EXCITEMENT, THE EXHILARATION OF WATCHING LIVE THEATRE. ANYTHING CAN HAPPEN.

AND ITS THAT KIND OF EXCITEMENT THAT WE'RE GONNA BRING TO HACK/ SLASH. I MEAN, COME ON. TWO BIG, MONSTROUS DUDES FIGHTING WITH OVERSIZED MEAT CLEAVERS AND A GIANT METAL CROSS? YOU JUST KNOW SOMETHING EXCITING'S BOUND TO HAPPEN...

THE LUNCH LADY

Real name: Delilah Hack
Death by: Hot gravy
Pre-Slasher Occupation: School Cafeteria chef/server
Slasher type: Vengeful Ghoul/Psycho Mommy

Special Abilities: resistant to pain and damage.

Slasher weapon: Kitchen knife, various pots, pans, blenders and other implements.

Body Count: 11

The story: Delilah Hack was always eccentric, but after the birth of her daughter, her bizarre behavior accelerated until her strange emotional fits drove her husband to leave them. Left to the task of raising Cassie, alone, Delilah became very protective of the young girl. Observing her daughter's school hardships from her job as the school lunch lady, she eventually began to eliminate students she felt treated her daughter unfairly. After murdering them, she disposed of their bodies by introducing a new "mystery" meat to the school lunch menu. She was eventually discovered, but killed herself by stuffing her head into a pot of boiling gravy. But, Delilah eventually came back, choosing to continue her undying murder spree at Cassie's new all-girl's school. A scarred and terrifying monster, Mrs. Hack was eventually destroyed by her own daughter.

Cassie's N~~~~

~~WHAT DO YOU WRITE ABOUT THE PERSON WHO FUCKED UP YOUR WHOLE LIFE? WHERE DO I START? WITHOUT YOU, MOM,~~ ~~TYPICAL AMERICAN TEENAGER, I'D BE~~ ~~DRINKING, SMOKING,~~ ~~AND TAKING PICS FOR~~ ~~GIRLS.COM,~~ EXPLOITING MY... ~~OCY...~~
-CASSIE

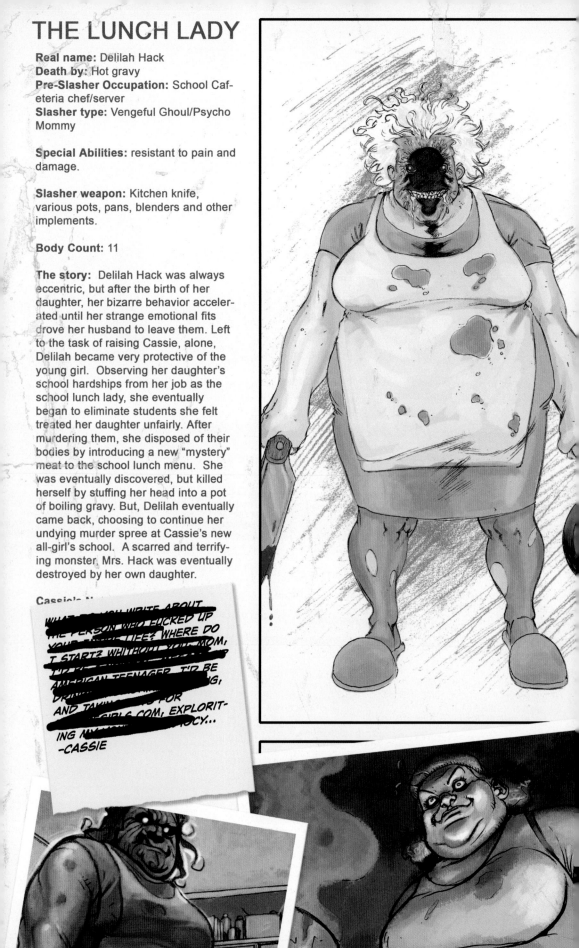

OBBY

l Name: Robert "Bobby" Brunswick
th by: Poison gas
-Slasher Occupation: Veterinary istant
sher type: Vengeful Ghoul

ecial abilities:
by can reanimate dead animals, ch obey his command. He is also newhat impervious to damage, ugh the always handy "zombie d shot" put him down.

sher weapon: Shovel

dy Count: 5

story: Bobby Brunswick was a et, mentally handicapped child loved his job working at the local nal shelter, euthanizing unwanted s. He had great affection for the ner and veterinarian of the clinic, a Elsten. The head nurse, and a's boyfriend, Kyle Raymond disap-ved of this affection and constantly gered Bobby with remarks and de jokes. One day, a prank went far, and Bobby was gassed and d. When Bobby returned as a sher, he had the ability to control undead animals he had once "put leep." Now a relentless killer king justice, Bobby stalked the n until stopped by Cassie & Vlad.

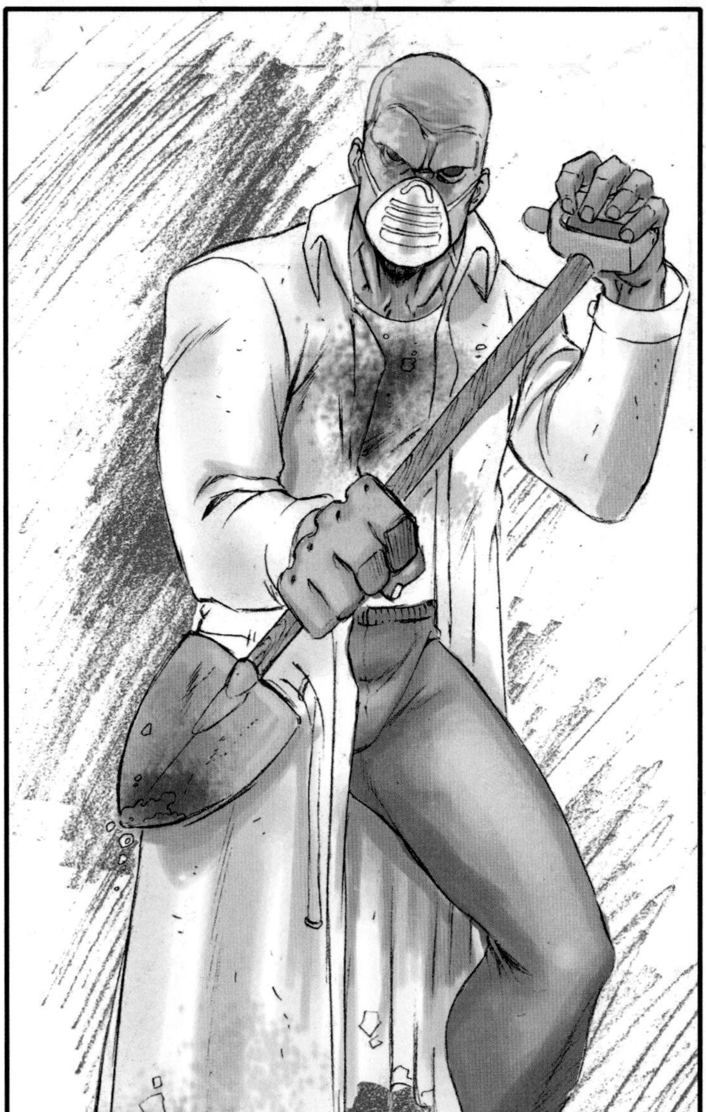

OOR BOBBY. USUALLY I
N'T HAVE MUCH SYMPATHY
R SLASHERS, BUT THIS WAS
PRETTY SAD CASE. IT JUST
LWAYS AMAZES ME HOW
RUEL PEOPLE CAN BE TOO
ACH OTHER. BOBBY WAS AN
NNOCENT CAUGHT UP IN THE
RUELTY AND INSECURITIES OF
OTHERS. ON THE OTHER HAND,
I WAS CLEANING DEAD CAT
GUTS OUT OF MY CLOTHES
FOR WEEKS, SO I CAN'T BE
TOO SYMPATHETIC"
-CASSIE

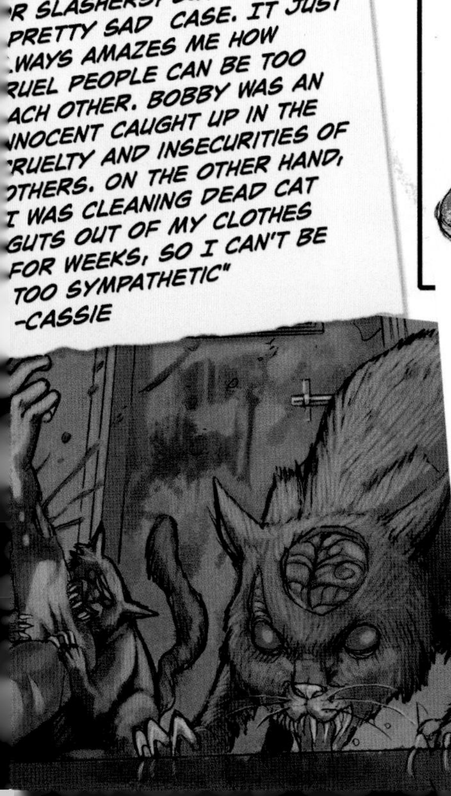

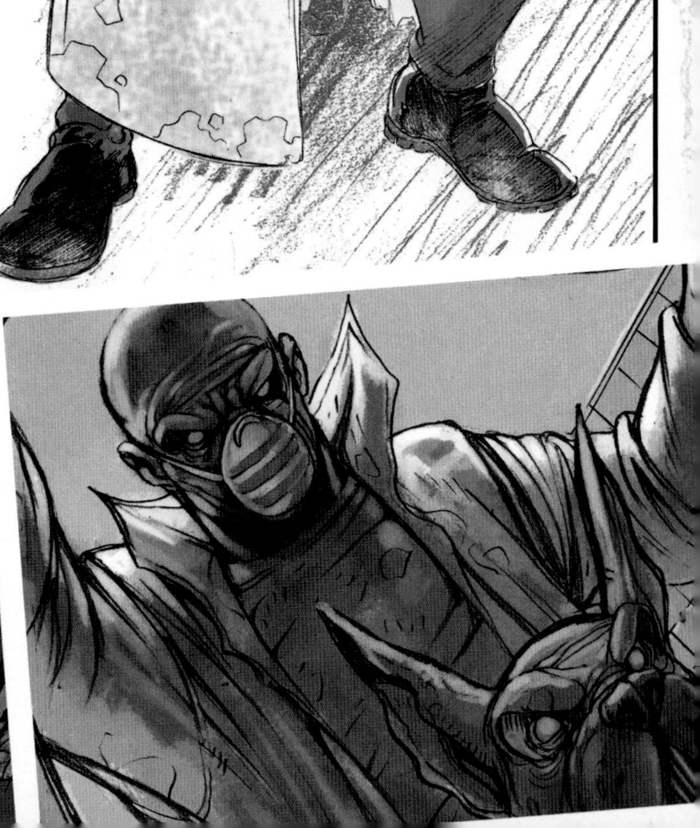

LAURA & FATHER WRATH

real names: Laura Lochs / Niles Rafferty
Death by: N/A / Bludgeoned with cross
Pre-slasher Occupation: Student & Cheerleader / Traveling Preacher
Slasher type: Scorned woman / Vengeful Ghoul

Special Abilities: Laura has no inherent powers, though she is fairly adept at the use of her arcane spell book, and has several spells memorized, allowing her control of Father Wrath.
Father Wrath is resistant to pain and damage.

Slasher Weapon: Big Ass Cross

Body Count: 12

The story: Laura Lochs was a student at an all-girls school in southern Georgia. Her boyfriend, Jeremy, attended a nearby school, and they dated for three years. During his spring break trip to Panama City Beach, a drunken Jeremy cheated on his girlfriend with a girl who had just won a wet t-shirt contest. Out of guilt, and looking or a reason to break up with her, Jeremy revealed his indiscretion to Laura. Distraught, Laura threw herself into her studies, spending hours at the school library. One night, she discovered an ancient book, which contained evil spells. The book corrupted Laura's already fragile psyche and she became determined to get revenge on cheating men and the women she blamed for them doing so. Using the book, Laura located the murderous Father Wrath, killing Bible students in rural Tennessee, and they traveled to Florida to make an example of the spring breakers there.

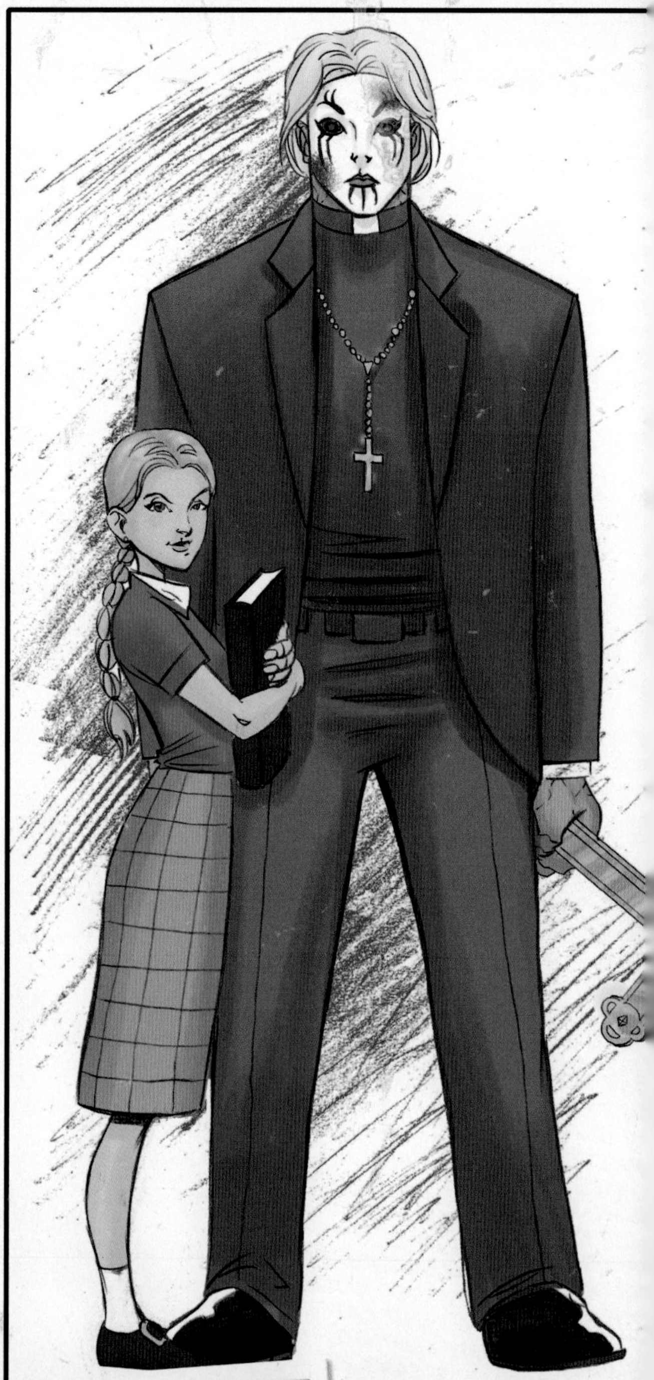

Cassie's Notes from The Sl

"LAURA LOCHS WAS THE KIND OF CHICK I HATED IN HIGH SCHOOL. WELL-OFF, PRETTY, SNOTTY.TURNS OUT, I HATE THAT KINDA CHICK EVEN MORE WHEN THEY COMMAND UNDEAD PRIESTS AND TRY TO SHOOT ME. MAYBE WORST OF ALL, HER PAIN MADE HER ALMOST...RELATABLE. KINDA SCARY THAT IT TOOK LOONY LAURA TO MAKE ME RELATE TO GIRLS LIKE THAT..."
-CASSIE

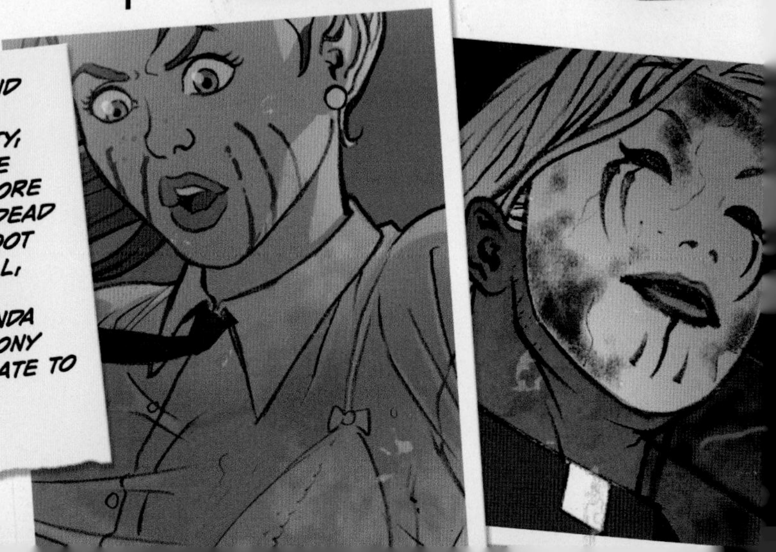

.OYD & JIMMY

l names: Lloyd and Jimmy dermann
th by: N/A
-slasher occupation: Lloyd ked as a short order cook. my operated v.wunderkindfansunite.org, and known on message boards as ndertwin103."
sher type: Obsessive Nut job, er Freak

ecial abilities: Jimmy and Lloyd e are a very rare from of a para- twins known as "fetus in fetus." my never developed and main- ed his fetus size, though he could ve and re-enter Lloyd's body never he wanted.

sher Weapon: Blow gun, knives.

dy Count: 4

story: Lloyd Sundermann was ays a strange child. He preferred e alone, where he could read his ic books, most notably, his favorite nderkind. But, little did anyone w, Lloyd was not alone. Lloyd was with his twin brother inside him, a that even Lloyd's mother was ware of. Jimmy, Lloyd's brother, an speaking to Lloyd while he was in Lloyd's body. Hyper-intelligent, underdeveloped, Jimmy stayed in Lloyd until they were 11 years Lloyd's mother gave birth to their er. Enraged at the attention given is new child, Jimmy convinced d to kill the baby. At first, horrified is action, Lloyd cut himself open eventually tried to remove Jimmy. two reconciled, and realized they ded each other. The two felt a cial kinship over their mutual love Wunderkind, a comic book they d relate to, since it featured a ng boy who could become a grown . They hoped to one day be as d and admired as their childhood).

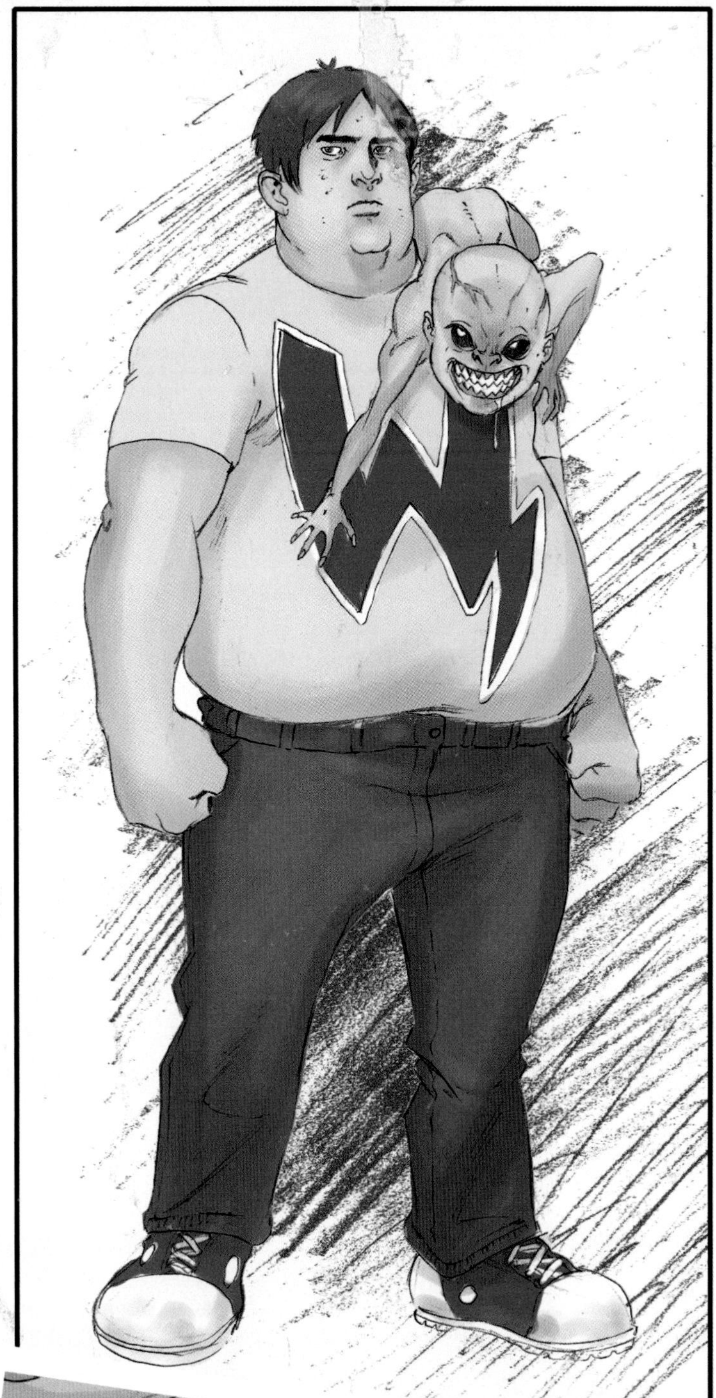

LY LIVING FUCK! I WAS PRETTY T OFF BY THE CONCEPT OF ILDREN BEFORE, BUT NOW THAT VE SEEN, WELL, WHATEVER THE LL THAT WAS, I'M GOING TO ECOME A NUN OR SOMETHING. OH, AN, WITH MY LUCK, I'D GET NOCKED UP... THEN I'D BE A PREGNANT NUN! AAH! OKAY, TIME TO TELL VLAD TO STOP OFF AT A ARCADE OR A ROADSIDE ATTRACTION..HELL...EVEN A 7-11 WILL DO... MUST. TAKE. MIND. OFF. ANGRY. FETUS. HMMM... I WONDER IF IT'S TOO LATE IN THE YEAR FOR CADBURY EGGS...?
-CASSIE

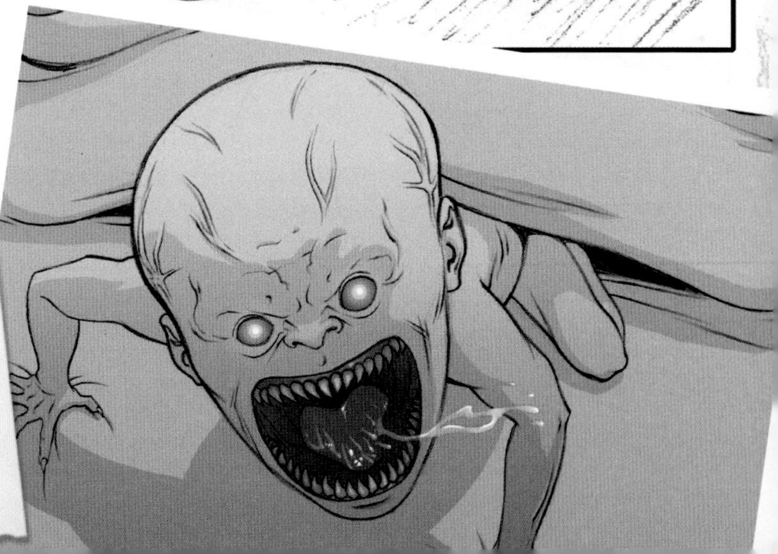

PROFILES

Tim Seeley is the writer and creator o Hack/Slash. He hails from a small tow in the middle of Wisconsin, where he spent too much time drawing the adve tures of angsty superheros and their scantily clad female sidekicks. He began his art career as a children's book illustrator, and eventually found himself drawing 3 3/4" men in the G.I.JOE comic. He spends his time watching slasher movies, chasing bea tiful, noncommittal women, and sitting in the bathtub formulating more comic book ideas. He lives in Chicago, Illino where he keeps his heart and his Trom movie collection.

Stefano Caselli At the tender age of 12, Stefano Caselli decided he wanted to be a superhero. But he didn't have powers, nor had he tragically lost his parents to crime. Briefly considering finishing them off himself, he instead turned to drawing. Taking advantage of his lustful Italian nature, Caselli began his carrer illustrating for Playboy and other erotic stories. Eventually, he was contacted by Tim Seeley, who utilized Caselli's fixations to co-create Hack/Slash. Caselli lives in Rome, Italy.

Sunder Raj, a ninja-pirate-samurai-barbarian-warrior from the little peninsula known as Malaysia, this mighty man stands at an incredible 5'8". An action hero by nature he is known to make his friends worried whenever a tsunami or earthquake occurs over "in that part of the worl He likes to color and paint even whe he's not making money. He's awesome. Love him.

Federica Manfredi is the penciler and the colorist of HACK/SLASH # 2-3. As far as she can remember, she always wrote and drew comic books. Her room has always been full of characters pleading, flattering and even blackmail-ing her into drawing their stories. For years she also enjoyed playing guitar and she regrets she lacks the time to do that. She is also very fond of hamsters. She works and lives in Rome, and loves to skate throughout the whole city in her spare time.